GOLD DIGGERS

WELCOME TO THE HAUNTING

AMY SUNDBERG

Cover by MibliArt, 2024.

To Lee. This is entirely your fault.

One

EMERSON COURTLAND WILL LOOK FOR HIS HAPPILY EVER AFTER IN THE 2ND SEASON OF LEOGAMI'S HIT ROMANCE REALITY SERIES LOVE STORY IN JANUARY 2019

With his dreamy smile, defined jawline, and piercing blue eyes, Emerson Courtland is the fairy tale prince every woman is hoping to meet. At 32, Emerson seems to have it all: a senior vice presidency at Courtland Industries, a glamorous apartment in Manhattan's Tribeca, and a shining social life among New York City's elite. The only thing he lacks is a love that will last forever. Emerson is ready to capture hearts across the nation as he embarks on a once-in-a-lifetime journey to find his soul mate, starring in the 2nd season of Leogami's hit romance reality series "Love Story" when it premieres in January 2019.

The announcement was made during Emerson's exclusive appearance on "Good Morning America." This season of "Love Story" will be set on the Courtland family island in the Bahamas, where Emerson's great-aunt Margaret Courtland, former Vice President and Editor-in-Chief of Imagination Books, as well as author of the cult favorite novel *This is the End*, currently resides.

Emerson was born and raised in New York City, part of a loving blended family with four siblings, father, stepmother, mother, and stepfather. He attended Harvard University and earned his MBA at Stanford. Emerson truly comes with the whole package.

But a few years ago sudden tragedy struck Emerson's charmed life. His beautiful fiancée was killed in a devastating car accident, changing his future forever. In his grief, Emerson wondered if he would ever find love again. It's only now, after years of mourning and at the insistence of his friends and family, that he's finally ready to search for a lasting love.

When Emerson isn't supporting one of his favorite charitable causes, including Big Brothers Big Sisters of America and Doctors without Borders, you can find him traveling around the world, appreciating fine dining, enjoying a pick-up game of squash at his gym, or rooting for the New England Patriots. He's looking for a partner who will join him for a life of adventure, family, and romantic bliss. Encouraged by the success of Season 1's star, Alex Martell, he's confident he too will find his true love on "Love Story."

Heralded for combining suspenseful competitions with the search for romance, Leogami's "Love Story" dominated its two-hour time slot during its 1st season among Adults 18-49 and was Monday night's top show among Women 18-34.

Hosted by reality star Cannon Murphy, "Love Story" is a production of Outgrow Entertainment in association with Bulk TV. Seth Booth, Miles Dabrowski, Maxwell Yee, and Jennifer diCardio are the executive producers. "Love Story" is broadcast in 720 Progressive (720P), Leogami's selected HDTV format, with 5.1 stereo surround sound.

Two

Even after forty years, my NDA holds force, and as such, I've never written at any length about my experience as a contestant on the second season of the reality television series *Love Story* back in 2018. While it inarguably changed the course of my life and exercised a major influence over my subsequent work, I've avoided mentioning it in essays and interviews. During the initial success of the *Sherlock Chronicles* series and then later when *The Other Sister* won the Newbery Medal, I have held my silence. The work was enough. Indeed, I've been relieved the world moved on so quickly and forgot what I cannot.

But lies have a weight to them, and the days, the months, the decades of malice whispering in my ear have coalesced into an iron ball shackled to my soul. I understand what Margaret meant now when she spoke of the great fatigue she bore. I understand why she chose to go back to that island. I'm as old as she was when I met her. And I would be a fool if I continued to refuse to learn from her mistakes.

Here we are then, Darwin, just you and me, as you said you wanted. Read these words of truth as I write them, and know you have never succeeded in breaking me. Know I understand exactly who you are and what you've done, and I understand my own role in these events, in all my youth and folly and impotence but also in my basic humanity, which I refuse to allow you to strip away.

This morning I pulled that old diary from under the bed, its leather cover scarred, its pages faded and fragile like autumn leaves. You may relish playing with my memory, whispering your sibilant falsehoods and amplifying my doubts, my regret, my grief. But this is my story, and I have a lifetime of practice spinning narratives that you cannot match.

Let me remind you, dear Darwin, how this all began.

"I'm giving you the opportunity of a lifetime." My older sister Kennedy, producer extraordinaire, had been attempting to persuade me to be on her show for weeks. I didn't question her dogged pursuit of the idea, assuming she simply wanted me to stop mooching off her and sleeping on her couch. We both agreed I owed her, and she was sure being on her show would help transform me back into a productive member of society. "Like being tempered in the fire," she said repeatedly. I didn't appreciate the metaphor; it made the show sound more like a painful trial than a bid for freedom.

But she finally stumbled upon the perfect argument. "What would you say if I told you being on this show would give you the opportunity to finally use that expensive creative writing degree of yours?"

Kennedy had never been fond of the magic words "please" and "thank you," but these were even better. "I'm listening."

"If you do well on a show like mine, you become a minor Instagram celebrity. You could build your platform and make it irresistible to publishers. They'd jump at the shot to work with you. You could do an authorized memoir"—she saw me open my mouth to object and kept right on going—"but you could probably sell whatever you wanted. Name recognition sells books, does it not?"

She had me there. But I didn't want her to see she'd piqued my interest. "It's not really the way most novelists do things," I said.

She jabbed her finger at me in triumph. "And that's one of your problems right there. Who says you need to do things like everybody else? The important thing is that you jumpstart the writing career you've always wanted. Who cares about your methods as long as they work?"

This was Kennedy's philosophy down to a T, and it did seem to have merit: she was a successful producer while I was struggling to leave the couch every morning. "I don't really think I'm the reality show type," I tried. "I need my alone time."

She snorted. "The island will be your playground. You'll be able to get away sometimes, I promise. And get this: remember that book you loved in high school? What was it called again? *The End Times*, *At the End*...?"

"*This is the End*," I corrected her. The perfect dystopia for my teenaged self, I'd read that book until the binding broke and I had to get a new copy.

"That's it. Well, it just so happens the author, Margaret Courtland, is the leading man's aunt, and she'll be in residence during the show. What would you say to meeting one of your writing heroes?"

An unfamiliar pulse of excitement rushed through me, but I did my best to throttle it. "She only wrote the one novel, you know, and that was a long time ago."

"Yeah, but she went on to become a top editor, didn't she? Think of the career boost she could give you if you make a good impression." Kennedy had done her homework, I'd give her that. "This could be just what you need to start producing words again."

I glared at her. My lack of output was a sore point. I hadn't been writing regularly since I finished my MFA. Between being the sole financial provider for Joe and I while we lived in Brooklyn and Joe's painful revelations that my new work was subpar, my motivation had floundered while his work had thrived. He was on track to be on the *New Yorker*'s prestigious *20 under 40* list, and his first novel had made the *Times* bestseller list...right before he'd called off our engagement. Now, a few months later, I was still raw and bleeding inside. Nobody could write under these circumstances.

But Kennedy didn't care about my excuses. "You know, you play your cards right, you'll end up more famous than Joe. You do realize the size of our audience, don't you? This is TV numbers we're talking about, not publishing." She paused a moment to let that sink in. "This is your chance to show him just how wrong he was about you."

Those were the words that convinced me. I'd do anything to give Joe the middle finger and get my life back on track. Anything.

At least that's what I thought at the time.

Which was how I found myself lying on an overly soft bed, sliding into its undignified sag in a complimentary but meager bathrobe. The only window in the stuffy room faced directly out onto a dense thicket of tropical brush. No vaunted ocean view for me, private island or no. The sunlight filtered into my room in a sad and feeble stream, but even the dim light did nothing to diminish the fetid humidity in the room. I had kicked the tired AC several times upon arrival, but it refused to be coaxed to life for someone of my minor talents.

The show, in keeping with others of its genre, tried to keep its contestants off balance through isolation and forced inactivity. No internet, no cell phone, no TV, no books, nobody to talk to, and the door was locked, trapping me inside. "Don't worry about it, it's protocol," Kennedy had said right before she left me alone. "Soon the fun will start, and then you'll hardly notice." All I had was an empty journal and a leaky pen that left the occasional annoying blot at the beginnings of sentences.

I hated it. In enforced solitude I couldn't escape the repetitive maelstrom of my own thoughts. My physical body felt like just another prison, a form Kennedy had spent a lot of time molding in preparation for the show. My transformation had begun with extensions to give me a wistful forest of dark hair, every other hair on my body carefully trimmed or waxed or plucked, nails carefully painted and buffed, every inch of skin so moisturized I didn't understand why I hadn't turned into one gigantic zit. I'd been dutifully spending half an hour a day doing "power abs" exercises. In spite of those crunches and Kennedy's obsession with every little bite of nourishment I consumed, my stomach still pooched out in stubborn revolt.

"The camera adds fifty pounds." How many times had Kennedy said this to me?

The first time I thought I could argue her into civility, or at least silence. "I look better than I have in years," I said. "Throw me in a black dress and everything will be fine." Even in my wretched post-break-up state, I knew I didn't want to become neurotic about my weight on top of everything else.

"You think I don't know my job?" Kennedy said. "You want to weigh the most of any of the Gold Diggers?" Gold Diggers was shorthand for the contestants amongst her production staff, their level of respect for the female participants who made the show possible underwhelming. "Someone has to be the fat one. You want it to be you?"

I shut up after that. I'd gotten over the starvation period of my grief, and all I wanted was pizza warm from the box, dripping with cheese and grease and calories, rich gooey brownies with frosting I could lick from my fingers, heavy pastas rich with cream sauce and seafood and sin. Instead I lived on fruit, grilled chicken, and plain lettuce for weeks. Romaine until the recall, and then I had to switch to baby spinach. The sound of my own mastication repulsed me.

My new sterilized body disgusted me too, even while it made me hate my old, normal one. I'd stand for hours in front of the mirror, looking at myself in horrified fascination and wishing in spite of my self-respect that my fiancé could see me now. Ex-fiancé. Ex. I was so used to thinking of everything in reference to him. What he'd think about a decision I was making. What he'd want to do, to watch, to eat. What position he'd want to fuck in. And now when it was too late I'd become who he'd wanted me to be, a worthy substitute for the porn stars populating his fantasies.

He would see me with the rest of America in all my drama-filled glory, but he'd have to wait for my season of *True Love* to air. I wondered if he'd watch. I wondered if he'd regret what he could have had. I even imagined he'd contact me after the show aired and ask to get back together. These hopes embarrassed me even as I clung onto them for dear life.

I wanted to win just so he saw that someone wanted me. And then I could throw my hefty book contract into his face.

One of the most important instructions Kennedy gave me before we left LA was to lie my ass off. According to her, that was what was necessary to dupe America—and its proxy, Emerson Courtland, Prince Charming extraordinaire—into falling in love with me. Kennedy was the expert, and I hated myself with a passion right around then, meaning...I bought into her bullshit one hundred percent.

"Don't tell anyone we're sisters," she warned me. "Nobody. Cast or crew." Everyone knew her as Kennedy Brown. She'd kept Wesley's last name even though their marriage had fallen apart after five months. Kennedy Roberts had been a nobody. As Kennedy Brown, she'd become a force to be reckoned with.

"Are you sure that's a good idea?" I was doubtful. "What if I last awhile? Won't it be hard to maintain the charade for any period of time?"

"Oh, I'll keep you on the show, never fear, but people can't know we have a personal connection. The crew wouldn't like it, they'd call it favoritism"—Kennedy rolled her eyes—"as if I don't work my ass off to earn everything I get. And the other Gold Diggers will try to sabotage you if they find out, talk about how you have an unfair advantage and make your life a living hell. Trust me. I won't be your personal producer so it's not like we'll see a lot of each other anyway. The only person who can know is Jen." Jen, the superwoman showrunner who'd brought Kennedy with her when she started *Love Story*. To hear Kennedy tell it, this woman was a ratings whisperer, giving audiences what they didn't even know they wanted.

"And you don't think I'll actually have an unfair advantage?"

She gave me the same devilish grin I'd seen our whole lives, only most of the time I wasn't on its receiving end. "Do as I say," she told me, "and you won't be sorry. This show will change your life."

And wasn't that all I wanted?

Kennedy told me she planned to sell me as the "artsy one" on the show. Never mind I was a washed-up writer with only one proper credit to my name. Never mind I'd never finished that elusive novel. Never mind I was a genuine artistic fuckup.

No surprise, I loathed her idea.

Kennedy didn't care. She sat me down on a chrome stool at her breakfast bar like I was a spy going into the war zone and gave me instructions. "You can go for the passionate label, and that means you can get away with crying," she told me. "But don't cry all the time. If you do, the viewers will make fun of you and eventually they'll get annoyed. And then—" She drew her finger across her throat.

I didn't learn until later that how much I cried was irrelevant.

Through editing they could show whatever they wanted. They could present me as the most together woman on the planet or they could re-cut the same isolated crying jag and present it as continuous emotional wreckage. When I signed the pile of papers some executive assistant shoved in my face, I gave away any chance for self-determination.

For public consumption, Kennedy planned to present a Zoe Roberts who was a budding talent. Step by step she laid it out for me, sun snaking through the blinds making me squint, all while she chowed down on chips and dip I wasn't allowed to eat. The show would tell the world I still lived in Brooklyn; the website would mention my MFA as if it were a feature instead of the failing it felt like in my heart. Confident but modest, I would write love letters to the show's Prince Charming to show how articulate and tender I could be.

I finally gave up and blocked the light with my arm so I could see Kennedy's face. "Will you expect me to talk about Joe?" I knew she wouldn't want to bring up our mom. She barely ever spoke about her. But my wounds from Joe were fresher and bloodier.

Kennedy shrugged. "We'll figure something out." I gave her my skeptical sister look. "We'll say something tasteful that makes you look good, swear to god."

I had never been a fan of reality TV, but I'd mainlined a season of *His Engagement* once when I was sick with the flu and I knew how this went. My ex-fiancé Joe would be an irresistible topic to stoke drama. "I don't want to talk about him. Not on camera." Not ever, really. If I could have erased those years from my life, I might have in spite of everything I would have lost in the process. Anything to stop the ongoing pain.

"Welllll." Kennedy's phone conveniently buzzed, and she began rapidly texting. I took the opportunity to steal a single chip. "It's a romance reality show, Zoe. You're going to have to talk about your dating history." She looked up long enough to turn on her grin. "Of course, what you say is entirely up to you. Think about it this way: it will be your turn to tell your story instead of letting that bastard have the last word."

She knew exactly what I wanted to hear. But still I pressed her. "Will you promise not to fly him to the island to confront me Jerry Springer style? Because if you do, so help me, I'll never speak to you again." I pretended I was kidding, but we both knew I wasn't.

"Cross my heart." She drew an X between her boobs. "Besides, I wouldn't want to draw focus away from Emerson. Scandalous backstories are all fine and good, but we don't want to get distracted from the main storyline."

The main storyline was Emerson finding the love of his life. For the amount of fame I was hoping to garner, I'd have to be one of his main love interests. The entire experience on the island would be a carefully crafted story, but one that felt real while it was happening. Not so different from how I already felt; ever since Joe and I had broken up, my life felt like it was happening to someone else with my name while I watched in bafflement.

Who decides to go onto reality television shows? It's a valid question, and there's no pat answer. But I will say this. Everyone who voluntarily goes on a show like that is looking for *something*. You don't sign up to have your entire life put on display if you're sleek and content and satisfied. Why would you subject yourself to that kind of judgment?

And anyone could see I was searching. All my life I'd been Zoe Roberts, the girl who never lived up to her potential, a deep, bone-aching embarrassment. I was thirty years old, due to turn thirty-one soon after the show wrapped filming. By that age I was supposed to be well on my way to establishing myself as a writer. Be someone like Kennedy, with an impressive list of accomplishments to tout in my resumé. But all I'd done was trash my prospects and settle into aggressive mediocrity.

Finally, here was my chance to alter my course. Become the critically acclaimed writer I'd always wanted to be. Maybe even score a movie deal or two.

At least that was the plan.

Kennedy spent the flight to Ft. Lauderdale nagging me about hydrating because of the potential effects on my skin. From Ft. Lauderdale we were flying to George Town in the Bahamas, where we'd catch a boat to Emerson's family's private island—the real reason he was chosen as that season's Prince Charming.

While waiting for our connection in Florida, I met my first fellow

Gold Digger: Lucy Miller. Lucy was younger than me, twenty-four at most, an eager look in her eyes like she was on a permanent mission to please. She wore a halter top and miniskirt showing endless limbs as honey-colored as her hair. Kennedy had pushed me to wear a similar outfit, but I'd insisted on jeans and a hoodie. "No cameras yet, right?" She'd hemmed and hawed and eventually let me have my way.

Kennedy approached Lucy immediately, all smiles. "It's so great to see you again," she gushed. Seeing her switch into producer mode gave me a jolt. As her sister, I got the real Kennedy, or as least as much of the real Kennedy as she gave anybody. But Lucy...well, Lucy got whatever Kennedy decided was the most beneficial to her goals.

Lucy smiled too, and allowed Kennedy to hug her, but I caught her looking surreptitiously around the busy terminal. "Where's Pearl?"

Kennedy didn't miss a beat. "Oh, she's back in LA. She's not working with us on location this time around, but don't worry, I'll take the best care of you, and we're all going to have a total blast this fall."

Lucy gave a nervous laugh that made me clutch my shoulder bag tighter. An almost motherly instinct awoke inside me, wanting to protect this willowy girl from Kennedy's machinations. But she knew what she'd signed up for, right?

Lucy turned to me and held out her hand. "Hi, I'm Lucy Miller. You must be the competition."

My pity increased in that moment. She was trying so hard to be simultaneously perky and thick-skinned, but she was so very wrong. We weren't competition. We were fellow victims...or beneficiaries, depending on how you looked at it. Sisters-in-arms at the very least. "Zoe Roberts." I took her hand, and the three of us sat down in a row with Kennedy in the middle.

"Not to be a buzz kill or anything," Kennedy said, "but you guys shouldn't really be talking to one another until the show starts. We want to capture all that fresh energy on camera, don't we?" Lucy nodded with enthusiasm, and I swallowed my sigh at the commencing of the bullshit. Filling out all those psych questionnaires and being screened by the show psychiatrist had been bad enough.

But then Kennedy got a call, and midway through, she winked at me and stood up. "I'll be right back," she said. "Be good!"

She walked rapidly down the concourse, leaving me to watch Lucy, her foot tapping rat-a-tat-tat against the cheap linoleum like the frantic wing beats of a hummingbird. She glanced over at me from time to time as if scoping me out, the two of us caught in a rivalry over a man neither of us had met. Hell, she hadn't even learned his *name* yet. Kennedy had obviously set up this opportunity for me, so I leaned over to murmur in Lucy's ear. "I know we're in kind of a weird situation, but I hear on these shows you get to know the other girls really well. Make life-long friends, even. It's good to have people around who really get it."

This time Lucy's smile was real. "Have you seen all the photos on Instagram of the girls from season one hanging out together? Carlie, Brenda, and Tayisha seem inseparable, don't you think?"

To this day I've never watched season one of *Love Story*. I preferred to rely on Kennedy's inside advice. But now I prepared my first lie of the show. "Totally."

Apparently that was enough for Lucy to decide I was her new best friend. She began to spew out her entire life story: her parents' rough divorce, her time at the University of Texas studying communications, her inability to break into on-camera work for the local news, her last boyfriend's reluctance to pop the question. What did this girl want? Time in the spotlight, for sure; anything to break onto the TV airwaves. She oozed a desperate kind of wince-worthy charisma that made me want to look away. Kennedy suppressed a smile as she returned and Lucy fell silent.

When boarding was announced, Lucy pulled me into a swift hug. "I'm so glad you're the first one I met," she said into my ear. Then she sashayed out the door to the plane.

Kennedy held me back. "Don't get too close to her," she warned. "Lucy's the Crazy One. She'll be a constant center of drama. Don't let her tears be contagious, yeah?"

"Got it." I didn't envy Lucy. If the producers stayed firm with their typecasting, she could kiss that broadcasting career goodbye. I wasn't thrilled about being the Artsy One, but at least it would get me where I needed to be. I could succeed on this ridiculous show. I wasn't a doe-eyed innocent like Lucy.

I was so naïve to think I was any different.

My second Gold Digger meeting was not as auspicious. Trapped in my small bungalow room, I was writing a desultory entry in my journal, trying and failing to get the words flowing. A sudden rattle interrupted me, a connecting door I'd barely noticed bursting open and disgorging a young woman. When she saw me sprawled on my bed, she stopped, her mouth making a comical "O" shape.

We took a good look at each other, and if I hadn't already felt inadequate, I would have immediately begun. Her long blonde hair fell in lustrous curls, framing her heart-shaped face, and her blue eyes could melt the hardest of hearts. She looked like a living Kewpie doll, the kind of girl who wouldn't hesitate to play helpless to get attention, who might carry a four-pound dog in a ridiculous purse, and who probably never had a single blemish on her skin. She wore a cute little hot pink dress with high-heeled sandals that laced halfway up her calves, and she looked like she'd been relaxing in a cool spa instead of roasting in an airless room. She finished her assessment of me with a small sniff of derision, and I checked to make sure my robe was covering my boobs.

"I have an ocean view." She drawled the words, but I recognized the challenge underneath.

"Good for you." I turned back to my journal.

"I can't believe they've kept us waiting this long." She wrinkled her nose. "These rooms are so cramped."

"Personally I'm enjoying the privacy," I lied. This woman didn't need to know I'd been crawling out of my skin. "When they move us into the main house, we'll all have to share." I couldn't entirely repress the glee I felt at being the bearer of bad news for this seraph.

She tossed her hair to the side, and it bounced and settled like it was starring in a shampoo commercial. "We'll see about that."

Game on. I'd met women like her all the time in New York, and I knew what drove them up the wall: not being the center of attention. Being stuck in these drab little rooms had to be eating her up inside, and I could add fuel to the fire. I ignored her and read over what I'd been writing.

The gorgeous blonde walked over to my window and pretended to peer out, then turned to stare at my grimy purse, the fake leather peeling on the strap. I had a feeling if they'd delivered our suitcases, she'd be going through mine now, making snarky comments about my wardrobe options. "Do you think you'll make the first cut?" she asked.

I shrugged. "I hope so." I was the only woman who didn't have to worry, but she'd never know that.

Our first meeting with Emerson, a highly engineered affair, was scheduled to take place in a few evenings. Before that, we'd be filming the opening sequence and any extra footage for the bio sections of the first episode, which meant I'd be sitting around doing nothing, since I wasn't getting one of the long bio treatments. "You don't need it, and the less anyone knows about your real life, the better," Kennedy had declared.

So most of my focus was on the overdone cocktail shindig up at the mansion where we'd all get our first shot to charm Emerson. A shocking number of women would be cut at the end of the night at a monstrous ritual called, fittingly enough, the Culling, and those unfortunates would hop right back on the boat, waving their chance at reality TV notoriety goodbye. Whoever remained would try their luck winning time with the elusive "Prince Charming" through competing in various challenges.

"That makes no sense," I'd complained to Kennedy when she first explained the show's concept the year before when they'd received the network's green light. Back when I'd been secure in my old life, when Joe and I were engaged and questioning her new show was simply an intellectual exercise. "Shouldn't the leading man be the one choosing how to allocate his time? Isn't that how it's done?"

Kennedy had laughed throatily over the phone. "He gets some say, silly, but this is a more interesting way of guiding his choices. It's a fresh take on the tired format of most romance reality shows. Besides, watching competitions between the individual women that actually result in full dates? Think of the drama. It will make for some fucking great TV."

Season one's ratings had agreed with her assessment. And now I had to compete with this arrogant princess. A splinter of doubt pierced my heart that someone I already disliked so much was in the exact same place I was.

"I'm Zoe," I said when it was clear she wasn't leaving.

There was a pause while she pondered whether I was worthy to hear her name. "Vivian." There was no question she was one of the candidates for the villain this season. "Your job gave you time off for filming? Your boss a *Love Story* fan?"

Trying to place my economic status already. "I'm unemployed." Best to disabuse her of any interest in me as quickly as possible. "You?"

She gave a fake tinkle of laughter. "Oh, I make my own hours," she said with an airy wave of her hand. "I'm in real estate so...."

It took me a moment to realize she wasn't going to finish her sentence. "Real estate," I said. "How goal-oriented of you."

"I have to say, this isn't what I thought it would be." She said the words in a slow, measured way, overemphasizing her consonants just a little bit as if she'd worked with an elocution coach.

"Oh?" I tried to sound as disinterested as possible.

She sniffed. "I thought there was going to be some real competition."

I actually groaned. This was her idea of tearing me down? I'd spent hours being savaged without mercy at writing workshops. Too many adverbs, Zoe. Your language is so pedestrian. Your female protagonist isn't likable enough, no one wants to read about *that* kind of woman. That might have happened in your real life, Zoe, but it doesn't read as realistic. And now this child wanted to give me attitude because we wanted to fake-date the same person? "Tell it to someone who cares," I said. "I have better things to do with my time."

Her eyes narrowed, but other than that, her resting bitch face didn't change. "Let me give you a little piece of advice. If you're planning on going the villain route, do everyone here a favor and forget it. You're not pretty enough to pull it off." She posed, hands on her hips, like the power player she thought she was.

I smiled sweetly. "Don't worry, your sunny disposition has obviously already cornered that market."

She opened her mouth, no doubt to deliver another stinging retort, but all that came out was a cracking wheeze. She clutched her throat with both long-nailed hands and tried again. No sound emerged, and she began to cough.

"What, cat got your tongue?" No way was I going to be nice to this nightmare. She could get her own water.

She swallowed several times, and I thought I caught a glint of fear in her eyes. She tried to speak again, but all that came out was an inquisitive croak, an unnatural sound that sent a shiver through me. It was strange, her voice going out just like that, but really, she was probably talking so much trash all the time, was it any big surprise? I couldn't resist goading her, not after the attitude she'd given me. "It might not be the easiest to win over our Prince Charming with laryngitis, but I'm sure you'll rise to the challenge."

She glared at me and tossed her gorgeous blond hair around before stalking back into her own room. I closed the door firmly behind her, turned the lock, and fell back onto my bed with a pained moan.

This was only the beginning.

Three

Transcript of a *Wake Up Happy* segment featuring Emerson Courtland and Cannon Murphy, aired on October 1, 2018

Host: From the upcoming season of *Love Story*, please welcome star Emerson Courtland and host Cannon Murphy.

(Upbeat canned music plays as the two suited men saunter onto the set, the audience applauds, an unidentified female voice shouts "You're beautiful, Cannon" and receives his trademark wink for her efforts.)

Host: Emerson, you lucky dog, are you ready to make a tough choice between...wait, how many beautiful women are on the menu? It's hard to keep all these shows straight.

Emerson: (laughing) I don't know how many either, Tom. I just go where they tell me, smile for the cameras, and listen to my gut. (He pats his appropriately flat and hard stomach through his crisp button down and several ladies in the audience cheer.)

Host: Fair enough, fair enough. But in all seriousness, what made you decide to search for love on national television?

Emerson: I figured my hit rate would be better on TV than it would be through a dating app. (audience laughter) But to tell the truth, I'm looking to meet the love of my life, and as long as we have a good thing together, I'm not picky about how I find her. There used to be matchmakers, you know, women whose entire profession was to know everything about everyone so they could—poof!—waggle a pinkie and bring together two compatible people. But now with the hectic pace of modern life, everyone has a million and one choices of people to date, and nobody wants to stop and really get to know each other. I think *Love Story* can change all that for me.

Host: We've all heard the tragic story of how you lost your fiancée in a car crash several years ago. Has that complicated dating for you as well?

Emerson: Of course, without question. You know, for a while, maybe even a couple years, I just wasn't ready to settle down and make a commitment to anyone else. I couldn't help comparing any woman I met to Melanie, and to the relationship we'd had together. And that wasn't fair to anyone.

Host: You needed time to grieve.

Emerson: Exactly. So I took that time. And there's a part of me that will always love Melanie. I wouldn't want it any other way. But there also comes a time when you have to let go of the past and move forward, and I want to enjoy the future with a partner by my side. I'm ready to find love again, and I know Melanie would want that for me.

Host: So—correct me if I'm wrong—how it works is you jet off to your family's private island in the Bahamas where a large number of lovely single women are waiting to meet you and find out if you're their one and only? And they don't even know you're the man they'll be meeting?

Emerson: That's right, the women are already on the island and without an internet connection, so I'll be a big surprise. (He laughs nervously.) I'll be taking a couple months off work to focus entirely on the journey, and by the end of that time, I fully expect to have fallen in love with the girl of my dreams. And because we're filming in the Bahamas, I'll get some quality time with my aunt at the same time.

Host: Got to get that all-important family approval, am I right?

Emerson: (strained laughter) You got it.

Host: So your aunt approves of your quest for love?

Emerson: Well, she's not too enthusiastic about the show, I have to admit. She's old fashioned that way. I can't really blame her since we'll be upending her daily life while we're filming. But at the end of the day, she just wants me to be happy.

Host: Of course she does. And what about you, Cannon? Are you ready to shepherd Emerson through this experience?

Cannon: I was born ready. (another wink)

Host: When *Love Story* was first announced a year ago, a lot of us wondered if there was any space in the market for yet another reality TV show about romance, and I have to admit, I was one of the skeptics. Finding true love on television isn't an easy path, and surely a guy like Emerson doesn't need that kind of help in the first place. Plus for some of us it's a lot to swallow that the show might end in an actual love connection. What do you have to say to that?

Cannon: I like to let the evidence speak for itself, Tom. I'm still good friends with Alex Martell, our leading man from season one, and I'm happy to say he and his final choice Kaylee are still going strong almost a year later. Can we guarantee a happy ending? Of course not, and we've never said otherwise. But we do everything we can to help our leading men find what they're looking for. And while we all know Emerson doesn't need help getting a date, this experience will give him the time and space to focus on that special connection that can truly last a lifetime.

Host: Can you tell us if there are wedding bells in the future for Alex and Kaylee?

Cannon: If I did know anything, I'd be sworn to secrecy. (mimes zipping his lips, then winks at the audience) All I can say is I'm one hundred percent ready to help Emerson go on his own journey of romance and discovery.

Host: Speaking of romance, I've heard a rumor you and a former flame (he turns to the audience and mouths "Jillian" in a comically obvious way) might be in the process of patching things up. Care to comment on that?

Cannon: It's absolutely not true. (no smile, no wink) I can’t afford any distractions while I help Emerson on his own quest for love.

Four

The island was officially not what I signed up for.

Don't get me wrong, the stretch of pristine beach where we spent the day filming the opening sequence was an idyllic delight: its sand ground so fine and white you knew you'd never get a pebble stuck between your toes, water so blue it looked like the tourism board decided to invest in food coloring. The sun shone bright in a vibrant blue haze, and the sea breeze cut through the heavy humidity overlaying everything like a wet blanket. This was the tropical paradise we'd been promised.

But away from the beach, the oppressive heat surrounded me like a living thing. Sweat collected in every possible crevice and cranny of my body, sticky and salty, attracting swarms of tiny bugs. The damp air offered a soupy resistance, heavy and stale, and I tried in vain to shield myself from the relentless sun with my sunglasses and sunscreen.

At least on the beach, I could ignore the persistent discomfort. I met the other producers and shook hands with the show's medical doctor and the resident psychiatrist. I did not officially meet any of the other Gold Diggers—that treat was being saved for the all-important cocktail party—but Lucy and I stuck together, and I couldn't help noticing Vivian's continued muteness. Kennedy explained that aside from the producers and the two doctors, the rest of the crew and the contestants weren't supposed to talk to each other. "It's best if you pretend they're not even there," she told us.

We spent hours pretending to laugh and play together in the surf, tossing beach balls and frisbees. We had to wait, sitting under umbrellas, water bottles being continually pressed upon us, feeling our makeup begin to melt on our faces as if they were made from plastic instead of flesh, while each woman had her own individual shot on the beach taken. Returning to the bungalow in the evening, I fell asleep by nine o'clock in spite of the oppressive heat.

Kennedy came to unlock my door the next morning. "Go ahead and take a look around," she told me. "Get a feel for the island, find a romantic spot in the mansion to take Emerson during the cocktail party. But don't tell any of the other girls. They'd all kill for a chance to explore before the show officially begins."

I understood the favor she was doing me. Maybe I'd even get a glimpse of Emerson's aunt Margaret Courtland. The sooner I could begin to build a relationship with her, the better.

I decided to explore the island first, making my way slowly towards the mansion, the epicenter of our experience. After spending the first few minutes beaten by the unrelenting sun, I entered an overgrown forest, the shade ineffective against the heat and humidity. The branches interlocked over my head like a net, not the barest hint of wind stirring them. I trudged on the dirt path, my toes slowly turning brown, strange bird calls and insect noises keeping me alert.

The trees thinned, and as I emerged back into the unforgiving sunlight, I realized the Courtlands were *weird* rich. Rearing from a slab of concrete and positively dwarfing the trees surrounding the clearing on all sides, a full-sized replica of a landlocked pirate ship stood before me, complete with a Jolly Roger flag hanging limply from its mast. A long rope ladder hung all the way from the deck to the ground.

Two complete skeletons lay in unnatural poses by the ship's prow, stark white against the dark cement, arranged to look like the two individuals in question had died in a sword fight. One rapier stuck from a bare ribcage, the other abandoned almost within grasp of the knobby finger bones. A gleaming pile of gold coins separated the two, and I almost started laughing. Whoever had arranged this little scene certainly had a sense of drama.

I picked up one of the coins, weighing it in my palm. Plastic, just as I'd suspected. I clutched the fake prop in my hand, knowing this was just the beginning of my season of pretense. A strange scraping sound drew my attention back downwards, where the skeleton's finger bones were now touching the rapier's hilt.

I blinked. I must have been mistaken as to where the hand had been posed, distracted by the absurdity of the vessel beached high on land. I had a lot on my mind, after all. But even so, I put the coin back with its fellows, a lump suddenly constricting my throat, and hurriedly left the clearing to make my way down to the beach.

After the relative gloom of the trees, I cringed away from the baleful gaze of the sun as I jogged down to the ocean's edge, eager to feel its coolness. I kicked off my sandals and waded into the surf. The warm water washed over my feet and calves, the sand sucking hungrily onto my toes. I could almost pretend I was on a solo tropical getaway to recover from the debacle with Joe.

As if I could ever afford to travel to the Bahamas under my own power.

When I turned inland, I saw it for the first time: the Courtland mansion, perched high above me on a bluff as if surveying its territory. Huge, brutal, and unrelieved in its façade of dark concrete and glass, it looked more like a prison block than an island retreat. A scar on the landscape, it menaced like a bird of prey. "We've had to do a lot of work to soften it up," Kennedy had told me, and now I marveled she'd thought such a thing was possible. Apparently wealthy educated men with island estates weren't lining up to appear on reality television, and the producers had been forced to settle for what they could get.

In front of the house, a variety of colorful tropical plants and flowers grew—no doubt the "softening" Kennedy had referenced—a riot of life and brightness that contrasted with the grim building. I could picture this house in a wealthier Soviet-era neighborhood, sterile and utilitarian, but placed in such lush landscape it created a cognitive dissonance that made me want to look away.

A figure—a gentle blur of white--appeared amongst the shrubs on the edge of the bluff, looking down at me. I froze, the water still lapping around my ankles. I half expected a siren to rent the air or some black-clad crew members to burst out onto the beach to detain me, but nothing happened. Even at such a distance, I could discern the woman's ramrod straight posture, along with the soft glory of her perfectly white hair. We stared at each other, and at that angle, it looked as if she might be consumed by the house rising up behind her.

For a moment I fully expected the stranger to call down to me, in spite of the great distance between us, but instead a bird's mocking cry echoed in the air above us. I tried to catch a glimpse of it, and by the time I'd turned back, she'd disappeared back up the bluff. Where I should be going myself.

After a long series of stairways and a steep hill, I was breathing heavier than I liked to admit as I approached the concrete stronghold. In the middle of the grand circular drive stood a large fountain featuring a woman kneeling, the water arcing up and out of her pursed lips as a winged angel looked down on her in grim disapproval. The house itself was a blot of gray against an otherwise vibrant landscape. This, I thought, is where people came to wait for death.

The large double front doors expelled two women deep in conversation. It was too late to evade their notice, so I continued gamely forward. I couldn't avoid everyone if I wanted to investigate the house.

As I drew closer, I recognized Jen diCardio, the showrunner of *Love Story* and Kennedy's boss, looking like the epitome of a successful career woman, even in the stultifying heat. She wore sharp gray slacks, a bright yellow shell that complimented her brown skin, and stilettos that looked like they could do real damage if deployed as weapons. Her long black hair was pulled back in a sleek high ponytail, her lips painted ruby red. An earpiece rested in her ear, the wire discretely curling around her neck and under her hair, but all her attention seemed focused on the woman in her company: a red-haired vixen with a pale peaches and cream complexion and almost nonexistent eyebrows who I remembered from the shoot the day before.

The two ignored me, and I gave them a wide berth, circling around to climb the steps behind them, feeling like I was getting away with something. I was halfway up before Jen called to me without looking back. "Zoe. Come and let me look at you."

Busted. And since Jen made all the final decisions about the show—including the all-important editing, which would determine if America thought I was a sweetheart or a villain—I came back down to join them by the grotesque fountain. This was the woman my sister worshipped. More than that, this was the woman she wished to become.

And I could see why. Jen gave me a cool gaze that seemed to assess my absolute worth in five seconds flat: the sweat collected at my hairline, the chaos of my hair caught back in a plastic clip, the fact I hadn't shaved my legs yet today. "So you're our sensitive little artist." She extended her hand. "We didn't get a chance to speak yesterday, but I've heard so much about you."

"Not as much as I've heard about you." Her hand was dry like snakeskin.

"Getting over some recent heartbreak, I hear?" Yes, striking fast as a rattlesnake. "I do hope it won't bring up any painful reminders for you to be here. I hear your ex is quite the up-and-comer, just like our Prince Charming."

I hadn't expected to *like* Kennedy's boss, but I also hadn't expected to wish for her painful death quite this soon. "They move in very different circles," I said.

"Yes, your ex is the literary type, isn't he." It wasn't a question. I knew she'd read a complete dossier about me. "How did you meet him?"

"We were both pursuing our graduate degrees at NYU."

She pursed her lips. "Ah yes, before you washed out as a writer."

I had to give it to her, she knew how to make me fighting mad with only a few short ripostes. I knew she was doing her producer thing and manipulating me, but I couldn't help taking the bait. "I completed my MFA," I said stiffly.

A little smile curled the corners of her lips. "Of course. Well, I hope you read your NDA closely. No unauthorized memoirs about your experiences on the show. But if you want to write a tell-all about your life afterwards, well, we might be able to negotiate something."

Her condescension was a slap in the face. "You're too kind."

She gave me a gracious nod, as if we both believed what I'd just said.

"Allow me to introduce you to one of your fellow Gold Diggers." Jen gestured over at the gorgeous redhead. "Giselle, meet Zoe."

Giselle gave a little awkward wave completely at odds with her supermodel appearance. "So good to meet you. This is quite the place, isn't it? It's hard to believe we're not all in some bizarre dream."

"Well, as you know, Giselle, we're in the business of making dreams come true," Jen said.

One look at Giselle's face and I could tell she wanted to roll her eyes as much as I did. After meeting nervous rabbit Lucy and stuck-up princess Vivian, it was nice to know there were at least a few other Gold Diggers who were down-to-earth and had senses of humor.

Jen turned back to me. "Here's a fun fact. Giselle's parents know our Prince Charming's parents socially. Isn't it a small world? I'm sure Giselle and our suitor will have plenty to talk about." They were both from money, she was saying, and none too subtly. Jen's attitude made clear Kennedy had called in a big favor to get me on the show.

Giselle gave me an apologetic smile. "I still don't know who he is," she told me. "Just that he grew up in Manhattan. I'm from Boston myself."

Jen patted Giselle on the arm. "You two will hit it off, I just know it." She looked me up and down, disapproval dripping. "Don't let us keep you." I might have been beneath her notice, but she was also giving me tacit permission to break the rules, and I'd take what I could get. I gave Giselle—the name made her sound like a Disney princess slash fawn—a last nod before running up the stairs and entering the maw of the house.

An unexpected blast of freezing air caused goose bumps to instantly rise on my skin. My eyes struggled to adjust to the dark, the tall windows on either side of the door sheathed in thick draperies, the only light coming from a small Tiffany lamp on a side table and the ambient light from deeper in the house's bowels. A large staircase, its bannisters garlanded with flowers, dominated the space. I listened for sounds of the crew setting up for filming tonight, but the house was unnaturally silent. I couldn't even hear the tinkling of the fountain outside.

I continued deeper into the structure, my sandals clicking against the hard floor. The crew had obviously been here at some point, as evidenced by a lighting rig built into the ceiling and equipment already partially set up in a large reception room. A small V-shaped platform covered with red carpet stood between two gigantic flowering plants on one side of the room, surrounded by unlit candles on large sconces. Beyond that was a lounge with another lighting rig along with several large sectionals all strewn with red rose petals. A small bar stood in one corner, stocked with a massive number of flutes and wine glasses. French doors led outside to a heavily landscaped tropical paradise complete with palm trees, polished wooden bridges over water features, and tiki lanterns, completely at odds with the stark utilitarianism of the house.

I gazed at myself in the heavy gilt-framed mirror over a fireplace so large I could sleep in it, trying to picture myself there this evening, heavily made up, in the black gown chosen by Kennedy, champagne in hand, surrounded by all the other butterflies the producers had collected for their precious exhibition. Trying to flirt with Emerson, some faceless entitled New Yorker I could never love, given Joe had devoured my heart before we broke up. That's what I was now, a heartless bitch competing in a tasteless romance reality TV show.

It was while I was musing and wondering if I might be able to catch a boat and get the hell out before the whole spectacle had begun that I saw the figure in white flit by behind me in the mirror. By the time I turned around, the person had vanished, presumably out into the garden. It hadn't been Jen, unmistakable in her bright yellow. Maybe another contestant? I followed after her to have a look at yet another poised beauty.

As I stepped into the sudden heat a white flutter retreating through a door further down the house caught my eye. I hastened my steps, eager to get back into the chilly AC. I'd met two beautiful blondes and a redhead; I guessed I was the raven-haired beauty in this scenario. The absurdity of this idea made me laugh out loud.

I'd reached a different wing of the house, one that didn't seem to match the rest, perhaps a later addition. Instead of dreary concrete, the wall in front of me was constructed of slightly foggy glass, stretching upwards to a peaked glass roof. An unassuming green door interrupted the expanse of glass, and when I reached to turn its knob, it wouldn't budge. When I tried again, it burst open with a sudden pop like a cork from a champagne bottle.

The familiar icy cold didn't embrace me as I stepped in. In its place was an aggressive humidity, the air so damp I could feel it pouring into my lungs. Sunlight shone through the glass ceiling, a profusion of lush green plants spilling from all sides to greet me. A conservatory. One of the better perks of being rich.

Large leaves caressed my arms and interrogated my face as I made my way forward. All the vegetation gave the space a privacy that might be useful for my time with Emerson tonight. The idea of several gown-clad women wandering around in loopy circles, slowly becoming sappy and pollen-sprinkled, searching for a man with the means to make sure they'd always have a greenhouse at their disposal had me shaking my head at the absurdity of it all.

And then I saw the woman hovering over some orchids with a spray bottle in hand. She wore a white linen suit, sensible low heels to match, her silver white hair pulled back at the nape of her neck. A large amber-colored pendant nestled in the hollow below her throat.

I must have made a rustling sound when I drew closer. She turned around, bottle brandished, and I realized she was much older than my initial guess. Her carefully applied makeup couldn't hide the lines and sun damage on her face, the narrowed lips, the loosened skin of her throat. She had to be at least seventy-five, but her bright blue eyes burned with the intensity of youth.

This was no fellow contestant scoping out tonight's hunting grounds. This was...

"Mrs. Courtland?"

"In the flesh." She said it as if she were making a joke, her voice low with a gentle rasp. "Which one are you again?"

"Zoe Roberts, but we haven't met."

"Indeed. I might be retired, but I haven't gone senile yet. You think I haven't read the biography of each girl coming to stay in my house and try to convince my nephew to marry them?" She tapped her lips with her finger, then nodded. "Ah yes. The writer."

I swallowed, nervous to be facing one of my idols. I'd been dreaming of this moment for more than a decade, and now it was here, I had no idea what to say. "I didn't mean to bother you."

"No, no, I'm interested in you. There are more commonalities between you and I than with most of the Barbies I'll be meeting." She set down her spray bottle and drew closer to me. "Remind me, what do you write?"

"Fiction."

She snorted. "Yes, I remember that much. What kind?"

"Literary."

She clicked her tongue. "You and everyone else with an MFA. Well, I can't say I approve of you as a match for my nephew. Let me spare you some disappointment. Odds are you're too neurotic for his taste. Emerson has never been a particularly refined boy, you know. He likes his women simple." She shrugged. "What can you do? The Courtland men have never been particularly progressive. They have absolutely no reason in the world to improve upon their empathic capacity, and they, like most human beings, are profoundly mediocre when it comes to their moral compasses." She collapsed into a nearby wicker chair with a sigh. "I don't approve of all this nonsense, such a lot of fuss to get the boy a girlfriend when he could take his pick in New York. But Emerson's always wanted to make a splash, be on TV, that kind of thing." She shook her head. "Wanted to be the center of attention since he was a little boy. And here we all are." I had no idea what I was supposed to say to this, but she kept going. "I guess since you're willing to play this game, you have at least one thing in common. Tell me, have you been published?"

I grimaced. I wanted this woman to think well of me. "I had a story in *the New Yorker*."

"Hmmph. When?"

Here came the painful admission. "2013."

"And nothing since?"

"No." I didn't elaborate. What was there to say? I gave up, I ran dry, there were bills to pay. Excuses all. I could have written around the edges of my job like so many of my colleagues. I could have chosen not to give up so much for Joe's sake. But instead I'd stopped.

She gave a gentle, almost musical sigh. "It's never pretty when something gets in the way of our art. To truly succeed, you must fight against those obstacles, whether they come from without or within. The main trait that distinguishes the successful artist from the pack is a certain ruthless drive. You must never stop writing. Never. No matter what happens."

I had already failed. I looked away, only for my eye to fall on a small camera concealed in a bush across from us. Its little red light shone like a singular eye. Joe's voice spoke in my head. *"I'm not going to lie to you, Zoe. This work is mediocre. Not your best. Don't embarrass yourself with the editors over this piece of tripe. Do better."* He'd always been a harsh critiquer in grad school, but afterwards, when it was just the two of us in our tiny Brooklyn apartment? He'd shredded my work into participles of misery.

The red light blinked its savage judgment of me.

I focused back on Margaret, her tired eyes and stubborn jaw. "You stopped."

"Oh yes." She shrugged. "The first time was for love. I was young and stupid, and eventually I woke up and went back to the calling to which I'd been born."

"And the second time?"

"I lost my focus, my passion for words." She reached up and fingered her pendant. "I guess you could say I became...haunted." She gave a dry little laugh. "Be sure you don't follow in my footsteps, Zoe Roberts."

She fixed me with her eyes, so wide and so blue, as if she could see right through me and all my weak excuses: for not writing, for being dumped, for being so desperate I'd decided to come on this show. I held my breath, frozen in the judgment of her regard. The sweet odor of the flowers surrounding us seemed suddenly cloying, stifling, as if masking some deeper decay

Margaret leaned forward as she spoke. "At the end of the day, women like us, we're fighting a losing battle. The world wants our primary focus to be a man, and the world will have its way in the end."

I was the first to look away. "Surely you don't believe that." I said it against my better judgment. This woman was one of my childhood idols. I wanted to drain her wisdom from her to satisfy my own enduring hunger. But I couldn't keep my mouth shut. "You never married. And after writing *This is the End*, you went on to become one of the most influential editors in New York."

She blinked and shook her head slightly. "Of course." Her voice sharpened. "I was, wasn't I? It seems like a very long time ago."

"Two years," I said helpfully.

"Someone has done her homework. And yet here I am, presiding over this three-ring circus at the insistence of my nephew. So perhaps I'm right after all." She stood up. "I find myself tired. Until this evening, Miss Roberts." She walked more slowly than I'd expected, as if she were carrying a great weight. She stopped with her hand on the door handle. "Keep in mind, my dear, there are even worse things than artistic failure."

"Like what?" My artistic and romantic failures were like twin anchors weighing me down.

She tapped her sternum gently. "Like forgetting who you are. Good luck, Miss Roberts."

I was going to need it.

Five

When our mother abandoned us, Kennedy and I had very different reactions.

I was in fifth grade, a child still. A small tube of baby fat remained stubbornly wrapped around my stomach, and I wore my long hair in a ponytail every day. I played with animal figures and dolls, and I dominated the tetherball court at recess because I didn't mind a little pain if it meant winning.

When my mom left, I was convinced she was coming back. I constructed elaborate fantasies I'd share with anyone who'd listen. "When my mom comes back, she'll take me to Disneyland," I'd tell my recess friends, who'd laugh at me behind their hands when they thought I wasn't looking. "When Mom comes back, we'll go to that Indian place with all the elephant statues," I'd tell Kennedy, who would roll her eyes and look heavenward. "When Mom comes back, we'll have Friday night movies again," I'd say in the direction of my father, who gave no sign of hearing me.

Everywhere I went, I kept an eye open for her. For a long time, I was convinced she'd come and meet my school bus coming home, so every day on the bus I'd tighten my ponytail, sit up straight, smooth any imaginary imperfections from my clothes. I was ready.

I also cried myself to sleep every night. I had terrible nightmares where I'd watch her die over and over again. Then I'd wake up in the morning and pretend nothing had happened, that today was going to be the day everything would change and she'd come home.

Kennedy, on the other hand, was thirteen. She wore lots of black eyeliner and red lipstick and shaved her legs. She was the lord and dictator of a small group of girls at school who constantly called her and asked her to the mall or the movies. They had sleepovers on Friday nights, swapping between every house but ours. If she wasn't bored by something, she hated it, and she hated our mom most of all.

She wasn't my biggest fan either.

It must have been five or six months after our mom left that I got sick. Really really sick. I thought I just had a cold. I stayed home from school by myself, curled up in feverish misery in the middle of my bed for several days. And then the wheezing began. Every breath was a painful struggle. I don't know how long I lay like that, little hands tensed into fists, time measured in oxygen I managed to suck in. It might have been forever. It wasn't like anyone was paying much attention.

Except Kennedy. She came home from school that day, Tootsie pop in her mouth, took one look at me fighting for air, and called an ambulance. No hesitation, no wondering whether she should consult with an adult, no fear Dad would be angry with her (he was). She was looking out for me first, herself second, and no one else in the world mattered at all.

She sat next to me on the bed while we were waiting for the ambulance to arrive, and she held my hand and rubbed my back, and in between strained breaths, I gasped out, "Mom. I need Mom." I thought I might be dying, and I couldn't bear the idea of not getting to see her one more time.

And for once Kennedy didn't roll her eyes or tell me to shut up. "Forget about her," she said. "You don't need her. You have me. I'll always take care of you, Zoe."

"You...hate me."

I broke into a fit of wracked coughing, so strong I thought I might throw up. Kennedy waited until I was finished. "Don't be silly." Her voice sounded different than it usually did. "I'm the big sister, and I'll take care of you, Zoe. You have to remember that, no matter what happens. Because we're the only family we need."

Things were never the same between us after that. In the end, however awful Kennedy might be on a day-to-day basis, I knew she loved me. It was us against the world. And that's what really mattered.

Six

The night of the fateful cocktail party found me queasy with both anticipation and hunger. Were they withholding food so the alcohol would hit faster? I wouldn't put it past Kennedy.

First, the dress. Chosen by Kennedy, it was slinky and black, hitting below the knee. The back plunged into a giant V, revealing my pale skin and making wearing any kind of comfortable bra impossible. It was sleeveless, much of the bodice a translucent black mesh. Spanx underneath forced my body into the proper shape, and in spite of the discomfort, my greatest worry was how I would go to the bathroom. Silver waterfall earrings, a silver wrap-around bracelet, several rings, and Kennedy forced me to wear four inch red stilettos, which made walking an adventure sport. "Accessories are crucial," she'd said several times back at her apartment, dumping bags of borrowed merchandise onto the couch for me to comb through.

Kennedy gave me her seal of approval after insisting on additional bronzer. A sound guy had already helped me secure my mike pack in as unobtrusive a way as possible. "You're one of my girls now!" Kennedy broke into maniacal laughter, which didn't exactly increase my confidence.

"I thought you said we'd hardly see other."

She wrinkled her brow. "Don't worry, you won't have to hang out much with your old sister. I'm going to spend the next several weeks being run off my feet."

I followed her to a big black SUV—apparently we couldn't be trusted to walk up that huge hill in all our finery, which, given the alarming way my ankles were already wobbling, was fine with me. Four other girls and a camera guy wearing a baseball cap already waited inside, including Lucy and Vivian.

Lucy patted the seat next to her, and I slid in gratefully, glad to have at least one person in my corner. Kennedy climbed into the front seat and addressed us as the car began to move. "Looking fabulous, everyone. Our Prince Charming is one lucky man."

All the girls cheered, including Vivian, who seemed none the worse for wear after whatever weird throat disorder had been plaguing her. All the other women held half-empty champagne glasses, and a full one was pressed into my own hand. I prayed there would be food when we reached the mansion, even if it would be hard to fit inside my newly squeezed body.

"My girls are the best of the best," Kennedy continued. "This is a once-in-a-lifetime experience, and"—she cupped her hand around her mouth as if telling a secret—"none of my girls ever get sent home the first night. So relax, enjoy, and really live in the moment, you know what I mean?"

The other girls nodded along as if the words coming out of Kennedy's mouth weren't one big load of bullshit. Lucy giggled and leaned close to my ear. "I'm so glad Kennedy is our producer," she whispered. "I'd be way too nervous to meet the Prince Charming otherwise. I mean, I don't even know his name!"

None of the girls knew it was Emerson except me. Having a producer sister did have its fringe benefits. Although it looked like Giselle was getting some kind of leg up as well. Who was she? A relative of someone important to the show? A family friend of a network bigwig?

Kennedy had only told me the basics about Emerson: that the man came from money, that he loved being the center of attention, that he spent a lot of time partying, that I didn't need to worry about his dead fiancée. "So we have absolutely nothing in common?" I'd asked. After all, I was still hung up on my very much alive *ex*-fiancé.

Kennedy scoffed. "Let me tell you, sister mine, common interests mean nothing on shows like these. Toss that idea into the garbage right now. It's chemistry, chemistry, and more chemistry. That's all that matters. Anyway, you're well set up to double team him with mysterious artist and manic pixie dream girl. Default to the dream girl and then when you can't figure out what to say, lapse into the mystery. Easy."

Years of producing romance reality TV shows had completely warped Kennedy's ideas about relationships. Well, that and her five-month marriage that ended with a restraining order. We Roberts girls didn't exactly have the best track record when it came to matters of the heart.

Kennedy kept trying to pump us all up in the SUV by asking inane questions. "Aren't you excited?" she'd say in a fake voice, and then we'd all squeal and wonder who Prince Charming could be. Vivian gushed about how she might be meeting her future husband tonight, all while swishing her perfect blond curls. Her deep blue gown matched her eyes and showed about a mile of cleavage. Did I look too grim in black? I could already feel myself freezing up in front of the camera, showing too much teeth and laughing too loudly.

The SUV pulled up in front of the mansion, and we all piled out, only to be rushed into the foyer now lit bright as day, up the stairs, and into a large holding room where at least ten girls already waited. Several makeup stations with large mirrors surrounded by light bulbs were clustered on one side of the room, along with three floor-length mirrors. A few plush couches were arranged on the other side, along with a large supply of booze.

The five of us rushed with uncanny herd instinct to the mirrors to check our makeup, left unobserved for ten whole minutes. Kennedy uncorked a bottle of champagne with a large pop, holding it aloft as the fizz frothed unchecked like effervescent semen. "Let's get this party started," she shouted. All the girls cheered again. They spent the entire evening cheering at the slightest provocation. I'd never been around so much forced pep in my life.

Producers kept arriving with girls in tow until the room was exploding with silk and hairspray, perfume and perfectly tanned legs, curls and stilettos and lipstick. I lost count of how many of us were waiting. I perched at the far end of one of the sofas and pretended to sip my champagne while I watched everyone primp and drink and circle around one another, trying to suss out who presented the most serious competition. Two cameramen were in the room with us at all times, their red lights glowing, just in case anything juicy happened. The whole display made me sick.

I couldn't stop staring at the women wearing novelty outfits. Giselle was dressed as a sexy leprechaun in a short green dress puffed out by white lacy petticoats, a white apron tied around her tiny waist. One girl wore a penguin onesie. Another wore a white lab coat over a slinky red dress. Still another wore cowboy boots and a cowboy hat along with a skimpy brown dress that was all leather and fringe.

The couches began to fill as women tired of staring at their reflections, and the one in the lab coat came to sit next to me, not making eye contact. Her long brown hair fell into ripples as silky as Vivian's, but her pale skin told me she didn't get the memo about going to the tanning salon. She too held a half-empty glass that she nervously tapped with her fingernails. Eventually she shook her head and whispered, "Fuck me."

"Enjoying the view?" I asked.

"I can't believe I took a leave of absence from my PhD program for this." She closed her eyes, showing off the luxuriant fake lashes they made us all wear tonight. "What was I thinking?"

"Well, if it makes you feel any better, it looks like you and I are the only two people in the room having second thoughts. Maybe everyone else knows something we don't?"

"Here's hoping." She put down the glass and slumped back into the couch. No Spanx required for her, and I hated myself for noticing. "I'm Michelle."

"Zoe."

She started blinking furiously. "Oh my god, these eyelashes! They're so uncomfortable. I wonder if I put them on wrong." Blink blink. Blink blink. "I feel like I have spiders growing on my eyelids."

I cracked up in spite of myself. "Insect eyelids, bloody lips,"—I wave my manicured fingers in front of us—"and don't forget our sharpened claws. Guess we're ready to hunt our prey."

"Heaven forbid if we're not married by the time we're thirty."

Ouch. Every road of conversation led back to Joe. We could have been married by now, if I'd just kept my mouth shut and given him what he wanted.

"Speak for yourself," I said. "Thirty has already come for me, and in a few months, it will have gone as well."

Her hand flew to cover her mouth. "I'm so sorry. I didn't mean...it's just what my mother says all the time. She's the one who submitted me for the show in the first place. I haven't had a boyfriend for years and years. It's hard enough to be taken seriously in the hard sciences as it is. Especially when you look like this. My mother just doesn't get it."

"What are you getting your PhD in?"

"Astrophysics."

Damn. I didn't understand why she was here either. My MFA had been a waste of paper, but a PhD in physics? This girl had some serious brainpower going on behind her pretty hazel eyes. "Hence the lab coat."

She rolled her eyes. "They're making me wear it. It's ridiculous. I never wear these. I don't even own one. I feel like I'm a freak they're trotting out before the public for some good PR: see, even female scientists are on board."

"Well, you are here," I pointed out. "So it's not exactly false PR."

She gave a little sigh. "Yes, I'm here. It would be nice to meet someone who isn't a physicist, you know? With them, first things first, we have to engage in a mean-spirited dick measuring contest. And I can't just be above it all, not unless I want to be professionally screwed."

"And you think being on this show won't do the job of fucking you over?" I'd read a story about a woman who wanted to practice as a psychotherapist right after being on reality TV. No one would hire her. No one wanted that hot mess helping them sort out their own problems.

Michelle laughed. "You think any of my colleagues would ever watch a show called *Love Story*? Please. I'm more incognito here than I'd be anywhere else." She blinked again. "How often do you think they'll make us wear these things?"

I found myself batting my own eyes in sympathy. "Kennedy says they're very camera friendly."

She rubbed her eye. "This is fucking fantastic. I'm going to be sent home on the first night because I can't handle cosmetics." She began laughing. "Is that a trenchant commentary on the state of objectification of women's bodies or what?" She stopped suddenly, looking self-conscious. "What about you? What do you do?"

That was the million-dollar question. "I have an MFA in creative writing." I had to begin presenting myself as a credible writer if I was going to use this show to build my platform.

"God, am I going to end up in your next book?"

I gave her a side-long look but thanked my lucky stars she didn't tell me she had her own idea for a great book she'd always wanted to write. "I signed the NDA the same as everyone else."

Another woman approached us, this one with light brown skin, smooth black hair, and perfect eyebrows, dressed in a simple orange gown that made her stand out from all the reds and blacks and blues. She raised her eyebrows at both of us. "And here we have the bitches with the brains, am I right?" She lowered herself carefully onto the couch next to us, probably another Spanx victim, which cheered me up. "Lord save me from the amount of petty talk going on in this room right now."

"I love your dress," Michelle ventured.

She had said the right thing. The woman beamed. "I designed it myself." She held out a hand. "I'm Simone."

Michelle introduced us, and we sat in silence for a moment. "You enjoying your free vacation?" Simone asked. "This is my first time in the Bahamas, and I've gotta tell you, I hope they give us plenty of time to hang on the beach."

"You're going to get the idea that I'm a workaholic," Michelle said, "and you wouldn't be wrong, but I'm already missing my laptop. There's nothing to do here. No phone? No books? I'm going to lose my mind after six days, let alone six weeks."

"Unless you're too busy falling in love to notice." The way Simone said it, I could tell she was kidding. "They let me bring my sketch pad, so I'm planning to do some work if I can. Find some island inspiration."

"They let me bring my journal," I offered. I was going to have to guard that book like it was made of gold.

Another pause. "Do you think he'll send you home tonight?" Michelle asked.

This was what we'd been reduced to. Competing for the favor of a stranger who would determine the course of our lives based on whether he thought we looked hot enough in our evening wear.

As much as she drove me up the wall, thank God for Kennedy. Because if it weren't for her promise I'd be staying, I would already have been losing my shit.

Another measure of Kennedy's influence? I was one of the first women to meet Emerson. They let us out of our holding room one at a time to make a dramatic entrance down the staircase, greeting Emerson at the bottom. Do something memorable, they told us, you only get one chance at a first impression. Emerson mattered, sure, but even more urgent was the necessity of shining for the American public, the invisible participant in this particular threesome, represented by the ever-present cameras. Be witty, say something cute, make a connection.

Three minutes, they kept saying, three minutes and then you have to move on. We'd get more time with Emerson later...if we were lucky. "Five, tops," Kennedy hissed in my ear as she escorted me out of the room. She'd relayed my instructions to make a lasting first impression this morning. I was third, after Giselle and a blonde bombshell named Grace. Did they stagger hair color on purpose?

God, I was nervous. I hesitated outside the door, and Kennedy gave me a little push. With the unaccustomed heels, it was enough to make me lurch forward, and then I was going down the stairs whether I liked it or not, steadying myself on the banister while trying not to disarrange the flowers. I couldn't see Emerson or the cameras, only the glaring lights as I groped for each stair with the heel of my shoe and tried not to blink as much as Michelle. I don't think I breathed the entire descent.

When I reached the bottom, I looked up into a man's smiling face. Emerson Courtland in the flesh.

He was handsome, I'd give him that, and he did look more or less like the photos Kennedy had shown me. He wasn't as tall as I thought he'd be, but then I was wearing higher heels than normal. His hair, a shade between blonde and brown, flipped up in a way that suggested lots of hair product, a rugged five o'clock shadow graced his strong chin, and his smile revealed a small gap between his two front teeth. His gray suit fit impeccably.

"I'm Emerson," he rumbled. I held out my hand just as he went in for a hug, and in my haste to adjust, I ended up knocking my forehead against his ear. Smooth, Zoe, really smooth. He enveloped me in a scented cloud of citrus and wood.

I pulled away, gave him the obligatory smile, and began reciting as Kennedy had told me to do:

"Had I the heaven's embroidered cloths,
Enwrought with golden and silver light,
The blue and the dim and the dark cloths
Of night and light and the half-light;
I would spread the cloths under your feet:
But I, being poor, have only my dreams;
I have spread my dreams under your feet;
Tread softly because you tread on my dreams."

I looked up at him through my fake lashes as I intoned the familiar lines, trying to give my voice a husky quality. After the first few lines, his surprised smile began to stiffen. Not a poetry lover then. As Kennedy must have known when she pushed me to do this.

At least I chose something short.

"You wrote me a poem," he said when I'd finished. "How sweet."

This was the man I was supposed to fall in love with? Someone who had never heard that iconic last line? Jesus Christ. "It's actually a poem by Yeats," I said. "I'm not much of a poet myself." Make that the understatement of the year. I'd reminded Kennedy as much when she'd insisted on this plan, but she didn't care. She wanted a love poem, and she was going to get a love poem. "I'm more of a fiction writer."

His eyes shifted up above my shoulder, as if he were already anticipating the next girl down the stairs. "Oh really? I only read nonfiction."

I was surprised he read anything at all, but I kept that charming impression to myself and decided my best course at this point was to change the subject. "How has your night been so far?"

That's when I noticed the cameras, two of them, perched on the shoulders of two beefy guys including my baseball cap friend from the SUV. There was something utterly demoralizing about knowing my lackluster introduction to Emerson had been caught on film. No wonder all the women on these shows cried all the time.

"Great, I'm excited to be here." He said it like it was a line in a script, and hell, for all I knew, it was.

"Well, I look forward to getting to you know better." Ugh. Really, Zoe? Could I be any more awkward? At that point I just wanted to get out of there, the sooner, the better.

I was already heading out of the room when he said, "Um, what's your name?"

I stopped, mortified, before forcing myself to turn. "Zoe." I gave him the biggest smile I could muster. "My name is Zoe."

"Nice to meet you, Zoe."

All captured on camera for posterity. Soon everyone in the United States would know I couldn't even remember to introduce my sorry-ass self.

Cringing, I paused by the risers before entering the lounge. I couldn't hear Giselle and Grace chatting, and I didn't want to sit there in silence staring at Giselle's Disney princess beauty or making small talk about how great Emerson was when I hadn't learned a single meaningful thing about him. I'd fucked it up so badly, if it weren't for Kennedy, I'd have known for sure I'd be leaving this island tonight.

As it was, I still wasn't confident. After all, it wasn't like she could force him to pick me.

I saw a door off in the corner, and I took my chance to escape. Just to collect myself. I knew I'd have to push hard to get more one-on-one time with Emerson tonight and do a better job interesting him. No more talk about literature or poetry, that was for sure.

The door led to a hallway with several closed doors. God, my dress was tight. And the AC was still going full blast, making goose bumps stand out on my bare arms. I chose the first door and slipped inside.

I'd entered a library, the kind I'd only dreamed of, with walls lined with floor-to-ceiling bookcases complete with sliding ladder. The bookcases were built around a fireplace at the end of the room, sadly devoid of a fire to lift the artificial chill. Draperies covered the single large window, giving the room an intimate and isolated feel. It no longer felt like I was on a tropical island.

A large table dominated the center of the room, and at the table sat a man in a suit, his head in his arms. He didn't appear to notice I'd entered. I almost snuck right back out, but I needed to be somewhere away from the other women where I could pretend my life hadn't taken a sudden weird turn into reality TV.

I walked as quietly as possible to the sofa in front of the drapes, but my horrible heels clacked on the hardwood floor in spite of my best efforts, and the man looked up, running a hand through his curly hair. I recognized him immediately as Cannon Murphy, the show's host and veteran of several seasons of the *Engagement* shows. He was more handsome than I'd expected him to be, with a carefully groomed goatee and a humorous glint in his brown eyes. He gave me a crooked grin. "Hiding already?"

"Just for a minute." I sank gratefully onto the couch, my feet aching.

"Your introduction with Emerson went that well, huh?"

I prepared to lie, but then I shrugged. Why bother? The camera had caught every painful second. "It was a disaster," I admitted. "I recited Yeats's *Cloths of Heaven* and he thought I'd written it myself."

He laughed. "'Tread softly because you tread on my dreams.' Nice choice, but yeah, I can see that going over Emerson's head. He's not exactly a poetry kind of guy." He cocked his head. "I don't suppose you play golf?"

I groaned and rubbed the top of my nose before remembering I shouldn't be touching my makeup-covered face. "Would it shock you to learn that's not my scene at all?"

"You can always let him teach you. Have him embrace you to correct your swing, that kind of thing. It could be romantic." His eyes danced.

No matter how hard I tried, I couldn't picture myself spending the next forty years of my life on a golf course. "Only if I can take him on a nice romantic tour of a huge library."

Cannon laughed again, the corners of his eyes crinkling. "I can already tell you two are soul mates."

"Make sure to remind him of that when he's making his choices tonight," I joked. Well, I was mostly joking. I tried to get more comfortable on the couch, a hopeless proposition in my outfit. "It must be nice being the host. Nobody's going to send *you* home."

"Very true." He stretched like a cat. "Instead I'm stuck here on an island for six weeks with nothing to do but work work work."

"Not to be unappreciative, but couldn't you fly in when you're needed and spend the rest of your time in LA?"

"You'd think so, wouldn't you?" He got up and began prowling around the room. "But no. The idea for *Love Story* is that the host is supposed to become a kind of best friend to Prince Charming, here to guide him through the entire process. After all, I've been through similar experiences, so who better to help this season's chump?"

"Wow." I didn't expect him to sound so negative about the whole thing. He'd done so many seasons of these shows, I figured he'd have drunk the Kool-Aid.

"I'm just thanking my lucky stars the network didn't decide on eight weeks of shooting. Or ten. Can you imagine? Ten weeks stuck here listening to some rich dude complain about which girl to date for the next few months? The things I do for fame." With that he collapsed dramatically on the couch next to me. "So what's your deal? No themed outfit, I see. I guess the producers took pity on you, what with the whole reciting poetry thing. Your idea?"

I gave him a look. "Are you kidding? That was all Kennedy. And get this: she also wants me to start writing him love letters." The embarrassments never ceased. "I think after his reaction to the poem, I might have to rebel."

Cannon snorted. "I support your rebellion. That Kennedy's a real piece of work. Last season I thought she was heading for a breakdown. You know she was one of my main producers for my second time on *Her Engagement*? She's good. Too good. That woman could make a piece of furniture think it was in love. But when I finally got home, suddenly"—he waved his hands in the air—"the fog cleared." He shot me a look. "Watch out for her.

Kennedy hadn't always been that scary good at manipulating people. But once Mom bailed, she studied people like her life depended on it. Kennedy always thought she knew better than anyone else. And she was so hyper competent, maybe she was even right. But falling within her scope of attention held a cost. The debt would always come due in the end.

Like the stupid poem I'd be shown reciting on national television, as one tiny example.

"You have any other advice for me?" I asked.

He shrugged. "Remember it's TV. It's all a game. It's make believe, but the feelings are real enough. Eventually you'll go back home and sort everything out. Each season did a real number on my head because I'd lose sight of what to believe." He paused. "Remind yourself why you chose to come."

"I have no idea why I'm here." Even though I was putting on an act for him, the words gleamed with unexpected vulnerability.

"You're an honest one, aren't you? I remember when I was your kind of naïve." He stood and walked to the window. "The producers have probably been telling you ad nauseam this experience is going to change your life, yeah?"

I laughed. That part was true enough. "They won't shut up about it."

Cannon pulled the draperies aside, but we couldn't see anything out there in the dark. "Well, they're right. You want my real advice? Take this seriously. Being on reality TV can crack your life wide open, give you opportunities you never imagined. But you have to be smart about it, and you have to be ready to jump on whatever is offered to you." He tapped the window. "If you're at a dead end, this show could be your ticket out. But only if you let it."

I joined him at the window, trying to see anything moving out there in the darkness. I was banking on exactly what he was talking about, a way to catapult my writing career above Joe's. I didn't want all my past mistakes extending indefinitely into the future, pinioning me with regret.

Cannon put his hand on my shoulder, and I leaned into him without thinking about it. "Also," he said quietly, "and I doubt you need this advice, but be careful what you admit to out loud."

He nodded his head towards one of the bookshelves. It took me a while to find it, but there it was: the angry red light, the only sign the lens was watching. I reached around and fingered my mike pack, attached securely to my dress. The red light from the camera blinked. *"You don't belong here,"* it said. In Joe's voice. *"Do you actually think you're good enough to surpass me?"*

I swallowed. Was that the voice I was going to listen to for the rest of my life? "I guess I should get back out there." I offered Cannon my hand. "I'm Zoe, by the way."

"I know." He took my hand gravely, pressed his other hand on top of it. "Starting tonight, I'm Emerson's perfect best friend. I know who you all are."

"Well then." Not disconcerting at all. "I guess I'll see you out there."

He stopped me when I reached the door. "Zoe." I turned. "Don't be satisfied with stories, how things have gone with others. Unfold your own myth." At my confused look, he said, "Rumi. You're not the only one who can quote poetry." He gave me his dimpled smile and for a second I wished he were the Prince Charming I was competing for.

The night became a blur of alcohol and hair and perfume and verbal dances cut short by tipsy laughter. Every time I turned around another glass of champagne was being shoved into my hand, and if I declined, whichever producer had targeted me would run through a list of my other alcoholic options. I kept Kennedy's advice in the forefront of my mind: "If you're going to create some drama, and let me tell you, I live for that stuff, make sure you're making a conscious choice about it. Let the other women booze too much and make emotional decisions. You, my dear, have the luxury of being strategic."

And she was right, it wasn't just me being plied with alcohol. All the women were being targeted in the same way. The huge lights rigged above us counteracted the AC, and we were all hot and flushed and high on nerves. The producers wanted a party atmosphere, and by God they were going to get one. And if one of us couldn't hold our liquor and erupted in inappropriate emotions or unexpected drama, so much the better. I began sneaking off to the bathroom to empty my glass in the sink.

When all the women were crowded into the room, Emerson entered with Cannon and gave a cheesy speech about how great we all were, how excited he was to go on this journey with us, and how he'd never felt more ready to fall in love. At one point Cannon even clapped him on the back in a show of male solidarity. Michelle and I exchanged pained looks, which made the whole spectacle more bearable.

Right at the end of the speech Cannon looked directly at me and winked. At least I had the host on my side.

The producers also trotted out Margaret Courtland. She looked as elegant as she had earlier in the day, but the bright lights gave her face a sepulchral quality, her eyes deep-set and shadowed and her cheekbones prominent. She only spoke a few words welcoming us to her home before retreating gracefully from our Bacchanalian festivities.

Michelle and I stuck close together making sardonic comments about the zoo around us until Kennedy arranged for me to have the coveted one-on-one time with Emerson. I took him to the conservatory as planned, trailed by the omnipresent camera person, but he seemed oblivious to the beauty surrounding us. He looked tired, bags visible under his eyes, and he kept looking past me as if expecting to be interrupted. The camera stared at us from its all-seeing lens as I tried to make successful small talk, mostly by getting Emerson to talk about himself.

I knew none of this footage would make the final cut. In spite of the adrenaline coursing through my body, the conversation was nothing special. If I'd agreed to go on this show hoping for sparks, I'd have been vastly disappointed.

I was still disappointed, even though falling in love wasn't part of the plan. Would never *be* part of the plan.

I didn't want to go through that again.

And now I didn't have to worry about it. The only challenge would be convincing Emerson to keep me around long enough for me to develop my brand. And with Kennedy in my corner...well, let's be honest. Kennedy was the only reason I had any shot at all.

At the end of the night, that still stretch of time when the sky's darkness feels a little less absolute and the world stands on the edge of a precipice, the sense of waiting permeated the pre-dawn, and nowhere was that stronger than in the mansion's reception room where all of us contestants stood in our tiered rows, waiting to hear our fate. Anyone sent home tonight had failed absolutely; no one would remember them, not the producers, not their fellow contestants, and certainly not the American public.

I chose a place between Michelle and Lucy, women I hoped would be chosen as well. Kennedy had emphasized how important it was to make friends. "You want to find a couple people who will have your back in the first few weeks," she'd said.

"And then?"

"And then you've already won and anything goes." So very Kennedy. Loyalty wasn't exactly her strong suit.

We stood there, all twenty-five of us in our elegant gowns and hair-sprayed curls and uncomfortable shoes. Four camera people stood with their cameras pointed at us to capture our every reaction. I didn't want to say anything, knowing every word would be picked up by my microphone. Its pack taped to my back helped remind me to be cautious.

Emerson took forever to arrive, and when he did, Cannon by his side, it was obvious he'd just had a makeup touchup. Most of us looked wilted, especially under the stark lighting, but he looked more energetic than he had in the conservatory several hours earlier. Maybe they'd given him some caffeine.

I scanned the faces of the women on the platform opposite me. The woman in the penguin onesie gazed at her feet with large sad eyes, blinking back tears, and an unexpected stab of anger ran through me. "What does she have to cry about?" I thought. "It's not like *she's* wearing heels."

Emerson gave another bullshit speech and then paused dramatically before announcing the first person who would be staying another week. I tried not to shift my weight, knowing it wouldn't decrease the throbbing in the ball of my right foot. Someone coughed. A sickly sweet stench hit my nostrils. It was all I could do not to cough myself.

Everything around me—the women's heavily made-up faces, the highly polished wooden floor reflecting the lights, the intent work ethic of the camera people even after a long night—came into sharp focus. Michelle brushed the back of my hand with hers, and I could feel every little hair bending at her touch. Emerson took a breath, his shoulders rising, and began to open his mouth to announce a name. We all held our breath in collective anxiety and anticipation.

Into the void of the evening, a scream shot like a spear. Everyone froze in confusion until another scream followed the first, breaking us into splinters of action. The women around me shifted, craning their heads, trying to see what was happening. The camera people's focus sharpened further as they slowly advanced on their prey, one hanging back to record Emerson's confusion. Kennedy stood at a cameraman's shoulder, grinning like a wolf. A few other producers hovered beside her, letting the scene play out but ready to step in if necessary.

Finally I found the source of the scream. It was the woman in the penguin onesie, her face screwed up in an unattractive rictus of emotion. Wearing all that sweltering plush, her face shone bright red in the suit's cowl, and strands of straw-colored hair clung damply to her neck.

As she screamed she did a ridiculous little penguin dance and rubbed her hands compulsively down the front of her onesie as if trying to get them clean. No one moved to help her. Was she having some kind of allergic reaction? Was there an insect trapped in her suit?

Or was she simply incredibly wasted? Several of the women looked woozy.

As I stood paralyzed, wishing Kennedy or one of the other producers would intervene, the woman reached up and began to unzip her suit. Maybe it *was* a bug. I hung back, horrified at the thought of something alive and wriggling about to erupt from her clothes.

The penguin woman scrambled out of her suit and threw it on the floor in front of us. I couldn't help backing away, waiting for some nasty scorpion thing to stick its head out. But the suit just lay there in a crumpled mess, and the woman, now wearing only a skimpy little tank top and boy shorts, kept screaming and pointing at it. "It's my skin," she shrieked, tears running down her face. "It's my skin, and it's too big for me!" Followed by more screaming.

The camera people kept doing their job, and the producers kept hovering, and Kennedy kept looking like someone had given her a free ice cream sundae, and in that moment I hated them all. My disgust included myself; I remained rooted to the spot. I'd had that uncharitable thought about her right before she'd broken down. What on earth had I been thinking?

It was Cannon who finally broke ranks, Cannon who stepped

forward, took off his suit jacket and slipped it around the girl's shoulders, Cannon who spoke softly to her and gently led her away. When one of the cameramen tried to follow, he glared and shook his head, and the guy actually listened and turned back around. A few producers did follow, and I wondered if they had Valium on hand for just this kind of emergency.

The rest of us looked at each other uneasily, as if Penguin Girl's nervous breakdown might be catching. Another producer led Emerson out of the room, and we were allowed to take a break. A plate of sandwiches materialized, and Vivian complained bitterly about not being able to eat carbs. I decided not to care about my new sleeker body and dug right in. It had been a long night.

When we reconvened, the ceremony took over two hours. Emerson called my name about halfway through and tied the red ribbon around my wrist, the bow lopsided and as cranky as I felt. And that was it. I was in for at least the first week. Michelle congratulated me, happy from the ribbon already around her own wrist, but I felt weirdly deflated. The whole process was so artificial, so sterile, so...lacking in any kind of actual romance or feeling. I knew they'd edit that all in, but the gap between reality and appearance had never felt so wide.

Those of us staying were ferried back to our bungalow rooms to collapse in bed and obsess over everything that had happened. Penguin Girl's screams kept replaying in my head. I'd never even learned her name.

I needed to do better to make it to week two, that was clear. Kennedy's carefully crafted artsy persona wasn't going to cut it. I couldn't even fake being an artist with any kind of success.

But I kept thinking about Cannon's advice to me. That this show could lead me to unexpected opportunities. Everything happened for a reason, didn't it, and however unlikely it seemed, here I was in the ranks of women competing on this show.

If this was my second shot for a writing career, I wanted to give the cameras a show the American public would remember.

Seven

Transcript from *Love & Bubbles*, episode 10, hosted by Olivia Childs for *Everything Entertainment Online*, January 15, 2019:

Olivia Childs: We've got a gorgeous tropical island, we've got a formidable and disapproving aunt, and we've got...a penguin having a nervous breakdown? (laugh track)

Hi everyone, I'm Olivia Childs, and we are here for more down and dirty dishing at Love & Bubbles recapping Emerson Courtland's season of *Love Story*. (She raises her full champagne flute in a toast gesture.)

And damn, do we have a lot of dishing to do today! This episode was not what I expected at all. Sure, we got the glamour, we got the gowns, we got to watch first impressions being made and sparks already beginning to fly. But that was the tip of the iceberg!

First off, didn't Emerson look drool-worthy? I can't resist a man in a tux. And his tribute to his dead fiancée brought tears to these jaded eyes. Yeah, yeah, we all know I'm actually a total marshmallow on the inside. I think the show handled the whole thing with a lot of sensitivity and class, didn't you? Let me know what you think in the comments. I'm definitely rooting for Emerson to find another love as deep and true as the one he lost.

And with that, we move on to the beautiful belles in this season of *Love Story*. I always love seeing all the girls meet their potential sweetheart, don't you? It makes my heart go pitter-pat, pitter-pat (she beats the rhythm on her heart), and when they crash and burn, wow, do they blaze out in a fire of glory. Whew! For this first night we needed a fire extinguisher! But let's talk about the winners first, shall we?

First up was Giselle, and can I just say, she reminds me of a young Nicole Kidman. And it's not just the long red hair, although she does have one magnificent mane. (She shakes out her own glossy brown hair.) This lady has charm and poise up the wazoo. She had Emerson wrapped around her little finger in less than a minute, and did you see the smile on his face after she left? Adorable, am I right?

Other ladies I think we should keep a close eye on, at least until we get a better idea of Emerson's type? Well, we have Lauren, our sporty girl next door who can keep him company on the golf range, if that's what he wants. And I liked Simone. That girl is funny; she has a gift for one-liners that's going to keep us entertained all season long. And then we have the bevy of knock-out blondes: Grace and Summer and my personal favorite, Vivian. Why Vivian? Well, Summer has two little kids, and at the end of the day I don't know if I can see Emerson going for a single mom. And Grace is gorgeous, but she didn't show us anything behind that dazzling smile. But Vivian is the complete package: beautiful, confident, well-spoken, and I think it was really sweet that she went to the trouble of bringing an entire box of Emerson's favorite candy bars all the way from the good old US of A since he can't get them on his private island. That's the kind of gesture that screams girlfriend material.

Speaking of the island, I'd sign up to be on the show just for the free beach vacation, wouldn't you? And that house! What is going on with that hulking piece of concrete? But the interiors are gorgeous: the crown molding, the marble floor in the entryway, the massive chandelier in the Culling room. Seriously, if they put any more lights on that thing it would be a fire hazard. And I've always wanted to make an entrance down a double staircase like that. Are these women fulfilling our deepest Cinderella fantasies or what?

The first season of *Love Story* really leaned into its opulent surroundings, and they're doing the same thing again this season. I really like some of the touches they've included: the cute little rose Tiffany lamp in the Hot Seat room, the glowing sunken lights and tiki lamps in the garden, the bright pink and orange and white accent colors. I really felt the move away from the manor house rich burgundies and chocolates of last season.

And what about that conservatory? You could fit about five of my apartments in that space! And all that lush tropical greenery? They even put a freaking waterfall in there! Pure decadence all around, and that's one of the reasons we adore *Love Story* with all our hearts. Not that Emerson isn't absolutely delicious, but his family's private island has to be a huge reason the producers courted him for this season.

All right, what did we think about his Aunt Margaret? Let me know in the comments, but I thought she was a trip! I loved her little speech to the women when she talked about how a partner is one of the most important choices in life and they should never settle or depend on a man to give them the things they can get for themselves. The irony, in a show designed around its wealthy leading man! That woman is not kidding around, and I hope we see more of her. Can't you see her giving relationship advice to Emerson and being a complete hard-ass about it? (imitates Margaret's rounder vowels and lower voice) "It's not all about a beautiful face, Emerson. Focus on someone worthy of you." That would be priceless. She's going to see right through some of those girls, and I can see her making some of them *very* uncomfortable, so I hope she's on board for playing a greater role on the show.

Now, before we get to the girl in the penguin suit, let's talk about some of the other drama of the evening. What do you all think of Thea? I love that Southern drawl of hers, but my, my, did she have some nasty things to say about some of the other girls. I don't know which was worse, openly laughing at Giselle's outfit or calling Grace an empty-headed plastic prude. Actually, scratch that, we all know which was worse, and that was Lucy joking Naomi had to be angry in order to stay on the show. If she had been deliberately calling out potential racism, that would be one thing, but it came across as insensitive and tone deaf. Not cool, Lucy. Of course then she went on to cry during her Hot Seat. That girl isn't going to be able to hold it together for long, that's my prediction and you can hold me to it.

Naomi, on the other hand, rose to the occasion and then some. When Lucy made her racist comment, she simply raised her eyebrow higher than I thought it could go and left it at that. She had one of the most compelling conversations with Emerson, complete with a small good night peck on the cheek. Plus that blue gown she wore was to die for, one of the best outfits of the night. That slit was just high enough to say danger. I'd put her in the "Women to Watch" category.

What about Eva with her cut-out dress? The moment when she told Emerson she was a tigress in the bedroom, I didn't know whether to laugh or cry, but he seemed to be into it, at least enough to keep her another week. And Michelle mixing Emerson his favorite cocktail in that lab coat? I actually thought that was kind of sweet.

And then there was that poor waif Zoe of the huge eyes and dramatic eyebrows. Can't you see her as the sad Goth girl in high school who wrote dramatic poems and wore too much eyeliner? And did you see the look on Emerson's face when she started reciting that poem? He was not impressed. And she looked so sad afterwards. Something emo's going on inside that one, and personally, I'm here for it. There's going to be some drama there pretty much guaranteed, and I'm betting that's why she was allowed to stay.

Even with all the dramatic personalities on display here, I don't think any of us expected poor Willa to tear off that penguin suit right in the middle of the Culling. When Cannon teased that this season would be full of surprises, he wasn't joking. Let's face it, Willa didn't have the best shot of being chosen to stay by Emerson anyway. We didn't see any clips of them bonding, and their introduction was almost as awkward as Zoe's poetry debacle. But Willa's outburst clinched her dismissal from the house and seemed to shake up the rest of the women in the process. Even Emerson looked a little gray by the end of the ceremony.

Looking at the women as a whole, I think this is shaping up to be a strong second season. But it all depends on Emerson Courtland. I like the rich guy angle, I really do. It makes a nice change from the Every Man we're so used to seeing on these shows, and we can use a touch of fantasy in our reality TV, am I right? For now Emerson's a bit of a mystery: tall, handsome, his thick tousled hair, that roguish smile. But what makes him tick? What is his type? And will he be able to rise above his tragic past? I'm looking forward to finding out.

Who are you most looking forward to seeing more of this season? And who do you think has the best shot at winning Emerson's heart? Let me know in the comments, and you know my Instagram DMs are always open to you. I love you guys so much, thank you for watching, and ta-ta for now!

EIGHT

The next morning a sound guy came knocking on my door to wire me up, and then those of us who made the cut—twenty in total, most of whose names I couldn't remember—moved into the big house. They'd set up several bedrooms dormitory style with bunk beds. I roomed with Lucy, Michelle, and Simone. The information quickly circulated there were hidden cameras all over our areas of the house.

With insufficient closet space, we only hung our seven gowns each. Twenty-eight dresses barely fit in the wardrobe, and brightly colored silks and satins burst forth whenever we opened the doors. Our other stuff was regulated to piles in our suitcases or on the floor. And with eight of us sharing one bathroom, forget about counter space. Just getting everyone showered every day was a feat of Herculean proportions.

All the contestants were in one wing of bedrooms on the second floor, with Cannon and some other crew members in another wing on the same floor. Kennedy had her own room in one of the bungalows, along with some of the other senior crew, and from something she let slip, it seemed like the regular staff of the house also lived down there. The third floor was Margaret Courtland's domain, strictly off limits to everyone from the show.

All the common areas on the main floor were at our disposal, including the enormous kitchen manned by an incorrigible chef who served buffet-style meals three times a day. We could grab snacks whenever we chose, and alcohol was encouraged at all times of day and night.

Extensive manicured grounds surrounded the house, including a swimming pool and hot tub, and a punishing flight of stairs went all the way down the bluff to the beach below. It took less than twenty-four hours for the women to start bragging about how many times they'd taken the stairs to keep their physiques in television-ready shape.

After the house tour and a late lunch, my three roomies and I trooped back up to our room, and Simone immediately started stripping and changing into a bikini. "So soon?" Michelle quipped. Even without her uncomfortable fake eyelashes, she blinked more than normal.

"You have any better ideas?" Simone pulled on the skimpiest white bikini bottoms I'd ever seen. "You want to lounge around on the couches downstairs and snipe at the other women, be my guest. There aren't going to be any challenges or dates today, so I'm going to grab me some precious beach time."

"Don't you want to try to catch a glimpse of Emerson?" Lucy sighed like she'd magically already developed feelings for the guy, even though she'd spent all of ten minutes alone with him last night.

Michelle rolled her eyes. "I'll join you," she told Simone. "After the way that girl lost her shit last night, I'm in for a little extra self care."

"You worried you gonna go the same way?" Simone asked. "Because if that's true I wish you'd told me before I agreed to room with you. A girl needs her beauty sleep." She swished her long black hair, making me wonder how many of us sported fake hair.

Michelle snorted. "Are you kidding? If I could survive all these years in my physics program, I can survive a few weeks here. It's not as if my entire future is at stake."

I hated her a little for saying that because that's exactly how it felt. This was the end of the road for me. I had no plans beyond using this show to catapult me forward.

Michelle fingered her mike pack before removing it to change into her suit. "We should probably check in with sound before we head down."

Lucy gave me her best puppy-eyed look. "You'll stay in the house with me, won't you, Zoe? At least until we find out what Emerson's doing today?"

I already had regrets about my new bestie, but mindful of the watching cameras, I tried to play nice. "We can hang out by the pool," I offered.

Lucy's face lit up in her typical over-the-top fashion. "I brought the cutest cover-up," she gushed. "After all, we can't afford to get sunburned, can we? Imagine what that would look like on camera."

She had a point, and when we went downstairs, I chose two recliners shaded by a large umbrella. Giselle was already lying out in a black bikini, wearing huge glamorous sunglasses. She gave us a nod as we got settled. The fancy infinity pool looked like it was falling into the ocean, its water a sharp camera-friendly blue. I closed my eyes, trying to relax after the absurdity of last night and only a few hours of sleep. I was drifting through the world like a half-corporeal ghost, more spectator than participant.

But Lucy wanted to chat. A sound guy held a boom above our heads in case we said anything juicy, as a camera guy filmed our every move. "Didn't you just want to melt when you saw him for the first time?"

I didn't need to ask who she was talking about. And no, I'd been concentrating very hard on not tripping and falling down the stairs on national television.

"And he laughed so hard when I made my breaking news joke. He told me later he thinks I'd make a sexy newscaster." Forget about any actual qualifications, he went with the physical compliment. Why was I not surprised? I kept my eyes closed, hoping she would leave me alone.

But Lucy was nothing if not persistent. "Did you know he and I have the same favorite movie?" She'd mentioned it at least four times already, and each time I bit my tongue and didn't tell her how asinine picking *Forrest Gump* as your favorite movie was. I also didn't tell her I suspected Emerson was lying just to get her to shut up. "I can't believe we already found something we have in common. And he's such a gentleman." My restraint was so great I didn't even make a small gagging noise. "What's your favorite movie, Zoe?"

Damn. A direct question. "Tie between *Edward Scissorhands* and *The Truman Show*," I muttered through clenched teeth.

"Oh, I remember *Edward Scissorhands* from when I was a kid. With a baby Johnny Depp, wasn't it?" She clapped her hands. "Such a weird movie. I don't know the other one though."

Yes, because who in their right mind would love *The Truman Show* and then come on a show like this one?

Guess that said something pretty deep about me right there.

Lucy babbled on, enumerating Emerson's many fine qualities. When I couldn't take it anymore, I shut my eyes again, took a deep breath of salty sea air, and tried to pretend she was the radio playing in the background. I'd begun to fall into a light doze when Lucy's monologue came to a sudden abrupt halt. I cracked open one eye.

Vivian and Thea walked toward us, worse luck, carrying full margarita glasses and being trailed by another camera guy. They sported matching belly button piercings, Vivian a butter-could-melt-in-her-mouth angel and Thea an edgy Southern Belle, a delicate silver chain circling her stomach to highlight its concavity.

"Hi guys!" Lucy gave a nervous wave like we'd been blasted back to our first day of high school. Neither of them responded but settled onto loungers within earshot.

"I can't believe some of the girls that made the first cut." Vivian delivered her opening salvo in a confident, carrying voice. "Good news for us, it means we'll have an easier time, but I do relish a challenge." The angel had teeth. "Still, we're all here for Emerson, and that's the important thing."

"For sure," Thea said. "But you're right, this isn't what I expected either. No offense, but some people need to watch what they eat. Doesn't everyone know the camera adds ten pounds? At the very least don't call attention to it. Wear black or some neutral color, not, like, bright orange."

My bikini was bright orange. Thea wasn't even bothering to be subtle. Lucy turned away, embarrassed. Yes, my thighs had meat to them; they were limbs meant to support my body. Thea's extended from her torso more like precarious stilts.

I didn't rise to the bait though, just closed my eyes again as if I were bored. And in a way that was true. They might have been surprised, but I wasn't. All my negative stereotypes about just how superficial people could be were being borne out.

"Hey, did you know there's a gun room here?" A note of excitement had entered Thea's voice. "It's back by the library. I asked Emerson about it last night, and he told me his grandfather collected all kinds of guns. When I told him about my shooting experience, he offered to take me out to give some of them a try one of these days." Gloating oozed from Thea's voice, and I braced myself for Lucy's dismay.

But luckily Giselle chose that moment to interrupt. "I'm sure we'll all have a chance to get to know Emerson better." Lucy took a deep breath and relaxed back on her recliner.

"Undoubtedly," Vivian drawled. "By the way, Giselle, you know that story you were telling me last night about this house? You should fill the other girls in. We don't want them to think we're withholding information from them or anything like that."

Giselle wrinkled her nose. "Oh, it's nothing important. Just silly kid stuff."

Thea snorted. "Or maybe you don't want everyone to find out you already know the Courtlands."

Lucy gasped and sat back up. "You knew Emerson before?" Her lower lip trembled as if the mere thought made her want to cry.

Giselle's sunglasses obscured her face, but I could have sworn she glared over at the troublemakers. "No, I met him for the first time last night, the same as everyone else." She paused. "But it turns out I did go to college with his sister."

"Go on and tell them," Vivian said. "I think everyone deserves to know."

"Know what?" Lucy had absolutely no ability to play it cool. She rolled over onto her side to give Giselle her full attention. "You have to tell us. Please!"

I suppressed a sigh. Lucy was playing right into Vivian's hands. Not that I wasn't curious, but showing weakness in front of Vivian was like giving her the scent of your blood.

Giselle took a careful sip of her drink. "Well, his sister Nadine told everyone this story once at a party. We'd all had a little too much to drink, and she was probably just joking around. You know how it is." Lucy nodded vigorously, and I caught Vivian smirking. "Anyway, she happened to mention her family owned a haunted island. Back then we all had a good laugh about it."

Imagine hanging out with a group of people where it was normal to talk about your family island.

Lucy's eyes had grown. "Haunted how?"

Giselle shifted in her lounger and took another sip of her drink. "She said there was a big scandal back in the day. It had to do with their aunt Margaret."

"Good old Aunt Margaret." Thea raised her glass in a mock toast.

Giselle seemed to be warming to her story. "I guess Aunt Margaret moved out to the island sometime back in the 60s, and she brought a bunch of friends with her."

"And a boyfriend. Don't forget about the boyfriend." Thea giggled.

"Yeah, and a boyfriend. He had a kind of unusual nickname. What was it? It was some famous scientist." She clicked her nail against her glass, thinking. "It wasn't Einstein, wasn't Newton....I think maybe it was Darwin? Yeah, Darwin. The group of them were fresh out of college and established some kind of free love colony out here in the old house."

"Sounded more like a cult to me," Vivian said.

"Well, maybe. It sounds like they got up to some pretty crazy stuff. And get this: except for Darwin, it was all women. Can you imagine? And then things started to go...wrong."

"What happened?" Lucy was hanging on every word.

"Nobody knows exactly. Aunt Margaret was off island at the time, lucky for her. But what we do know is that somehow the house caught fire, and everyone living here died: Darwin and all those girls. The house was completely gutted, the family was scandalized, and it was more than a decade before Emerson and Nadine's grandfather decided to rebuild."

"Oh my god." Lucy leaned back into her lounger with a sigh. "That's so tragic. Poor Aunt Margaret. I had no idea."

And then she'd gone on to write her one and only great masterpiece. No wonder it was such a dark and painful book. It had felt like she'd known what it was like to be lost.

"Nadine said the kids used to joke that the island must be haunted now. They didn't want to come out here for vacations; they were always pushing to go to some plush resort instead. All those girls, their lives cut violently short right where we're sitting now." Giselle gave a little shiver.

"And Darwin," I said. I didn't mean to. I hadn't wanted to engage in whatever little game Vivian was playing out through Giselle. Trying to scare us and weed out the faint of heart. That sounded like Vivian. But the idea of them all choking on the smoke, burning to a crisp....my own skin felt hot in sympathy.

"It makes you think, doesn't it?" Vivian raised her eyebrows suggestively.

But Lucy just laughed. "Yeah, it's a good story to tell around the campfire." She was still watching Giselle. "So, would you say you and Nadine were close?"

"Just acquaintances." Giselle rose gracefully to her feet. "It's getting hot out here. Think I need a little bit of AC." And with that, she escaped Lucy's intense scrutiny, drifting into the house with her empty glass.

I took a breath and closed my eyes, glad Vivian hadn't been able to do any real damage. "Don't you think Emerson is great?" Lucy asked. I winced; couldn't she leave well enough alone? "I can't wait to see him again."

"He's everything I was hoping for," Thea said. "Handsome, sophisticated, a true gentleman."

"And just a little bit naughty," Vivian said. I opened my eyes in time to see her sly smile. "But then, where would the fun be if he wasn't?"

Lucy's face fell. "Did he...did you guys...I mean...." She stammered to a halt, but we all knew what she wanted to know.

"I'm sure he kissed all the girls last night," Vivian said. "After all, he needs to figure out who he has chemistry with as quickly as possible. And let me tell you, he and I definitely have a spark together." She made a fake sympathetic face at Lucy's obvious shock. "Oh, sorry, did you not kiss him yet? I just assumed...but don't worry, I'm sure you'll get another chance." Her tone implied the opposite.

Lucy pulled in on herself, becoming physically smaller in her dismay. "Oh," was all she managed to say, and I could imagine what she must have looked like when she was four years old.

"At least you didn't make a fool of yourself last night," Vivian continued. "Kennedy told me there was a girl who actually recited a love poem to Emerson. Can you imagine?"

I met her eyes directly, calmly, without changing my expression. Did she know she was talking about me? She had to. After all, I was the "artsy" one.

"You're kidding." Thea's laugh sounded like barking. "How did he take it?"

"Like a gentleman, of course," Vivian said. "After all, he wasn't going to be rude. But she must have seemed so pathetic. Kennedy says she tried to change her mind and persuade her not to do something so embarrassing, but some people"—she shrugs—"you can't help them, even with the best of intentions."

I took a slow breath. Sure, this felt like a betrayal from Kennedy, and to Vivian, of all people. But Kennedy had her job to think about. This was just a normal part of the show. Nothing personal.

"Kennedy must not have tried *that* hard," Thea said. "After all, she has ratings in mind. And watching some chick bomb with love poetry is going to be pretty entertaining, you have to admit. I wonder who it was."

"She probably got eliminated," Vivian said. "Why would he keep a girl like that around when he has so many options?"

"She might be hot," Thea said. As much as I hated both these girls, I was beginning to develop a certain grudging respect for Thea's clear-sighted take on reality.

Vivian shrugged. "Well, if she's still here, she won't last long." She raised her eyebrows at me, erasing any shadow of a doubt. She knew. Kennedy must have told her. And the viewing audience would know she was talking about me too. I'd been put into an impossible situation, set up by my dear sister with no warning whatsoever.

One of the sound guys adjusted slightly, reminding me of the boom over my head, the cameras zoomed in on my every facial expression. We were supposed to be ignoring the cameras, but my eye was caught by that sneering red light. *"Vivian's right."* Joe's voice came straight from the camera. *"You aren't in her league. Emerson would send you home tomorrow if you weren't hiding behind your big sister."*

I sucked in a strained breath. Anger mixed with shame in the pit of my stomach. "It was me." I enunciated as clearly as possible. "Guess he wanted to keep me around in spite of my dumb love poetry." I wanted to tell Vivian what a bitch she was, to call her out for making me look bad, but I knew what magic they could perform in the editing room. If I used any provocative language, I'd be cast as this season's villain without a second thought. And the hatred of so many viewers seemed like an impossible weight to bear.

I stood as gracefully as I could and stalked off, trying to look dignified. I knew even as I placed one foot in front of another that I was failing. Which was worse: to be the villain everyone hates or the patsy everyone laughs at?

And why did I keep hearing Joe's voice? I'd have given anything to stop thinking about him, but instead he'd wormed his way deep into my subconscious. The ringing contempt he'd expressed when we'd broken up for good continued to echo and spread.

He was an addiction my brain had no intention of quitting.

Nine

Hot Seat transcript: Zoe Roberts, October 5, as aired in episode one

Have I been in love before? Well, yes, I guess you could say that. It's funny because once the relationship is over and your heart is broken, you begin questioning yourself. Was it really love, or was it just some kind of weird addictive...malignancy? But I think it was love. At least on my side. You can never truly know someone else's heart.

Hot Seat transcript: Vivian Green, October 5, as aired in episode one

I'll do whatever it takes to win Emerson. I like the other girls here, I really do, but I'm not here to make friends. After all, this is the rest of my life we're talking about. And the minute I saw him at the bottom of those stairs, I knew." (She puts her hand over her heart.) This is how I always am, I'm very deeply intuitive. When I test-drive a car, when I tour a new house, when I got my acceptance letter from USC...I always listen to my gut. And this time, my gut isn't just telling me, it's literally screaming, "This is it! This is the man you've been waiting for!" All I have to do is take what is mine.

. . .

Hot Seat transcript: Zoe Roberts, October 5, as aired in episode one

Maybe the poem wasn't the best idea. We think of poetry as being so romantic, don't we, but not everyone is into that, especially right off the bat. I think maybe I came across a tad strong. I do think Emerson appreciated that I put myself out there and wasn't afraid to do something corny for him. I mean, confidence is sexy, right? (Long pause.) Right?

Hot Seat transcript: Lucy Miller, October 5, as aired in episode one

(Nervous laughter.) Wow. (She covers her face with her steepled hands and closes her eyes for a long moment.) Just wow. I can't believe I'm here. (More nervous laughter.)

Hot Seat transcript: Simone DuPrade, October 5, as aired in episode one

I have to admit, Emerson is a real looker. That gap-toothed smile is the clincher. Time to find out what's behind that pretty face. (Hair toss.)

Hot Seat transcript: Zoe Roberts, October 6, as aired in episode two

I don't think Vivian knows what she's talking about. I mean, she wasn't even there when I met Emerson. It wasn't *that* bad. So what if he doesn't like poetry. I'm not even a poet, I write novels, the two forms are completely different. I just don't know. (Looks away from the camera, bites lip.) Maybe coming here was a terrible mistake. I try not to believe you only get one chance in life. Because if that's true, I've already had mine and that's it. Thirty with a dead-end future and no chance of happiness. (Pause.) Oh god, I really (beep) up last night, didn't I?

Hot Seat transcript: Vivian Green, October 6, as aired in episode two

I have nothing against Zoe. She seems like a little lost lamb. But she doesn't belong here. Emerson needs someone who—how can I say this? —has superior social skills. Someone who can help him entertain, who will accompany him to business and charity events and look like she fits in, who can help him get where he wants to go. And I'm sorry, but that girl is *not* Zoe Roberts. As long as she's here, she's wasting time that should be spent on more deserving candidates is all I'm saying.

Hot Seat transcript: Giselle Wallace, October 6, as aired in episode two

How do I feel about Emerson? Well, he's funny, he's smart, he's knock-me-off-my-feet handsome, what's not to like? The first time I saw him, my mind literally went blank. I could hardly string two words together. And I haven't been able to stop thinking about him since. (Dreamy smile.) I really wasn't sure about all this. (She gestures, but whether at the red backdrop and tropical plants or at the camera recording her every move, we can't tell.) But maybe it's not such a crazy idea after all.

Ten

My biggest rival from my NYU days was Ida Snow. She would wear shapeless shift-like garments in dark browns and olive greens, she pinned up her black curly hair in a haphazard fashion, little red pimples dotting her hairline, and her teeth were slightly too long for her face. But her appearance didn't matter, not the way mine did, and the reason cut through my heart like a machete.

Ida Snow was a genius. You've all heard of her, although at the time of the show taping, she'd only had one bestseller, just like Joe. I heard a professor call her "the next Jonathan Franzen," and he wasn't exaggerating. That the next Jonathan Franzen could be a woman was mind-boggling, and it also meant it was my own damn fault I wasn't good enough.

Ida also had the good sense not to fall in love with Joe, the other wunderkind in our class, so her brilliance extended beyond the written word.

My growing resentment of Vivian reminded me of my jealousy of Ida. Vivian had Ida's scathing contempt in her voice whenever she talked to me. One thing I learned with Ida was that I could never beat her. My only chance lay in pretending to play a different game altogether. Right now that meant I needed to collect myself away from the scrutiny of my fellow contestants.

Unsure where to escape, I made my way back to the pirate ship. It stood in the tangle of jungle like a beacon. Someone must have been putting in some effort to keep it clear of growth because the ship's hull was pristine, no branches impeding the upward progress of its towering mast. The size of the Courtland fortune was a moving target I found difficult to visualize.

I began my ascent up the rope ladder hanging over the side, a scent like jasmine in the air. The sun beat against my back, and I was glad Emerson wasn't here to see me now, my all-too-human sweat another strike against me. In spite of Kennedy insisting I'd be recorded at all times, I couldn't see a single camera. I'd even left my battery-powered mike back in the room, a move strictly against protocol, but nobody had stopped me. Maybe Kennedy was cutting me a little slack.

I was panting by the time I reached the deck and pulled myself over the railing. A door into the cabin beckoned to me, but then I saw the flimsier ladder leading up to the crow's nest and I couldn't resist. From there I might be able to see the entire island.

A slight breeze ruffled my hair as I ascended rung by rung, reminding me of its sudden extra inches. I'd been feeling like an alien in my own body, and I welcomed the opportunity to do something simple like climb.

When I could go no higher, I wrapped my hands in a rope tethered to the mast and looked out. Much of the island was covered by trees, but I could see the sprawling footprint of the mansion, the pool, and the beach and ocean beyond. The orange roofs of the bungalows and other buildings peeked out between patches of dense forest, and I saw a stone tower off in the distance. But most of the island ran wild, fecund growth over many layers of decay.

I clasped my arms around the center pole and leaned against it, taking in the vista. Surely knowing the lay of the land would be useful in the show's upcoming challenges. I needed to impress my audience if I wanted to capitalize on being on TV.

I studied the surrounding area until a shout came from below. "Ahoy there!" I jumped and gripped the pole more tightly before venturing a look straight down. Damn, I was high. A man peered up at me, his eyes obscured by sunglasses. One of the crew maybe? I was too far up to see. The distance made my head spin, and suddenly I was terrified of moving.

Slow, careful breaths. I'd survived worse than this. No way was I going to fall. But I kept picturing one of my sandal-clad feet slipping on a rung, rope burns on both palms, the slow teetering effort to hold on—no. My imagination had always gotten the better of me.

The man started shouting something else, but I couldn't hear him. I took a deep breath, knelt down, and forced myself to send one foot downwards to quest for the first rung. Slow and steady was fine. I had nowhere I needed to be.

Breathe, Zoe. Another step, and then another. Don't look down, don't you dare look down. My hands squeezed around the rungs above me with a death grip. How long could this ladder go?

And then it happened. My foot slipped and I let out a terrible scream as I tried to grab harder with my hands and...felt someone's arms wrap around me from behind. "It's okay." His breath against my ear made me shiver. "I've got you."

I finally allowed myself to look down. I'd made it to the bottom of the ladder without realizing it. Typical Zoe. I flushed with embarrassment as I stepped down to the solid deck and looked at my would-be rescuer.

Cannon was laughing at me, showing his straight, brilliantly white teeth. He must use special strips to make them so bright. "Get a little carried away there?"

Let him laugh. At least I'd had the courage to go up in the first place. "Great view," I managed. "You gonna check it out?"

He shook his head. "Nah, I'll leave the adventure sports to you and your fellow Gold Diggers." He peered around the deck as if it might start tipping at any moment, spilling us out onto the ground below.

"Wait a second, don't tell me you're afraid of heights? You jerk." I swatted him on the arm. "You don't get to make fun of me then."

He grinned. "I most certainly do."

"Hypocrite."

He didn't seem bothered by the accusation. "Guilty as charged. Hollywood is crowded with us. I'm surprised New York isn't the same way."

"Oh, it is," I assured him. And I was one of them, participating in this show, pretending I was here for the right reasons. Maybe three of the twenty remaining Gold Diggers weren't hypocrites, and that was a generous assessment.

"Can you see the mansion from up there?" I nodded. "What about the tower?"

I gave him a sharp look. "They give you a tour of the island when you arrived?"

"Not yet. I've been stuck like glue to Emerson, and he's not exactly interested in doing a Greatest Hits recap of his childhood."

"Poor you." The mockery dripped from my voice like the sweetest shade.

"It's a living." He gazed up at the crow's nest and shook his head. "So tell me, Zoe, why are you out here all by yourself instead of making life-long best friends and stirring up trouble with the rest of your cohort?"

I looked around uneasily. Kennedy has drilled the idea of hidden cameras into the depths of my psyche. "I could ask you the same question. Shouldn't you be with your new best friend giving him trenchant advice?"

"Touché. But you know what they say about all work and no play."

I raised a disbelieving eyebrow at him. "Seriously? Like you don't have anything better to do?"

"At present I'm busy being charmed by your prickly company." At my look, he continued, "Besides, Emerson and his aunt have jaunted off to another island, and they won't be back until tomorrow. Funny thing, they didn't invite me along. I can't imagine why not." He shook his head in mock worry. "I'm sure he must be missing me terribly."

"Lucy is going to be so disappointed," I said. "She was hoping to catch a glimpse of him today."

"But you weren't?"

This man was too sharp for comfort. "I didn't expect to see him. But I guess you never know. We *are* sharing a house with him."

Cannon clicked his tongue. "Not true. When he gets back, he'll be taking up residence in the guesthouse down the ridge. Has its own pool and everything. The proper protocols must be observed, after all." I remembered seeing another much smaller house from the crow's nest, its blue pool shaped like a kidney. "You need to work on your intel sources, babe."

"Why bother when I have you?"

"Why indeed?" He gestured at the door to the cabin. "Care to investigate further? It seems the latest family patriarch was a bit on the eccentric side, wouldn't you say?"

I thought the door would be locked, but it opened easily, revealing a luxurious hideaway. A huge bed draped in red dominated the space, a mirror tacked to the ceiling above. Large sconces bracketed the bed, and a classic captain's trunk sat at its foot. A small galley took up the far corner, complete with a wet bar, and there was even a tiny working bathroom. My mouth fell open. This wasn't what I'd been expecting at all.

"An illicit love nest." Cannon pushed his sunglasses back on his head. "Maybe not so eccentric after all." He opened the trunk, and a bunch of sexy costumes spilled out: feather boas, masks, a French maid's outfit, a few whips, and more, all silk and ribbons and lace. "Then again...."

I laughed and picked up a leather-embossed book on the nightstand. A journal. I flipped it open, a newspaper clipping falling out. Sprawling loopy writing in blue ink filled the first several pages, and the name "Adelaide Vance" was written on the flyleaf. I read the first line: "I might have sold my soul to the devil to be here, but goddamn, this is better than I ever dreamed."

"Anything juicy?" Cannon asked.

The journal would make some great forbidden reading material for me back at the house. I tucked the loose article carefully back in between the pages. "I'll take a look later." I walked over to the mini-kitchen, turned on the faucet, and gasped when water flowed out. "How is this possible?"

"Babe, money makes all things possible." He opened the small fridge and pulled out two beers. "You want one?"

"Why not?" He popped open the tops and handed me one, and we clinked our bottles together. "What shall we toast to?"

"I always toast to surviving the season in one piece."

"This is only your second season of *Love Story*, and you're already this jaded?" I teased.

He looked away. "You forget, I have plenty of prior experience."

Bantering with him made me feel more myself than I had in ages. "So from a battered survivor to one of the fresh pieces of meat: what's the best strategy?"

For a moment it was as if he'd discarded his usual public mask, and the lines of his face and the anguish in his eyes spoke of an inevitable bleakness. "Detach yourself as much as you possibly can," he said. "From anyone and everyone involved with this show. I don't care how great of a relationship you think you have with someone. Don't trust anyone."

His sudden dark shift made me uncomfortable, and I tried to lighten the mood. "Including you?"

He made an appreciative noise. "I'm just like everyone else. My goal is making sure I have this gig for as many seasons as possible. Nobody here has your best interests at heart, Zoe. Except maybe you." He shrugged. "But then again, you chose to be here, so who knows. Contestants on these shows have a couple different profiles: Innocent as fuck. Self-interested to a fault. Or laboring under a vicious self-destructive streak."

"Which one were you?" I couldn't help asking.

"Oh, I went through all three stages before I was done. And now I'm so entangled in this whole world, I can never leave." He drained the rest of his beer. "Does that sound like bullshit to you? Because it won't sound so weird when we're done filming."

To be honest, it did sound like a cop-out of sorts, but one I understood all too well. It was so easy to become trapped: in a routine, in a subculture, in a relationship, in a dream of the future that would never happen but was impossible to release. "You think I'll make it long enough? My performance last night didn't exactly inspire confidence."

Cannon returned to the fridge, pulling out a bottle of champagne. I was only a quarter done with my beer. These people never stopped drinking. Not so different from the literary scene, but with champagne and pinot gris instead of G&Ts and Scotch, and starting earlier in the day.

"You'll make it." He said it with a confidence I wished I had. "You just need to relax. Stop focusing on not having anything in common with Emerson and play to your strengths."

"The poem wasn't my idea." I didn't know why I cared that he remembered that. Vivian's words still stung.

"Yes, you told me. Kennedy strikes again." He popped the cork from the champagne bottle. "But what's done is done. And you learned something from it."

"Oh really? What's that?"

He poured too quickly, and champagne foamed from the glass. "That I'm right. Nobody here has your best interests at heart. Now you know, so you can take the power back."

I took the wet glass from him and watched as he poured himself another. Damn, he was attractive, all bronzed skin and muscle and Hollywood polish. I wanted to reach out and run my fingers through his curls. Not that I ever would. "Why are you telling me this?"

He held his glass up. "To paying it forward, one deluded contestant to another." He winked at me. "And, of course, to love."

"To love." I clinked my glass against his, but I didn't buy it for a second. His own advice told me he was playing some deep game of his own.

Eleven

Excerpt from Adelaide Vance's journal:

September 23, 1974

I might have sold my soul to the devil to be here, but goddamn, this is a better opportunity than I ever dreamed. The ship's finished, and Leland's going to be over the moon when he sees it. It is truly beautiful and reflects all the research I put into the design. And all the fuss over the plumbing! I could tell the workmen think I'm a crazy person.

Everything is exactly as we discussed: the way the mast reaches high into the sky; the traditional mermaid figurehead perched on the prow, painted so brightly; the polished wooden deck and brass trimmings; the cabin retreat where Leland can disappear from the stresses of daily life. Seeing the blueprints come to life, not the same old office buildings the rest of my cohort are working late to design but an honest-to-God pirate ship, helps with the difficult times.

And geez Louise, is it sometimes tough! Leland's been away for over three weeks this time. I know I'm not in love with him. I know at the end of the day what we have is strictly a business relationship—intelligent and willing female companionship for him, a generous budget and interesting design experience for me—but I have to admit I've allowed myself to be won over by his charm.

And it's so lonely on this island. The workmen and the servants are friendly enough, but I can't really talk to them, not about anything but business. They know why I'm here, they can't help but know, and I feel their judging eyes following me, watching me act both the boss and the lady when we all know I am neither.

All of this is me trying to make excuses to myself, because the truth is I once again have an imaginary friend. I don't remember when I stopped believing Samantha was real, but I must have been, I don't know, five or six years old? Now, between designing pirate ships and fairy tale towers and having an imaginary friend named Darwin, I have definitely regressed.

At first I thought I was making him up to keep me company, an act of desperation if I do say so myself. But now I'm not so sure. Grandma always said I was too rooted in the concrete, in facts and figures and measurements. Which makes for a great architect! But Grandma seemed to think I was missing out on something. I always thought she was just disappointed I'm not as religious as she was. I've always had trouble taking things on faith.

Until now. Darwin knows things I don't know myself. And he... understands me. It's uncanny how much he seems to know about me. "Your whole life, people have been overlooking you, haven't they?" he said to me.

"We just call that middle child syndrome," I joked.

But he refused to let it go. "It started in your family, yes. But it didn't get any better in school, did it? Everyone always took you for average. Never quite pretty enough, never quite loud enough, too much going on upstairs for people to feel entirely comfortable with you. A formidable woman who everyone underestimated."

"Except for Leland," I couldn't help saying.

"Ah yes, the chivalrous Leland. He's paying for your genius, is he?"

"That's right." I can't talk about Leland without instantly going on the defensive.

"You feel that he respects your abilities?"

I couldn't answer that. Because the truth is, it's complicated. He *does* believe in my competence as an architect, I believe that. He wouldn't let me design this new house for him if that weren't true. But would he have given me the job if I'd turned down his advances? No way. He would have chosen someone more celebrated, someone more experienced, let's face it, an older man. There is respect, and then there's *respect*, and I only have the first kind. Darwin's been the only person I've ever talked to who understands the difference.

Just like my old imaginary friend Samantha, who shared several pertinent characteristics with my cousin Sally who lived across the country, Darwin did actually exist once upon a time. He was the boyfriend of Leland's oldest daughter—the one who is older than me now, the one I hope and pray I never meet—and they used to live here on the island together with a bunch of their hippy friends. Darwin died here in some kind of tragic accident, and he says he's thrilled to finally talk to someone. And he chose me—ME—when he had his pick from all the servants and workers.

He tells me stories at night to help me pass the time. Stories of how he and his friends used to strive to become closer to what he calls the Great Flow. It's all pretty typical stuff: vows of silence and various fasts, along with some dream work along the lines of taking control of your worst nightmares. Things that help you gain a different perspective on yourself and how you fit into the world around you. I've tried fasting a few times myself since he and I started talking, and I swear his voice gets louder after I've gone thirty-six hours consuming nothing but water and sweet tea and melon.

Sometimes I daydream that Darwin is a real man, not a ghost who I cannot touch. I miss him when he doesn't talk to me. Sometimes he falls silent for hours, and when I ask him why, he avoids the question.

Sometimes I imagine Darwin is actually here, in the flesh here, and this is his island, not Leland's. I can't let myself picture it for too long though. It reminds me exactly why, in spite of this opportunity I've unearthed for myself, I have failed to be perfectly happy.

Twelve

Kennedy warned me about the treasure hunt, our first challenge of the season, after my roommates had already been wired up and gone downstairs for breakfast. I'd stayed up late reading Adelaide's journal, fascinated by her growing obsession with this Darwin character, Margaret's old flame that Giselle had told us about by the pool. The further into the journal I got, the more Adelaide gushed about him. Finally I'd had to put the book aside and sleep, but I was running behind everyone else.

"This first challenge will be the toughest," Kennedy told me. "We want to weed out the less committed, separate the wheat from the chafe, capture the cream that rises to the top—"

"I get the picture," I interrupted. "Today will be difficult."

Kennedy folded her arms. "Exactly. This will be your chance to show the viewers what you're made of. The Gold Diggers who stay will be the ones who can roll with what we throw at them."

I made a face. "You're not going to make us do anything truly gross, are you?"

"Don't worry, you can trust me." Her words reminded me of what Cannon said: Trust nobody. It was almost as if he knew I had family on set. "None of you will be in any true danger. Just remember that and you'll do fine. You need to make up some lost ground after your less-than-stellar debut. No pressure, but if your team wins the challenge, that would help you a lot. Get you some much needed one-on-one time."

I swallowed. "Has he chosen his dates for this week?"

She nodded. "Giselle. No surprise there. We knew those two would hit it off. And Grace." She snorted. "Also no surprise, not with the way she displayed her tatas on night one. We'll send them out on a yacht for the obligatory on-camera make out session."

I couldn't even remember Grace's face. "And the rest of us?"

"The rest of you will compete for him. Six teams of three. Do me proud, little sister. I saved you the first night, but it would be nice if you could pull your own weight this time."

Neither of us mentioned I'd only bombed so badly by following her instructions. I couldn't risk getting on her bad side. Kennedy had always been the master of retaining the upper hand and not having to face the music when one of her ideas went sideways.

But in the end we were family, and we looked out for each other. That belief had to be my touchstone now.

We gathered in the lounge right after lunch. Giselle and Grace were there too; they didn't yet know they wouldn't be competing in this week's hunt. Grace was one of the blondes who had blurred together for me on the first night, from...Denver? Or was it Chicago? It didn't matter. Several separate camera operators, all but one a man, watched us with their blank lenses, along with several sound people with their headsets and booms. Two producers hung out behind them, whispering to each other. Kennedy was nowhere in evidence. She was probably watching on the monitors in the control center.

Most of the women were dressed in short shorts, bikini strings poking from underneath tank tops. A few even wore strappy sandals. I'd taken Kennedy's words seriously and was wearing long pants and sneakers. I'd also taken the precaution of dousing myself liberally with bug repellent. Vivian and Thea wrinkled their noses as I walked past, but the television audience would never know.

Cannon strolled into the room, looking relaxed and casual in a Hawaiian shirt and khakis. "Hello, girls. How are we all feeling today?"

In spite of his addressing us as if we were a kindergarten class, we all cheered and gave the obligatory excited smiles. Then Cannon started reading out the teams. I was assigned a team with Lucy and Thea. Thea and I hated each others' guts, and Lucy looked close to tears from not being picked for a solo date this week, so the producers were sniffing for drama.

Both Giselle and Grace gave convincing performances of being surprised and delighted by the news they had romantic dates planned instead of having to do the challenge. Everyone else beamed enthusiastic smiles with sour edges. Michelle quirked an ironic eyebrow at me. We'd been hoping to pick our own teams and work together, but we should have known better.

Each team gathered into its own cluster. Our fates rested upon one another's shoulders now. At least Thea and Lucy were both wearing cute sneakers instead of Grace's kitten heels or Naomi's towering sandals. Giselle and Grace stood off to the side, queens of the day with their places assured.

"And now ladies, let me give you some background about the hunt." Cannon spread his hands and leaned forward, and we all drew in. "This island is known as Eleizer's Promise. A promise of what, you may ask? Pure white beaches, crystal blue water, a tropical paradise? You'll find all these things here, but that's not what the original Eleizer had in mind. Eleizer, you see, was a pirate, one of some repute, and legend says he hid the bulk of his treasure right here on this island."

A few women gasped, and I held back a groan. Did the show's team really think this kind of overt cheese would fly with the viewers? On the one hand, a pirate theme made sense for a treasure hunt, but surely everyone knew any theoretical treasure would have been found and claimed ages ago. On the other hand, on a show on which almost everything was manufactured, what was one more layer of lies? I braced myself for the terrible pirate puns that were inevitably going to fly.

"You ladies will be searching for Eliezer's fabled treasure. Each team will be following a set of clues that will hopefully lead you to your goal. The first team to find their treasure wins the challenge and will enjoy an intimate cocktail party with Emerson tonight. The runners-up will get a small amount of time with him before the main event. Any questions?"

Cannon didn't need to say that the poor teams that didn't come in first or second wouldn't get to see Emerson at all until the next Culling Day. We understood the real stakes at play, and they were much higher than some stupid fake treasure.

"Your clues, ladies." Cannon handed out six gleaming golden envelopes. Lucy clutched ours in her hand like it was the only source of her salvation. "May the best team win. Be warned, your hunt today will bring you face to face with your worst fears. And remember: dead men tell no tales."

There it was. I glared at him, and it might have been my imagination, but I think his smile grew even larger at my reaction. I ran my fingers over my mike's battery pack until Lucy tugged at my arm. "Come on." Pure desperation colored her voice. "We've got to get started if we're going to have any chance of winning."

Thea gave her a derisive glance, but she followed us fast enough. Cannon caught my eye as I left the room and gave me a wink. He sure was enjoying himself.

Lucy hurried to the far side of the pool where we might hope to have a little privacy from the other teams. One of the cameramen, Curtis, peeled off to follow us. He balanced the camera on his shoulder as if it weighed nothing, and a sound guy ran after him and made us re-start our conversation, boom properly in place. Elaine, a tiny Chinese-American producer who was new this season, showed up a minute later, already looking harried and hot in her black jeans and T-shirt.

Lucy slit open the envelope and pulled out an embossed card. In neat calligraphy, it said: "Follow the pieces of eight to the bridge you must cross." Next to the words was a cheesy skull and crossbones stamp. Thea and I forgot we hated each other long enough to share a weary look, but Lucy was already running around looking for clues like an overeager puppy.

"I can do this, guys," she shouted back to us. "I have excellent eyesight, and I've always been great at noticing things. Like, you know those picture puzzles in kid magazines? Find the banana in the drawing of a jungle? I'd always solve them before anyone else."

Her words didn't fill me with confidence, but then, I didn't have any better ideas. I started to look around too. I'd only seen one Jolly Roger on this island so far, but I was loathe to reveal the location of the pirate ship to these two women. Thea stood hands on her hips, refusing to make herself look as ridiculous as Lucy and I doubtless did.

My heart was beginning to sink when Lucy let out a squeal. "I've found one, guys! We're on the right track." A small Jolly Roger had been painted on the side of the house, right next to a true eyesore of a fire escape, an unwieldy construction of black iron that made me think of an insect hovering above us. "I think we should go that way," she said, pointing toward the front of the house. "We already looked in the other direction, and I have a good feeling about this."

A moment later, she squealed again. And then again. It began to feel like Thea and I were following a hound on the scent. We made our way past the fountain and the curving front drive, none of the other teams in sight, and walked into the forest. I spun around, looking at the web of branches and leaves above me. Finding small skulls would be a lot more difficult out here.

But the familiar cry came again. This time, Lucy was kneeling down and looking at something on the trail. "Pieces of eight!" she cried. "We're definitely in the right place."

Thea and I exchanged another glance. "I guess they didn't want to make it too hard," she said.

But I knew how devious Kennedy could be. "At least not yet," I countered. Elaine tried to hide a smirk under her hand, and I knew I was right. We'd reach the real challenge soon enough.

We pushed our way down the steep overgrown path, Curtis huffing to keep up with us, the sound guy frowning at the sky, Elaine bringing up the rear. Lucy was almost trotting in front of me, head bent in order to see smatterings of pieces of eight in the dirt. We all felt the pressure of time passing, knowing some other teams might be quicker.

Lucy stopped so abruptly I ran right into her. Thea halted with what I was beginning to recognize as characteristic grace. The three of us stood at the edge of a steep ravine; a rope suspension bridge that had seen better days appeared to be the only way across. Some of its boards were cracked or missing, and the ropes looked awfully threadbare, as if they'd been withstanding the elements since the days of Cannon's mythical pirate. Thea took several steps backwards.

A small pile of golden coins glistened from the middle of the bridge, and at the far end stood a tall Plexiglas box. I could just barely make out the embossed envelope inside. "We've come to the right place," I said, and I stepped out onto the bridge.

"Wait!" Thea cried, and the whole bridge shook with my weight. I grabbed at the rope handrail to keep my balance and froze until the ripples had passed through the structure. A single gold coin toppled into the crevasse below. It took a long time to fall.

I gritted my teeth. "It's fine." After all, Kennedy had said we'd be in no real danger. However dilapidated this bridge might look, it must be structurally sound enough for us to cross.

But Thea was frantically shaking her head and looking at me with real fear. "I can't do it." Her voice rose with a note of hysteria. "I can't, I can't, I can't."

Lucy sighed. "I think she's afraid of heights," she told me.

"No shit."

"Maybe the challenge isn't to cross." Thea was almost gibbering. "Maybe we're supposed to find a way around. That must be it. We should find a way around."

Oh hell. I'd never have expected Thea to go to pieces like this. It made me realize how little I knew any of these women. I gazed at the swaying bridge in front of me. "Don't worry. I'll go get the letter and bring it back." Thea didn't seem to register what I was saying, her breaths coming in short gasps. "You hear me, Thea? You don't have to cross, okay?" Still no response. "Keep her from doing anything stupid while I'm gone," I told Lucy, and then I took another step forward.

Curtis didn't follow me, and I tried to ignore the sinking feeling in my stomach. If he'd followed, I'd have known for sure it was safe. Elaine surveyed me from a safe distance, arms crossed. But the viewers would love how plucky I was being, wouldn't they? That thought kept me going.

I didn't pause until I reached a gap near the middle where two of the wooden planks were missing. The view downwards into the craggy ravine was dizzying, and I looked up quickly and took a few deep gulps of air.

The bridge might not crumble beneath my weight, but nobody could save me if I fell. It's not like Kennedy was God.

I knew I was being silly; I could easily span the distance. And we were racing the other teams. I reluctantly let go of the rope handrails before launching myself over the empty space. My feet hit the next plank with a reassuring thud.

When I reached the far end, I gave Lucy and Thea a thumb's up before kneeling in front of the Plexiglas container. It stood waist-high and was too heavy to lift. Maybe not Plexiglas after all. An electronic keypad controlled the lock mechanism, and the instruction text flashed red: "Three fingerprints to unlock."

I stood up and kicked the container. The pain in my toe was worth the satisfaction. I looked at the two women standing on the other side waiting for me. There was no way Lucy would be able to get Thea across on her own. With a sigh, I started back.

Elaine hurried up to me when I returned. "You're going to have to convince her to cross," she whispered. "You can't give up this close to the beginning or Emerson will cut you all for sure."

I was quickly coming to dislike Elaine. "Thanks for the tip."

Between the two of us, Lucy and I eventually convinced Thea to cross as a group. She was terrified the extra weight would put more strain on the bridge, but going by herself was obviously never going to happen. Now I understood Kennedy's promise that we'd never be in any real danger. Thea's fear was just as real as if we faced actual jeopardy.

We shuffled across the swaying bridge, first Lucy, then Thea, then me bringing up the rear. I arched an eyebrow at Elaine before we left. "Coming with?" She snorted but stayed where she was, flanked by Curtis and the sound guy, whose name I still didn't know.

Thea squeezed her eyes shut and kept a death grip on the ropes on either side of her. She took the smallest steps imaginable, testing each one as if she thought she'd drop through the wood and fall to the bottom of the ravine at any moment. Tears streamed down her cheeks, and her chest heaved as she walked, more like she was running a marathon than crossing a bridge at a snail's pace.

And then we reached the dreaded gap. I'd deliberately not told her about it, but now she had to face it, like it or not. Lucy hopped over easily, and I patted Thea on the shoulder. "You're going to have to open your eyes now," I told her. "It's a very small gap, I promise, but you're going to need to see to get across."

She went rigid, her breathing even faster, and I thought that might be it. We were going to fail. Emerson was going to send us all home. My only consolation was that most viewers would forget our failure quickly since we'd washed out so early in the season.

But then Thea opened her eyes, took a deep breath, and leapt. She overestimated so badly she jumped way too far, landed poorly, and pitched forward. She fell on her hands and knees, looked through the space between the slats, and screamed.

I'd never heard such pure terror given voice before. Before I had time to think I'd jumped myself and grabbed onto her shoulders. "I've got you. I've got you!" I insisted into the void of her scream. With Lucy's help I pulled her to her feet. "We're almost there."

Thea was full-on sobbing by then, her makeup running in black rivulets down her cheeks. I turned around to see Curtis right on the other side of the gap from us, capturing everything on film. I whispered, "Keep looking straight ahead." No one needed to see Thea's private horror on their television screen.

Traversing the last third of that bridge felt like it took at least an hour. Thea had to stop and hyperventilate at least three times. When she finally put her feet on solid ground, I wanted to fall to my knees and kiss it myself.

"Hurry up," Lucy said. She'd been hovering, trying to chivvy Thea into moving faster the entire time with almost no success. I wanted to slap her eager, Emerson-obsessed face, but Kennedy's advice ran through my head like a mantra: "Think of the optics. Always think of the optics." The optics of me being thoughtful would win out over Lucy's show of impatience.

Which begged the question: knowing that, had my behavior to Thea been kind in any meaningful way? Less than a week in, the show was already bankrupting my soul.

With all three of our index fingers pressed to the screen, the box popped open, allowing Lucy to snatch the next envelope. She read while Thea wiped her face in vain and I wondered about the wisdom about letting the shows' producers have access to my fingerprint. Elaine hovered behind Curtis, just waiting for her chance to manage us.

Manipulate us, more like.

"Where to next?" I tried to keep the exhaustion from my voice. Who knew how many of these envelopes we had to find?

Lucy handed me the envelope without a word. The paper inside had an actual map marking our next destination. I sighed. This wasn't a treasure hunt after all; they were making it way too easy for us. Instead it seemed to be shaping up into a "what terrible experiences can we force you to endure while being filmed" contest. I'd never been so glad I'd lied on the battery of tests I'd taken prior to my acceptance on the show. I'd said my biggest fear was public speaking. Not that I loved talking in front of a crowd, but I'd take that over Thea's ordeal any day of the week, and how could the producers conjure a crowd on this isolated island anyway? My spirits lifted, and I continued down the trail with Lucy and Thea, smug and secure in my knowledge that I wouldn't be suffering the way they would.

I told you I was naïve.

THIRTEEN

The Miami Reporter, November 3, 1964

MASS SUICIDE DISCOVERED ON MILLIONAIRE'S PRIVATE ISLAND IN THE BAHAMAS

Tragedy struck last week on New York millionaire Leland Courtland's private island in the Bahamas. Authorities arrived after receiving reports of smoke sightings from a nearby island and found Mr. Courtland's summer home burnt to the ground.

Further investigation revealed a small free-love cult led by American citizen Stewart Price, known to his associates as "Darwin," had taken up residence on the island and had participated in a mass suicide that resulted in the fire. It was initially unclear whether the fire itself had caused some of the fatalities.

Mr. Price had lured twenty young women to this isolated location, where it appears they catered to his every need. The authorities found large quantities of illegal drugs, along with lurid photographs and other party paraphernalia, extant on site.

There were no survivors.

Fourteen

Following the map, we quickly reached our next stop: a dilapidated wooden cabin. The paint peeled from its walls in putrid green-white strips, and one of the stairs up to the porch was rotted through. A funky smell I couldn't identify hung in the air: dry rot, maybe, or some kind of fungus. Thea had retreated behind a blank stare, and Lucy wrinkled her nose as she pushed the door, half off its hinges, the rest of the way open.

Only to instantly squeal and fall back, running to the far corner of the porch. Well then. Guess it was her turn to sweat. Curtis had a shit-eating grin on his face, and standing on that sagging porch on a godforsaken private island, I realized exactly how sordid this undertaking was.

Kennedy must know. Had years of doing this rendered her blind to the repulsiveness of torturing these women?

Joe's voice intruded in my thoughts. "How can you be so selfish?" he'd raged during one of our last fights. "Sometimes I think you don't truly care about anyone."

Doubt crept in. Maybe I couldn't believe in this show because I was so fucking broken.

I poked my head through to see what had upset the previously indomitable Lucy. Newspapers and cardboard covered the windows, the only light filtering in from the doorway, but it was sufficient to see the writhing mass of furry bodies congregated in the middle of the room. Rats, or maybe mice. Even with no special fear of rodents, I had no desire to get any closer.

Poor Lucy huddled over the side of the porch, gripping tightly to the railing. Elaine had directed Curtis and the sound guy to hover right in her face, the boom hanging over her head. She hadn't made a single sound since her initial scream, and she didn't fall to pieces either. Her makeup remained unmarred. Her mouth was screwed up in a moue of either determination or defeat, I couldn't tell which. "I need to go in there." Her voice sounded almost robotic.

"Okay," I agreed.

"I need to go in there," she repeated. "Did you see the box in the far corner?" I had not. "I'm sure it's just like the last one and needs all three fingerprints to open."

"That seems likely."

"Where is Thea?"

"Here." Thea surprised me by coming up behind my right shoulder. It was the first word I'd heard her speak since she got off the bridge.

A pause. "I can't do rats." Lucy shuddered all over. "They're such nasty creatures. And one time, when I was really little...." Another pause. "I can't do rats."

Thea shoved past me and grabbed Lucy's face. "Yeah, and I can't do heights. But somehow I got over that fucking bridge, and I'll be damned if we fail now because you're afraid of a few wriggly noses."

In the face of her fear, Lucy's new-found assertiveness failed her. "But did you see how many there were? There must be thousands."

"We might be able to walk around them," I said. "I'll go check." Anything to avert another emotional breakdown.

Curtis kept his camera focused on the other two women, probably hoping to catch Thea being catty during Lucy's time of need. Elaine leaned in and whispered something into Thea's ear, no doubt egging her on. Nobody was paying me any attention.

The door to the cabin had been jammed open, off its hinges as it was, and I couldn't budge it in either direction. I braced myself to look inside at the desperate knot of seething furry bodies. But there were no rodents in sight. At first I thought they must have moved into one of the back corners where the light didn't reach, but as I walked further inside, it was clear they'd disappeared altogether. How could that many rats be moved so quickly? Maybe there hadn't been that many to begin with. Maybe our minds had begun to play tricks on us.

I ventured further into the small structure, looking for a hole in the baseboard that might have served as the rats' exit point, when the door slammed suddenly shut. The room was plunged into darkness, and I immediately became deeply obsessed with the idea that the rats were still here and I'd somehow missed seeing them. The hairs on my arms and legs stood on end, and I blessed my past self for being one of the only Gold Diggers to opt for pants today. I froze, trying to hear any movement.

Nothing. I couldn't even hear the women outside talking or crying. It was as if I was in my own private bubble. And how had the door shut anyway? I wasn't sure I could have pulled it closed even if I'd put all my strength to the task.

The producers had to be up to their tricks, trying to scare me. Was Elaine standing on the other side of that door right now, internally cackling? Were cameras tracking what they hoped would be my slip into meltdown?

Well, I'd show them. I walked cautiously back towards the door, arms outstretched, each step a test in case I was forgetting about some obstacle that would result in a stubbed toe or worse. When I reached the edge of the door frame, I stopped, held my breath, and listened.

I've read that when you're deprived of one sense, your remaining ones become more acute. But in this case I felt like I had cotton wool stuffed into my ears. No sounds reached me from outside the cabin, and the thoroughness of the dark unsettled me. It was for Lucy, I kept telling myself. This test was designed to freak her out. Not me. And Kennedy had said there would be no real danger. That would be a lawsuit waiting to happen. But the longer I stood there, the less sway my rational arguments seemed to carry. My fingernails wore half-moons into my palms as the blackness insulated me in its chill.

The door swung open as abruptly as it had closed, letting in a long draught of warm and fragrant air. I blinked from the sudden light. "What's taking so long?" Thea asked. "Can we get around the rats or can't we?" Lucy hovered at her shoulder, eyes hopeful.

I turned around and the rats were back as though they'd never left, a great mass of them crawling around and over one another as they chittered softly. I stared at them for a long moment.

Losing my mind on national television was not exactly what I'd planned for the day.

I had to pretend everything was fine. "I'm not sure." The words came out creaky.

"Well, Lucy is ready." Thea didn't look back at Lucy as she said it, and I wondered what had gone down between them. How much time had I waited in my silent paranoia?

Thea tugged Lucy forward, and the three of us headed towards the wall, away from the pile of bodies in the center of the room. The rats extended all the way to the wall, but they were more thinly dispersed than in the middle. Still, we wouldn't be able to avoid contact with them. Thoughts of rabies flashed in my mind, and Lucy's breathing had taken on a loud, rasping quality. Her fingers dug into my hand like claws.

"Let's count to three and then make a run for it," I said, and the claws tightened further. Neither of the women said anything. "All right, here we go then. One...two...three."

At first I thought Lucy wasn't coming along with us, but a low moan just behind me told me I was wrong. Little rat feet skittered over my shoes, and I knew Lucy could feel their warm furry bodies against her bare legs. But we were moving through the narrow swathe, and we quickly made it to the other side. Lucy didn't stop moving until she ran into the far wall, and there she stayed, her hands pressed up against it as if she needed to be propped up.

"You okay?" I asked her.

Thea didn't wait for her response. "The envelope," she said. "Hurry up." I heroically restrained myself from mentioning how long Thea had taken to get across that damned bridge and walked over to the large cube. Lucy followed reluctantly, not taking her eyes from the floor. All three index fingers out, and snick snick snick, the cube popped open.

"God, now we have to go back," Lucy whispered, and she shut her eyes. I hoped the rat pack would magically disappear again, but no such luck. The all-too-real feeling of little claws scrabbling over my sneakers had convinced me they weren't just a clever special effect.

That was probably the first moment I began to question myself.

The final letter consisted of a single sentence: "Go to the tower and you will find what you seek." I guess it was Kennedy's way of helping me out. It might have stumped a Gold Digger who hadn't done any exploring the day before—like Lucy and Thea—but I knew exactly where we were supposed to go.

Well, at least in theory. I'd seen the tower from my perch on the mast, but I had to figure out our location in relation to the ship, and then guess how to get to the tower from here. Not exactly an easy task.

We ended up wandering around the island for a couple hours, for all intents and purposes lost. The crew kept pace with us, doubtless hoping the stress and heat would make us crack and start really digging into each other. Elaine kept pulling one or another of us aside, delivering various snide comments and suggestions, but in spite of her, both Lucy and Thea were being weirdly helpful. They pointed out holes and rogue branches, didn't say anything mean when we repeatedly failed to make progress, and Thea even shared some fruit snacks. We should have been freaking out that we were losing our chance to win time with Emerson, but Emerson had receded into a fictional shadowy figure. What was real was the three of us and what we'd been through together so far.

And all three of us knew I was the next target. Even though I'd lied on my initial tests, that didn't mean Kennedy hadn't come up with something particularly diabolical for me. If anyone knew me well enough to harmlessly torture me, it would be her.

I clung to her promise that she wouldn't bring Joe to confront me. Anything would be better than that. Bring on the rats and the dizzying heights. Make me give a lecture to some high school students. It all paled in comparison.

Finally, more from dumb luck than skill, we crested a hill that gave us enough of a view to find the tower, which was in a completely different direction than I'd thought. Twenty minutes hard hiking later, we emerged from the forest to see the moss-covered stone tower at the other end of the clearing.

"It really does look like something out of a fairy tale," Lucy murmured.

"Emerson's grandfather sure was eccentric." Thea shook her head.

"Just think, he had to make a conscious decision to have that built. Some random tower in the middle of nowhere that nobody needs or wants."

"People can spend their money however they want," Lucy said.

"Whatever. He built that, but there's no working A/C in the bungalows? Please."

I stepped forward toward the tower, but Lucy put a hand on my shoulder. Her eyes darted nervously from my face to the tower and back again. "Do you know what it will be?"

We were finally voicing the unspoken belief that this trial—hopefully the last—would be mine. "On the form I said my biggest fear is public speaking," I told her.

Lucy laughed. "And you chose to come onto reality TV? You're braver than I thought."

"Well, there's no time like the present." Thea took off ahead of us, head held high.

"You think there's a huge group of people in that thing?" Lucy sounded as dubious as I felt. "Think you'll be forced to give a speech?"

I shrugged. "It doesn't seem likely."

Lucy bit her lip. "Maybe it won't be you after all. Maybe it's heights again, for Thea. It is a tower, after all." We watched the hard lines of Thea's back. "Poor thing." Lucy shuddered, and I knew she was thinking about the rats.

I squared my shoulders and followed Thea into the fray...while secretly hoping it was just more rodents.

But of course, it wasn't. Kennedy would never make it that easy for me.

No, it was a dumbwaiter. An old-fashioned, charming, cramped, and utterly terrifying dumbwaiter.

We didn't have to go up a dizzying circular staircase, which might have sent Thea into full panic mode at this point. Instead there was a large downwards red arrow spray-painted on the wall above a set of cupboard doors. At first I thought it might be some kind of weird old-fashioned oven. But when Thea flung the doors open and we weren't set upon by another deluge of rats, the inner operations of the dumbwaiter became clear.

"Well, that's not so bad." Thea's relief echoed against the hard stones even as I leaned weakly against the damp wall. "Look, it's not even the manual kind that needs someone to haul you up and back. It goes down with a press of a button. It's basically an elevator." The large green button next to the opening seemed to back up her words.

I peered into the dark space again. "It's a little...small, don't you think?" It took all my self-control to keep the strain from my voice. I'd hoped Kennedy had forgotten.

Lucy stuck her head inside. "Is this really...it?"

"Seems easy enough." I said it as if I didn't have a care in the world. "As long as there aren't rats at the bottom." Lucy pushed away from the dumbwaiter like a shot, and I felt a momentary pang at my betrayal. "Thea, you want to go first?"

"Let's get this over with," she agreed. She made an undignified scramble into the dumbwaiter and gave a little wave as we shut her inside and pushed the button, which turned red. A low hum was the only sign it was working. The dumbwaiter was obviously in excellent repair. Kennedy had been right. There was nothing to worry about here. No danger, no potential lawsuits. Everything was going to be just fine.

"I wonder what's at the bottom," Lucy said. She didn't know the dumbwaiter itself was my test, and I wasn't going to enlighten her. It would be easier to cope if I pretended it wasn't happening in the first place.

Elaine was watching me with a knowing look. How could Kennedy have told her my most private fear? I tried to focus on the feeling of betrayal instead of the continuous clenching of my stomach. The sound guy held the boom above my head as if he expected me to break down any second. No doubt a stationary camera was positioned inside the dumbwaiter to capture my inevitable embarrassment. I gritted my teeth and took a breath through my nose.

The button changed back to green, and I swung open the doors. "After you." I gestured grandly at the entrance.

"Trying to put off your speech, are you?" Lucy gave a weak laugh before crawling inside. If only she knew.

Now it was just me and the crew. I let Curtis get a nice shot of me waiting patiently by the dumbwaiter before turning and giving Elaine my best charming smile, trying to channel Kennedy. "This is taking forever, isn't it? I don't suppose I can take the stairs so I don't have to wait for this old thing to come back up?" There had to be stairs. Fire codes were a thing, weren't they?

Elaine oozed faux pity. "I'm afraid the successful completion of the challenge requires the dumbwaiter. But don't worry, it's only a short ride."

Desperate, I turned to Curtis. "Won't you be taking the stairs down?"

He shook his head. "Can't interfere, sweetheart. Can't talk to you. You know the drill." He smiled with his refusal, showing beautifully straight teeth. I didn't know how everyone in LA afforded such good dental care.

I wandered around the room, trying to be appear disinterested for the camera, as if I was just trying to pass the time before the dumbwaiter came back. But there was nothing to find. The few doors were locked. With limited slits for windows, it was a shadowy circular room, completely empty apart from some lighting installed in the ceiling in front of the dumbwaiter, the better to get shots of me balking and crying.

The button turned green. I took a long shuddering breath and opened the doors to take a look.

The dumbwaiter was lit up like a fancy jewelry display case, but I didn't know if the light would turn off once the doors closed. I couldn't decide if it would be worse with light so I could see exactly how small the space was, or in the dark not able to see anything at all. Not that I would get a choice.

The sound guy brushed my shoulder with the boom, and I jumped. Guess he wanted to make sure the sound quality of my incoming sobs was up to snuff.

My heart had started beating faster, and a pervasive feeling of dread coiled up from the pit of my stomach. I was suddenly aware of the thousands of pounds of stone above my head, just waiting for their chance to cave in and bury anyone unlucky enough to be inside.

No, that was my fear talking. It was just a dumbwaiter in a stupid scenic folly built by Adelaide Vance for her rich lover. Thea and Lucy had taken it with no problems.

At least I assumed so. But then my imagination began to get the better of me. I imagined Thea at the bottom of a long shaft, neck at an unnatural angle, limbs all akimbo; Lucy trapped in a room teeming with rats and no exits except a tiny window high up on the wall, letting in just enough light to see their fat brown bodies covering her feet, then her ankles, then her knees, until—

"Enough!" I didn't realize I was going to speak out loud until the word rung out. I blushed. They'd show a clip of me talking to nobody. The humiliation gave me the strength to crawl into the tiny dumbwaiter.

"I'll push the button for you," Elaine said. And without waiting for me to respond, she slammed the doors in my face.

The light remained on, and with a lurch, the dumbwaiter began its descent.

I stared at the white wall right in front of my face, trying to take slow, calm breaths. How airtight was this dumbwaiter anyway? Was I in danger of running out of oxygen? Another picture sprang to mind, this time of Thea and Lucy unconscious and blue around the lips, laid out in an icy crypt. I began to breathe faster, as if I were already having trouble getting enough oxygen.

And if I had thought it was hot before, it was ten times worse in this cramped, airless space. I could feel the back of my tank top getting even wetter, and my arms made damp patches against my legs as I held them close to me. And still the dumbwaiter continued its crawl downwards.

I began to count to give myself something to do. It worked for the first hundred and fifty numbers, and then I began to panic. Why wasn't I there yet? Was the dumbwaiter really moving or was its descent an illusion? Was something wrong with the lowering mechanism? A small whimper escaped me, and I clenched my jaw even more tightly to keep any other noises from betraying me.

Kennedy was probably laughing in the control center. She was probably rooting for me to crack more visibly to help out the ever-important ratings god she worshipped.

But I was stubborn. I squeezed my knees ever tighter; every muscle in my body was ripcord taut. My own tangy odor suffused the space. And the dumbwaiter lurched to a stop.

I'd done it. I'd foiled Kennedy and ruined this whole segment of the treasure hunt in the process. There were so many teams, she didn't need more footage from mine. Let her torture the other poor Gold Diggers. I was ready to chortle with glee.

The doors didn't swing open.

That was when I noticed there was no latch or knob on the inside. The door was stuck fast.

I wasn't going to allow Kennedy to get the best of me and make me panic. Lucy and Thea simply hadn't noticed the light turn green. Any minute, they'd see. And I could speed things up by delivering hard repeated thumps to the door.

Any second now....

I paused my knocking, straining to hear anything outside my small box. Nothing but my own labored breathing. God, what about the oxygen running out? The fear that had seemed silly a moment ago suddenly engulfed me. I needed to keep my breath controlled, but it rushed through my lungs at an ever-increasing pace. There wasn't enough, I knew there wasn't enough, I was hyperventilating, the seconds stretched out to eternity, my face wet from something besides sweat, but all that mattered was my labor for air. My rapping became louder, more frantic. Maybe I could break the door open. Didn't desperate people get sudden bursts of strength? Hadn't parents been able to lift entire cars when their children were caught underneath them? Surely this situation counted as dire enough to give me unearned super powers.

The dumbwaiter didn't even shift as I repeatedly threw my weight against the exit. I didn't have room to maneuver. I was going to die in this tiny white cube. A heartbreaking keening noise made its way out of my chest and filled my ears. I didn't want to die. I wasn't ready. What had I accomplished in my life? A fat lot of nothing. Despair added strength to my flailing.

And then the lights went off. In the sudden darkness, I understood what it was to be beset by unknown horrors. Anything seemed possible. Kennedy was capable of any and all trespasses. Even though I had just seen the blank walls, I no longer trusted my senses. Anything could be in that dumbwaiter with me, and meanwhile I was still running out of air, and pain shot down my arms from all the slamming I was doing with my hands and shoulder.

I began to get dizzy even though I was lying down. This was it. Soon

I'd be put out of my misery, lapsing into a glorious unconsciousness. Maybe it wouldn't be so bad. Maybe the acidic taste of shame would finally dissolve without a physical body to inhabit. Maybe all mistakes would disintegrate into blessed irrelevance. Maybe—

The door swung open, and I fell halfway out with a huge wheeze as if my lungs were being pumped by bellows. In the painful brightness my eyes stung with tears and sweat and rogue sunscreen, and I couldn't see a thing. My body kept making weird rasping noises, a stray croak scraping my throat as I pushed myself forward and fell down onto the hard floor below. A new agony bloomed between my right hip and knee, which had borne the brunt of my flopping like a beached fish.

"Jesus, what happened to her?" Footsteps. "Zoe, are you all right?"

I couldn't respond, tried to peer up out of swollen eyes, but it was all too much.

"Forget about that." A different voice. Thea? It must have been Thea. "Get her up." Hands prodded me and they wouldn't relent, no matter how hard I tried to curl in on myself, so eventually I allowed them to chivvy me up.

My sight was beginning to clear. We were in another white room, a gigantic version of the dumbwaiter, which made my breath start speeding up again. Had I actually escaped or was this cosmic joke what death was? A peal of hysterical laughter bubbled from my lips.

"Jesus," Lucy repeated. I leaned on her heavily, limping the entire way to the corner where the hated safe waited. Thea grabbed my right hand and pushed my finger against the screen. They added their own fingers, and the door clicked open.

I was already collapsing when Thea said, "It's the treasure! We did it!"

In that moment, I no longer cared.

Fifteen

LOVE STORY: The Female Torture We Can't Help But Watch

—January 22, 2019 by lacey, www.dontcallmegirl.com

After two episodes, the new season of *Love Story* is proving to be as riveting as the previous season, even as it's more of a walk on the dark side. You'd think watching these women perform like lab monkeys receiving random shocks would lose its novelty, so kudos to the talented producers involved for continuing to make us care.

Love Story does a scrupulous job giving lip service to ideas that will attract the modern professional woman, and for good reason: their target demographic has the disposable income to spend, attracting lucrative advertising deals and winning *Love Story* a coveted (and highly marketed) spot on Leogami's schedule. But watching the drama unfold, I can't help asking myself, "Why do I love to hate-watch this show so very much?"

It's become a cherished personal ritual for me. I set my calendar reminder, I look forward to chilling out in front of this hot mess with a glass of Chardonnay and some Gouda and crackers. I become mildly obsessed with the cast of the show, to the extent that I *may* indulge in some cyber-stalking from time to time.

Confession: my fascination encompasses everyone on this season except Emerson Courtland himself. He's pretty enough, I won't argue with that, and he has the prerequisite tragic past to milk for his story arc, but so far he seems like a bland stand-in for a romantic interest. Does he have a personality? So far he's just your typical straight-laced old-money type who needs a sense of humor transplant stat. You can tell if it weren't for the antics of the show forcing his hand, he'd be all over the trophy wife types in lieu of any of the women who make the show interesting. And this asinine taste makes it tough to be too invested in his choices.

Take, for example, Naomi Butler. She's fierce, she's funny, she runs her own accounting business and she must be doing all right for herself if she can afford to take this amount of time off. And like every woman on the show, she's drop-dead gorgeous. I'd take out a second mortgage to have such smooth, creamy skin. But what remains mostly unspoken is the fact that Naomi is black. And I'm sorry, but can you imagine Emerson Courtland ending up with a black woman? He'll keep her around long enough to belie any racism claims, sure, but will he keep her till the end? Will he seriously consider confronting New York high society with her on his arm? What about bringing her to the family Christmas celebration? A quick skip around the internet suggests most of the family might not be particularly liberal-minded, and we can't expect poor Aunt Margaret to hold them all off.

(I'm being flip, but Margaret Courtland is actually a formidable and accomplished businessperson in her own right, much more so than Emerson himself. And she insisted on venturing away from the considerable shadow cast by the Courtland family fortune and business empire in order to do so. Although those priceless family connections of hers couldn't have hurt. But I digress.)

Or take poor Zoe Roberts, who had such a rocky start I felt sure she'd be eliminated right off the bat. She'd make the perfect manic pixie dream girl for Emerson if she learns to be a little less earnest and a little more quirky, but you know that woman has some serious shit in her past. I'm willing to bet a season's supply of wine she slept with one of her creative writing professors and was his muse, or hung out all alone in high school while giving everyone tragic dirty looks, or used to live off coffee, cigarettes, and cheap wine. She's not one of the stereotypes these shows usually lean into, but she's a stereotype all the same. Zoe the Young Bohemian.

Zoe is a mixture of contradictions that makes her interesting to watch: she cares, sure, but she doesn't care in the same way most of the other women do. She's the cool girl without even trying. And in spite of her waif-like appearance hinting at emotional wreckage, she has an unexpected core of steel. Watching her try not to lose it in that dumbwaiter? She totally had it together until they locked her in and made her wait for it. A lot of viewers are only going to remember her breakdown, but the fact is, most of the women broke down during that treasure hunt, and most of them didn't hold out as long as Zoe did.

A strange side note: before writing this post, I very naturally hopped onto Instagram to do a little stalking and see what these women are posting now the show has started airing. The answer is: nothing. It's normal for contestants' Instagrams to go quiet during filming and before the show airs, but usually the embargo against posting is lifted by now. How else can the contestants launch their careers as social media influencers and get a crap-ton of free stuff?

Well, not this time. It looks like Leogami has asked contestants to continue staying mum. For how long? It's anybody's guess, but I wouldn't be surprised if it's for the entire run of the show. Talk about locking things down to prevent spoilers!

At the end of the second episode, after we've watched these women go through some producer's idea of hell to be on television, we're forced to ask ourselves, "Where could this show possibly be going?" Sure, some of the women were more aggressively tortured than others. (Simone had to *get dirty*. That was literally her challenge, which, when juxtaposed with women facing serious phobias and general disgustingness, really makes you wonder if she slipped someone a bribe.) But many of these women have already been stripped down to their raw emotions. Beginning the season this way is either plain foolhardiness or dizzying ambition.

Only time will tell.

Xoxo Lacey

Sixteen

In spite of our suffering, we were not the first team to complete Kennedy's sadistic treasure hunt. Vivian, Simone, and Cassidy had won the private cocktail party with Emerson. But as the second place team, we were thrown a bone: twenty minutes of private time each before the real party began.

So instead of curling into the fetal position and making strange moaning noises like a beached whale, which is what I wanted to do, I was jockeying for position in front of the bathroom mirror with five other women, all of whom seemed refreshed and bubbly and ready to go, as if they could simply shed the traumatic events of the day like a snake's skin.

I don't know how they bounced back so quickly. In hindsight, several of them were probably suffering as much as I was but keeping it hidden for the benefit of the cameras. But in the moment, it felt like I was the only one struggling. My five-minute shower made me feel every ache and strain in my body, and the effort of fixing my newly augmented hair felt even more onerous than usual. I'd already made a poor impression on Emerson, and now I was in danger of falling asleep during our precious few minutes together. Somehow I doubted that would convince him to keep me around another week.

Elaine escorted me down for my twenty minutes in heaven. If it had been Kennedy I might have launched myself at her throat.

Someone had gone to a lot of trouble setting up a lovely bower on the beach, complete with carpets, tiki lanterns (in addition to the lighting rig), and a wicker loveseat overwhelmed with red cushions. Emerson stood when I approached, hugged me and gave me a dry peck on my cheek. "Zoe, it's good to see you." I was surprised by the genuine warmth in his voice. "I heard what happened today." He led me over to the loveseat, which I sank into with real gratitude, my knees wobbly from the combination of my sandals' high heels and my general feeling of being a wrung-out and filthy hand rag of a human being.

"It was nothing." That was a joke, but what was I supposed to say? I was hardly going to relive the whole thing for his benefit.

He smiled and took my hand. I looked at our interlocked fingers with hazy confusion. "I wouldn't say that." I stared down at the light brown hairs covering his forearm, not sure how to reply. "I have to say, I was quite impressed by your courage. Have you always been so claustrophobic?"

And here it was, my chance to open up, let Emerson get to know me, show him a deeper, vulnerable side of myself that had nothing to do with poetry. He never needed to understand everything about me was fodder for my internal love affair with words. And for all I knew, that fire had been extinguished for good. I flashed on Joe's face for a disconcerting moment and felt a small burst of uncharacteristic rage. He'd left me stripped and bare of what was most important to me, defenseless not only to Kennedy's ploys but to the world at large.

"Since I was a little girl," I told Emerson and the expectant camera's eye. "I got trapped in one of the kitchen cupboards by accident when I was, oh, three or four."

This was the story I always told, the socially acceptable version of my insignificant little trauma. It hadn't been an accident. My mom had done it on purpose, and Kennedy had known, and she had let me rot in there. She'd had no choice; it was leave me or bring down my mom's wrath. I'd sat curled up in the smallest ball for hours, wet with my own filth, until my mom finally let me out again and gave me a sharp scolding for the mess I'd made.

The only one who knew the story was Joe. While I'd told him, he'd gotten a funny look on his face: wrinkled nose, an almost smirk marring his full lips. When I'd finished, he'd laughed at me.

I should have left him right then. But instead I waited for years until he cast me aside as casually as he would an unpaired sock.

But Emerson was being held accountable on camera, and my sanitized version made it easy on him, so he put on a suitable sympathetic expression. "How long were you stuck in there?"

I gave a light laugh. "Oh, I don't know. I was so young, I can barely remember."

Nine hours, it must have been. She shut me up right after my dad left for work, and she only let me out when she knew he was coming home. My dad might have been a piece of work, but even he would have balked at keeping me under the sink all evening.

"But your body remembers."

I started. It was such an unexpected thing for Emerson to say, and yet it was completely true. Squeezed into that dumbwaiter, it had been like I was four again. "That's exactly how it feels," I told him. It might have been the first time genuine warmth crept into my voice while we were talking, and his body responded instantly, relaxing and opening up. "The years fall away."

"And it feels like it happened yesterday." He looked directly—fiercely—into my eyes for the first time. He actually had a personality! Here it was, under all the layers of convention and privilege and ossified wealth.

"Exactly." We shared shy smiles even as I wondered what had happened to him that he knew this the way I did. He reached out and touched the back of my hand, and I didn't pull away.

Only to be interrupted by Kennedy. "Emerson," she said, "I'm going to have to take you away for a few minutes."

"But Zoe only just got here." His protest warmed my heart more than it should have.

"Sorry, but it's important." She didn't sound sorry. Her voice was a strange mixture of somber and excited that made my arm hairs prickle. "Zoe, stay here with Elaine. She'll walk you back to the house in a little while, okay?"

She didn't look guilty or even a little self conscious about what she'd put me through earlier in the day. Her lack of concern stung even though it wasn't a surprise. "Will I get more time with Emerson later?"

She'd already put her hand on Emerson's arm to lead him away. "What? Oh, I don't know. Just sit tight, okay?" She'd already dismissed me from her mind. I wasn't one of the major players in whatever little drama she was orchestrating right now. I was just a bystanding casualty, an inconvenience to be swept off the board. I glared at her departing back as she and Emerson hurried up the hill, heads bent close together as she filled him in on whatever part she needed him to play, the crew members scurrying behind them. Nothing more to see down here at the beach.

Not fair. Emerson's and my sudden connection, along with the lingering aftershocks of adrenaline still spiraling through my system, made me bold. I crunched over the sand to where Elaine stood, slightly hunched and holding a hand up to her earpiece, as if that made it easier for her to listen.

I clutched my stomach right around my belly button. "I think I ate something bad." I tried to add a certain tension to the words, a little hiss of discomfort. "It's pretty obvious Emerson's not coming back, so can I just go back up to the house and um...you know...."

Elaine's face squinched in embarrassment. "Do you think you can hold on for a little while?"

I shook my head and made a show of looking around desperately for bushes or any other shielding. But it was, conveniently, a beach, and sand offered no cover whatsoever. "If I run, I might make it back in time," I said helpfully.

"Oh, all right, go, go." She flapped her hands at me. "And hurry."

I took off at a sprint up the beach to the cliffside stairs. I could see Kennedy and Emerson nearing the top; if I was lucky, I'd be able to see where she was taking him and follow along, maybe even insinuate myself in the current drama. After what had happened that day, I took a certain vicious pleasure in the idea of throwing even the smallest spoke into Kennedy's machinations.

But I was thwarted in my desires. By the time I reached the top of the stairs, short of breath and disheveled, Kennedy and Emerson had disappeared from view. I stood with my hands on my hips, surveying the romantically lit landscaping in front of me and puffing in a vain attempt to get enough air in my lungs.

Someone grabbed my elbow, and I jumped back with a little shriek.

Margaret Courtland stepped out of the shadows. In the dim lighting her face looked like a specter's head, drawn and gaunt with enormous sunken eye sockets. She smiled at me, her teeth weirdly large behind bared lips, and I took another step back.

"You want to know where my nephew went, don't you?" She leaned towards me, rubbing her hands together like we were co-conspirators. "Your time got cut short. That producer must not like you very much."

I rubbed the bridge of my nose, sudden fatigue permeating every pore. "No, it's not that." I stopped myself before I said too much. "I'm sure she has a plan."

"Don't we all?" Her eyes glinted in the darkness.

I shook my head. "I'm just along for the ride."

Joe's dry laugh echoed in my head. *"Poor little Pooh Bear. Always being left behind."* I started and looked behind my shoulder, but there was no Joe in sight. Just the memory of his nickname for me and the painful vise it created around my heart.

"A kindred spirit then. Come, watch with me." Margaret took my hand as if we were schoolgirl friends and led me across the grounds, into the house, and up a back flight of stairs I hadn't known existed. Her grip was unrelenting and uncomfortably tight, and when I looked down in the unlit stairway, her hand reminded me of a claw, the knuckles swelling monstrously, the nails little pinpricks in my skin.

Up two flights of stairs, down a narrow hallway of closed doors and around the corner, she shoved me into a small stuffy room and shut the door behind us. An array of monitors covered the entire wall, a single fancy office chair facing them. Margaret Courtland settled in the chair and made a sweeping gesture with her hand. "This was part of my deal with the network. They want to use my house, I want to be able to see what's going on."

Holy shit. I scanned the monitors, and as their pictures shifted, I saw the entryway, two different angles of the lounge, the conservatory, a few of the pool area, the kitchen, and each of the Gold Digger bedrooms. She fiddled with the control panel in front of the monitors, and murmured conversation came out of the speakers. She even had audio access.

But my surprise was quickly cut short by a heavy panting. "No no no no no." A rhythmic repetition from someone in distress. I looked from screen to screen, trying to figure out which one we were listening to.

Ah, there it was. The camera was zoomed in on a young woman hunched over in the middle of one of the bedrooms. She rocked gently back and forth while making her continuous stream of denial. It took me a minute to recognize her: Cassidy, one of the multitudes of blondes.

The camera drew even closer. Cassidy moved her hands to her head, and a huge hank of hair came loose in her hand. I gasped, and only then did I notice what I'd missed: several locks of blond hair were scattered around her on the floor. "Holy fuck."

Margaret clucked her tongue. "I'm afraid it's just the beginning."

"What's wrong with her?" I found my hands patting my own head, making sure my hair was firmly attached.

Margaret shrugged. "They're not sure."

At least the producers had had the presence of mind to isolate Cassidy, keeping the other women from seeing her. What if—horrible thought—she was contagious? But the angle and movement of the camera work didn't suggest a stationary camera, which meant there was at least one person in there with her, recording her distress.

Was this another trial like the ones on our treasure hunt? And I'd thought my dumbwaiter experience was bad.

I didn't want to watch. "All these monitors...does this mean you're a fan of the show?"

Margaret's laugh could have scraped a barnacle off a hull. "Hardly. Exploiting naïve young people and commodifying their experiences for the entertainment of the masses? That's never been my cup of tea."

My hackles came up. "We get something out of it too. It's not like we're being forced to do this."

Margaret looked back at me, eyebrows raised. "And now that you're here, the constant surveillance doesn't give you pause? The need to play for the camera at all times, no matter how extreme your emotions or your suffering? You think this is psychologically healthy for you?"

There was a heavy pause. "It's not so bad," I finally muttered.

She wheeled her chair around to face me. "I was very much like you when I was young. Wandering around lost, not sure where I belonged. Valuing other people's opinions above my own. Not able to stand on my own two feet."

I gave my feet a pointed look. "Seems like I'm doing okay."

"I thought I was willing to give up everything for the sake of love." She reached up and touched the amber amulet around her neck. "This was a gift from Darwin, you know. My first and only true love. He had one that matched, and we both wore them all the time. They were like our wedding rings, his way of showing I was on a different level from the other girls. At least that was what I wanted to believe." She gave a bitter laugh. "He was so sweet at first. Silver-tongued. He told me he'd been waiting to meet me his entire life. I'd fall asleep to his endearments whispered in my ear. He asked me so many questions. For the first time in my life I felt like an interesting force in my own right."

I knew what she meant. When we first met, Joe and I had stayed up late into the night talking about writing, our classmates, our childhoods, anything and everything. I hadn't realized what it would be like to be so close to another person. To feel *known*. I'd never wanted to let that feeling go. "What happened?"

She released the amulet. "I didn't know him as well as I thought. He was never satisfied, playing people against each other for his own ends. Found my weakest points and exploited them to get what he wanted." She paused. "I'm not convinced he believed in the intrinsic reality of anyone but himself."

I found myself thinking of Kennedy. But she wasn't really like that. She meant well, didn't she? That was why I was here, after all, given this opportunity to resuscitate my writing career. "I'm sorry," I told Margaret. "He sounds awful."

She barked out a laugh. "That's one way of putting it." Cassidy still writhed on the floor. Why were the cameras still on? Why weren't they *doing* something? "You know, in some ways you remind me of myself back when I was young. I hope you won't mind me giving you a word of advice: most romance is as hollow as this show. If it forces you to consume yourself, it's not worth it."

No wonder she'd objected to having the show filmed here, if that's what she believed. "I'll keep that in mind."

"It's not too late to leave, you know. The boat will be coming in a few days, bringing supplies and taking a few young ladies back home. You could be on it." I didn't know what to say. Just because I reminded her of herself didn't mean she had the right to tell me to abandon my plans. "You should leave now while you have the chance."

Her words sounded ominous. "I'm happy where I am, thanks."

She sighed. "I would have stayed too. At least make sure you're doing it properly. Protect yourself, be careful, and remember, you're always being watched."

This lady was beginning to weird me out, childhood hero or not. "I'll keep that in mind."

"You're going to need to do better than you did today," she said. So she'd been watching as I melted down in that little box. For someone who condemned the show's premise so strongly, she sure liked being involved. "And how do you feel about my nephew now?"

I shrugged, remembering our moment of understanding. "He seems all right, actually. Even if he doesn't like poetry."

She snorted. "I'll be sure to tell him you said so." At the look on my face, she shook her head. "I'm joking. Emerson's sense of humor still needs some development. He's taking all of this very seriously indeed." She pivoted around to see the screen where Cassidy remained rocking. "He *seems* all right, and yet here he is, willing to play along with these producers. Keep that in mind once you're back at home recovering from the ordeal."

"Once I'm home, people will know my name. I'll finally be able to make something of myself." Locked away in her secret sanctuary I found myself accidentally speaking something close to the truth. Surely there couldn't be any cameras here? But I checked the corners of the room. Only a few days in, and my paranoia was in full bloom.

"And what do you know about fame, Zoe Roberts?" She waited as if expecting a real answer. "Not much, isn't that right? Fame is a well-dressed cage. Look at Cannon. He's a charmer, isn't he? And there's not an authentic bone in his well-honed body. Is that a sacrifice you're willing to make?"

"What do *you* know about fame?" I shot back. "You were born into a family that gave you everything." She didn't respond. "Fame isn't the only difficult road you can walk. And at least it gives you something back."

We both stared at Cassidy, who alternated between sobbing on her hands and knees and pulling out more hair. I wished someone would stop her. Look at me, powerless as always while her blonde hair kept falling like loose sheaves of wheat.

"We can help each other," Margaret said suddenly. "I need you to pay attention and tell me what you see."

As if this array of monitors weren't enough. "I don't know what you want to know."

"Anything strange," she said. "Anything at all. I need to know how things are progressing, that's all." I hesitated, but then she added, "I'll help you too."

"You'll put in a good word for me with Emerson?" I asked.

She frowned as if I'd said something inappropriate. "I won't be responsible for that. No, you write something, a novel, you finish it, you can send it to me. I'll read it, and we'll see. I still have contacts in the publishing world." She held up a finger. "But only if you keep me informed the entire time you're here. Is it a deal?"

Before I could answer, Emerson entered the shot. I watched open-mouthed as he hovered at the edge of camera range, a look of horror on his face as he watched Cassidy's transformation. "Cassidy?" They hadn't even had their cocktail party yet. This was a woman he barely knew. But he drew closer. "Are you okay?"

Dumb question, Emerson. She was very obviously not okay. She didn't look up, just began shaking her head. "No no no,"—her volume increasing with each repetition—"I don't want you to see me this way. Please."

"Cassidy." His voice shifted, became gentler. "Please don't worry. You'll always be beautiful, you know that, right?"

At his words, tears began to stream down her face. He knelt beside her. "Come on now. Come on. It's going to be okay."

He took her hands and brought them away from her head, more hair coming loose as he did so. I gasped at the huge bald spots that were revealed, raw and red, as if the hair had been forcibly removed. At this rate she was going to lose her all her hair.

In front of me, Margaret shook her own full head of hair. "It's only the beginning," she whispered. "I told him this was a bad idea. *I told him.*" She pivoted around, her face a terrible mask of urgency. "Is it a deal?"

"Sure." My voice felt like it was coming from a great distance. It was hard to think about myself, my future, any plans of surviving this show and what came after while looking at Cassidy's swollen eyes and pink scalp.

But I couldn't overlook the opportunity of having someone with Margaret's connections as a potential advocate. That was why I was here. "It's a deal."

Cassidy's hair would grow back, I told myself, trying to lessen the horror welling inside of me. It would only be a matter of time.

But I was wrong. It never grew back. I corresponded with her once, years and years later, and she told me she had a collection of the finest wigs, paid for by the network.

Seventeen

Description of footage from season seven, episode ten of *Her Engagement*, aired on July 13, 2009:

Cannon Murphy sits alone in front of the camera, the lighting giving him a haloed effect. He's clean-shaven, he wears a sharply cut navy suit jacket and tie with a crisp white shirt, his brown eyes meet the camera with an earnest look. He shifts nervously from side to side and occasionally mumbles his words. A discrete potted plant sits in the background.

"When I first came on this show, we all know how skeptical I was." He laughs without inhibitions, shows his perfectly even teeth. "But when I met Becca, and especially as I got to know her better, everything changed for me. I didn't think I would feel this strongly this quickly, but...." He spreads his hands, gives an endearing grin. "What can I say? Sometimes life surprises you, and you have to go along for the ride. Becca is everything I was hoping to find in a partner: she's gorgeous, of course, but more than that, she's a strong woman and she knows what she wants. And I couldn't be more excited to spend the rest of my life making her happy."

. . .

Cut to the Swiss alps, a gorgeous panorama of snow-capped peaks and clear blue sky. Cannon looks slightly dazzled by the brightness of the sun and the solemnity of the moment. He strides down the cleared stony path surrounded by clean drifts of snow, approaching a young woman standing at a vista point, looking out over the remarkable view. This is Becca Martin, the woman Cannon has been wooing all season. She wears an elegant shimmery dark blue gown that coordinates perfectly with Cannon's choice of suit, a look of deep contemplation on her face. The viewers can't help thinking these two are meant for each other.

Cannon's face breaks into a wide smile. We can see how besotted he is with this woman as he hurries his pace, not stopping until he's right in front of her, holding her hand and smiling down on her. They stand suspended in an aura of romance.

Cannon begins to kneel, fumbling with his free hand in his jacket pocket. We know what we're going to see: the small velvet box that makes this whole season worthwhile. We can't wait to see which ring Cannon has chosen to represent the personality of his beloved.

Becca tugs at his hand, does not allow him to kneel. The smile remains on his face even as he gives the quickest glance around him. "Becca," he breathes, "what is it?"

She turns away, a close-up shot showing the tears running down her cheeks. "I'm not in love with you," she gasps. "I thought I was, but I'm not."

"Jessie?" he asks. "You're choosing Jessie? He's not ready to get married. He doesn't even want to propose." The knowledge that this narrative isn't going to have a happy ending for him cracks onto his face.

"I have to give love a chance." Becca says the words breathlessly, almost as if they're a magic invocation to get her what she wants.

"But you told me you were falling in love with me!"

She sighs, and we get the sense she wants this little scene of the drama to be over, that this is the last obstacle between her and the ideal proposal she's hoping to receive from Jessie. "I have to listen to my gut."

He closes his eyes. "You sound like a (a loud beep) Hallmark commercial. I made love to you last week. Didn't that mean anything to you?"

Her mouth forms a perfect "O" of shock. Talking about what happened behind closed doors during their private evening together is a major faux pas. "I'm sorry, Cannon," she says firmly. Staying classy. "I wish you nothing but the best."

Jessie proposed to Becca, and they broke up eight months later. Becca later married minor country star Chad O'Brien in 2017, and the couple had two children together before divorcing. Becca went on to get married twice more. She and Cannon didn't stay in touch.

Description of footage from season eight episode one of *Her Engagement*, aired on May 9, 2011:

Cannon Murphy sits alone in front of the camera, a reddish cast to the lighting to cue his status as season villain. On the first night he's already clashed with several contestants on the show. He has a neatly trimmed goatee, he speaks with less hesitation, but he still occasionally slurs his words when talking too fast. His teeth are strong and straight, but now they're also almost blindingly white. He wears a sharp gray jacket but no tie, the top two buttons of his shirt undone. He runs his hand through his thick curly hair while giving a self-deprecating laugh.

"I really never thought I'd find myself sitting here again. If you'd told me this even three months ago, I wouldn't have believed you. But there's something different about Justine...something special. We'd been chatting for months after she was the runner-up on *His Engagement*; I'd reached out to offer the support of a fellow runner-up, and things just grew from there. We even met once or twice at a few charity events. But when I realized how important she'd grown to me and asked her if she was interested in seeing if it could lead to something more, she'd already agreed to do the show. I know I'm the first contestant to appear on two seasons of the same show, but I feel like I'd regret it if I let this chance pass me by. If this is what Justine needs to feel sure about what we have, then this is the journey we'll take together. At the end, we'll be stronger for it, and she'll be wearing my ring on her finger."

Description of footage from season eight episode ten of *Her Engagement*, aired on July 11, 2011:

Cannon Murphy is in front of the bathroom mirror in his hotel suite in Fiji, fixing his jacket lapels and checking his hair. We've already seen him slip the ring box into his jacket pocket, and we know he's about to go propose to Justine. No suit and tie for him this time, just a nicely cut shirt and linen jacket appropriate for the tropical location.

Cannon flashes a nervous smile when he hears a knock on his suite door. "I guess she just can't wait," he jokes as he goes to answer the door.

Justine comes in, wearing pedal pushers and a bright pink halter top. Not a proposal outfit in the slightest, and Cannon instantly has his guard up, joking and laughing and offering her something to drink. She's having none of his deflection though, taking his hand and leading him to the extremely neutral hotel couch.

"We need to talk," she says, and we all flinch along with Cannon at the infamous words. "I can't go through with this. I just don't feel confident in our relationship moving forward."

Cannon swallows, takes a moment, is visibly upset. "Of all the guys, I'm the only one here because you asked him to be. I'm the only one you can be sure is here for the right reasons."

"I'm sorry," Justine says, "but that's just not good enough."

Dillon proposes to Justine later in the episode. They stay together for two and a half years before breaking up. Justine falls in love with another alumni from the franchise, and they get married a year and a half later. They are still married and have three children. She and Cannon didn't stay in touch.

Description of footage from season fifteen episode ten of *His Engagement*, aired on March 9, 2015:

Cannon Murphy sits in a pool of soft lighting, eyes closed. The plant has made a reappearance in the rear of the shot. He's kept the goatee, still has the shock of light brown curly hair, but the mumbling has disappeared except in moments of especially high stress. No visible signs of increasing age mar his boyish good looks, but the way he carries himself is indefinably different. More at ease with himself, perhaps, and more accustomed to giving the camera a good sound bite at will. His season as the center of attention has been jam-packed with such moments, and his approval ratings with the fans is the highest it's ever been: 86.6% of polled viewers say the network made a good choice in casting Cannon, and 91% say he is "deserving" or "very deserving" of finding love.

Cannon sighs and gives a guileless stare to the camera. "I've come a long way since I started this journey back in 2009. If I'd known what was waiting for me, I would have hesitated to take the plunge. But now I know it was all worth it, because at the end of the road, Jillian was the one waiting for me. I wouldn't change anything that led me to meeting her, and to making the proposal I'm about to make."

"Of course I've had such bad luck with my past proposals it's only natural I'm feeling a little nervous right now." He gives a self-deprecating laugh but otherwise fails to look apprehensive. "Jillian says she's fallen in love with me and I think she'll say yes, but"—he shrugs—"I've thought the same before, and I was obviously wrong. So I'm hopeful right now and trying to stay focused on the future I want to build with Jillian, but I'm also aware that at the last minute, everything could fold like a house of cards. I sincerely believe this time is different, that Jillian and I are soul mates. I've never felt as sure as I do today. But I'm also in suspense. I won't breathe easily until I've asked her the question and heard her response. Could today be my happily ever after? I can't wait to find out!"

Cannon poses confidently in front of the camera in his stylish purple-black tux before we see him getting into a nondescript town car in New York City and being whisked away. After a commercial break, we see him waiting on a rooftop. Night has fallen, and a sea of lights stretches out behind him. He's leaning against the barrier as if he doesn't have a care in the world until Jillian appears, and he stands up straighter. Her long brown hair is curled and she's wearing a beaded red gown, an excited smile plastered over her face. The viewers can tell just by looking at her that she's going to say yes, and we have to assume Cannon knows this too.

As soon as she reaches him, he drops to one knee. He holds up the little velvet box. "Please make me the happiest man in the world," he says. "Jillian, will you marry me?"

She gives a little giggle, eyes wide at the huge diamond on display, before saying yes. He stands up, leans down, kisses her passionately. The ring goes on the finger. Cannon Murphy has finally gotten engaged on primetime television. Maybe this process works after all.

Cannon Murphy and Jillian Prince break up ten months later with the usual bland statement regurgitated by dozens of celebrity gossip sites. Cannon says he won't consider appearing on another iteration of the franchise ever again.

He is announced as the host of the new romance reality television series *Love Story* less than two years later.

Eighteen

I couldn't stop thinking about Cassidy's hair falling out in huge chunks, accumulating around her on the floor like tumbleweed. The producers whisked her off the island without telling anyone why she'd left; as far as I knew, Emerson and I were the only cast members who knew anything.

I'd never given Kennedy's career in reality TV much thought, but now I was seeing it up close and personal, I had questions. The scheming, the meltdowns, the constant surveillance, the way producers would storm into our bedrooms at all times of the day and night, interrupting our sleep, the subtle putdowns of our appearances, both from fellow contestants and from producers, the less subtle push for us to be drinking alcohol at all times, the lack of anything to do with ourselves except muse in our journals and exercise. I'd thought I had what it took, mental fortitude and all that, but I already wanted to leave.

Which is why I didn't tell Kennedy what I knew. Not about what happened to Cassidy, not about Margaret Courtland's secret room of monitors, and certainly not how I felt about her exploiting my claustrophobia. After that first rough patch when my mom left, I had learned how to keep my own counsel.

Coping mechanisms exist for a reason.

I didn't see Emerson for a few days, or Margaret Courtland, or even much of Kennedy. I spent most of my time with my roomies, although Thea would abandon Vivian to join us from time to time. Whether Thea liked it or not, our manufactured adventure together had bonded us.

We spent most of our time lying by the pool or on the beach. It wasn't that we were restricted from leaving the house, but after that savage treasure hunt, none of us wanted to leave the relative safety of our manicured environment. Even the chance of running into Cannon didn't sway me. Boredom for safety seemed like a reasonable tradeoff. We slathered sun lotion on one another, sipped fruity drinks, told each other our life stories. I told just enough to make it seem like I belonged, but the only place I was really honest was my journal, which I tucked under my pillow at night and hid in the conservatory when I wasn't using it. The words began to flow a little easier, a small improvement, but I'd take it.

Mostly we waited. And eventually Kennedy appeared by the pool to announce the next Culling would be held that very night.

Thea sighed dramatically. We'd come to learn in the last few days she had a flair for the dramatic when she wasn't using her sly wit to skewer someone. "I still haven't gotten my promised time with him," she said pointedly.

Kennedy shrugged. "Something came up," was all she said. "Emerson's schedule has been packed all week, and he hasn't been feeling well."

"We were promised time with him," Thea repeated stubbornly.

Kennedy raised her eyebrows. "You want time with him? Do better next time. Win the competition."

"Is Emerson feeling better?" Lucy interrupted. "Does he need anyone to keep him company while he's laid up?"

Kennedy gave an insincere smile. "He's doing fine now. Nothing a little rest couldn't fix." I wondered if she'd had a lead man with cold feet on her hands. Watching Cassidy fall apart would be enough to shake anyone.

Thea was undaunted. "Both Lucy and Zoe got their time with him. And in season one there were group activities every week." She knew I'd only gotten a few minutes, but in this situation, even those brief minutes seemed like a crushing advantage. Emerson might actually remember my name tonight, but Thea would have to depend on whatever previous impression she'd made on him.

Kennedy rolled her eyes. "You'll get to talk to him tonight before the Culling. If he really likes you, you have nothing to worry about. Seven pm, girls. Make sure you look your best."

I was the last one to finish getting ready for our big night. The other women had descended downstairs like a horde of locusts, and after days in such close quarters, the quiet felt unnatural and oppressive. I kept looking behind me, expecting someone to be watching. Maybe it was because I knew someone *was* watching. Margaret was probably ensconced in her little room monitoring the cameras, not to mention all the producers looking for drama to exploit.

A burst of girlish laughter filtered from downstairs. I finished blotting my lipstick and turned to reapply my mascara. Kennedy was going to give me a lecture later about not using fake eyelashes, but seeing Michelle's reaction to them had turned me off.

I was fluttering my eyes, assessing the mascara's effects, when I saw him reflected in the mirror behind me. I dropped the mascara brush onto the floor. "Joe?"

I almost expected him to fade into nothingness, another trick served by my grieving mind, but he leaned against the door frame, tall and lanky, arms folded, just like I'd seen him do a hundred times. He looked just as I remembered him: same five o'clock shadow, same dark hair falling into his eyes, same tortoiseshell glasses. "Hey Pooh Bear," he drawled. The pet name hit me like a strike to the throat.

What was he doing here? Kennedy must have arranged this reunion. All eyes in the producers' control room must be on us right now. Would I take him back, or would I refuse in hopes of making something happen with Emerson, a man I barely knew? The absurdity of my position hit me full force, along with a healthy dose of anger. Kennedy had promised to look out for me. She'd promised not to bring Joe into it. She'd *promised*.

But here he was, looking at me like he wanted to devour me. Just like he had at the beginning of our relationship, back before the switch flipped and everything changed. "I can't believe you're here."

He grinned. "You look good. I like what you've done to your hair." I couldn't help the glow in my chest at his approval. "I've missed you, Pooh Bear."

I sucked in a painful breath. "I don't understand. Was this Kennedy's idea? Did she fly you out?"

"Kennedy has nothing to do with this." He came forward into the room, reminding me of his dizzying height, how he took up so much *space*, not just physical but energetic. If the other women were here, they'd be buzzing around him, asking him questions, trying to take care of him. They wouldn't be able to help themselves.

I'd certainly never been able to resist him. A hope sparked in my heart. If he'd come all this way, maybe we could work things out after all. Get married and have a real partnership. Maybe that beautiful future I'd spent so much time envisioning wasn't irrevocably lost.

After all, was it really so awful taking care of him? He couldn't help it that he was a better writer than me. He had sat down and done the work to get where he was. Maybe I'd just been suffering from a severe case of sour grapes. But with him here in the flesh, all of my frustrations seemed to melt away. I wanted to be with him. I wanted to touch him. I wanted....

I took a step back, glancing up at the ceiling fan where I was pretty sure one of the omniscient cameras was hidden. "I need to get down to the party." But I could hear the lack of conviction in my voice.

"You can give me five minutes, can't you?" I knew that smile so well, the dimples flashing seductively, the tinge of hurt in the crook of the lip. "I think you owe me at least that much after everything we've been through together."

I took obscure comfort from the fact I was television pretty and therefore looked better in this moment than I had during our entire relationship. If things were about to get tragic, at least I'd look good for it. "Joe, you were the one who wanted to break up," I reminded him. "You said we weren't good for each other. You said I'd never be anything but a writer groupie and a hack. You said you didn't love me anymore." Saying his words felt like regurgitating poison. But if he was here now, did that mean...he'd changed his mind?

"Oh, Zoe, you've always been so dramatic. I didn't say those things."

I blinked. I'd replayed his words over and over in my mind, wallowing in my searing inadequacies. He had absolutely said those things.

This wasn't the first time he'd denied his own words. It had happened all the time when we were together. This rising feeling of confusion and panic and desperation was sickeningly familiar.

"I always said you were the best thing to ever happen to me," he continued. This was true. He had said that many times. Especially when I stayed up late editing for him, rewriting huge swathes of his prose, or came home bone exhausted after a dreary day at work and mustered up a smile while I served dinner from the slow cooker I'd had running all day. "Don't you miss me, Pooh Bear?"

I thought I was going to choke. "I'm doing okay," I managed to get out.

He took another step closer. "The truth is, I'm worried about you." He glanced around the room, and I saw it through his eyes: the unmade dormitory-style bunk beds, the piles of clothing, the array of makeup cases and beauty products scattered around my feet. It smelled of sunscreen, lotion, and overly sweet perfume, a cross between a freshman college dorm and a beauty pageant. "Here you are, on some island in the middle of nowhere, mooching off your big sister, trying to get some stranger to profess his love to you on national television. You've hit rock bottom, Zoe. I know you, and this"—he waved his hand at the door, indicating the party going on right beneath us—"isn't something that will make you happy."

Crap. So much for keeping Kennedy's and my relationship a secret from the other producers. I hoped they'd edit that part out.

God, what would viewers think watching this conversation? Would they think it was romantic? Would they think I was playing Emerson false? Was I really ready to quit and leave the show behind?

"I've written about you," Joe said.

Another sickening plummet for my heart. "You...what?"

"You're the star of my next novel."

He meant it as the ultimate compliment, I knew he did, and yet... Joe's writing was always cruel. Brilliant, yes, with fluid prose and witty dialogue. He always picked just the right details to bring his characters and settings to life, but he never flinched. He flayed the truth to the surface with his words.

I didn't want the world to see me the way he must.

"I made a commitment, to Kennedy and to the show," I stammered out. "I can't leave now. I just can't."

"This has come as a real shock to you." I'd expected a burst of impatience, but his voice was soft, soothing, as though I were a child. "I can understand that. But think about it, Zoe." He held my gaze without blinking. "We're meant to be together. I think you know that. Everything else is just noise."

With that, he turned and walked to the door with me gaping after him. He never ended a disagreement until he got his way. Never. Was it possible he had really changed?

"We'll talk again soon," he said, and then he disappeared through the doorway.

The cameras were watching, always. I couldn't let myself fall apart. Not again. I might be forgiven for my claustrophobia, but not for being hung up on an ex-boyfriend. I willed myself to feel nothing, to see my life as a television show unrolling and nothing more. None of this was real, and I could become an empty vessel.

This blessed numbness lasted until I went downstairs and saw Kennedy whispering to Lucy in the kitchen. It all fell away all in a swift second, replaced by a burning anger, and I marched up to her. "We need to talk. Now."

Kennedy didn't blink. "Of course, Zoe. I want to hear all about it, and then maybe we can film you in a Hot Seat segment."

"Fuck the Hot Seat." If there was any time I had to worry less about being filmed, it was in a shot like this where it would be hard to remove Kennedy. The producers were rarely shown in the final cut of the show.

"Okay then." She gave an apologetic smile to Lucy. "Give me a moment, okay? You're doing great. Really. You have nothing to worry about."

Leading me away from the party, she hissed around her smile. "Calm down."

I kept my own smile pasted on my lips. We'd both had a lot of practice with this sort of thing growing up. "Don't you fucking tell me to calm down. Not tonight."

She pulled me into a bathroom, all high-brow with its bronze faucets and marble bowls for sinks, and locked the door behind us. I opened my mouth to let her have it, but she pushed me around, fumbling with my microphone pack. Once she got the whole device free, she placed it, along with her own earpiece ensemble, next to one of the absurd bowls and turned on the water. Then she made a beeline for the separate room for the toilet, turned on the fan, and beckoned to me.

It was only when I squeezed in with her, sitting on the closed toilet seat, and the door was shut behind us that she leaned in and whispered directly into my ear. "There aren't any cameras in here. We can speak freely."

Her idea of speaking freely was so absurd I almost burst out laughing. But being trapped in this little space with her leaning above me, thinking she knew what was best, just made me madder. "You promised." I wished my words had sharp edges that could hurt her. "You fucking promised. You said you wouldn't bring Joe on the show. The dumbwaiter, that was bad enough, you knew exactly what you were doing and you didn't hesitate to use your inside knowledge to hurt me in front of everyone, but this? This is a low blow even by your standards. You promised!"

As if promising had ever stopped Kennedy from doing what she wanted. All she cared about was higher ratings for her stupid show. Would the mikes in the main bathroom register it if I started screaming at the top of my lungs? Because that was what I felt like doing.

Meanwhile Kennedy was looking at me like I'd morphed into a monster right in front of her. "Zoe, what the hell are you talking about?"

"Don't give me your innocent act. It might work on these other poor women, but it won't work on me."

Kennedy leaned back against the wall. "I promise I have no idea what you're talking about."

"You. Brought. Joe. Here." Each word was like spitting out a tooth.

She stared at me for a minute, and then she had the gall to actually look concerned. "No, I didn't."

This only made me angrier. "Then why did I just talk with him upstairs? It's not as if he could have arranged travel here by himself. Somebody had to bring him."

"We've never discussed bringing Joe out. We want all the focus to be on Emerson, not on some writer. Believe me, I would have known if he were here. Besides, there wasn't even a boat today. Are you telling me that Joe has been lurking around this island since yesterday without me knowing? Seriously?" She arched her eyebrows in that big sister way she had.

"He was here," I said stubbornly. "He came up and found me in my room. I'm sure you filmed the whole thing."

Kennedy pursed her lips. "I'll go look at the footage. When did you say this happened?"

"Just now!" I hated how reasonable she was being. I wanted to yell at her, not have her pretend to be concerned.

She glanced down at her watch. "Okay, that should be easy enough. I can't get away until after the Culling, but I'll look into it, okay? If one of the other producers is fucking around on my turf, I want to know about it."

This was Kennedy's way of feeling protective of me. "He talked about us being sisters too, so I guess that cat's out of the bag."

She sighed. "I'll take care of it, okay? Nobody knows we're sisters and no one's going to find out."

But that wasn't one hundred percent accurate. "Your showrunner knows."

Kennedy actually laughed. "Now you think *Jen* is involved? There's no way. Trust me, you and I being sisters is not the story this season. You think the viewers care? They don't even know who I am. We have way bigger fish to fry."

My righteous rage was crumbling into confusion. "Then why was he here?"

She gave me a condescending pat on the shoulder. "This is a stressful process, Zoe. You know I warned you about that. You Gold Diggers have it tough, and let's face it, you're one of the underdogs. Tomorrow's going to be a downtime day, so maybe you can take some time to relax. Go on a nice quiet walk, think about something not related to the show. Just don't tell any of the other producers I said that, all right?" Another pat. "You're doing just fine. You have nothing to worry about."

Did Kennedy really think this was about my stress levels? "He was here, Kenny. It's not as if I thought I saw him from a distance. I had an entire conversation with him."

"And I'll look into it. But right now you need to get back out there, remind Emerson you exist so he'll want to give you a ribbon. Okay? Can you do that for me?"

Would I always be seven years old in Kennedy's eyes? "Sure thing, boss." She stood up and stretched, revealing the butt of a gun stuck in the waistband of her jeans, another unwelcome surprise. "Jesus! Since when do you have a gun? Isn't that thing dangerous?"

"Emerson's grandfather collected guns and has a whole display of them here, big surprise." She rolled her eyes. "Don't worry, the rest of them are locked up. I'm just making sure we're all safe."

I suddenly doubted everything she'd told me about Joe not being here. "And what exactly are you keeping us safe from?"

"Chill out, okay? Stop complaining and let me do my job."

She turned as if about to leave, but I barred her way with my arm. "Kennedy. You don't even know how to use that thing. Lock it up with the others where it belongs."

For a moment I thought she would argue with me, but instead she simply shrugged. "Okay, fine. Maybe you're right."

I let my arm drop. That had been too easy. "Okay, then. Good," I said weakly. I hoped she meant it.

She strode over to the sink and shut off the water. "Oh, and Zoe? Get one of the sound people to help you get that mike back on, will you? I don't want your sound quality to suffer."

That was classic Kennedy. She needed to feel in charge at all times.

Later that night, I stole a few moments of Emerson's time to stroll along the cliff with him. He put his arm around my waist, even though we were basically strangers. The camera following us demanded it.

"I'm sorry our time together earlier this week got cut short," Emerson said. A gust of wind punctuated his words, and I shivered. "It really was a bit of an emergency or I would have come back."

He couldn't know how well I understood, but I tried to express it all the same. "I know there are a lot of demands being placed on you right now. And hey, I'm glad to see you now."

The sound guy interrupted us. "The wind ruined your audio. Can you repeat everything you just said?"

I looked to Emerson, who simply sighed in a way that made me realize he'd probably had to do this repeatedly tonight. "Yeah, okay, should we go somewhere less windy?"

The sound guy and cameraman exchanged a look and then looked out toward the ocean as if it would answer the question for them. "The visuals here are great," the cameraman finally said. "Let's just try again."

The repeat of our conversation was not as heartfelt, but it didn't change that Emerson had been thinking about me. Maybe I'd be able to get a ribbon on my own merits this week.

"Have you spent a lot of time on this island?" I asked him.

He shrugged. "There was a period of time in my childhood when my grandfather became obsessed with rebuilding, and we were out here more often. There was an architect in residence and everything. That's why there are so many weird buildings scattered around; my grandfather was trying to keep her employed. But I've only been back once as an adult. Aunt Margaret hasn't been living out here all that long, and before that, there was really no reason to make the time to come."

Time to do a little digging. I'd been reading Adelaide's journal with fascination. It gave me something to think about besides my own problems. "Trying to keep his architect employed? That sounds generous."

Emerson laughed. "It does, doesn't it? The truth is, Grandfather was having an affair with her, and he wanted an excuse to keep her around as long as possible. And the thing she most wanted was her own design playground. So here we are. Romance at its finest, huh?" He gave me an engaging grin.

"That's one way of putting it." Once more the foibles of the wealthy were on display, putting a price tag on romance. And Adelaide's journal didn't make things sound so cut and dried. She vacillated between wanting the professional opportunities and having real feelings for Emerson's grandfather, both states interwoven with her odd obsession with Darwin. "Personally I've always paid my own way."

"I respect that." He looked out at the ocean, a stray gust of wind ruffling his hair, and for the first time I noticed a hint of gray at his temples. "I have a similar take on things myself. I certainly know people who have sinecures at their family's companies, who don't really work for what they're given. I've tried not to be like that." He frowned. "Sometimes I think about striking out on my own and doing something completely different. Escaping the shadow of the Courtland name. That's one of the reasons I admire Aunt Margaret. She's managed to live on her own terms."

Poor little rich boy. "She's an impressive woman."

"You've spent some time with her?" I nodded. "Yeah, out of all my family members, she understands me the best. If it were anyone else living here, I might not have signed up for"—he waved his hands—"all this."

I wondered why he *had* signed up for this. He wasn't unattractive, and he seemed personable enough. I hadn't been single in New York, but I had a hard time imagining him having trouble finding a date. And if he was worried about someone marrying him for money, going on a show where the women were unofficially called Gold Diggers? Probably not his best move.

But I couldn't ask him, not and get a truthful answer. "I like her a lot," I said instead. "She's been very kind to me." Granted, her viewing room was a touch obsessive, but she seemed harmless enough. Plus she gave me a glimpse outside this environment of intense scrutiny: the freedom of being old and not needing to give a shit was vastly underrated.

"I'm glad to hear it." He laughed. "When I'm with her, she won't shut up about canceling the whole thing. Never mind the ramifications involved, the contracts I've signed. "Emerson," she says, "it's not too late to call the whole thing off. You can go back to dating with the swiping.""

I laughed too. I could hear her saying it. "Dating with the swiping. That's adorable."

"I know. She has no idea what it's like to date in modern New York. She probably hasn't been on a date herself since the seventies."

"A confirmed bachelor then?"

He laughed at my joke. "You could call her that. For as long as I can remember, she's been very career-focused. Never interested in romantic entanglements. Although I suppose she would have kept any racy stories to herself." He shook his head. "It's easy to forget we only get to know certain sides of a person."

"Really? Filming a reality TV show, I find myself thinking about little else."

"Touché." He laughed again. "I like you. You're sharp."

"I like you. You have a sense of humor."

We grinned at each other in something like mutual recognition, and then he leaned in for a kiss.

I wasn't ready for it. I wasn't ready for any lips that weren't Joe's lips, this clear signal it was really over. Joe had come to this island to see me, hadn't he? He was still thinking about me. We were still tied together. But this...this was a clear marker that time moved forward regardless of any feelings I might continue to harbor.

This was what I was on TV to do. I didn't stop him.

His lips were dry and a little tense, like kissing all these women on TV maybe wasn't the most natural thing in the world for him. He smelled like peppermint, and I suspected the producers had slipped him something before this little chat. Maybe even encouraged him to kiss me. This was all so staged, it was hard to stay in the moment.

He deepened the kiss. On the other hand, he'd definitely chosen to kiss me. It wasn't as if anyone could make him do this. Which meant someone in the world liked me enough to kiss me. Publicly, even. That was something. After everything with Joe, I'd thought maybe I'd never be with anyone again.

I began to kiss him back. And so what if it was for the wrong reasons? This was all fake anyway. If we could find one moment of truth, of actual connection amongst the weeds, so much the better for both of us.

And then as quickly as it started, it was over. We stared into one another's eyes. His were hazel flecked with gold. This is all a game, I reminded myself.

People actually fall in love on these shows all the time, Kennedy had told me. The intensity of having your entire focus be on love and romance, the forced intimacy of the set, the heightened emotions from being filmed all the time. People fell in love all the time.

But I didn't want that to be me.

The Culling. The same room, the same candlelight supplemented with overhead lights invisible to the viewers. The same ranks of women, all thin, all shorter than Emerson, all high heels and cleavage and cakes of makeup hiding any possible blemish. We each wore another in the array of flattering dresses we'd stuffed into our suitcases, a weird sort of rainbow favoring black and red and sequins. My own dress was an emerald green Kennedy had decided would pass muster. Standing next to Lucy on one side in red and Thea on the other in black and silver, I felt like part of a band of demented Christmas elves.

I wasn't as nervous this time. Emerson had kissed me, and whatever confusion that awoke inside me, it seemed like a good sign. Even though she'd gotten her full twenty minutes with him post-hunt, Lucy stood shifting from foot to foot, biting her lip. "I don't know that we've connected enough," she whispered to me. "I just don't know how he feels about me."

"It's going to be fine," I whispered back. I wished I were in bed. I knew from the prior week that filming the Culling could easily take hours, and my calves burned just thinking about it.

"Maybe I should have talked more about my family so he understands where I come from." Lucy was literally wringing her hands. "Tonight we were just joking around, but maybe he would rather have had a serious conversation."

"The poor man must be exhausted. I'm sure he was happy to keep it light."

"Oh, do you think? That might be true. But on the other hand, this is all about building a connection, and sharing deep confidences is an essential part of that, isn't it?"

"Lucy. Breathe."

Our conversation went on like that in fits and starts with Thea visibly rolling her eyes on the other side of me, until Emerson finally showed up. He did look tired; whatever makeup he was using, it didn't quite hide the shadows under his eyes. We were all tired. Being constantly on alert did that to a person, along with the odd hours and the constant drinking. It was squeezing down on us, our deeper reserves beginning to run dry.

The crew set up the shot. Emerson called out Giselle's name and tied the ribbon around her wrist. No surprise there. They set up another shot, and he spoke another name. Then another.

I was fourth, and I was grateful. Not much time spent waiting in suspense. He gave me a warm smile as he tied the bow around my wrist like he was decorating a Christmas tree. Lucy gave me a sickly smile when I returned to her side.

The night wore on, and it felt like we would be standing there forever, focused on the ribbons and Emerson's tired face. Cannon stood off to one side, and without even the suspense to keep him going, I wondered how he stayed awake. But whenever I looked at him, he stood straight, shoulders relaxed, arms behind his back, a slight smile on his face. As if this was what he routinely did for fun.

I wondered if Margaret Courtland was sitting upstairs watching us. It seemed like a lot of effort when she could hear the elimination news in the morning, but somehow I couldn't imagine her anywhere but in that ergonomic desk chair, eyes constantly scanning each of our faces, looking for...something. I wasn't sure what she was so eager to discover.

Lucy gave a little squeal when her name was called and hurried to Emerson as if she were afraid he'd change his mind. The ribbonless women started to turn into statues, afraid to breathe for fear of making the wrong impression at the last minute and changing Emerson's mind. Those of us who were already safe shifted at will, moving the weight from one sore spot of our feet to another. We'd earned the right to express our discomfort, however quietly.

Thea's name hadn't been called. She began to sag downwards as if she were melting. Each shot began to take longer as everyone's fatigue grew. Kennedy wasn't there, and neither was Jen. Were they watching us from the control room? Or did they have things well in hand and not expect any surprises tonight?

Finally there was only one ribbon left. Thea, still ribbonless, vibrated beside me, so subtly nobody but me would notice. Her aura of entitled success had fallen away from her, leaving her naked in her skimpy silk dress. Vivian stood several women away from us, a ribbon perkily tied around her wrist. She had been ignoring Thea all evening, almost as if she'd known something unfortunate was about to happen.

"Summer," Emerson said. And that was that. Thea was going home.

I was the one who went up to the bedroom with Thea. Her actual roommates, Vivian among them, seemed to be giving the place a wide berth, as if they were afraid Thea's exile might be catching. I was the one who made sure all her clothes and toiletries ended up in her suitcase. She deserved at least that much.

I didn't want to talk. I knew the cameras were watching, that Kennedy was listening, and besides, what was there to say? We'd all come onto the show knowing this moment was bound to come. Only one woman stayed until the end. Even the most optimistic person would have trouble feeling confident with odds like that.

Thea got my email address and then hugged me tightly at the front door. "I'll write you," she said, and I was surprised at the passion in her voice. "We'll stay in touch, okay?"

"Of course," I lied. I couldn't imagine being friends with Thea in real life. What would we have to talk about?

"You're the only ones who will understand," she said.

That was when it dawned on me we'd be leaving this island different people than when we arrived. And we'd have one crucial thing in common: surviving this show.

NINETEEN

Reality TV can harm participants' mental health, but do they really understand the risks involved?

—by Yvette Dupres, June 20, 2018, ourtimeillustrated.com

Reality TV has been receiving an increasing amount of criticism in mainstream media recently after several suicide scandals involving former participants, including Jessica Durham from *His Engagement*, Matt Brooks from *The Game*, and Melanie Yu from *If the Shoe Fits.*

A spokesperson for *If The Shoe Fits* says, "There are a lot of inaccuracies when people speak about our show. We take our participants' health incredibly seriously, both mental and physical. Each participant undergoes a rigorous screening process before being invited onto the show, and we even provide mental health support after the season has finished filming. We are committed to supporting our cast through every step of their journeys with us."

When asked about the stress and strain of appearing on reality TV, Cannon Murphy, former star from the *Engagement* franchise, had this to say: "Does it take a mental toll being on these shows? Of course it does! After all, you're there to search for the love of your life, not relax and have a nice little vacation. And what's more important than finding the woman you're going to marry? But it's not like I didn't know what I was signing up for when I did *Her Engagement* that first time. I'd seen the show. I talked at length with several different producers and a psychologist as part of the screening process, and they explained all the details. I even had a complete medical checkup. I went into it with my eyes open, and I have no regrets. It's been the experience of a lifetime."

But psychologist Dr. Bridget McMillan has a different take. "The level of scrutiny and intensity on most reality TV shows is so much more than in a typical life, most participants can't possibly know how they'll hold up under that level of pressure. Those shows go to great lengths to romanticize their process, but the truth is that latent psychological problems will often manifest during times of increased stress, and participants are encouraged, both implicitly and explicitly, to put the good of the show before their own mental health."

And what does the good of the show entail? In the fight for ratings, drama is essential, and certain reality TV producers have been accused of trying to stir up as much drama as possible. And it turns out they have a lot of tools at their disposal, everything from emotional manipulation and lying to the participants about what's actually happening to physical tactics such as keeping the participants sleep-deprived, drinking plenty of alcohol, and cut off from their normal means of support. Some shows even have a strict policy that participants may not have any access to current media, including no internet access, magazines, books, phones, and no talking to friends or family unless a producer specifically arranges it.

"Being so thoroughly and suddenly isolated can lead to all kinds of aberrant behavior," Dr. McMillan said. "Participants can lose touch with reality when they are removed from their daily lives and all of their focus is forced onto one object of desire. They can become unhealthily obsessed with this object. Being filmed all the time can also cause a person to become fixated on appearances, on how other people will view them or judge them, instead of on their own emotions, comfort levels, and moral centers. In some cases, they might even change or lose touch with their own identities to try to compensate for the amount of stress they're under."

Yet in spite of these drawbacks, reality TV seems to have no trouble attracting potential contestants. As Adam Yaffa, 26, who has applied multiple times for romance reality TV shows, told me, "Hey, man, I just want to be famous. How cool would it be to end up on TV?"

After which he could end up with a lifetime of mental health problems. How cool indeed.

TWENTY

Kennedy slipped into my room as Michelle and I were getting ready the next morning. "I need to borrow Zoe," she announced, and then gave Michelle a pointed look until she left.

I looked up at the ceiling fan. "Is now a good time?" Would we have to go into the bathroom and do that whole routine again?

But Kennedy just shrugged. "He was never here." I'd like to say Kennedy looked concerned that I was seeing nonexistent ex-boyfriends, but in truth she looked more impatient. The subtext was clear: I was wasting her time. If I weren't her sister, she would never have stuck her neck out this far for me.

And she was lying to me on top of everything. "That's not possible," I said. "I had an entire conversation with him. A very upsetting conversation."

Kennedy shrugged. "I looked through the recordings. Once the other Gold Diggers went downstairs, you were alone the entire time."

I didn't know how to respond. "Did you listen to the audio?" I finally asked. "Maybe he stood outside the visual range of the camera or something."

"Your microphone cut out. Some kind of technical difficulty. Believe me, heads rolled. What if we had missed something important?" What were the odds my audio would stop working right when my ex came to visit? But Kennedy wasn't even trying to convince me. Her mind was obviously on other things. "I need to talk to you about the other frontrunners."

Oh, so I was officially a frontrunner now? In spite of the fact I might be having some kind of psychotic break? Great news. "What about them?"

"You need to figure out a way to neutralize a few of them."

I looked at the ceiling fan again. "You can't be serious. You think one or two fewer women is going to make any difference? Emerson will never choose me in a million years. You know that, I know that, everyone working on this show knows that."

"He kissed you."

"What are we, twelve? That's what he signed up to do. It doesn't mean anything." Had I felt a small thrill when his lips touched mine? Sure. Had I daydreamed about a scenario in which he chose me at the end, with the two of us walking into the sunset? Maybe once or twice. But the show wasn't real. Kennedy had been warning me about that nonstop.

She pursed her lips in annoyance, and I comforted myself by focusing on her crooked nose. "Look, Zoe, are you serious about this or not? The longer you last on the show, the more exposure you'll get, the more time you'll have to win over the viewers. And no offense, but after your performance at the beginning, you're going to need that time."

Setup after setup. But I'd put in too much effort to give up now. "Fine. What do you want me to do?"

"Take down Vivian."

I laughed until I realized she was serious. "No way. She's ruthless. Even if I wanted to take her out, I'd fail, and then I'd be in serious trouble."

Kennedy walked over to Michelle's pile of clothing and started sorting it into random piles. "Nah, she's isolated now that Thea's gone. No one likes her. She's ripe for the picking."

"Emerson might choose her for a personal date no matter what I do," I objected.

Kennedy shook her head. "He doesn't get to choose his own dates this week." She looked positively gleeful. "Or rather, he will, but only as a judge for this week's competition."

More arbitrary rules. "Maybe someone else will take care of her?" I made the suggestion halfheartedly. I already knew what Kennedy would say.

"You're the one we've chosen," she said. "Jen is excited about the idea. We haven't had enough contestant conflict yet this season. And you and Vivian are both so..." She paused, and I wondered if she was trying to spare my feelings. "Divisive," she finished. No, apparently not. "The viewers will love it, I promise."

I sighed. "Are you sure it can't be someone else?"

Her grin was pure evil. "I'm sure." Her eyebrows drew together. "And no matter what happens, you can't tell anybody I'm involved. Not any of the other women, and no one else in production either. You understand?"

This didn't sound good. "Kennedy...."

"Look, you worry too much. No one's going to get hurt, I promise." She scowled down at her stubby bitten fingernails. "But I can't keep pulling rank to keep you safe so this is what it's going to take. You don't want to be kicked off the island this week, do you?"

I should have refused. But I wanted to show Joe up so badly. I decided to do as she asked.

Which is how I found myself sneaking through the mansion later that afternoon while everyone else was down in the lounge waiting to do Hot Seats. Hopefully if anyone noticed I was missing, they would think I was busy answering intrusive questions and trying to come up with snappy one-liners that would later become memes.

I tiptoed into Vivian's bedroom, making sure it was empty. With Thea gone, she'd taken two mattresses out of the bunk bed frames and pushed them together on the floor to create a double bed. I tried to remember who her remaining roommates were. Maybe Summer? Or Lauren, the most inoffensive and bland woman I'd ever met?

It didn't matter. I knelt by Vivian's bed, the sheets pushed back and twisted every which way, and I pulled the packet of powder Kennedy had given me from my pocket. It was unexceptional, no smell, looked like baby powder. "Be careful not to get it on your skin," Kennedy had said.

But really, how bad could it be?

I carefully teased open the packet, pulled back the loose sheet, and sprinkled the powder over the bed, trying to get an even spread so it would make contact with her skin whichever side she slept on. Then again, she was probably one of those people who sprawled over the entire bed. Someone born to take up space. I flung the rest of the powder with careless abandon and got the hell out of there before I was caught.

Only to be stopped in my tracks by Joe in the hallway. He was still here! He greeted me with a low laugh, as if he could tell what I'd been doing. "Getting into trouble?"

"No." I crumpled the empty powder packet into my fist. "I don't understand what you want. Kennedy said she didn't bring you."

"Well, Kennedy doesn't know everything, does she?" He smirked. "You're in over your head, Pooh Bear."

I held my incriminating fist behind my back and desperately tried to hold onto my self-possession. How had he gotten up here without a single crew member seeing him? And how did he see right through my façade? "I'm doing fine, thanks."

"That why you're sabotaging your fellow contestant?"

How did he know? It was like his cool blue eyes could see right through me and my bullshit. "I...what...I...don't know what you're talking about." I shut my mouth around my pathetic splutters before I made things any worse.

"You need a strong man to look after you, Zoe. You know it's true. No"—he held up a hand"—you don't need to tell me, I know you have doubts. But look at you, involved in petty games, letting Kennedy play you like a fiddle. This isn't who you are." He leaned in closer. "When we were together, you had something that mattered."

I hated him because he was right. I had found purpose in supporting him, in encouraging him, in editing his manuscripts again and again so he would realize his full potential. In his success I had found a kind of completeness of my own, and without having to take any real risks. I wasn't putting myself out there, after all. I was presenting Joe. And he had enough confidence for both of us.

I was trying so hard to put that version of myself behind me. To believe in myself and my work enough to start writing again, to push harder when I failed instead of turning away. But it was so damned difficult.

"Remember. The cameras see everything." He sauntered past me down the hall. When I came to my senses a moment later and tried to follow him, he was already gone.

Cannon had a new announcement for us. "I know last week was a real struggle for many of you ladies." I don't know how he managed to keep a straight face. "So this week, we want to keep things light. To that end, we're going to have a fashion show." Leo, possibly the most enthusiastic of the producers, clapped his hands from the sidelines as if we were being offered a special treat.

We all squealed as required by our contracts, while I studied Vivian from the corner of my eye, wondering what exactly the powder would do to her tonight. "Here are the rules: no one will be allowed to wear anything they or any of the other women brought with them. You'll have to search for appropriate materials. We'll provide you with needle and thread, safety pins, tape, whatever supplies you need to pull an outfit together. Then Emerson himself will judge your turn down the catwalk tomorrow evening. Any questions?"

Another cheer, inevitable as the sunset. I joined in with actual enthusiasm because I wouldn't need any magical crafty seamstress skills. I'd just head to the stash of dress-up clothes on the ship. Surely I could find something suitably artsy yet revealing in that trunk.

Cannon had made a little joke about that trunk too, hadn't he? Almost like he knew what was coming and didn't want me to forget. Maybe Kennedy was leaning on him to look out for me.

As soon as Cannon had left the room, Lucy started having a full-on meltdown. "Guys, guys, I don't know how to sew." Her voice was high, breathy, like she was ten years old. "I'm not a crafty person, that's just not my thing."

Michelle's mouth formed a grim line. "We'll Scarlett O'Hara our way out of this shit," she said. "God, I can't wait to get back into the lab. This has been the best cure for burnout ever."

Vivian stood a little apart from the rest of us, a small smirk on her face. She obviously had something up her sleeve, but whether it was a secret stash of designer clothing or a hidden talent for clothing design was anyone's guess. She sashayed up to Lucy, who was working her way up to full-on hyperventilating. "Don't worry, honey. It's not just about the clothes you wear, it's about the body underneath. If you don't have that, it won't make any difference that you can't sew."

Perfect Giselle gasped at this, as if she couldn't believe Vivian had said it out loud. But I could. Vivian was committed to her role as villain. A bold move: it could lead to greater prominence, sure, but it could also lead to mass hatred. Not everyone's careers benefited from being on shows like these.

Of course, with all her family money, she could afford to risk it.

I suddenly felt less guilty about whatever that white powder had been.

I waited until the group had broken up. When only Michelle and Simone were left, loudly discussing curtains while eyeing the drapes in the room, I took the opportunity to slip out, an empty tote bag slung casually over my shoulder.

None of the camera people followed me, for which I was grateful. Much easier to be inconspicuous without a shoulder-full of heavy electronics following me around. Instead my constant monitors would just have to listen to my heavy breathing as I climbed the next hill over. I wasn't going to make a direct line for the ship, just in case anyone was watching.

I stood on the hilltop, panting and relieved to be more or less alone. The moist air wrapped around me like a sodden towel, my hair trailing down my chest in limp strands. Impossible to look good in so much humidity. Lucy was probably already working herself into another tizzy over that, if she'd managed to recover from the all-important wardrobe question.

I sat cross-legged on the ground. Just sat. Nobody could see me, and I couldn't see them. I wasn't making any sounds for the mike to detect. They probably knew where I was—there must have been a GPS tracking system in the mike pack—but as long as they thought I was being very boring they might leave me alone.

Bliss. I wanted to hide in the mist forever. If only at the end of filming I could stay behind, live a quiet reclusive life here, writing and taking long walks on the beach. It would beat the media storm awaiting me in LA once the show began airing. To turn my back on that, to disappear....

It would defeat the purpose of my being here, but a person could dream.

The ship was waiting for me, another solitary oasis on this island of drama. I half-expected to see another Gold Digger—I couldn't have been the *only* one who explored the island in my spare time—but the ship appeared to be blessedly empty. I ditched my mike pack in an empty bin on-deck before heading into the luxurious cabin. I'd take what privacy I could.

When I opened the trunk, costumes burst from it, just as I'd remembered: a pirate wench costume, a mermaid's get-up, various period dresses complete with voluminous skirts and corsets and cleavage-baring necklines. No men's costumes. Presumably this was Adelaide and Leland's love nest, but with only Adelaide doing the dressing up. I wondered whose idea it had been.

I began pulling costumes from the trunk and holding them to my body. Not the mermaid, definitely not the French maid. A huge nope to the skimpy Native American costume. Can-can girl, Southern belle, and oh look, a dress like the one Dorothy wore in *The Wizard of Oz.* Not alluring enough.

"That's the one."

I jumped. Cannon leaned lazily in the doorway, looking as sexy as always. "Hello to you too." I put the dress aside and pulled out a furry peignoir.

"Trust me, you should wear that blue gingham get-up."

I gave him a look. "You are aware of what everyone else will be wearing, right? Are you *trying* to get me eliminated?"

"Hey, I'm on your side, Poet." He ambled inside, crouched down beside me. "I made sure you knew about these costumes, didn't I?"

"Your generosity is overwhelming." I pulled a red feather boa from the pile, struggling as it got stuck under the mass of remaining costumes.

"I'm just saying you can trust me." He moved some entirely inadequate bikini armor out of my way.

"Weren't you the one who told me not to trust anyone?"

"That doesn't mean you should turn down free advice."

His voice was like a caress, and I paused to look at him. His face was only inches from mine. "And your advice is to wear a *Wizard of Oz* dress?"

He moved his face even closer. "Our boy has a kink for Dorothy," he whispered. "Watched that movie repeatedly during his formative years, and he still likes them innocent, if you know what I mean. Trust me, you wear this, you'll get one of the private dates. He won't be able to resist."

Was this another trick, like the whole "recite a poem and make a great first impression" thing? And if it wasn't, why was he bothering? "Why are you helping me?" I asked.

He shrugged, slid down to sit on the floor beside me. "Nothing better to do?"

I raised my eyebrows at him. "You're going to have to be more convincing than that."

"I remember what it was like, okay? I don't know why you're here, but I can tell you think you need to do this. So, fine, let's make sure you stay as long as possible. That's all. No hidden agenda. I promise." He showed me his empty hands.

"All the Gold Diggers want to stay here as long as they can. It's not like I'm unique."

"Yeah, but I like you."

And there it was, the reason he was asking me to believe. Because he liked me. And I definitely liked him back. He knew it: the charisma rolled off him in maddening waves that were almost impossible to resist. He'd had two women turn him down on shows like these, but only just. I wanted to touch his curly hair. I wanted to feel his lazy smile as he kissed me. I wanted...

"Well, that's very nice of you." I stood up abruptly. I had to remember where I was.

"It's true, what I told you before." He took my hand and began lightly stroking my fingers. "No cameras on the ship. And it looks like you lost your mike somehow." He made a tsk sound with his tongue. "This is our one chance to relax, Zoe." My name sounded like a caress. "I've got just as much to lose here as you."

More, if we got right down to it. I didn't want this to be my permanent career. If I had my choice, I'd never appear on television again. On the other hand, turning my back on possible true love in order to dally with the host? Not exactly a reputation builder. "I'm going to try this on." I waved the Dorothy dress in the air. "It probably won't even fit."

He ran his eyes over it and then me. "Oh, it'll fit."

"Turn your back."

"If you insist." He went to inspect the mini-fridge while I stripped and pulled the dress over my head.

"Oh." It was a *sexy* Dorothy dress. What a shock in a boudoir like this one. It was cut mid-thigh, and the bodice clung pleasingly to my breasts, a few white frills highlighting my cleavage. I couldn't pull the zipper all the way up by myself, but it was clear the dress would fit just fine.

Cannon gave a satisfied smile. "What did I tell you?"

I was still struggling with the zipper. "I need help."

He came around behind me, pulled the zipper firmly to the top, then pushed my hair in front. "Find a few blue ribbons, give yourself pigtails, and voila." His voice was a little huskier than usual. "He'd be a fool not to choose you." He said the words right into my ear, and I shivered.

"Cannon."

"No one ever needs to know."

I threw caution to the winds.

Some time later, I scrambled around the love nest trying to find my underwear while Cannon looked on from the bed. He had the same lazy smile on his face, but he sure hadn't been lazy in other ways. My body shuddered again just thinking about it. Had it ever been that good with

Joe? It wasn't classy to compare, and yet...this had been something else all together.

"Did you hook up with any Gold Diggers last season?" I asked. I wanted evidence that this was no big deal, that this was just what Cannon did.

"Are you kidding? And risk biting the hand that feeds me?" He didn't take his eyes from me. "It might not be the career I dreamed about, sweetheart, but I still care about it."

"And yet here we are."

"It's true." He gave me a salacious smile. "And if you want we can go again."

I threw the mermaid outfit at him and began getting dressed. Of course he'd hooked up with someone last season. What a stupid question to ask. This was both of us letting off steam from the constant eyes on us, that was all.

But I did take his advice and bring the Dorothy costume back to the house.

Twenty-One

Hot Seat transcript: Lucy Miller, October 15, as aired in episode three

So Vivian's basically bullying me, which really sucks. I thought about telling Emerson. After all, open communication is a key part of a successful relationship. But then I thought, no, Lucy, you should focus on your relationship with Emerson, not on Vivian's attitude problems. Because let's face it, he probably spends enough time thinking about her as it is. She's gorgeous, after all. He'd have to be blind not to notice.

Everything happens for a reason, and this is my chance to show Emerson I can handle myself and not be distracted by petty jealousy. In the end, Vivian's true colors will shine through, and Emerson will know who is here for the right reasons. (Her eyes shine.) He'll realize we're meant for one another. I can't imagine anything else happening.

Hot Seat transcript: Vivian Green, October 15, as aired in episode three

I'm not here to make these other women feel good about themselves, I'm here to win Emerson's heart. Nothing else matters. All of this rah-rah bonding and singing around the campfire bullshit is a waste of time and energy. And yes, I definitely don't think everyone who is here deserves to be here. It's not as if Emerson would ever choose to date a nervous wreck. Please. Confidence is sexy as hell.

Some people simply need to develop thicker skin. News flash: we don't get to spend our entire lives in kindergarten.

Hot Seat transcript: Michelle Howard, October 16, as aired in episode three

I love to sew. I'd do projects with my grandma all the time when I was a kid. You should see some of the quilts we made. Lately I've been too busy, and honestly I'm pretty constrained in what I can wear if I want to be taken seriously as a scientist, so it's not as fun as it used to be. But this time I can let loose. I'm excited to show Emerson a different side of myself.

Hot Seat transcript: Simone DuPrade, October 16, as aired in episode three

No, I don't have any problem with Vivian. She's here to win, it's as simple as that, and if some of the girls can't hold their own against her, well, did they really think this process would be easy? That's the problem with being sheltered; eventually the real world is going to find you wherever you're hiding, and then it's going to kick your ass if you're not ready for it.

You know what I do have a problem with? All the *Gone with the Wind* references. That book is racist as hell. But you don't hear anyone complaining about that now, do you?

Hot Seat transcript: Giselle Wallace, October 17, as aired in episode three

I can't stop thinking about him. I keep playing our date back in my mind, remembering how magical it was up in that helicopter, and when he reached to take my hand.... (A long pause.) It already feels like a long time ago, and I can't wait to see him again. I know he can't choose me at the fashion show, it wouldn't be fair to the other girls who haven't had as much time with him. But I want to see his jaw drop when I walk out, and I want to know he's thinking about me too. (Another long pause.) He is, I know he is. When we're together, it's impossible to ignore the sparks.

Hot Seat transcript: Zoe Roberts, October 16, as aired in episode three.

What do I think of Vivian? She's a condescending bitch. She thinks she owns the universe, you know? Or, I mean, I guess it's her *daddy* who owns it. Same thing as far as she's concerned. Vivian's the kind of person who needs to tear people down in order to build herself up.

What Vivian said to Lucy was uncalled for. Lucy didn't deserve that. Someone has to take a stand against cruelty, but we all know we can't go to Emerson to talk about it without being eliminated ourselves. When the game is rigged, you have to play by your own rules. My mother taught me that.

Twenty-Two

I sat with Michelle while she sewed. She'd found some beautiful emerald green fabric, I don't know where, maybe it used to be curtains. Lucy and Simone were downstairs, drinking and talking shit and hoping to catch a glimpse of Emerson so it was just the two of us.

After Cannon's and my interlude, Emerson was the last person I wanted to see. We were all pretending, I knew that, and he'd probably made out with all the women here by now, but I felt guilty all the same. When we'd stood together under the night sky, I'd almost been able to pretend we'd met in some normal way, that he'd asked me out and we were taking an evening stroll after drinks. That if it went well, we'd be getting together for another date next week.

But Emerson and I would never have met in real life. We moved in different layers of New York, and the only time we might have intersected was at a literary event where his family was donating money and I was giving Joe moral support.

Joe, who was skulking around the house hiding from the cameras. Nothing was making sense. I knew I was still messed up in the head from the breakup, but this? Did Kennedy really think I'd hallucinated talking to my ex? Surely I wasn't that close to a complete mental breakdown.

But a little nagging voice in my head said otherwise.

"I think this might have been a mistake," Michelle said.

Knowing nothing about sewing, I tried to be as diplomatic as possible. "The fabric is lovely. It's a good color for you."

"That's what Simone said. And she helped me figure out a pattern too. But all this hand-sewing is killing me." She took a few more stitches. "That's not what I meant though."

I looked up at the ceiling fan, then gave her a warning look. She laughed. "It's okay, Zoe. I don't have anything to hide. It's not like I'm here for the wrong reasons or anything like that. It's just...different from what I expected. I don't even know what I *was* expecting, to be honest. I was so ready for something—anything—different, but now I realize I could be gallivanting around Europe, doing whatever I want, you know? And instead I'm sitting here stressing out."

"Why are you taking time off, anyway?"

Now Michelle did glance up at the camera. "My advisor thought it would be a good idea for me to take a break for a semester. There were some...departmental politics, and it's convenient for me to be somewhere else for a little while, that's all. Until it has time to blow over."

Damn. I'd had no idea. Were we all here to escape the shambles of our misfiring lives? Trying to compensate for our failures with the fleeting fame and notoriety reality TV would bring us?

It made sense, actually. I hadn't thought very hard about why the other Gold Diggers were here. But they wouldn't be here if they didn't want something, if something hadn't been missing in their lives up to this point.

Of course, some people couldn't resist the lure of being in the spotlight. Like Cannon. Grab a quick few moments of bliss in the sack and then smile for the cameras again.

"Think of it as an all-expenses paid vacation," I suggested.

Michelle jabbed her needle into the fabric. "But it's not really free, is it? We're paying to be here. Not with money, but we're paying."

They wouldn't air this, would they? It would sound so creepy. I didn't know what to say. Something chirpy and upbeat about Emerson and how it would all be worth it? I didn't have the heart for that, not when Michelle was being so brutally honest.

"Maybe it's okay to take a break from your life and give yourself a chance to reset," I said instead. "Obviously this is a bizarre experience and it's not for everyone, but maybe we can cut ourselves some slack. We're all just trying to figure out what to do next, aren't we? Maybe this will help."

So many maybes. There was nothing like knowing my every move was being filmed to make me inarticulate.

But Michelle put down her sewing and hugged me anyway. "I hope you're right." She dabbed at her eyes. "I know you're right. I miss my program. I've been doing mathematical equations in my journal, just to show myself I can still do them. We've been here, what, less than two weeks, and I'm already bored out of my mind. I could never make it the full six weeks. I think my brain would atrophy. I need to keep fighting for my future. And once Emerson sends me home, I intend to do exactly that."

"He might choose you." I felt obligated to say it, but then we exchanged a look and burst out laughing.

"And global warming might not be a serious problem," Michelle said. "God, I really don't know what I was thinking coming on this show."

Me neither. I'd let Kennedy's arguments go to my head.

The evening of the fashion show, a catwalk had been set up outside by the pool, and a peek through the window confirmed Emerson and Cannon lounging like kings at the far end, wine glasses in hand. The lighting made it bright as day, and crew members in black moved with purpose all around us, more than I'd seen in one place since the last Culling.

Michelle sidled up to me in her green dress, which she'd ended up sewing herself into. "Don't worry," she'd said, slightly breathless. "I can cut myself out when it's over." Her hard work had paid off; she looked even better than she did in her off-the-rack clothing. Meanwhile, Simone's design experience showed in the mini dress she'd made from what I was pretty sure was a burlap sack. It accentuated her curves just as well as anything else she'd worn since we arrived.

Not all the Gold Diggers had fared as well. Poor Lucy had found some yellow polka-dotted fabric that she'd tried to fashion into a fun skirt and bandeau outfit, but it looked like she'd just knotted it on, shapeless and lumpy, at the last minute. She looked close to tears as she came up to me and fingered my skirt. "Where did you find that?"

She didn't bother to hide her jealousy, and guilt crept in as I remembered all the other outfits still in the trunk on the ship. "All's fair in love and war," Eva said as she sauntered by. She wore a burgundy towel with nothing underneath, showing off her smooth brown skin. That was one way to go.

Elaine rushed over with her tablet in hand. "Are we all here? We're a go in ten minutes."

Lots of murmuring and looking around, then Summer said, "We're missing Vivian."

"Crap." Elaine looked around the room as if she expected Vivian to spontaneously appear before turning and saying something into her headset. I pretended disinterest while trying to overhear, but before I could get closer, she made a sudden exit.

My conscience stabbed me, and I made to follow, but Lucy grabbed my arm. "Do you think she's hiding because her outfit is even more hideous than mine?" I stood frozen, appalled by how pathetic this all was, until Lucy burst into laughter. "Kidding, I'm kidding. She's probably just doing her makeup. Come on, Simone is going to show us how to do a proper model walk."

It was just setting in that at thirty years old I didn't know how to walk when Kennedy interrupted us. "Zoe, those shoes aren't doing you any favors," she said. "Run upstairs and choose a slightly lower heel, and you'll do better." As a nod to our complete inability to become cobblers overnight, the producers had told us the night before we could incorporate our own shoes into our outfits, and Kennedy had a point: I had never been great in these stilettos, even though they were a sexy version of Dorothy's red ruby slippers. I'd wobbled around her apartment for a few weeks practicing, but I hadn't been wearing these for years like some of the other Gold Diggers.

"You're probably right," I conceded, sitting down to remove the offending shoes before I hurt myself.

"I always am. Hurry it up, will you? We'll be starting in a few minutes." She didn't give me a chance to respond before she moved over to shove a glass of wine into Lucy's hand.

I padded up the stairs and had just reached the landing when I heard a large crash. Something had just become very broken. I rushed down the hall, past my own bedroom. Another crash led me to the correct doorway, where I stopped dead and dropped my shoes with a thud that was drowned out by incomprehensible shrieking.

Vivian stood in the center of her bedroom, shoulders heaving. Both mirrors in the room had been smashed, and Elaine stood cowering in the corner behind the cameraman. Vivian had wrapped herself in what looked like yards of toilet paper that left very little to the imagination. But that wasn't the first thing you noticed when you looked at her. Oh no.

All her bare skin—and there was a lot of it—was covered in swollen hives. Even her face and neck had the angry red marks, and there was one particularly painful one pushing up beneath her eye. A few of the larger ones on her legs were oozing some kind of clear liquid.

So this was what that white powder did.

Fuck.

Was this how far I was willing to go for Kennedy's approval? Was this who I'd become?

A shuffle behind me, and I turned to see another cameraperson, the only woman. They wanted to catch my reaction from several angles. I could imagine how this would play out on the TV screen. The Villain title had just fallen squarely on my shoulders, and I one hundred percent deserved it. I'd fallen for Kennedy's manipulation with hardly a struggle. I'd believed in our sisterly bond, but it was hard to see how this convoluted scheming could end well for me. None of the viewers would know this hadn't all been my own idea.

God, I was a shit human being.

"Turn off the cameras," Vivian screeched. "Turn off the fucking cameras."

I scooped up my shoes and left before I had to witness any more of the carnage of my actions. The second camera woman stayed behind to continue to film Vivian.

I retreated to my room to replace my offending shoes and try to get my incipient tears under control. I was staring at myself in the mirror and taking deep breaths when Joe came up behind me, making me jump. Every time I saw him a jolt ran from my heart outwards, as if it was reminding the rest of my body it wasn't allowed to just give up and die in his presence. "A coward through and through," he said. And then he laughed. "Nice work, Pooh Bear."

I spun around. "Why won't you leave me alone? You said you didn't want to be with me. You can't just keep changing your mind." He'd gone back and forth about us several times in the years we'd been together; would it never end? I gave him a wide berth as I fled the room.

Why did Joe keep appearing when I was by myself? No one else had mentioned seeing a tall dark man with tortoiseshell glasses, and I had to ask myself: was I seeing things? Or was this all some kind of reality TV trick designed to give Kennedy the most memorable season yet?

It said something that I really wasn't sure which possibility was more likely.

I went through the fashion show like a zombie, putting one foot before another pretending to be a dutiful little Gold Digger, doing the twirl that showed off my skirt's flounce, giving one shy little smile right before I strode back off the cat walk. Cannon gave me a wink, which I ignored. I didn't deserve a wink. I didn't deserve to be there.

When we all returned to the catwalk at the end, Michelle and I were announced as the two winners of private dates. Apparently all it took to succeed in love was wearing something I would have never chosen myself, sabotaging the competition, and not giving a flying fuck about the results.

Oh, and fucking the guy's advisor and pseudo-best friend. Don't forget about that gem. Just because it was still a secret didn't mean it didn't count in the tally of my failures.

After my win, Shep Sloane, a producer I barely knew, pulled me aside for a Hot Seat. I knew what was expected of me. I produced the tears, the guilt, the self-recriminations on cue. Yes, I felt remorse for using the powder on Vivian. Yes, I was afraid of what the other hopefuls would think of me were they to find out what I'd done. Yes, yes, grovel grovel, this was just the beginning of my penance. Kennedy had me between a rock and a hard place, and it was getting harder and harder to trust her, even if we *were* family.

Yup, everything was going stellar, all right. I was really turning my life around, just like Kennedy had promised.

Twenty-Three

Transcript from *Love & Bubbles*, episode 12, hosted by Olivia Childs for *Everything Entertainment Online*, January 29, 2019:

Olivia Childs: We've got a Culling, we've got a catwalk, we've got oceans of Lucy tears, and we've got Vivian finally being sabotaged...and maybe a new villain in our midst?

Hi everyone, I'm Olivia Childs, and here we are for more down and dirty dishing at *Love & Bubbles* recapping Emerson Courtland's season of *Love Story*. (She raises her full champagne flute in a toast gesture.)

And wow, this episode started out a little slow, don't you think? Lucy wasn't the only one crying. (She dabs her eyes daintily with a red silk handkerchief.) I guess a little let-down was inevitable after the grip-your-seat spectacle we saw last time. How can you possibly match an episode that has the contestants being forced to face their fears, more than one full-on panic attack, and a girl who goes bald? (She strokes her own sleek mane as if to make sure it's still there.) I want you guys to know I've had legitimate nightmares about losing my hair since watching this show. (She takes a gigantic gulp of champagne and smiles glassily at the camera.)

We begin with a yawn-fest of a pep talk from Cannon to Emerson.

Normally I could listen to Cannon talk all day long, but they aren't giving him much to work with here. I could tell both men were uncomfortable talking about Cassidy losing her hair, and Emerson was obviously shaken by the experience. (Another shudder.) And who wouldn't be?

I do wish the show was using Cannon more. If we could have a spin-off with Cannon trying to find love however long it took, I would be all over that show. Granted, it would probably run several seasons. After all he's been through, that boy has commitment issues. But who wouldn't? And with those eyes and that body, he can afford to be a little choosy. Don't get me wrong, I do like the choice of Cannon as host. He can understand what our leading man is going through better than anyone else, and it's always interesting to hear his take. What do you think about Cannon as host? Let me know in the comments.

Then we move right along to the next Culling. No real surprises here until the end when Emerson chooses to eliminate Thea by giving the last ribbon to Summer instead. I thought Lucy might be a goner, but no such luck.

Having Thea leave has shifted the dynamic in the house, depriving Vivian of her one main ally. And of course a Culling wouldn't be complete without Lucy breaking down in a Hot Seat right afterwards, telling us how convinced she was that she was going to be sent home and how grateful she is to be given another chance to get Emerson's attention. I'm all for knowing what you want and going after it, but that girl takes that idea to the next level, and you can see all the other women visibly cringe when she speaks.

And then finally—FINALLY!—things begin to really liven up with a showdown between Little Miss Perfect Vivian (screen shows photo of Vivian looking gorgeous on the first night) and...(trumpet fanfare plays) Sad Little Goth Girl Zoe (screen shows photo of Zoe crying on her hands and knees after the dumbwaiter incident). Not the head-to-head I was expecting this time, what about you?

And I have to say, it did not play out the way I thought it would. Vivian has always seemed like a piranha in a pool of guppies, and I expected things to keep getting bloody. Even the loss of Thea didn't seem like it would break her stride. But in a surprise twist, it turned out poor little Zoe was a cold-blooded shark this entire time. Who knew she had it in her?

But personally, I think Zoe went too far. Sure, Vivian is a bit of a snob, she can be really nasty to the other women, and she interrupts their time with Emerson pretty consistently. But she's not the only one playing that game, and she's got style, you have to admit. She's fierce about going after what she wants, but at least she's not a fountain like Lucy. Zoe's poem debacle has been hanging over her head since her introduction to Emerson, and I think it's impaired her judgment. Tell me what you think below: are you Team Zoe? Or do you think she crossed a line?

Granted, Vivian's hives don't seem to be life threatening or even particularly serious. No dramatic air vac sequence for us. But they had to hurt. And directly threatening the health of a fellow contestant? That's just not right. I'm surprised the producers didn't disqualify Zoe right then and there. I guess they fell for her tearful "I didn't know what that powder would do, it was just a prank" confession. She does seem pretty naïve, so I guess it's possible, but frankly? (The *Jaws* theme plays in the background.) I think my shark theory is closer to the truth. (She winks.)

Meanwhile the other women remain in the dark. No one suspects Zoe of anything. Every single woman seems to suspect a different person is responsible, and then we have sweet-as-pie Giselle insisting none of them could have done such a thing. Which means there's nobody to cue Emerson in on this latest drama, and unless the producers drop him a hint, he's likely to remain in the dark. Poor guy. As the season progresses, I get the feeling he had no idea what he was signing up for. Or rather, what the women were signing up for. His time on the show has been filled with yachts and beach days and zip lining and fancy dining, while the women are tearing curtains from spare rooms and crawling through dark vermin-infested spaces. There's not exactly an equal amount of investment here.

And not an equal level of difficulty for the women either. Giselle and Grace lucked out in missing the "face your fears" treasure hunt, and coming up with an outfit from scratch is a laughable challenge in comparison. Not only that, but they both had to know they'd never win, so they just had to avoid making fools of themselves and spend the rest of the week relaxing. Do you think it was fair for them to get to skip the face-your-fears treasure hunt? Let me know what you're thinking below. My DMs are always open to you guys!

The women are all game to whip up some outfits out of not much, which leaves us back with poor Lucy. I would feel sorry for her—I *want* to feel sorry for her—except she's so damn annoying. I swear that woman cries enough to solve Southern California's drought problem. And she believes so sincerely in her connection with Emerson, which leaves me thinking, "Girl, have you ever been in a romantic relationship? Do you know what a connection looks like?" We haven't seen anything that makes me think Emerson is even considering her. Of course, on a show like this, it's always possible her meaningful moments with him just aren't as interesting as everything else and ended up on the cutting room floor, but come on, girl. Get a hold of yourself. No one finds that level of single-minded obsession attractive.

To her credit she doesn't completely break down when she trips in that—what was she wearing, exactly? (Screen shows photo of Lucy mid-fall on the cat walk.) A DIY project gone horribly wrong. She smiles bravely and carries on, but once she gets back inside, wow, the waterworks! (A gurgling sound effect plays.) All the other women have started giving her a wide berth. And her best friends in the house, Michelle and Zoe, both won the individual dates, so she doesn't even have her best gal pals to commiserate with. That eye roll from Simone after she tries to talk Lucy down is classic. (Cuts to a short clip from one of Simone's Hot Seats where she's saying, "That girl needs to take a chill pill.") I love Simone, her classiness, her attitude, her style, and I wish we got to see more of her.

Finally we get the teaser for the next episode, and...are you as confused as I am? The women running around in the dark, and the old aunt wearing some kind of dark hooded cape deal. What are they doing? It looks like things are about to get a little weird on the island, and as long as that gives me some more distinguished old aunt time, I'm completely here for it.

In spite of its slow start, did you enjoy this episode? And what do you think is going on in that teaser? Another challenge for our intrepid ladies? Let me know in the comments. I love you guys, you're the best, thanks for all your messages, and ta-ta for now!

Twenty-Four

After the hive incident, I wasn't sure where I stood with Kennedy. She'd promised to look out for me, but my faith in her was beginning to crack. The truth was I'd barely seen Kennedy since she left home to go to college. She'd always had very important things going on: school, career opportunities, travel, various sleek and self-satisfied men. I knew we'd been through a lot together when we were young, but I was beginning to have some doubts.

But when she found me sitting with my journal in a nook in the conservatory the day after the fashion show, I smiled as if I were actually happy to see her. What choice did I have? She had all the power here.

"You killed it at the fashion show," she said. "Where'd you come up with that outfit? Did the old lady help you?"

I shrugged. Safest to say nothing at all.

"Well, I have great news." Somehow I doubted it. "Margaret has asked if she can host a little séance. Can you imagine anything more perfect? She wants to have it outdoors in the middle of the night, and for only a select group of you. And here I was worrying this next episode might be on the dull side." Her smile took on a vulpine edge that made me nervous.

"Really, full body hives aren't enough for you?"

She ignored my comment. "She asked specifically for you. The four of you that Emerson has chosen for private dates so far, to be precise."

"Great, it will be like a cutthroat slumber party."

She grinned at me. "See, I told you you'd come around and see them as the competition."

"Yeah, I can't wait to see what crazy things we do to each other next. All for the dubious honor of getting to be a stranger's plus one at his next fundraising event."

My bitter words didn't seem to bother her. She held up a finger and cocked her head, a sure sign someone was talking to her through her earpiece. "Sure thing, I'll be right there," she said. She switched her gaze back to me. "Complain all you want, but you're hungry for this, Zoe. We both know this will get you where you want to go."

She always had to get the last word. "Fun times," I murmured as she rushed off to orchestrate some other drama. A séance. I'd thought Margaret didn't want anything to do with the show. Had Kennedy pressured her into this?

I'd signed up to be exploited, but this was another thing entirely. It was time to pay Margaret another visit.

Margaret threw open the door to my gentle knock. "At last." She gestured for me to enter. Her thick white hair framed her face in a fuzzy halo rather than her usual perfect coif. She tugged the tie of her silk green robe tighter. Even in such casual attire she still wore the ever-present amber pendant. "You've come to report?"

I figured I might as well play along. "That's right."

She nodded at the desk chair, but I moved towards a new chair across from it, small and hard and wooden. "No, no, you take the comfortable one. I insist." But she didn't sit herself, instead hovering over me. "Now, tell me, what have you seen?"

I swallowed. I hadn't expected this to feel like a confessional. "Well, you know about Vivian and the hives."

"I do." She gave me a disapproving look. "That was a surprise."

I couldn't meet her eyes. "I know."

"The producers told you what to do." Margaret nodded sagely and paced over to the monitors. "MUTE," they all proclaimed. She was taking my visit seriously.

"Well...."

She interrupted me. "You don't owe them any loyalty. They certainly aren't on your side in all of this. I imagine you're seeing that more clearly now."

"Maybe," I admitted.

"They're on the side of the money," she said. "That's what you are to these people. Big dollar signs."

Her passion surprised me. After all, as a publisher, she had ultimately been on the side of the money too. Then again, she hadn't been causing emotional trauma to make it. "Sure."

"You remind me of myself when I was young. Naïve and with no goddamned backbone. You can't expect to maintain any sense of morality if you're so busy trying to make everyone else happy. You need to learn to stand up for yourself." She gave me a hard look. "Especially with the producers. They want you vulnerable. They want to crack you like an egg." Kennedy, she meant. But how could I defend myself after what I'd done? "What else?" She turned to a monitor and glared at Lucy, who was crying in the corner of our bedroom. Maybe she'd found out she wasn't invited to the séance. Any possibility of a missed encounter with Emerson seemed to shake her to her core. How she survived in the world outside this island was becoming a bigger and bigger mystery.

"I saw Joe. My ex-fiancé." I hadn't been meaning to tell her, but it fell out of my mouth. Such a relief to mention it to someone without Kennedy's agenda. "He came all the way out here to see me, and without the producers' cooperation, which...is something I can't explain."

"Hmmph." She walked over to me, hunched over, and stared directly at my face. "I didn't see him. Tell me more."

"The first time, he showed up while I was getting ready to go down for the Culling. Came out of nowhere."

"So you were alone?" I nodded. "And you first saw him—when? Did he knock on the door?"

"No," I mused, thinking back, "I saw him behind me in the mirror as I was finishing my makeup. At first I thought I might be seeing things. I'm completely over him, of course," I assured her. "It was just...a surprise."

She seemed completely uninterested in my disclaimer. "In the mirror," she murmured. "And he had crew members with him?"

"Actually, no." I hadn't realized at the time, but that was a bit odd, given how dramatic a moment our reunion was bound to be. "I figured they were just filming from the hidden cameras in the room, you know?"

She furrowed her brow and reached out to hold my face in her hands, staring at me almost as if she weren't really seeing me but looking for something else. I wanted her to stop, but I didn't know how to extricate myself. "Did you ask a producer about it afterwards?" she asked.

"She said...." I hesitated. I didn't want to admit this out loud. It made me sound too unstable. "She said it wasn't part of the show. That they hadn't brought him out here."

She released my face abruptly. "I see."

God, she thought I'd lost it. "He was here though, I swear. I don't care what she says." I shook my head, alarmed to find tears pricking my eyes. I'd been trying so damn hard not to cry since I arrived at this place. Let Lucy have the reputation for incorrigible sobber. I was made of stronger stuff. "The things he said...it had to be him. And I've seen him several times since. He must be staying somewhere nearby and sneaking in...." The idea of him skulking around sickened me.

"Several times? And there's no record on the cameras?" I swallowed, looked down, couldn't answer her. If there had been, surely she would have seen it as she kept watch up here.

"Do you believe in ghosts?"

I inhaled some saliva and began to cough. I'd been expecting her to gently inquire about my mental health, not ask a direct question about the supernatural. And with this séance tonight, maybe her question wasn't academic. "Why? Do you?"

She pinched her lips together. "I had someone in my life who I loved the way you must have loved this ex-fiancé of yours. Darwin. I may have mentioned him."

"You did."

"When he was with me"—she gave a bitter laugh—"well, it was difficult to think clearly. He was so funny, so joyful, so articulate, he could say the sky was orange and gravity was no longer a natural law, and I would have believed him. I felt like I'd do anything for him, be anyone he wanted me to be. Like he was the person I'd been waiting to meet my whole life, completely unknowing, and then, once I'd met him, everything else fell away, insubstantial and drab in comparison. When I wasn't with him, I felt like something was missing, like I was only seeing the world in black and white."

"I was so miserable with Joe," I whispered, "and yet somehow, I could never leave."

"That's what I believed too." She sighed. "But you can be stronger than you realize, Zoe. You can learn to choose yourself." She paused. "When you've seen Joe here on the island, has he...touched you?"

"Well, no." I paused, thinking back. "No, he hasn't." Thank God for small favors.

"Are you sure? Think carefully. Has he picked anything up?"

I saw where she was going with this. A ghost was insubstantial, right? If the Joe I'd seen here was a ghost, he wouldn't touch me. He'd be able to come and go as he pleased with no one being the wiser. "Are you saying..." I couldn't believe I was about to ask this. "Are you saying Joe is dead?"

She gave me a piercing look. "I have no knowledge of the well-being of this Joe. But given what you've told me"—she shrugged—"it sounds like a ghost to me. Oh, don't look so surprised." She actually had the nerve to laugh at me. "I've been haunted for decades. Why do you think I suggested we hold a séance?"

This woman kept surprising me. "Wait, you *want* to have the séance?"

Her smile didn't fade. "I've hired a noted expert. Penelope Eyer. She'll be running the show. Give the crowd what they want, that's what I always say."

"But why?" I couldn't understand it. "I thought you hated the spectacle of the show. Why would you help them?"

She closed her eyes, and I suddenly noticed how exhausted she looked, gray and lined. "Like I said, I'm being haunted. Have been for most of my life. Turns out Darwin is just as persistent in death as he was in life. If there's any chance this woman can succeed in ridding me of him, I'll take it. And maybe you can use the opportunity to ask about your Joe, hmm?" She stood. "But then again, you might not want to admit you're still thinking about an old fiancé on television." I winced as her dart found its mark. "Just so you know, you didn't need the hives to succeed in winning that date with my nephew. He would have picked you anyway." She held open the door and gestured for me to leave.

Her words, playing repeatedly in my mind as I walked back to my room, stung. But she was right to give me a hard time about using that powder. I'd known better than to trust Kennedy. I'd been acting from fear and spite, and I'd made a terrible choice. Now I'd have to live with that whether I liked it or not.

And what about this ghost business? I'd never believed in spirits or ghosts. I didn't even believe in Heaven and Hell. That wasn't what my parents believed, and if I'd ever asked them about anything supernatural, they would have laughed at me, and not in a kind way, either. I'd played the normal slumber party games: Light as a Feather, Stiff as a Board; Bloody Mary (only when Kennedy forced me); the Ouija board. I'd made cootie catchers, played MASH, and tried to determine which boy I would end up with some day. My favorite was the "Love, Hate, Friendship, Marriage" chant that involved the letters in your and your crush's names. I performed that ritual on every crush I had right up until I met Joe. We seemed so meant to be, I tossed aside my childish test, only to do it when we broke up: my name spit out friendship, while his produced hate. Was that the problem between us all along?

I rejected this thought. I'd never believed in the idea of another world, of something not observable to the naked eye, of something... uncanny and yet deeply true. I believed in science and the truth of my senses. And yet Margaret was an intelligent woman, and she'd been so thorough in asking me questions about Joe. I couldn't remember him touching anything, but he might have. Why would I notice something like that?

Margaret believed in ghosts enough to organize a séance. Or so she said. But it was just as likely she had other reasons, reasons she wasn't telling me.

I would just have to wait and see what happened next.

Joe's voice whispered in my ear as I entered the bedroom. *"Telling our secrets, are you, Pooh Bear?"* His words contained venom. *"Spending time with that meddlesome old hag?"*

"Shut up." I muttered the words out loud to give them more force. "Shut. Up."

He fell silent, but I suspected it would only be a matter of time before he came back. Was he a ghost or a manifestation of some kind? Could Margaret and I both be haunted?

Or had I simply created a version of him from my own troubled mind? I missed him so much, I could be sabotaging my own senses to believe he was here. It was like he'd hollowed out a place to live inside of me, and it didn't matter how much I wanted him gone. I was his home, and he was with me for good.

Twenty-Five

Excerpt from Adelaide Vance's Journal:

October 12, 1974

I almost shaved my head last night, but I faltered at the last minute. With my luck, it would turn out I have a bumpy head and I'd look completely ridiculous. Leland is gone again so it's not like it matters what I look like, but this is just another failure that shows the rot twisting inside me. Darwin says many of his acolytes shaved their heads to eschew vanity and demonstrate their devotion. I like how clean that sounds. I wish I had their strength.

All my life I've struggled to say the right thing and make the right choices. I wracked my brain to get into a good architecture program, but once I was there, it turned out being one of the only women in the program was harder than I'd expected. And here I am, after all that effort, having to fuck an old man to get permission to do anything worthwhile. Sometimes I feel so tired of the world I could just cry. The idea of having a clear list of guidelines that will take me where I want to go is so ridiculously comforting.

Darwin is less harsh than I am to myself. He says it's okay to wait. He says someday my path will clear, and I'll laugh at the things that seem like such insurmountable obstacles right now. But in the meantime, my focus has to be the house. It's so close to being done, and we all want to see the results. Darwin has suggested being bolder, leaning more heavily into the Brutalism he knows I love. Leland wants me to soften the exterior with stucco, with a sprawling front porch, foregoing the prominent black fire escape on the side and choosing something less obtrusive. But forget about Leland! I am keeping the stark concrete, the lack of porch railings, the functionality of those emergency stairs. I want to challenge and expose, not lull the world into further complacency.

Darwin knows how much I hate falling short of his previous acolytes. He says they were flawed and weak, that I should put them from my mind and focus on deepening our own connection. And I'm not *bothered* by them, not precisely. I just want to feel like I have something to offer. His previous acolytes gave him the raw materials from which to work his spells: not only their hair, but their teeth and their blood as well. I want to prove myself.

He says I can offer him a sacrifice soon enough. But first, the house. I must finish the house.

Twenty-Six

The night of the séance, the chosen contestants, along with our producer handlers and Cannon, made our way to the designated spot at the top of a nearby hill. We walked in silence, following the weaving beams of the producer-held flashlights. Knowing Margaret was expecting to commune with her dead lover had created a film of dread over the whole experience, and I wanted to get past this little thrill for the viewers as quickly as possible.

We crested the hill just as the blister on the side of my foot was becoming a real problem, emerging onto a large flattened grassy knoll with a dozen large standing stones, at least nine or ten feet tall, arranged in a circle. A ring of metal scaffolding surrounded the stones, the attached lights reflecting off their polished surfaces. The usual sweet perfume that accompanied the Gold Diggers wherever we went became overpowered by the strong stench of sulfur.

A short squat woman draped in voluminous folds of black silk knelt on her knees in front of one of the stones, bowing until her forehead touched the ground and then bobbing back up, muttering all the while. After a few moments of this, she rose and moved onto the next stone, where the fast flow of words began again.

Margaret stood in the middle of the stone circle, also wearing a black cloak, her back rigidly straight. She didn't smile when she saw us, or nod, or acknowledge our presence in any way. She stared out from the blinding ring of lights as if she could see something the rest of us couldn't. Grace, Giselle, and Cannon, who had been chatting away behind Michelle and I, fell silent.

Kennedy emerged from the cluster of crew, her hair pulled back in a messy ponytail. She wore a dark gray T-shirt with the word "BITCH" emblazoned in large black letters. "All right, you're finally here. Let's get this party started."

An anonymous crew member handed the five of us black cloaks. Grace looked at hers with annoyance. "Seriously?" But she followed our lead and pulled it over her cute outfit. I was glad for its warmth, the night air having an unexpected bite.

We gathered around Margaret, and I realized for the first time how tall she was. She barely had to tilt her head to meet Cannon's eyes. "What are *you* doing here?"

Cannon remained unfazed. "Not my call." He held out his hands in conciliation. "They tell me where to go, and I show up."

"Like a dog." The scorn in Margaret's voice was unquestionable.

"A very well-paid dog." Cannon's teeth gleamed as he smiled.

Luckily the new woman—the medium?—interrupted them. "I am Penelope Eyer," she intoned in a rich plummy voice. Rings flashed from every single one of her fingers, and she wore a large pendant that looked like a big shining eye. "It is time." A pause before a crew member gave a thumb's up, and then she was in motion, arranging us into a circle. "We will need to join hands." Margaret reached for me, deliberately ignoring Cannon right beside her. Her hand was frail and dry like rice paper. Penelope took her other hand, her eyes roving around the circle before she closed them and took a series of deep breaths.

I took Cannon's hand with my free one, and he gave me an amused look before running his thumb across my palm. Bastard. I needed to be focused, not thinking about the weight of his warm body pressing into mine. I bit down on my lip hard. Get a grip, Zoe. Beside me, Margaret was moving her lips without sound. It almost looked like she was praying.

Penelope gave a theatrical clearing of her throat and began. "We are gathered here tonight to gaze deep into the heart of the great mystery of the Hereafter. For thousands of years humankind has wondered what lies in store for us after our hearts stop and our bodies grow cold. And for thousands of years we have attempted to answer these questions." I tried to stifle a cough. "Rest easy, young ladies—and gentleman"—she gave a little nod in Cannon's direction—"you do not have to be believers here tonight in order for this ritual to succeed. And by the time we are finished, you may find you have opened your hearts and changed your minds."

God, she was good at laying it on thick for the cameras.

"Please close your eyes and think of the people you have lost to the great mystery of death. We request their presence and welcome their spirits. Here within the circle, we have created a container that exists outside space, one that recognizes the multi-directional nature of time. We acknowledge that now is but a construct of the human brain, something we can exist beyond if we so choose. Come join us. Come instruct us. Come help us see."

"I can see just fine," Cannon murmured, and I stifled a giggle.

"Come assist us in removing any evil presences from our midst. Help us purify ourselves and this land. Too long has this place been plagued by unrest, by suffering, by unaddressed trauma, but tonight we will leave this heavy history in the past and lay any who seek to harm to rest." I risked a peek at Margaret. Her lips were still moving in her soundless litany.

"I invoke you with the frozen cold of the glacier and the burning heat of molten magma. I invoke you with the violence of the hurricane and the struggle of the tempest. I invoke you with the power of the sinkhole, the darkness of the limestone cave, the shrieking of the gale winds, and the blood that has been spilled here on this very soil."

Cannon squeezed my hand. From his other side, I heard a quiet "Ew" from Grace.

"We offer you our deepest emotions, and our ugliest. Our fear of the dark and the things that go bump in the night. Our grief over those we have lost. Our jealousy for what others have that we do not. Our bitterness over the pains we have suffered. And our despair over who we are and why we are here." Her voice had gradually grown louder and louder until she was shouting. "We offer you a taste of the living!"

A sudden gust of wind whipped my cloak around my body, and the lights flickered. Kennedy hadn't told me they had a special effects budget. Grace gasped, and I think she might have flung herself at Cannon if Penelope's voice hadn't cut across us like a whip. "Do not break the circle. We must hold the things we have summoned inside. We must hold them until we can help them return past the veil."

The wind continued, and I was surprised the crew didn't stop us and make us wait until it died down so they could record better sound. Maybe even they were caught up in the spooky drama Penelope Eyer had created for us. My hair blew into my eyes and mouth, and I must have loosened my hand in Margaret's because she suddenly clamped onto me with a fervent grip.

"What can you tell us?" Penelope shouted. "What do we need to hear? How can we lay this haunting to rest for once and for all?"

A low moaning began, and even though I knew it was just the result of the way the wind was being channeled through the hills, I shivered.

The next voice was all too human. "Tyler?" A thread of uncertainty laced through Michelle's voice. "Is that...is that you?"

"Mommy?" Giselle suddenly sounded like she was five years old. "No, don't leave me, Mommy. I need you. I need you." She began to sob loudly, and I thought about breaking the circle, dropping Margaret and Cannon's hands, and making this stop. Both my hands were held so tightly I was beginning to lose circulation.

Joe whispered into my ear, *"My darling, my Pooh Bear. Soon we'll be together. This is what you've been waiting for."* I bit my lip so hard I tasted blood.

Beside me, Margaret began to quiver, and I could hear her loud gasps above the wind. I opened my eyes then—screw Penelope's instructions, what if Margaret was having a seizure?—and looked just in time to see her eyes roll back into her head so only the whites were visible. The pendant at her throat seemed to glow, gently enough that at first I thought it was a trick of the light. Her entire body vibrated as if she were conducting electricity, her face twitching spasmodically. Maybe she *was* having a seizure. Why weren't the producers intervening? My hand throbbed from the pressure she was exerting onto it.

"Margaret!" I shouted. "Margaret, are you all right?" Her pendant shone like a little sun around her throat.

I turned to Cannon, hoping for some kind of direction, but he was staring down in horror at his other hand. Grace's lips were moving, and I realized she was saying, "Let me go, let me go, let me go," again and again in a kind of monotone.

"I can't," Cannon shouted into the wind. "I can't release my hand."

Christ. I looked outside the circle of chaos and locked eyes with Kennedy, who stood right at one of the cameramen's shoulders, doing absolutely nothing to stop the turmoil around us. "Help," I mouthed to her.

She continued to do nothing.

Margaret's skin was undulating like gelatin, and I wondered if she would shake until she came apart. "Don't die," I found myself saying. "Don't die on me. Please don't die."

She was going to die, and there was going to be an enormous lawsuit against the network, and Kennedy had lost her mind, a look of rapt concentration pinching her face.

But Grace had other ideas. With a wild banshee cry, she ripped her hands free of Cannon on her right and the sobbing Giselle on her left and tore away from the circle, away from the lights, away from the chaos. The wind stopped as suddenly as it had begun, and the hands smashing my own went abruptly limp, releasing me from their hold.

I turned to Margaret just in time to catch her as she slumped, almost knocking me over. Cannon joined me, bracing us both so I could help lower her to the ground. The pendant around her neck had gone dead and dull, and I blinked hard. "We need a doctor!" I shouted. Thank God the show doctor was on site.

The crew burst into action just as a shriek pierced the air from down the hill. Grace. "Shit." Kennedy finally seemed to be emerging from her daze. "Shep, go after her and make sure she's all right. And bring Mike."

"That fool girl," Penelope said. Her voice had changed, and she was suddenly talking like a normal person, her shoulders slumped, her colorful makeup running from sweat. "We were so close." She looked down at Margaret's collapsed body. "And we only had the one chance. Too risky now. I won't have a death on my conscience." With that pronouncement, she strode off into the night.

Margaret's eyes fluttered. "It's too much," she whispered. "It can never be repaid."

"Margaret? Can you hear me?" I put my hand to her neck, making a pathetic attempt to find her pulse.

"I never wanted to come back here," she murmured. "But I had to. I had to."

Cannon had removed his cloak and padded it into a bundle to put under her head. "It's going to be okay," he said, and he patted the back of her hand. "Just rest, okay? We're going to take care of you." He gestured to Elaine, who was hovering nearby as if she didn't know what to do. "Someone needs to get Emerson," he told her. "He'll want to be with his aunt."

"Right, of course." She scurried off. Useless. I hoped she'd get fired after this season.

I knelt by Margaret, unsure what I could do for her. Giselle and Michelle still stood in their spots, Giselle sobbing into her hands and Michelle staring listlessly into space. None of the crew interfered with them. "Can you stay with her?" I asked Cannon. He nodded, chewing on his lip. I shed my own cloak and went over to Michelle, who I thought was the better bet of the two. "Michelle." And when she didn't respond, a bit sharper: "Michelle. It's time for you to go back down to the house."

"Tyler was my boyfriend. My high school boyfriend." She spoke rapidly, as if she had to get the words out or else choke on them. "He died while we were dating. Motorcycle accident. He wasn't wearing a helmet."

"I'm sorry," I said as gently as I could, "but it's still time to leave."

"I should have been with him." She continued as if I hadn't said a word. "We were supposed to be together that night, but my period had started and I felt terrible, and my sister convinced me to stay home and watch some stupid romantic comedy with her. *Never Been Kissed.* If I had been there, he would have been driving more carefully. Or maybe he wouldn't have been driving at all. I should have been there."

"You had no way of knowing," I told her. "If you'd been there, you might have died too. There's no use playing the 'what if' game, trust me. Now, do you think you can find your way back on your own?" In the dark, I didn't say. At this point I looked forward to escaping the glare of the lights.

"He didn't like romantic comedies," she continued. "Made fun of me for watching them. Called them girl movies, said they were beneath me. He made me so mad sometimes. I should have just let it go. Who cares about a movie, you know? Who knows when the most trivial thing will matter more than anything else?"

Well, okay then. I moved onto Giselle, who was still sobbing loudly. It was impressive how long she was able to keep it up. I wished I had tissue to offer her.

Shouts came from the darkness, and Mike reappeared with Grace in his arms, her head on his shoulder. Shep trotted beside them. "Sprained ankle," he announced.

Mike tried to set Grace down on the ground, but she clung to him like a limpet. I couldn't say I blamed her. He shifted her weight, and said, "I'll take her back down to the house. Get some ice."

Perfect. I could send the other two women with him. "Wait for us," I called, and he nodded. "Giselle," I said softly, "it's time to go back to the house now. You and Michelle can go together, okay?"

She nodded through her fingers, and I put my arm around her and led her to Michelle. They both followed me like little lambs to where Mike stood. If I stopped being useful for even one second, I was afraid I'd panic just as much as they were. "You two stick together, okay?" I hesitated, wondering if I should go with them, then looked at Margaret on the ground. Cannon stood beside her, staring down as he slowly clenched and unclenched his hand.

Michelle took Giselle's arm and they shambled slowly away from the lights with Mike and Grace, a single flashlight beam illuminating their path. I hoped they wouldn't fall down the hill in the dark and break their perfect little necks.

When I returned to Margaret's side, her eyes were shut. *"Never did know what was good for her,"* Joe said into my ear. *"Why don't you learn from her example, Pooh Bear? Don't bite off more than you can chew."*

Cannon continued to stare at his hand as if it weren't his own.

Twenty-Seven

Excerpt from "Conversations Beyond the Veil: An Interview with Penelope Eyer"

—by Manuela Jackson, July 13, 2024, ghosttruestories.com

Let's talk about your cameo on the short-lived reality show "Love Story." What did you think about your role?

Ah yes, one of my greatest and most public failures. There are some common misconceptions about what happened on that show, a lot of them based on the final edit. People think the producers invited me in an effort to make the show more dramatic. And I'm not saying that wasn't their goal or that they didn't eagerly sign off on the idea, but they weren't the ones who called me originally, and even though they did compensate me for my time, they weren't the ones I was ultimately working for.

Oh no? The episode shows it as a kind of sanity test for some of the leading contestants.

I know, and I didn't realize when I agreed to do the job they would portray my efforts at communication with the dearly departed in such a sensationalistic and negative light. But the actual purpose of the séance wasn't merely to gather information but to complete the exorcism of a particularly troublesome spirit who had been haunting that island and its main target for decades.

Who was this spirit's main interest?

Margaret Courtland, the aunt of the show's star who had already been residing on the island for some time when the show began filming. She had been haunted by her former fiancé since his death in a tragic fire on the island in 1965. She told me he had been speaking to her with regularity ever since, and she'd made many attempts to lay him properly to rest. But the case had gained a new urgency because she believed he meant the new inhabitants of the island harm, in particular the young ladies competing on the show. She'd read about some of my previous cases and thought I might be able to help, and I agreed to try.

How much of the famous séance scene was staged?

Almost none of it. Everything was being filmed live, and we didn't do any retakes. There was professional lighting and sound, of course, and I don't know exactly what they told the participants ahead of time. But I certainly didn't coach any of them myself, and the only one I'd spoken to previously was Margaret Courtland. The strange wind, the way our hands locked in the circle, the communications some of the participants received, that was all spontaneous. None of it surprised me; all were phenomena I'd witnessed previously when dealing with spirits of particular strength and malice.

Were you able to make contact with the spirit who had been haunting Margaret Courtland?

I was, yes. He called himself Darwin, and he was one of the strongest ghosts I've ever encountered. It was clear from his power and experience that while he'd been tormenting the poor woman for years, he'd also been interacting from time to time with other targets. While he seemed to be driven by fury, he had enough command over his emotions to exhibit a stunning power for manipulation. He was talking to some of those girls, masquerading as loved ones they'd lost, playing on their grief and guilt, feeding from their pain. It was truly horrific to witness.

Was he actually able to possess his targets?

Not in the classic way, no. He was more subtle than that. He was using their own weaknesses and assumptions against them to warp their minds to his own purpose. That being said, he did exhibit some control over bodily functions, as was evidenced by the seizure he induced in Margaret. Whether he was able to directly influence physical aspects of his targets or whether he used the power of suggestion to manifest his results was unclear based on what I observed, but Margaret had told me during our initial interview that she believed he'd used the power of suggestion to cause one of these girl's hair to fall out. If she was right, that was a particularly troubling manifestation of his power. And if unchecked, it is possible he could have eventually moved on to possession, especially if he had some kind of focus. Or a willing host. Either might have done the trick. Margaret was right to be afraid of him.

In the video clip, we see the moment when one of the participants is able to break the circle. How close do you think you were to a successful banishment at that moment?

It's really difficult to say. He was fighting hard against me, against all the people in that circle, and obviously he found the weakest link. But at that point he was attacking Margaret with particular force, and it's possible she might have died before I completed the banishment. I told her about the risks ahead of time, and she was adamant we move forward to protect the other people involved. I felt like I was close to sending him on, but you never know with a spirit like Darwin. He might have been fooling me. And of course, after the harm he caused during our attempt, it was out of the question to try again. Margaret wouldn't have had enough strength and we would have been doomed to a second failure. It was a tragedy all around.

So there was nothing further to be done then?

I told the person in charge—Kennedy, I think her name was?—that they should shut the whole production down and move to a different location immediately. I wasn't sure how important a factor proximity was, but from what Margaret told me, Darwin did seem to be much stronger on the island, and more able to haunt multiple targets simultaneously when they were physically present there. So it's possible if they had all left, it would have ameliorated the harm of which he was capable. But the producer just laughed at me and thanked me for putting on "such a good show." They hustled me off that island before I had a chance to talk to anyone else, and that was that.

Have you interacted with the spirit Darwin since then?

Thankfully, no. When you've been in this profession as long as I have, you learn not to court trouble.

Twenty-Eight

The mood in the house was dark. Gone was the cheerful day drinking, the constant giggling, the party atmosphere. Don't misunderstand, everyone was drinking even more than before, but it was the gloomy alcohol of anxiety and desperation. Summer began talking about going home of her own volition. "I have my little girls to think about," she kept saying.

Grace sat on a couch downstairs with her ankle propped up, Elaine running constant attendance on her. I kept catching Michelle with a weird glazed look in her eyes, but she went ahead on her date with Emerson. Giselle kept to herself and barely spoke a word. Lucy shut up about missing the séance, but she continued to sulk.

All the women who hadn't been included felt suddenly both lucky and superior. The women chosen by Emerson so far had been weak, I heard them whispering. They weren't psychologically tough enough. Just like the girl in the penguin onesie, whose name no one could remember. I could have told them about Cassidy and her hair loss, but I kept my mouth shut. Nobody had any problems with me—in spite of Kennedy's assessment of me as a frontrunner, they didn't see me as a contender for Emerson's heart, and I hadn't visibly lost it at the séance so my sanity wasn't in question—and I wanted to keep it that way.

Whispers began about Margaret Courtland. The women who hadn't been at the séance didn't believe anything supernatural had happened, but...they didn't entirely disbelieve it either. Michelle wouldn't shut up about that night, her story becoming more and more embellished each time she told it, and we all knew she was a scientist, which lent weight to her words. The rest of us kept quiet. Nobody knew exactly what had happened. And Margaret's current state of health was a mystery. Had her own doctor been flown in? Was she stable? When I asked Elaine point blank, she refused to answer. Kennedy and Jen were nowhere to be seen.

I was no better off than anyone else. I had huge bruises on both my hands from the unbreakable strength of my neighbors' grip. I had seen Cannon unable to control it. I had seen three women who had seemed perfectly stable have what appeared to be breaks from reality. It wasn't just me hearing Joe anymore. And the wind storm that had ended as suddenly as it had begun? I had no rational explanation. Whenever I played it back in my mind, my mouth went dry with fear.

This couldn't be the show, not anymore, could it? The producers messing with our minds? The séance had crossed some invisible line. Something else was going on, something inexplicable and sinister. What if Margaret was right? What if her old flame Darwin really was haunting her?

I finally understood why she'd been so vehemently opposed to this show from the beginning. And my worry about Joe's well-being continued to grow. If something had happened to him, I didn't know how I'd bear it.

Cannon cornered me when I came out of my room for my special date with Emerson. "Ready for your big day?" Was it my imagination or was his cheer more forced than usual?

"Doing my best." I had no idea what we'd be doing, so I'd tried to be as versatile as possible, wearing cute flat sandals and a comfortable little dress over a bikini, my hair in an artfully curled ponytail in case the day's activities called for it getting wet. I had a huge bottle of sunscreen in my bag, along with a truly absurd selection of makeup and hair products. A second bag held my evening change of outfit. I'd never gone on a date this prepared in my life.

Cannon fell into step beside me. "I heard his date with Michelle went well."

As if I weren't already nervous enough. "You would know."

"Guess she was able to put on a bright face after the shit that went down the other night."

"I guess so." And now I'd have to do the same, even though I was quaking in my sandals. I couldn't deny the awkwardness of having this conversation with a man I'd recently slept with, who was the confidant of the man I was about to go on a date with, who was dating several women at the same time. And people thought being on these shows was a good time?

"About all that...."

I stopped at the bottom of the stairs and looked up at him, trying not to show my panic. The last thing I wanted right now was a conversation about my feelings: for him, for Emerson, for anybody. I didn't want to be noticing the bit of stubble on his upper lip, the way his lower lip swelled slightly, the soft wiriness of his curls. I didn't want the cameras to capture my inappropriate reaction to his presence, to realize we were...what? Friends? Lovers? Something we shouldn't be.

"What?" It came out about as curt as you would expect.

"What the hell happened out there?" He kept his voice low, looking around to make sure we were alone. As if it mattered. We both wore live mikes.

The only safe choice was to play dumb. Surely he knew we couldn't have a real conversation, not here. "What do you mean?"

"I couldn't open my hand." He opened and closed it, stretching his fingers as far as they'd go. "It felt like it had frozen solid."

He waited as though he thought I had answers. Talking to me in front of the ever-present cameras, he must have been deeply disturbed by what had taken place. After all, he could be compromising his carefully cultivated image. "It might have been a stress response," I offered half-heartedly. "We're all tired, and it was intense out there, with so many people freaking out. And that weird wind." I paused. Neither of us believed a word I was saying. "I wouldn't worry about it."

"You didn't hear anything peculiar then? Not any...voices or anything? Nothing like Michelle or Giselle?"

I gave him a warning look. "Nope, nothing. Guess I'm not that sensitive to the supernatural. Doesn't seem like you are either."

His mask had slipped, but he shoved it back into place. "Yeah, yeah, that's not really my thing. You're right, I'm probably just tired. Lots of late nights when you're helping someone find the love of their life." He patted my shoulder in a fatherly way. "Good luck, Zoe." He strode into the bowels of the house, and I took a deep breath. God help me, but with even Cannon questioning what had happened, my newly born belief in ghosts was gaining a real foothold. I fussed with my sunglasses to buy myself a minute to recover before heading out the front door to meet the only man supposed to be on my mind.

Emerson hugged me in front of a Land Rover waiting to whisk us on our romantic adventure. Shep and Elaine hovered behind me. It looked like Kennedy was staying behind this time.

I spoke in Emerson's ear as if our mikes wouldn't catch everything I said. "We can stay here to be near your aunt, if you'd rather. I know she isn't well."

He squeezed me tighter. "You're sweet, but she's doing just fine. I'll check on her as soon as we get back."

Did I care about his feelings about his sick aunt? Definitely. Did I also care about rehabilitating my image post-hive incident by showing that I cared? You better believe it.

That's one of the things that got under my skin about reality TV. It was both real and unreal at the same time, driven by layer upon layer of motivations, only some of which were visible to the viewer. Only some of which were visible to yourself as a cast member, and that's where the biggest problem lay. You'd begin to question why you were doing what you were doing. You'd begin to forget where the real you ended and the fictional you began. When every minute of your life was being recorded, the boundaries blurred. None of your actions remained pure.

I smiled up at Emerson as if I was maybe falling in love with him, or at least nurturing a little crush (was I? no, impossible, my heart was still beating harder from talking to Cannon, and yet my feelings for Cannon ran into my feelings for Emerson, with Joe's insidious presence wrapping around us all like a python constricting my air supply) and slipped my hand into his. You're mine, that little gesture said. We're walking through this life together. I've got you.

I imagined the camera zooming in on our interlocking fingers, and my smile widened. I could play this part.

I had to.

The date was an idealized blur of arms squeezed, knees touched, smiles exchanged, doors opened, chests leaned upon, and me laughing too much. A helicopter waited to whisk us to another island, a populated one where we could play on the beach, wander through the marketplace, pop olives and small pieces of cheese into each other's mouths, and pretend we weren't being followed by a camera crew who occasionally made us stop and repeat things.

When we emerged from the SUV into the crowded central town square, I stared at all the people going about their daily lives. These people weren't competing with me for the dubious honor of having a very public relationship. These people weren't spying on my every move. These people had no vested interest in what I might decide to do in two hours, or later tonight, or a week from now. I wanted to hug them all.

I wanted to stay here. The idea of returning to the island filled me with a cold dread.

As the day progressed, I began to fantasize about never going back. About opting out of *Love Story*, walking away from both Emerson and Cannon, who, let's face it, probably wouldn't miss me once I was gone. I could return to the real world, without looming questions and creepy rituals and accidents I wasn't sure were accidents. Maybe I could move somewhere nobody knew me, to the anonymity of some big faceless city, and begin to pull my life into some semblance of order.

Sure, I'd be giving up a significant boost to my writing career. I'd be playing it safe, just like when I was with Joe. But the bruises on my hands screamed out the need to escape before whatever was happening on that island swallowed me whole along with everyone else.

Most of all, I wanted to check and make sure Joe was healthy and thriving, that hearing his voice was all a product of my overactive imagination. Every time I tried to consider the possibility of him being dead, my thoughts simply stopped.

"We aren't finished yet," Joe whispered as I splashed Emerson in the ocean. *"I'm waiting for you on the island. We can work things out."* Except he wasn't there. I knew he wasn't there.

I dreamt of escape the entire time I was flirting with Emerson, chasing him through the surf, trying fresh fish, keeping my chin angled so my face would look as thin as possible, sucking in my stomach, not complaining about the heaviness of my bag, discretely reapplying sunscreen when he took a bathroom break, laughing at anything remotely joke-like, and remembering to check that none of the treats we tried had gotten stuck in my teeth.

As the date ground on, I thought, "I can do this. I can go out on a high note and leave this all behind." Maybe I could get Elaine to help me. One night here on this touristy island, and then tomorrow...tomorrow everything could be different.

I carefully avoided examining the terror that underlay my new plan.

I had my chance before dinner. The show had rented an estate for the evening, and Elaine took me into a private room to give me a chance to change into a slinky dress and freshen my hair and makeup. This place would do nicely; there was no bed, but there was a soft-looking couch where Elaine lounged now, tapping away at her cell phone.

I decided the direct approach was best. "Elaine, I need someplace to stay tonight."

She didn't look up. "We'll take the helicopter back, but probably not until around eleven. That will give you and Emerson plenty of time to bond."

I took a big bite of the sandwich they'd provided me so I wouldn't have to actually eat dinner on camera. It took me a moment to force it down. Here it was, the moment of truth. "I don't want to go back to the house."

That got her attention. She put down her phone with a pained look on her face, and I almost felt sorry for her. "What?"

"I don't want to go back. You've rented out this place for the entire night, right?" She nodded. "I'll just stay here then, and in the morning I'll arrange my flight back to the States."

She got up, pulled up a chair, sat down right across from me as if I'd announced a terminal illness. "Zoe, I understand the stress is getting to you," she began. "All the women are feeling it, especially after...." She trailed off. We both knew exactly what she was talking about. "But things are going so well between you and Emerson," she continued. "I think it could be the real deal between you two. I'm not supposed to tell you this, but none of his other private dates have gone as well as today."

Maybe I'd been underestimating Elaine. Or maybe she was finally pulling out all the stops. Enough mistakes during her watch, and they'd fire her. I couldn't see Kennedy being the most understanding boss. "I'll go through with the dinner," I told her, "but then I'm done. If you want me to say something that helps you present a certain story, we can talk about that. If you help me out tonight and make sure I get back home okay, I'm happy to cooperate."

"But Zoe, I don't think you understand." She took my hands in her tiny, sweaty ones. "If we don't give you a redemption arc, the public is going to hate you. It can be really rough after the show airs, and I don't think you're going to like how you're presented. But if you stay, if you can convince Emerson to keep you around for a while longer or even to choose you at the end, the producers are more likely to show you in a positive light. We might even be able to swing some kind of "Come to Jesus" moment, you know what I'm saying? Trust me, I've heard all kinds of stories. You definitely want to stay."

I pulled my hands away and wiped them on the chair. "I think I know what I want. Will you help me or not?"

She sighed. "I'll have to clear it with Jen and Kennedy."

Oh God. Why hadn't I just snuck away without saying anything? The weather was so mild, I could have spent the night out on the beach and not be any worse for wear. "Do you have to tell them?"

"Everything goes to them for approval." She wrung her hands. "Everything."

Well, shit. Kennedy would never agree with my scheme. "Maybe you're right," I said. "Maybe I should try to tough it out." I would have to try Plan B and sneak off on my own. I glanced around the comfortable room with regret.

Her sudden smile cut through her face. "You won't regret it," she said. "Things will be more fun from now on, you'll see. And I'll do my best to tell a great story about you, I promise. Now, why don't you eat the rest of that sandwich? We wouldn't want you getting hungry tonight."

Emerson and I walked hand in hand onto the stone veranda that had been transformed into a scene of seduction. We sat on a comfortable damask sofa with a view of the sun setting over the ocean. Lit candles danced on every available surface, and a fancy bottle of wine sat in a bucket of ice. Beautiful food we weren't allowed to eat had been laid out on a coffee table in front of the couch. I surreptitiously grabbed a roll and slipped it into my bag for my beach campout later.

I hadn't wanted to break the carefree mood the producers were going for, but now I'd committed to my course of action, it didn't matter. They wouldn't edit this date to make it look romantic, not with me about to bail. They would be dragging my name through the mud. "How is your aunt doing?" I asked Emerson. "I'm worried about her."

"That's right, you were there when she collapsed, weren't you?" He took a sip of white wine. "She's been on bed rest, doctor's orders, and none too happy about it either. But she should be up and about soon. I'm trying to convince her to come back to New York once we finish filming. I don't like thinking of her all alone and isolated on that island, especially not now that her health needs to be monitored more closely."

"Why did she decide to retire somewhere so remote in the first place?" I asked. "I would have thought she was a New Yorker to the core."

"Yeah, I was surprised when she made the announcement." He took another sip of wine. "I mean, it's beautiful out here, no question. But she had such an active life in New York. Family, friends, a full social calendar, and a lovely home. Now she doesn't invite anyone to visit her and hardly ever leaves the island herself. One of the family will pop over from time to time to check on her, but"—he shakes his head—"it's not the same. My father said she's never recovered from what happened there when she was a young woman, but if that were the case, I would think she'd want distance and distraction."

From the corner of my eye I saw Elaine approaching, shaking her head and drawing a finger across her throat. They didn't want me pursuing this line of conversation. They wanted sound bites about past relationships and how we felt about each other, maybe some tender and heartfelt moment of vulnerability when I shared another challenging episode from my past. Hey, Emerson, feel sorry for me because my mom left the family when I was ten and no matter how much I hoped, no matter how I tried to be perfect, she never came back, never even checked up on Kennedy and me to make sure we were doing okay. Hey, Emerson, give me a pity ribbon at the next Culling and feel close to me because I've shared my secrets with a national audience to get your attention. Hey, Emerson.

"What happened to her on the island?" I asked.

He laughed uneasily and looked at the camera. "Well, it was a different time. The sixties. You know how it was."

Neither of us had been alive in the sixties, but okay. I decided to play dumb. "What do you mean?"

"Oh, sex, drugs, and rock n' roll. The free love revolution. All that stuff."

I wanted to keep him talking. "She was into that kind of thing?"

"Into it? Hell, she founded some kind of commune on the island right after she graduated college. Brought out a lot of her friends from Vassar. From what I hear, it was one big party."

"But then?"

He shrugged. "There was some kind of accident. I don't know exactly what happened, but the main house burned down. I think a few people even died. Aunt Margaret would never go back after that, not even after Grandpa had rebuilt."

No one would talk about how that fire started. I gave it up as a lost cause. Soon enough I'd be far away and it wouldn't matter. "Well, she seems super attached to the place now. It must be nice for her to have more company, what with the show filming."

"You'd think, wouldn't you? But she was opposed to the idea from the start. Gave me hell about it, and when she gets an idea in her mind... well, let's just say stubbornness runs in our family." He gave a proud smile. "But it's not her island, you know, it's the family's, so in the end, she had to give in. I thought she might hide up in her room and refuse to be a part of it, but she's a gracious loser, I'll give her that. Aunt Margaret has always been a class act."

So he'd decided to go through with the show when it meant upturning his elderly relative's home without her consent. Cracks were already showing in his made-for-TV persona, and we hadn't even finished our first date. Any qualms I'd felt about deserting him fell away.

I almost called him on it. After all, they weren't going to air anything that would mar his reputation and ruin their wish fulfillment fantasy. But the idea of the argument that would follow, of his defensiveness at the idea of taking anyone else's needs into consideration, of the sour grapes that would be attributed to me afterwards, it all felt too exhausting. I was leaving. That would have to be enough.

Emerson must have finally noticed Elaine's violent head shaking. "But enough about me. I want to learn more about the real Zoe." I kept my smile in place with difficulty at this announcement. "Tell me about your last relationship."

I didn't know what to say. That I'd never realized I could feel so destroyed? That I was still worried about Joe's well being? That I wasn't sure I was capable of loving again?

"It was serious." I'd give him the words, the right words, the words I knew everyone wanted to hear. "But in the end, we just weren't compatible. It's for the best, really. We're both happier this way." Never let them see the mess. Never let them see you cry.

"Were you in love with him?"

I raised my eyebrows in surprise. "Of course. How could it have been serious otherwise?"

Emerson took another sip of wine. "I don't know if I've ever been in love." A small pause, then, almost as an afterthought, "Except with Melanie, of course."

Ah yes, the dead fiancée. I thought of all his other ex-girlfriends who might watch the show and sent out a little prayer this conversation would end up on the cutting room floor. "I'm sorry. I heard about her accident. I can't imagine how awful that must have been."

"Thanks. It was a difficult time." He looked down, playing his part perfectly. Sad but strong. "I struggled a lot with survivor's guilt. I was in that car too, you know. But I'm still here."

"He was the one driving," Joe whispered. *"The guy wants sympathy, but he's not too eager to fess up to his share of responsibility for the whole mess."*

I dug my nails into my palms, keeping my eyes fixed on Emerson's face. How could Joe possibly know something like that? It was all I could do to stay quiet and keep breathing.

Emerson, oblivious, talked on. "Since then, I guess I just haven't met the right person. The One." He looked back up, met my eyes, gave me a small smile of promise. "But I have to tell you, I'm feeling hopeful."

"Well, that's why you're here," I said. "To find love." He had to at least pretend this show had a chance of working.

"It's why *we're* here," he corrected me. "True love is something we all deserve." He leaned in for a kiss, and I closed my eyes and endured. It was more slobbery than I remembered and less tender. I tried not to think about Cannon's urgent kisses as I underwent the endurance test of getting through the next few minutes of tongue and saliva and unwanted closeness.

I couldn't believe I'd been thinking I might like this guy. Even knowing it was an act, I'd been buying what the show had been selling me: that he was the grand prize, the one we all wanted, the guarantee of a Happily Ever After. Stupid, after hearing so many of Kennedy's stories. I should have known better. But the story was stronger than I'd thought, and my own mind was no longer entirely under my control.

Eventually I allowed myself to pull away. "Will you excuse me for a moment?" Now was my time to exit.

I went to the bathroom, just like I was expected to, and no cameras bothered to follow me. They were sloppier away from the island. I noted a side door exit as I wound my way through the building and into a small ladies' room with two stalls. It was only a few blocks from here to the center of town, where I could blend in with the tourists for a few hours before making my way down to the beach. Maybe even find a different bathroom to hide in for a while.

I washed my hands with cold water and stared at my face in the mirror. I forced myself to look at my makeup-enhanced features, my fake hair, my hollow cheeks. I was still there somewhere underneath it all. I had to be. But as I looked, my features morphed, elongated. My cheeks became even thinner, my chin more pointed, my nose more pronounced. My eyes looked like hollow pools, my hair wrapped around my own neck.

"You think you deserve to breathe?" Joe's laugh echoed in my head. I'd been suffocating ever since I met him, but now I was actually choking. I couldn't breathe, I couldn't see myself in the woman in front of me, not anymore. I brought my hands to my neck like I was in a dream, tried to pull the hair away, but it was held firm by an invisible force too strong for me to break.

"Zoe! There you are!" The hair loosened abruptly as Elaine burst into the room. "Sorry to interrupt, but we need to get back to the island right away."

I started coughing so hard I doubled over. My throat burned, and tears began to seep from my eyes. My lungs seized up with every breath of air, and I wondered if I was going to throw up.

"Oh my god, are you okay?" Elaine slung her backpack onto the ground, pulled out a water bottle. "Here, take some slow sips, okay? Just breathe."

I accepted the proffered bottle and took her advice. One sip, followed by tiny shallow breaths, then another sip. I could do this. I could take in oxygen. My hair was flowing down my back, not wrapped in a tight band around my throat. How could I have thought that was happening?

I was one hundred percent losing my mind.

I needed to get out of here. I stood up with difficulty. Let her tell Kennedy. She'd find out about my desertion soon enough anyway. "About this date...."

Elaine cut me off. "Forget about the date. The date is over. There's been...an incident. They need us back right away." She paused. "Kennedy's asking for you."

My churning thoughts instantly stilled. "What? Is she all right?" Kennedy had never asked for me in her life.

Elaine shrugged. "I've told you everything I know. They told me there's been some kind of accident, but it must be serious to cut things here short." She gave me a doubtful look. "If you're feeling better, we really should be going."

"Just give me a minute, okay?"

She backed out of the bathroom, looking at me like I might suddenly grow horns. "Come to the veranda when you're ready. We need to do one last shot out there before we go."

I didn't look in the mirror this time. I didn't want to know what I'd see. Instead I stared into the white porcelain basin. Black gunk had settled in a thin line around the rim of the drain. There couldn't be any cameras in here, right? I resisted the urge to start crying or hit my forehead on the edge of the sink.

Kennedy had asked for me. If she'd had an accident, someone should be with her, and who else was there but me? Our dad would never inconvenience himself by flying this far. She had no significant other to call. And her film school friends, if they could even be called friends, wouldn't care in the slightest. As far as I could tell, the only times Kennedy saw them was at pretentious little soirees where they wore slouchy black outfits, sipped wine from plastic glasses, and tried to out-do one another in the name-dropping game.

A knock at the door and Elaine came back in, phone proffered. "Here's Kennedy now." I gave the phone an uncertain look. I hadn't touched one since I left Kennedy's apartment back in LA. "It's okay," Elaine said. "Take it."

I held it to my ear. "Kennedy?"

"Zoe?" The line was full of static. "Is that you?"

"Yeah, what's going on?"

"Zoe. Thank God." Kennedy began to sob. I hadn't heard my sister cry since we were little girls. "You need to come back here as soon as possible, okay? It's all too much to explain over the phone, but...." More sobbing. "I need you."

The fear in her voice shook me, and I didn't have to think about it anymore. I had called her in much the same way not so many months before, and she had opened her home to me. How could I do any less? "We'll be there soon," I promised. "Just hold on, okay?"

"Please hurry," she said, and then the line cut out.

I pushed the phone back at Elaine. "Call her back."

She messed with the screen for a while, then shook her head. "She's not picking up. The cell connections over there are always hit and miss. Best to get moving. She'll fill us in when we get back."

What choice did I have? My sister had said she needed me. What were my vague fears and a few more weeks on this stupid show compared to that?

In a few moments, my escape plan had morphed into a malformed dream of something that never could have happened.

"I still have plans for you, Zoe." I couldn't tell if Joe was making a promise or a threat.

TWENTY-NINE

To: bruce.masters@leogami.com
From: kennedy.brown@goodmail.com
Date: August 23, 2018
Subject: I've found paradise

Hey Bruce, reporting in as promised. I've officially found paradise for the next season of *Love Story*. It's an idyllic private island in the middle of the Bahamas, near islands owned by Nick Cage, John Travolta, and Richard Branson. Pristine white beaches, sun-drenched tropical vegetation, perfect blue ocean, the works. It's exactly what we were hoping for.

It's owned by the Courtland family of New York, and Emerson Courtland fits the bill for the next Prince Charming. A little wooden, sure, we can't have everything, but he does have the good looks, the pedigree, and the aspirations to break into show business, which means he'll be easy to manage.

We're lining up the women now, and I've already got a Good Girl Goes Bad storyline in the works, along with all the usual neuroses, sweet things, and villains.

Best of all, the island has a dark history that I'll be able to exploit to give you what we talked about: something different, something explosive, something everyone will be talking about around the water cooler on Tuesday mornings. I'll make sure we get a girl who moves in the same circles as the Courtlands and knows one or two of the less savory stories about the island. And I have an ally in place who will help me deliver some truly mind-blowing chills and thrills. Our horror-romance cross will give the viewers an experience to remember.

I know you went to bat for me with Jen, and I plan to deliver. You're a prince, Bruce. Here's to bigger things on the horizon.

Xx,

Kennedy

THIRTY

Several producers and other crew members waited at the helicopter pad, along with three different vehicles. They whisked Emerson into one without even letting us say goodbye. He gave me an awkward wave over his shoulder, and that was it, the end of our vaunted private date.

Elaine stuck with me, and our SUV pulled up in front of a guest cottage on one side of the main property. I'd barely paid it any attention, cute and squat with a blue door and a fake thatch roof framed by matching palm trees.

Someone opened the SUV door from the outside, and Elaine gestured. "After you."

I climbed from the car and dutifully followed the stone path to the front door. Kennedy had to be recuperating inside, and I held my breath, expecting the worst but hoping for the best. Maybe she'd gotten some bad news about the show from the network? But I couldn't erase the picture of Cassidy clawing hair from her head. There was something about this show, this house, this island, something that left my skin crawling.

Inside the cottage, monitors covered the walls and stood on two rows of long tables, more and bigger than in Margaret's spy room. Keyboards and laptops and huge strands of black wiring cluttered the space. Kennedy sat hunched over her laptop, sporting large headphones and a messy ponytail. She wore the same black T-shirt and jeans combo she'd been wearing most days, and she looked...completely normal. Certainly not like someone in the throes of a nervous breakdown.

"Kennedy," Elaine began, but Kennedy held up her hand before returning to her frantic typing. The few other producers in the room took the opportunity to flee, sidling past me out the door without making eye contact. Elaine gave me an apologetic smile before doing the same.

Kennedy finally slammed her laptop closed and swiveled to face me. "So, I hear you tried to fly the coop."

I glanced at the door behind me and contemplated following the others out. But where could I go? There was nowhere on this island she couldn't follow me. I settled for folding my arms. "That's right." She stared at me, just the way she had when we were kids and I'd said something particularly stupid. And just as I did back then, I began to babble in pointless self-defense, even though she was the one who'd dragged me back here under false pretenses. "Look, I get this is your thing, this show is your baby, and that's fine, more power to you. But shit's been getting weird, you must have noticed that. Maybe it's normal weird for this kind of show, I don't know, but it's not normal weird to me. I should never have gotten involved, never come out here in the first place. Especially when I'm obviously not over Joe. I shouldn't be here. This isn't what I need, can you understand that?"

A pause. "No." The word exploded in the air like a gunshot.

"No?"

"You're just like all my other girls. You're stumbling through your life like some kind of deeply confused puppet. Not knowing what you want, doing what other people expect because you're incapable of tapping inside,"—she thumped her chest where her heart would be, if she had one—"of finding your driving force. Well, you need a guide, fine, that's my job. I'm here to give you a narrative with a beginning, middle, and ending, and *that*, Zoe, that direction is what you need."

Her face glowed with conviction, with such obnoxious certitude that she was right, that she knew best, even though she'd been mostly MIA for the last fifteen years of my life. I couldn't believe she'd lied to get me to come back...and at the same time, it was exactly the sort of thing Kennedy would do.

"You need her," Joe whispered. *"You know she has your best interests at heart."* I hesitated. However angry I was, I knew she loved me. And it wasn't like *she* believed in ghosts. She couldn't possibly understand.

I tried again. "Kennedy, I really don't think it's a good idea for me to be here anymore."

She gave a dramatic sigh. "Oh, give it up. Everything is always about you, poor helpless Zoe. You clung to Mom until you smothered her, then you transferred to me, and then later on you latched onto Joe. Maybe being on this show will finally turn you into someone with a fucking backbone, but I'll believe it when I see it."

I stared at her. "You think I smothered Mom?" Wait a second. "You think I'm the reason she left?"

She shrugged. "I thought you knew."

I struggled against the tide of hurt and horror, fighting back tears, glancing around for the hidden camera that might be filming me right now, taking my secret fear and making it large for someone else's viewing pleasure. Did Kennedy really believe that?

What if she was right? I'd loved Mom with all my heart, it was true. I'd spent hours and hours talking to her, telling her all the insignificant details of my life, crying over all the little wounds and doubts. Could I have been the one who drove her away? Because if she'd left because of my dad, as I'd always suspected, she could have taken me with her.

No. No, I'd only been ten years old. So what if I'd cried a lot? Surely....

But Kennedy thought it was true.

I cleared my throat. "I came back here because I thought you were in trouble." More the fool I. "Because you said you needed me. But it's all lies with you, isn't it? You'll say whatever you need to say to get what you want. What's another manufactured crisis, after all?"

"Oh, there's a real crisis." She said it matter-of-factly, as if she weren't about to drop a bomb into my world. "And not just the one where you lose sight of the prize."

"What do you mean?" I needed to know, and at the same time, I wanted to hop back into that helicopter and never see this godforsaken island or any of the people on it again.

"It's your friend Michelle," she said. "That's why we needed the helicopter. And she's been asking for you."

———

The house had been shocked into silence, with no evidence of the other Gold Diggers or crew members. I paused at the foot of the stairs, not wanting to find out what I'd see in our room. Elaine laid a hand on my arm; she was hovering as if she were afraid to let me out of her sight. Maybe the cameras were no longer enough to guarantee my containment. In another context it might even have been flattering. "Let's get this over with." She gave a nervous look up the stairs as we began to climb. "Why did I ever leave the talent agency?"

"Beats me," I said. "You mean you signed up for all this glamour?"

She didn't laugh. "My parents thought if I insisted on the entertainment industry, I should focus on the business side, and I tried, I really did. But I never wanted to represent actors. I wanted to be making something myself, you know? I wanted to be a part of it."

"She doesn't deserve to be here," Joe said in my ear. *"Ugly bitch."*

My subconscious was really going to town today. "So you decided to be a peon producer of reality TV." That shut her up. She'd played her part in Kennedy's deception, after all. I didn't owe her anything, not even sympathy. We'd all fucked up our lives in our own ways. And from what I'd seen, I'd be doing her a favor if I got her fired from this train wreck of a show.

I tapped lightly on the door to our room before pushing it open to see Michelle lying on her bottom bunk in a fetal position, wearing a baggy T-shirt and shorts, back towards us. "Give us some privacy, won't you?" The words were a joke, my glance going to the room's "hidden" camera even as I hissed them at Elaine.

She shrugged. "I don't have to come in, but..."

Curtis came puffing up the stairs behind her, a camera already balanced on his shoulder, his usual sound guy right beside him. I rolled my eyes. "Fine, I'll be sure to bring my A game and be as boring as possible." I glared at the man who had watched me climb into the dumbwaiter only to be trapped. "And you're not getting any second takes, do you hear me? I'm not repeating myself so you can jerk off to that woman's suffering."

Curtis didn't respond, as if I were speaking a different language. He must have been used to contestants mouthing off at him, deflecting my words as easily as if they weren't said aloud. After all, what was wrong with an honest day's work? We knew what we'd signed up for, oft repeated words that were beginning to ring hollow.

I gave Curtis a last warning look before entering. "Michelle, it's me. And there's a camera guy with me." No response. "I heard you were asking for me. Are you okay?"

At that last, her shoulders began to shake. At first I thought she might have started crying, but no, she was laughing in hysterical gasps. I perched on the bed behind her, the sound guy dangling the boom above me, and put my hand on her back. Her long dark hair had clumped into huge rats, as if she hadn't brushed her hair in weeks, even though I knew it had been groomed into flawlessness just yesterday. "Hey. What's going on? I heard you're leaving soon. Going back home."

The shaking became more pronounced. I looked back at Curtis, crouched down for the ideal shot. He gave me a pointed stare. I was on my own. "Hey. Michelle. Is there anything I can do for you?"

She reached backwards, her hand clutched into a tight fist, and when I touched it, she released her grip, dropping several pebbled-sized objects into my hand. They were smooth and white and at first I couldn't process what I was seeing. Dog teeth? Had she stumbled on a weird cache of another past eccentric Courtland?

But then she looked up at me, her lips pulled back in a grimace, several dark gaps in her formerly perfect smile, and I understood. "Oh Michelle. Oh no."

She covered her hand with her mouth, muffling her little sounds, half sob and half incredulous laughter. When she finally spoke, her words were slow and slightly slurred, no longer enough teeth in her mouth to speak clearly. "He had it. This same thing. All the teeth smashed from his mouth."

It was hard to remember I was talking to a brilliant physics graduate student. "Who did, sweetie? What are you talking about?"

"My boyfriend," she sniffed. "The one who...died...in the motorcycle accident. He had to have a...closed casket."

I was pretty sure there had been a lot more wrong with his dead body than some missing teeth, but I wasn't about to say that to her. "Did your mouth get smashed?" I asked softly. I looked again at the teeth lying in my palm. They didn't look damaged, nor was there any bloody residue.

"They just...fell out." Her voice took on a hysterical note. "I told myself to put him out of my mind, even though...I heard him, I thought he was talking to me, but I told myself, no, that's crazy, it's all the stress you're under, just try to relax, just try to act natural, don't break up in front of the cameras, not like what's-her-name, the girl in that animal suit, you can't be like her, not on national television, haven't you already made enough mistakes, just chill out. And then"—her breathing was becoming more ragged—"out they came, and I can't ignore my teeth falling out, I've been dreaming of that ever since I can remember, but it was never supposed to actually happen." She wrinkled her forehead in confusion. "Why did they come out? Am I being punished?" Her face crumpled further. "I should have been there with him."

I put my arm around her. "No, no, don't say that, this has nothing to do with what happened to your boyfriend. That was all a long time ago. I'm sure a good dentist can help you, it's amazing what they can do these days, it's all going to work out, okay?"

"Dentures at twenty-six." Her voice broke a little on her age. "No one will ever want to be with me now. Being so smart and nerdy and opinionated was bad enough. Can never keep my mouth shut. And now...." She covered her mouth with her hand again, then looked over my shoulder at Curtis and the sound guy. "Tell them to leave, Zoe," she whispered. "They can't show this on air, okay? They can't. Tell them."

I waved my hand at Curtis, and he rolled his eyes before they made their retreat. Guess they got what they needed, or maybe they knew the other cameras in the room would get whatever they might miss.

"I want you to win," Michelle whispered. "If it can't be me, I want it to be you."

Frankly I didn't think it would be either of us, but she gave me such a pathetic look, I nodded. "I'll do my best." Hopefully she wouldn't notice the irony in my voice.

She gripped my free hand. "You underrate yourself, Zoe. You can win this, I know you can."

I shrugged. The point wasn't to win. The point was to gain enough notoriety to be attractive to publishers. But I couldn't tell her that.

She looked down at my closed hand hiding her teeth. Between the hand over her mouth and her strange lisp, she was difficult to understand. "I can't stop thinking about Tyler. I haven't thought about him much for years, but now he's all I can think about. I guess I'm making up for lost time. He just...feels so close to me." She shuddered. "Hopefully it will stop once I'm home, and I'll be able to get back to normal. Or something. I don't know, this seemed like a good idea when I signed up, and Emerson is nice enough, but..."—her voice drops even lower than before, as if she's trying to beat her microphone—"I've never felt so inadequate in my life. Not even when I was the most awkward, nerdy eleven-year-old you can imagine."

We had an inferior complex in common. "I hope being home makes you feel better." Home. What a peculiar notion. Even in her current state I felt a twinge of jealousy.

"Tell me your email." I did, and she dropped her hand from her mouth long enough to write it on her inner arm with pen. "We're so close, we're sisters now."

I flinched, Kennedy's betrayal still chafing. "Better than sisters."

She shook her head. "I don't even know if you have a real sister. Or anything about your family." She began to giggle again, a mirthless sound. "Is anything on this island real in any way that matters?"

"She has no idea who you are," Joe said. *"You're all alone. Except for me. I'm the only one who understands you, Pooh Bear. I'm the only one."*

———

When I retreated to the library to decompress, Joe was waiting for me. He sat at the same place at the table that Cannon had when I first met him, only he looked straight at me as I came in the door as if he'd been expecting me. Which I guess he had.

He frowned, his eyes serious and wounded behind his glasses, and I thought of every time he'd demanded I fix things. All by myself, of course. As if I had some special lease on competence, a laugh-worthy idea. Here I was stuck on this horrible island, my best friend here was going home without her teeth in her head, I was embroiled in a pathetic fake love triangle between two men who didn't care about me, and my sister....

At the thought of Kennedy, I almost lost it. I'd given her every pass in the book because of our shared history. But when had we been close? Two decades ago? And now here I was stuck in this horror show. She'd known I wanted to leave, and did she ask me to reconsider like a normal person and then respect my decision? Oh no. Instead she'd lied to me to make sure I was stuck here.

I was surrounded by people who didn't give a damn about me. And Joe, whether he was actually here right now harassing me as I tried to get over him or whether he was some kind of tormented spirit, was at the top of that list.

I marched straight up to him. "I know you're not real," I said. "And you know what? I don't care because I'm still going to give you a piece of my mind."

He held up his hands in a placating gesture. "Pooh Bear, calm down. I was too hasty. I'm giving you a chance to make it up to me."

The way he sat there, so smug and self-assured, so certain I'd run back to him given a half a chance, made me want to scream. "And I guess you expect me to be excited at the opportunity to pay all our bills again? To keep our apartment nice? To make sure you're eating? To coordinate all our social plans? To remind you of your interview requests? To give you notes on everything you've written and then apologize for them when you're feeling discouraged about how the writing's going? You know what, Joe? No thanks. I don't exist to be your muse, and I'm certainly not here to be your mother."

"This isn't a good look, Zoe." He stood up and loomed over me. "You're just bitter because I broke up with you."

"Yes, I am bitter, and do you want to know the reason why? Because I gave myself away for you. I did, I gave up on myself. I thought the only way I'd have any value in the world was if you loved me and were happy with me. I let you lie to me, I let you make me doubt myself, I made every excuse in the book for you instead of having the guts to face the truth. And that is an empty bankrupt kind of way to have to go through life."

He shook his head. "You're under so much pressure here, it's made you confused. I only ever did what was best for you, you know that. Come on, Pooh Bear, be reasonable."

I snorted. "Are kidding me? You only do what's best for *you*. That's the way things have always been. And don't call me Pooh Bear. I'm not five. I'm a grown ass woman."

"Well, you don't act like it," he shot back.

Once that comment would have reduced me to tears, but now I was too angry. "Yeah, I get it. Poor little Zoe is always so sensitive. She's always begging for more attention. She's clingy, she's needy, she wants someone to save her. You know what? That's all true. I *did* want someone to save me. More than anything. I had no idea how to do it myself, and I did wish someone would swoop in and make things better. I wanted my parents to save me, I wanted Kennedy to save me, and I damn sure wanted you to save me."

I slammed my hand down on the table. "And look where that's gotten me! I have no real friends, I'm on a reality TV show that will make me look like a pathetic bitch in front of the entire world, my sister would sell me out for higher ratings without a second thought, I'm sleeping with a beautiful man who's only in love with himself, and I'm hallucinating demeaning conversations with my nightmare ex-fiancé in my spare time. This sure doesn't seem to be working out for me."

I looked up at him, so tall, so shining, my poor broken-down love in tarnished armor. We would never be together again. However wretched I felt about that fact, even knowing exactly how awful things had been between us, it was still true. "Goodbye, Joe," I said. "We're done."

I turned on my heel, ready to give myself the victorious departure I deserved.

"That's all very fine and good." This wasn't Joe's voice, but another man's, smooth with an edge of smoke, a Clint Eastwood voice. "But Joe's actually in New York right now, fucking his way through the literati."

I stopped, swallowed, counted to five before I turned around.

Sitting in the exact same position Joe had assumed when I'd entered smiled a man I'd never seen in my life. "Hi." He stretched like a large cat before putting his hands behind his head. "I'm Darwin. Nice to finally meet you."

Thirty-One

LOVE STORY: Taking a Dark Plunge

—February 5, 2019 by lacey, www.dontcallmegirl.com

I officially called it: the second season of *Love Story* is so dark, it gives *Black Mirror* and *The Twilight Zone* a run for their money. I know reality TV is far removed from actual reality—and even more so in this case, we have to assume—but damn! I don't know what showrunner Jen diCardio has up her sleeve, but I do know I'm in pain waiting till Monday night to find out what happens next.

After the parade of contestant phobias, I wondered where the show could go next. And now we have our answer: group psychosis! Served with a supernatural edge, when several contestants (and the host! Cannon, I believed better of you) lose their shit during an extremely fake-looking séance. Gusts of wind out of nowhere? Flickering lights? Really? And where did they find that woman who was running the ceremony? She probably reads Tarot at some major tourist center the rest of the year.

You'd think this twist would wreck havoc on any claim of plausibility for the show until you look at the polls and realize 45% of Americans believe in ghosts or spirits of the dead and 65% of Americans believe in the supernatural. What about the rest of us? Well, I definitely believe in the potent combination of the power of suggestion and reality TV's ability to alter its contestants' sense of reality, so hey presto! They might really be onto something here.

Never have I seen a reality show so eager to illustrate the wreckage it induces on its poor cast members. Watching the women confront their fears was bad enough, but when Cassidy broke down as her hair started falling out in episode three? That's when I realized this season is trying to do something different. True fact, I've started brushing my own hair less, just in case. And WebMD tells me hair can start to fall out from stress, just to give us all something else to worry about.

In its own way, it was even worse watching Zoe pivot from clueless tortured artist to ruthless and calculated schemer. I don't think any of us actually like Vivian, but to give her full body hives so she has no chance of winning the fashion competition? Damn, girl! Turn it down a notch...or ten. Notice too how the producers knew exactly what was going down but didn't intervene. Zoe got her precious (and super boring, natch) date with the bland Emerson, who's feeling more and more like a MacGuffin than a viable long-term romantic interest. And we finally got the Zoe tears I'd predicted, only shed with faux remorse instead of actual angst. At one point I found myself literally yelling at my screen, "Get it together, Zoe, you're better than this!" But when the show tries to redeem her what feels like two minutes later, it's so much whiplash I have trouble taking this plotline seriously.

But if Cassidy's breakdown was disturbing and Zoe's transformation disappointing, the season kicks into ultra high gear in the fourth episode with the sudden turn to the truly macabre: that bizarre séance in the middle of the night in what is becoming hard to think is any kind of paradise. The tone of the show, already uneven, went full Horror Show Central Casting. Who thought that was a good idea? And have they now received a promotion, because while on paper it sounds like a terrible idea —vibes of a pathetic *Blair Witch Project* wannabe—it gave us the best drama of this season yet.

This is the obligatory moment when I start to wonder how much the contestants were coached ahead of time. Okay, yes, the wind was too much, along with that medium—where the hell did she even come from?

—but I have to admit my blood ran cold watching all their faces, particularly Cannon and Michelle. The group ennui quickly transformed into disorientation and then outright panic, and the results were riveting to watch. Cannon has never distinguished himself as being much of an actor, which is why he has the gig hosting *Love Story* instead of trying to claw his way out of reality TV to something better. But he looked genuinely panicked. And you could tell when he pulled Zoe aside afterwards to talk about it that he was still upset. If the whole thing was staged, the producers didn't bring Cannon into the loop. Which I guess, given the aforementioned lack of acting chops, is understandable.

If the séance was inspired, Michelle's moment in the spotlight when she spits out all those teeth was more of a gross-out moment than anything else. I went to her Instagram to check on whether she's gotten implants since the show, but she, like her fellow castmates, isn't posting anything. Yup, not a single contestant has cracked thus far. Weird, huh?

Meanwhile, the ranks of women are being winnowed, and it's beginning to feel brutal. At this last Culling, Emerson cut two more potentials, so he's down to thirteen options. Several women are now hanging on by threads: how is Lucy still around? And Lauren is there based solely on her looks; she and Emerson have barely exchanged five words since the show began. The competition for the private dates next episode should be particularly fierce, and I can't help but wonder (cross fingers!) if the show will double down and become even darker.

Xoxo Lacey

THIRTY-TWO

My heart beat too fast in my chest as I contemplated the ghost in front of me. "It's been you all along," I said. Not my imagination. Not a sign Joe was dead and his spirit pining for me. No, this was Margaret's fiancé, Adelaide's secret passion, and the reason for this show's chaos. "I've heard a lot about you."

His lips quirked. "I know. I do seem to make a bit of an...impression, don't I?"

I hated him for being handsome: his wavy blonde hair, his strong jawline, the smirk on his face. His eyes were a little bit too close together, giving intensity to his stare, and he wore chinos and a lime green polo shirt like he was on vacation. "What do you want?"

"Never one to mince words, are you, pet?" His lips spread further, revealing blinding white teeth. "Or should I call you 'Pooh Bear?'" He was mocking me. "I've been waiting for you for a long time."

I fought against the fear making my heart race faster. "You didn't even know I existed until I showed up on the island a few weeks ago."

"So sure of yourself. And so entirely wrong." He stood up, and the chair didn't move even the tiniest bit. He wasn't physically present. But he looked so real. "I've been searching for my perfect mate my entire life and"—he gestured down at his illusory body and laughed—"a long time after that. The moment I saw you, I knew you were the one. We have so much in common."

I took a careful step back. "We don't have anything in common."

"We want the same thing, don't we? You're here on a show called *Love Story* and you want me to believe you're not looking for your own true love? Please. I know how you felt about Joe. I know how much you wanted that." He paused, leaned in. "And I know how it broke you to lose it."

"You're wrong." My voice quavered, and I wished so hard that someone, anyone, would come through the door behind me. Even Vivian.

"Am I?" He stopped his stalk forward. "We both know the truth that lives in your heart, Zoe. We both know what you need." His voice enveloped me, silky smooth. "You can't always determine the shape of true love."

"I know it doesn't look like you," I said sharply, and then I bolted before he could say anything else.

His laughter rang in my head. *"Oh, Zoe,"* he said. *"You should know by now it doesn't matter where you go. You can't leave me behind. And in time you won't want to."*

I slammed the door behind me, my whole body trembling. He'd chosen me. I didn't know what that meant, but it couldn't be anything good.

I knew ahead of time I'd survive the next Culling. Kennedy had made it clear she wasn't ready to let me go. And she was unknowingly playing right into Darwin's hands.

Besides, Emerson seemed to be becoming vaguely fond of me. He kept everyone he'd taken on an individual date—except Michelle, of course—and I couldn't help wondering if I'd have won the date like Margaret had insisted if I hadn't sabotaged Vivian. Surviving another week turned into its own justification.

Not that I wanted to stay. But I was the only one who didn't.

"Do you ever think," I asked Lucy and Simone as we were getting ready for the Culling in our room, "the price we're paying to be here is too high? Look what happened to Michelle."

Simone shrugged. "Poor thing." She continued dabbing on eye shadow. "She was so pleased after their date. Like, genuinely excited. If you had told me then that she'd be gone now, I wouldn't have believed it."

Lucy sniffed. "She didn't have what it took." She eyed her boob tape critically, turning to one side and then another to see if her boobs were even. "It's too bad she couldn't handle herself, but better for him to find that out now, right? He needs someone who can step up and support all his endeavors a hundred percent."

"Geez, how compassionate, Lucy," I couldn't help snapping. I could still remember the feeling of Michelle's teeth in my palm. "Besides, it's not like this house models real life in any meaningful way."

She remained fixated on her breasts. "You don't have to get all worked up about it. But this experience has been designed so Emerson can choose his ideal mate. And in order to do that, he needs to know how each of us responds under pressure." Simone and I exchanged a glance. "Really, this isn't about us. This is about what Emerson needs."

"Just another way to prop up the white supremacist, decadent capitalist, homophobic, transphobic patriarchy, all gussied up as an entertaining search for true love that tramples on the mental health of all the women involved." Simone put on her earrings as she talked, as if she weren't speaking fighting words.

"You guys take things way too seriously." Lucy grabbed her dress. "After all, we signed up for this. It's an amazing opportunity, so if you want to be culled tonight, fine, but I'm here to fight till the bitter end. And none of us should have to be distracted by someone who can't take the pressure."

"Her teeth literally fell out of her head," I said. "Did you see her afterwards? It wasn't her fault. Besides, she was our friend."

Lucy adjusted the bust of her dress to show a little more cleavage. "Them's the breaks." She smiled at her reflection, and I had to throttle the wish that I'd given her hives instead of Vivian. I hoped she'd get sent home in the Culling.

But she didn't, worse luck. For her more than for me.

Michelle's fate continued to bother me as we waited for the next challenge announcement. The remaining Gold Diggers sunned by the pool, relaxing and giggling as if they'd already forgotten Michelle. All except Vivian, who had been keeping to herself after the hive incident. With no friends remaining in the house, she didn't have anyone inviting her to hang out.

Even without Vivian's presence, I could only take so much of the good cheer and banal conversation. After lunch I changed into real clothes and hid in the conservatory, where none of the other women were likely to go. After all, they were on this show to be seen, not to hang out with some plants.

I was staring at an empty page of my journal, not sure what to write about Michelle and my aborted attempt to escape. My fear proved, once again, that I didn't have what it took to be a writer. A real artist would be willing to sacrifice anything, isn't that what Joe always said? And here I was desperately wanting to run away.

The blank page slowly filled with crossed-out false starts. When Margaret rounded the corner at a slow shuffle, brushing up against some of the giant ferns, I almost felt relieved.

A relief that was short-lived. "You haven't come to see me." The hand that held her cane shook.

Once I was sure she wasn't about to collapse, I took a good look at her. Her color was good, maybe a little high in the cheeks. The fussy draperies of her gray dress hid her body effectively, but her eyes looked as shrewd and bright as before. "I didn't know you were well enough to receive visitors." True enough. "And I've been a little busy."

She frowned. "Oh, I know exactly what you've been doing."

Already back to her spying. Although with a vengeful ghost stalking her, I guess I couldn't blame her. "I'm glad you're feeling better, but are you sure you shouldn't be resting?"

She laughed at me. "I've been in this body for seventy-four years. I think I know what it is I need." She narrowed her eyes, as if my appearance was giving something away. "Come along then, follow me." She started to wend her way back through the maze of plants, one slow step at a time. Right before she rounded the corner she turned back. "Unless you'd like to talk about everything out in the open?"

"Don't go with her," Darwin said. *"You have me now."*

But I refused to listen to him. "I'm coming." I gave her a rictus of a smile.

I followed her up to her surveillance closet like an obedient puppy. She locked the door behind us, then immediately settled into her comfortable chair and took a long breath. "How was your date with my nephew?" she asked.

For once I knew something she didn't. She could have watched all the footage from the cameras, but there hadn't been hidden cameras watching every second while we'd been off the island. No way was I going to say anything about my aborted escape attempt and Kennedy's machinations. "We had a good time," I said instead. "He was a perfect gentleman, right up until our evening was cut short."

"Yes, yes, less time for the two of you to get physical. How sad." She took a sip from an insulated water bottle.

"Not as sad as what happened to Michelle." My worry about Michelle was eating away at me. "I wish I could check my email, see how she's doing."

Margaret nodded at a laptop on the table in front of her. "Go ahead."

A connection to the outside world! The smooth silver laptop had suddenly become something I wanted desperately, a symbol of life outside this island. "What's the catch?" Because if there was one thing I'd noticed, it was that Margaret didn't tend to do things out of the kindness of her heart.

"Let me look over your shoulder while you're checking."

"This is a mistake," Darwin said. *"Nothing comes without a price."*

But I was done listening to that poisonous little voice. Margaret was already watching the rest of my life. Why not this too? "Done."

She took the laptop, guarded it jealously while typing in her password, then proffered it to me like a holy tablet. I didn't hesitate to pull up the other chair and log into my email, trying to ignore Margaret's inquisitive gaze as I scrolled down the screen.

Aside from the inevitable junk, I had a few emails from friends who were going to be passing through New York. No one knew Joe and I had broken up, or that I had fled to California completely wrecked. Nothing from Michelle, and nothing from my dad either. No big surprise there.

But there was an email from Thea. I felt like I hadn't seen her in a very long time.

To: zoezoezoe@goodmail.com
From: theacmasters@goodmail.com
Date: October 20, 2018
Subject: It's not the same.

I thought I could just come back home and resume my old life, but everything has changed, and not because I'm famous. I wish. No one will know who I am until the show airs next year, not that I lasted long enough to make a real impact.

But I'm not writing to you to bitch about my failure. Well, not much. The truth is I'm not doing well. My roommate thought I'd be gone longer and sublet my room for another month, so I've been sleeping out on the couch, what little sleeping I can do. I don't know if it's sleeping in the living room or what, but every night I have terrible dreams. I wake up gasping in the middle of the night, and once that happens, that's it. No more sleep for me. I have to turn on every light till the apartment's positively blazing.

And I think there's something wrong with my hearing. More and more when people speak to me I simply can't understand them. You know how I am, I'm not shy, so I ask them to repeat themselves, but it doesn't matter how many times they do. It's as if they're speaking another language. I need to go to the doctor, but I'm afraid of how much it'll cost.

I've tried to reach out to some of the other women who were eliminated to see how they're adjusting, but no one has written back. Well, except for Cassidy's mom, who wrote to say she's in a residential treatment center. I guess she's doing even worse than me.

Please be nice to Vivian, won't you? I worry about her all alone with no friends. She's not as bad as she seems, I swear. Not once you get to know her.

Please write when you get back. I feel like no one here can understand what I'm going through.

\- Thea

PS: I feel like I'm slowly going crazy, lol.

I pulled the laptop slightly away from Margaret, feeling like I'd showed her something unexpectedly intimate. But she'd already read Thea's words and was shaking her head. "It's spreading," she said. "I warned him this was a bad idea. *I warned him.*"

A sudden deep exhaustion swept over me. "Who did you warn?"

"My stupid blockhead of a nephew." She fell back into her chair with a little groan. "I told him not to do this show. Not here. I might have a penance to pay, but nobody else is supposed to suffer. This wasn't part of the plan."

"Penance for what? It's not your fault you're being haunted by a ghost."

She raised her eyebrows. "Oh, so the séance turned you into a believer?" I hesitated, wondering how angry Darwin would be if I told her I'd been talking to him. "You've heard about the tragedy that happened here. The first house, how it burned down and everyone died." It wasn't a question. She knew we'd all been talking about it. "Well, it's not quite true. Everyone didn't die. I was the sole survivor."

"You were here?"

She nodded. "I wasn't supposed to be. I was on my way home for my father's birthday. But there was a hurricane warning, my flight was canceled, and I decided it would be easier to come back here. To this day, sometimes I think, what if I'd stayed in George Town, waited for another flight out." She shook her head. "And what if, fool child that I was, I hadn't been here and had stayed with Darwin afterwards? Married him, even? Without seeing things for myself, I might not have understood."

I didn't want to interrupt her, but it sounded as if Darwin might have survived the fire and whatever had led to it. Might have, but didn't. And if she'd been there after all, a witness to everything that happened...she might be the only one who truly knew what had happened.

"You can't trust anything she's saying," Darwin whispered in his mind. I hated that I was actually finding myself agreeing with him.

But Margaret continued, unaware of my internal turmoil. "I might have *chosen* not to understand, more like. I was so in love with him back then, I had the judgment of a peahen. He was dabbling in dark forces neither of us understood." She ran her finger across the smooth face of her amulet. "I looked for his amulet afterwards, the one that matched mine. And I have to admit I was relieved to find it missing. He used it as some sort of repository for the power from the sick and twisted things he was doing." She shuddered. "I wear this one now to remind me to avoid hubris at all costs. And yet here we are, in spite of my best efforts."

I had an idea of what she meant by sick and twisted from reading Adelaide's diary. "The architect who designed this house...I found a journal she'd left behind, and she mentions a Darwin. You're not the only one he's been haunting."

Margaret didn't seem surprised. "Poor Adelaide. I told my father what would happen if he tried to rebuild. My life has been a series of men ignoring what I have to say."

"What happened to her? Did she end up having a successful career?"

"Oh no. Her only legacy is what remains here on this island. It swallowed her whole."

I felt a pang. Adelaide's diary had been strange, but she wasn't so different from me: floundering through life, ending up on this island by accident, trying to get her shit together and get something to work. "What happened to her?"

Margaret looked me straight in the eyes. "She killed herself. In that terrible boat you like so much. I can't stand to go there myself." She twisted her amulet around her neck.

God. Poor Adelaide. All those blank pages. Falling in love with a ghost, and then...killing herself to join him?

Margaret's eyes narrowed. "If Darwin ever starts talking to you, Zoe, just remember, he's a mass murderer. He's responsible for the deaths of all those women. My friends. And I will always bear part of the burden of his crimes. He's dangerous, and you can't trust a word he says."

"Tell her you're talking to me, and you'll be sorry," Darwin hissed in my ear.

The stories about him scared me enough that I kept my mouth shut.

Thirty-Three

The Chicago Globe, November 15, 2018

MICHELLE HOWARD, GRADUATE STUDENT IN PHYSICS AT STANFORD UNIVERSITY, DEAD AT 25

A native of Chicago, Michelle Howard made her friends and family proud when she was accepted to Stanford University's doctoral program in physics after graduating summa cum laude from Northwestern University in 2015.

"She had a real passion for science and mathematics ever since she was little," her mother, Irene Howard, said. "She always won first prize at the science fair, and her father started to teach her to program when she was only seven years old. Her first love was always space, which is why she was so excited to study astrophysics."

In addition to her academic studies, Michelle enjoyed playing the clarinet and competing in track and field. After her grandmother taught her to sew, she also helped with many of the costumes for Walter Payton College Prep's dramatic productions. Her high school physics teacher encouraged her to pursue her studies in science, and she decided to major in physics and mathematics at Northwestern University.

"The happiest day of her life was when she was accepted to Stanford to study for her PhD," her mother said. "When she opened the letter, she looked up at me and she said, "Mom, there's finally going to be a doctor in the family.""

"Michelle was a very promising student," her advisor at Stanford, Dr. Jeffrey Lewis, said. "Very bright and hard-working. Her early death is a tragedy for all those who knew her and for the scientific community."

Howard, 25, died October 31 at Northwestern Memorial Hospital in Chicago after being involved in a motorcycle accident six days earlier. She had been taking the semester off to spend more time with her family, her mother said.

"She was a brilliant scientist, true, but she was also a selfless and caring person," her mother said. "That's how her family would like her to be remembered."

In addition to her mother, Howard is survived by her father, Peter; a sister, Elizabeth Quinn; two brothers, Joshua and Eric Howard; her grandparents Peter and Gladys Howard and Beth O'Connor.

Services were held.

THIRTY-FOUR

We didn't expect the day to end in blood.

Tears, certainly, along with recriminations, sulks, snide remarks, and overdrinking: the normal aftermath to one of the weekly challenges, as all the losers commiserated and hated on the winners, who either attempted humility or stood aloof from the drama of it all.

The theme of the challenge was "Design Emerson's Perfect Date," and I had it in the bag. It was as if Kennedy designed it specifically for me. There were "clues" hidden around the house and grounds about Emerson's preferences, but I wouldn't have to bother looking. Between the time I'd already spent with Emerson and my inside knowledge from Kennedy, Margaret, and Cannon, I'd be able to give him exactly what he wanted.

Plus I had plenty of experience. I'm sure you can guess who did all the date planning in my relationship with Joe.

But in the end my experience didn't matter. Kennedy cornered me in the bedroom, where I'd retreated after the announcement while the rest of the house bustled with activity, and gave me a completed dossier. "This is your date with Emerson," she said. "It's already scheduled for Thursday."

I tried not to rise to her bait. "He might not choose it."

"Oh, Cannon didn't mention that, did he? The judging will be done by the producers. We need more advance planning than a day or two to make anything interesting happen." She waved the folder in my face. "Here."

I didn't take it. "That's cheating."

She shoved it forward. "You're welcome." I shook my head and she gave her long-suffering sigh. "This isn't an actual game show, you do know that, right? There are no rules here, no code of honor you have to live by. We're trying to tell a good story, that's all that matters. And you and Emerson have become a good story. Good enough and we might not even show who gave Vivian those hives. You never wanted to be the villain, did you?"

I took the folder and stared down at it balefully. "You know I didn't. You said I wouldn't be."

"How could I have known the lengths you would go to win a date with Mr. Dreamboat out there?"

I rolled my eyes. "Please. Let's not pretend this whole thing hasn't been masterminded by you." She was wearing a black T-shirt that said "Shut Up" that further illustrated my point.

"I think of it as doing the world a service." She tightened her ponytail and then cocked her head, listening to something coming in over her earpiece. "I gotta go, they need me downstairs. Have fun with your day off."

"Which other woman are you giving a date?" I called after her. There were supposed to be two winners, after all. But she continued down the hall like I didn't exist.

I sat down on the bed and flipped through the pages in front of me. Apparently Emerson had a passion for deep sea fishing, so I was going to dose up on Dramamine and spend a day at sea with him, after which I was going to personally prepare a fish dinner for the two of us. I hoped Kennedy had taken into account my basic skills in the kitchen, which covered pasta, baked chicken, breakfast foods, tacos, and not much else. Like whatever kind of fish we were hoping to catch.

In between these thrilling activities we'd have an afternoon interlude receiving a couple's massage. And of course the whole document was laced with references to Emerson's favorites: his favorite color, his favorite band, his favorite wine. I'd done this kind of thing for Joe all the time. I didn't really care about baseball but we went to games; I knew how to make his mom's pot roast; I'd watched six seasons of *The Walking Dead*.

Was I really ready to do that all over again?

I was sneaking down the hall, planning to leave the house before anyone noticed I wasn't franticly prepping my date, when I heard the sounds of crying from Vivian's bedroom. I stopped, almost kept going, then sighed and took a peek inside.

The room was dark, a single shaft of light falling across one set of bunk beds from a slight gap in the draperies. Not so dark I couldn't make out the long blonde hair draping over the pillow of the mattress in the center of the room. At first, flashing back to Cassidy's hair loss, I wasn't certain it was attached to a body, and my stomach gave a sickening lurch. But then a face swiveled to look at me.

"You. Go away!"

Vivian was nothing if not direct, and I almost did as she said. It wasn't like I had any love for her either, even if I did feel guilty about her hives. Now they'd faded, I wanted to pretend they'd never happened, like they were just another weird side effect of this distorted fun house.

I knew better though. They had been completely my fault. The desire to pass the buck and blame Kennedy was a gnawing sensation in my gut. But I'd been the one who did the sprinkling. I'd been the one who followed Kennedy's orders for the sake of keeping the peace. I'd been the one desperate to jumpstart my writing career.

God, I hated myself sometimes.

"Are you okay?" I asked.

The fact she didn't instantly tell me to go fuck myself gave me all the information I needed. I waded into the mire of discarded leggings, tank tops, sandals, and makeup bags and crouched down beside her bed. "Hey, what's going on?"

She looked up at me, and it was the most real I'd seen her. Hair messy, eyes rimmed in red, makeup cried off, cheeks damp. "What do you care?

Miss 'I think I'm better than everyone else because I know how to read a book.'"

"Hey now, I'm sure you've read at least one book in your lifetime."

She surprised me by laughing at my sad little joke. "My favorite book is *The Handmaid's Tale*. I read it over and over in high school."

I blinked. "Kind of dark for high school."

She shrugged. "Sometimes hard times call for dark reading, don't you think?"

"Yeah."

"I'm failing," she whispered. She wasn't looking at me anymore, but rather some indeterminate point somewhere past my shoulder.

"That's not true." What else could I say?

She shook her head. "Emerson doesn't know who I am. I have no friends in the house, everyone thinks I'm a bitch. Once this shitshow airs, the entire world will agree with them. And those hives, they're going to show those hives...." Her jaw hardened. "That was you, wasn't it?" I opened my mouth to deny it, but she didn't let me. "No, don't say anything, I know you won't admit to it, but it had to be you. I didn't think you had it in you, but the producers probably put you up to it, right? You pretend to be all hard, but at heart you're a big pushover. Besides, it's not like you would have thought ahead and packed some insane hive-producing substance ahead of time." A pause. "Unless you're crazier than I think you are."

"Never rule out insanity in your opponents."

She laughed again. "You're kind of funny, you know that? Ruthless and with a flawed moral center, but also funny."

"I decided I needed to have at least one redeeming trait."

She sighed. "That's more than I have. God, I haven't even managed to be an interesting villain. Turns out I'm not the queen of the bon mot I thought I was. I'm just...completely ordinary." She said the last as if it were a particularly disgusting form of disease. "Ugh, Ainsley's never going to let me live it down. Not like she ever has anything to worry about, she's everyone's favorite. Especially Dad's. I'm the family failure, I might as well just accept it."

"Ainsley's your sister?"

She nodded. "Married rich, has two disgustingly cute children who I adore to pieces, and she has her own successful lifestyle company. In the eyes of my parents, she can do no wrong." She groaned and collapsed back on her pillow. "Not that I have anything to complain about. I've lived a charmed life, I know that, I'm just so fucking sick of apologizing for it all the time." She put an arm over her head. "God, I'm a terrible person."

I couldn't believe I was comforting Vivian of all people, but here we were, and I owed her. "I don't think reality TV exactly selects for people who are well-adjusted and have all their shit together," I said. "Hell, we signed a piece of paper agreeing to allow our every move to be recorded for weeks on end so we could compete for a mystery man. We're all in this together." I gave her a tentative pat on the shoulder and considered it a success when she didn't jerk violently away.

And then I had what Kennedy would later refer to as a temporary fit of insanity. "Here." I gave Vivian the date dossier. "Turn this in as your planned date."

"You're already done?" Her mouth opened in an "O" of shock.

"Don't ask any questions, okay? Just...take it, turn it in, and trust me, you'll get a date this week."

"What are you doing?" Darwin was almost shouting in my head. *"Don't help that bitch out. Take the date. TAKE IT!"*

His distress gave me confidence. Vivian eyed the folder suspiciously. "What do you get out of it?"

"Finally doing the right thing." She kept staring at me. "Look, I've already had a date, okay? I probably won't be cut this week. You need this way more than I do." She wasn't wrong about my flawed moral center either. If this gesture would ease some of the gnawing discomfort I felt about the way I'd treated her, however big a bitch she was, well, that was my own business. "Also I can die happy having never gone deep sea fishing so maybe you're the one doing me a favor."

She opened the folder and started to read. "Oh, this is great. My dad does deep sea fishing, and I've gone with him a bunch of times." She looked up at me. "Are you sure you want to give this to me? Not that I'm giving it back, just so we're clear."

If she and Emerson could enjoy themselves, more power to them. No matter what Kennedy said, I was emotionally checked out. "Knock yourself out."

She went back to reading. "You could have given this to Lucy, you know." I didn't say anything. The last few days it had been all I could do restraining myself from plastering tape over Lucy's mouth to shut her up. After her callous reaction to Michelle's fate, I wanted as little to do with her as possible. But I wasn't going to admit that, not to Vivian of all people. It wasn't like we were friends now. We just weren't actively trying to sabotage one another in the present moment.

"Yeah, join the club, she annoys the hell out of me too," Vivian said. "I couldn't figure out why the two of you were friends. Why'd you choose her to cling to?"

What could I say? "She was the first person I met."

Vivian sat up, wiped under her eyes, and took a deep breath. "My mother says you are the accumulation of the five people you spend the most time with." She looked at me, green eyes glittering. "Just something to think about."

It wasn't my blood at the end of the challenge, although if looks could injure, it would have been; Kennedy was furious when Vivian turned in the deep sea fishing date instead of me. But it was as I had suspected; Kennedy couldn't pivot the planned dates fast enough to do anything but go along with it or admit to all the Gold Diggers present that the whole thing was rigged. And an insurrection of thirteen insecure and bored women against the producers wasn't what she had in mind for this season's storyline.

They had Cannon "announce" the winners back by the pool, which meant an hour of prep beforehand. When we were all casually draped on loungers in our most flattering bikinis, Cannon stepped outside with Emerson beside him, which meant we were contractually obligated to squeal with excitement and descend on Emerson in a hug-seeking hoard. Cannon took the opportunity to give me a lingering look, and I could feel my cheeks heating.

Once we'd all settled back down, Cannon got right to the point. "Ladies, I have to say, the amount of thought and creativity that went into planning these dates is impressive. I think you could even teach the producers a thing or two." Laughter. "I'm sure Emerson wishes he could go on every single one of these dates"—Emerson nodded—"but unfortunately, we only have time for two. And the selected winners are...." He paused for effect. Lucy clutched my shoulder, and even Naomi, the coolest of cool, looked on edge. "Simone and Vivian!"

"You really fucked this up," Darwin hissed in my ear.

The remaining Gold Diggers struggled to keep their smiles in place, a front to hide their disappointment. Being in week three meant there was a lot of pressure to get a date if you hadn't already had one or you were in real danger of ending up on the chopping block. For me to have a *second* date at this point...well, I would have definitely become the frontrunner by default, and everyone else would have hated me.

Could Kennedy be trying to isolate me? Exactly what kind of story was she trying to tell here?

Lucy hadn't stopped clutching my arm, and I turned to say something consoling. Her face was drained of color, her blue eyes blinking rapidly, reminding me of a camera shutter.

A small whining sound, high, like a mosquito, and then blood erupted from her face.

It all happened so fast. One minute I was sitting there, trying to think of something inane to say to keep Lucy's tears at bay, and then I was springing backwards, away from the bright torrent. I couldn't even tell if it was coming from her nose or her mouth, just that there was a never-ending gush of red. She doubled over, pressing her hands to her face in a futile attempt to stem the flow. It spread out in grotesque patches on her thighs, on the towel we'd been sitting on, on the stone tiles.

In a moment Lucy was surrounded by a circle of black-clad producers, a flock of carrion crows hunched over her body. I stared, motionless, every second stretched out to its breaking point, until I eventually gave into the persistent tugging on my hand and allowed myself to be drawn away.

Cannon led me with decision, guiding me inside, up the stairs, and down a long hallway, into a part of the house I'd never seen before. My mind had gone into a kind of frozen fugue, making a slight twitch every several seconds, almost as if to see if it were safe to wake up again. No, the answer kept coming back. No. Too much blood. Too much. The hair, the teeth, the great swollen hives on Vivian's body like over-ripened apricots, Margaret Courtland shuddering in some kind of fit, all for the benefit of the always watching cameras. It was too much.

So as long as he kept leading me away, I'd follow Cannon anywhere he wanted to go.

He unlocked a closed door, revealing a bedroom with a four poster, pillows flung everywhere, a huge fireplace, a laptop thrown carelessly on a sofa. The rug bloomed with flowers under my bare feet. He removed my mic pack from my bikini, pulled off his own, threw them out the door, and shut it with an authoritative click.

"Don't worry," he said, crooned really, in his trademark sexy drawl. "No cameras in here. It might not be a fancy guesthouse like Emerson's, but it's safe, I promise."

I stared at him in his crisp blue button-down, his perfectly creased khakis, the leather shoes with all the tiny holes in it as if someone had sat there punching them with a needle all day long. It was as if he were speaking a foreign language.

"Zoe. We need to get you cleaned up."

I looked down to see a spray of blood across my chest. My cleavage, shown off to best advantage by my bikini top, looked like it belonged in a slasher movie instead of a hot summer romance. I tried to remember feeling any kind of splash, any wetness, but the evidence in front of my eyes seemed entirely removed from what had happened down by the pool.

I wondered if I had blood on my face. I was afraid to look.

Cannon had already gone into the adjoining bathroom and turned on the shower. He kicked off his shoes, stripped off his perfect khakis, one button at a time until the shirt was off, peeling away the socks, the tight black boxer briefs, the whole time with me watching as though he were not a man I'd once had sex with but some kind of machine wholly removed from me.

He brought me under the hot water and began lathering my body with soap. I looked up at the shower head and imagined the water as the flow of blood exiting Lucy's body. I began to shake in spite of the heat, and somehow Cannon noticed. He wrapped his arms around me, resting my chin on his shoulder. "You've had a shock, Zoe, that's all this is." He spoke right next to my right ear. "But you're not hurt, you're just fine. Do you hear me? You're going to be just fine."

I stared up at the water for a long time. I kept forgetting to breathe. Now that he mentioned it, I didn't think I'd been fine for quite some time.

Thirty-Five

Transcript from *Love & Bubbles*, episode 13, hosted by Olivia Childs for *Everything Entertainment Online*, February 12, 2019:

Olivia Childs: We've got redemption, we've got blood and gore, and most importantly, we've finally got a hot tub!

Hi everyone, I'm Olivia Childs, and here we are for more down and dirty dishing on *Love & Bubbles* recapping Emerson Courtland's season of *Love Story*. (She raises her full champagne flute in a toast gesture.)

Can you believe what happened on our romantic tropical island this episode? It's been a bizarre season, I have to say. Hair loss, a creepy séance, contestants dropping like flies. And this episode didn't disappoint in the weird department.

I liked seeing Zoe realize she'd taken her rivalry with Vivian too far and actually attempt to make amends for it. She must have put a lot of thought into planning the perfect date with Emerson, and then to just hand it over to Vivian, knowing she'd get zero credit? I thought it was a classy gesture. And props to Vivian for suspecting Zoe was behind the hives and not being afraid to say so. What did you guys think? Do you appreciate Zoe trying to make amends for her bad behavior or do you think it doesn't matter unless she comes clean and apologizes? Tell me in the comments, m'kay? Either way, it worked out well for Vivian, who finally got a private date with our leading man.

But first, Lucy's spectacular...I was going to say melt-down, but it was hardly her fault. I'll never forget the look on Zoe's face when that first gush of blood sprayed across her. And Emerson just stood there as if he were frozen in place. Poor Lucy. She's been trying all season to make an impression, and love her or hate her, you have to admit she is genuinely dedicated to Emerson. She must be absolutely mortified with how her time ended. Although I think we're all taking a big sigh of relief that we'll no longer be drowning in her tears every week.

Meanwhile, while everyone was busy trying to help Lucy, Cannon came out of nowhere and whisked Zoe away. Thank goodness someone did because it looked like she was about to collapse, but I have to say, I wasn't expecting Cannon to go back to his knight in shining armor roots. I mean, you can tell he means well, but he's always been a bit in his own head, and he's the first to admit it. So what was going on here? Was this just an example of good producing? Or is Cannon finally developing more of a nurturing side? Let me know what you think about Cannon and how he's handling his job as host. (Takes a gulp of champagne.)

Well! After all that drama, the show must go on, and Vivian gets her long-coveted date. And what a date it was! (Another sip of champagne.) Vivian has been a dark horse in this race so far. Gorgeous, of course, and sharp as a tack, but wasting a lot of time fighting with Zoe over being the villain of the season. But she flung herself wholeheartedly into this date, showing Emerson she can fit into his world, and it turns out the couple have some serious chemistry! I'm pretty sure that was the steamiest make out session so far this season. Whew! (fans face) Vivian's going to give Giselle and Zoe a run for their money, that's for sure.

And then we had Simone's date with Emerson, which was sweet but lacked some heat. It also felt more generic: who doesn't love a romantic horseback ride along the beach followed by an elaborate picnic and a secluded Jacuzzi soak? But we've seen that date so many times before, it made me wonder why she won the date in the first place.

I will say, it's a pleasure to watch her. She's so collected and direct, she doesn't let Emerson get away with any of the tricks he plays with the other women. (Cuts to clip of the hot tub, with Simone batting her fake eyelashes and saying, "Let's cut to the chase, Emerson. I know you're dating a bunch of fabulous, sexy women. But let's see if I can make you forget them for a moment." She then leans in to kiss him, pressing her mostly bare body against him in the process.) Yes, that woman has confidence and poise to die for.

And then finally, another Culling. It went about how I expected. All the frontrunners remained: Giselle, Zoe, Vivian, Simone, and Grace, who we haven't seen much of since she sprained her ankle. Nine women left in total. It will be really hard for the other four to catch up with the progress the frontrunners have made, but look what happened last season. Anything's possible!

So everyone, let me know where your heads are at and who you're thinking is going to make it to the end. Do you think it will be one of the frontrunners or do you think we'll have another upset? Let me know in the comments. I love you guys so much, don't forget to DM me and tell me your theories. Thanks for watching, and ta-ta for now!

Thirty-Six

After our shower, Cannon and I slept with each other.

Yes, we were swept away in the moment. Once he'd washed away all the blood and held me for a very long time, I let him comfort me in another way. And you know what else? I have zero regrets. I'd do it again.

Afterwards, I rested my head on his chest and he stroked my hair until I felt like maybe I wasn't a mere inch from losing my sanity. His body was warm, his touch was gentle, and he knew when to shut up. "I don't know if I can keep doing this," I whispered. Not that I had much choice, but it still felt good to say out loud, out of reach of the mocking cameras.

"I could tell you it gets easier, but I'd be lying. Each week is harder than the last. Do what you can to rest."

"Unless I get eliminated." Hope sprung eternal.

"You know that's not going to happen yet. Emerson likes you."

The absurdity of being naked in the arms of another man reassuring me about Emerson's affections was not lost on me. "He doesn't know me."

"Do any of us really know one another? How many times have you been completely surprised by something a boyfriend of yours has done?"

My silence was answer enough. "Exactly. In some ways this isn't so different from what we do to each other all the time."

"You're full of shit." I didn't expect the affection I heard in my own voice.

"That I am. Look how well you know *me* already." He kissed the top of my head. "Just be careful, okay? You know why things get harder as you progress on these shows?"

"I have a feeling you're about to tell me."

He didn't let my sarcasm stop him. "Sure, you get more tired, but the key thing is your emotions become more and more involved. Most people decide to be on a show like this, they think they're going to have fun, they're going to be a big shot back home once they're on TV, maybe they can even leverage it into something better for themselves career-wise or relationship-wise. But you don't get a lot of true romantics showing up. I mean, sure, you get the occasional Lucy, but in general, nobody thinks they're actually going to fall in love. That's why everyone is talking shit about how they're "open to it" and "what if they could be meeting their future wife" and about how the love interest is "the complete package." It keeps them detached from the whole thing."

"You're not going to get any argument from me." I knew I'd said similar things during my Hot Seats. With the producer sitting right there priming you, asking you pointed questions, what else were you going to say? They'd keep you sitting there for hours if you didn't give them what they wanted.

"Yes, well, as the days go by, that changes." I looked pointedly into his eyes, then down to my naked breasts, and he laughed. "Yes, well, maybe it hasn't changed for you yet. But this is a stressful situation, and whether you like it or not, going through the fire together makes you bond. You can find yourself in love with someone before you even realize it's happening."

Like he and I were bonding? But I didn't say it out loud. "I'll be careful."

"Just remember you're being manipulated by the show, and those romantic feelings you have? They're not real."

How many of the women from his seasons had he thought he was in love with? Only to be rejected or have the relationship crumble once it was off camera? Once I got through this season, I couldn't imagine returning. "Did you have fun on *Her Engagement*?" I asked. "Is that why you went back a second time?"

It might have been my imagination, but it seemed like the muffled thumping of his heart sped up at my question. "I went back because I was arrogant and stupid and embarrassed, and I thought I could construct a better ending for myself if I got a second chance."

Ouch. What could I possibly say to that?

We lay in silence for a moment. "You have to understand," he said, "the public scrutiny is intense. You haven't experienced it yet, but you will once the show airs, and then you'll see. All that attention, even the negative stuff, it's like a drug. It gives you a high like nothing else, and believe me, I've tried. And you think, what could I do to get another hit of that spotlight? How can I get them to care even more? And what you really don't want is their pity, you know? They can love me, they can hate me, that's all good, but to feel sorry for me? That's not the way I wanted to go out."

"So instead you just never left?"

"This is my life now. This is what I do."

What he left unspoken: that there was nothing else remaining.

I'd agreed to visit Margaret again that evening, and I had to hurry to get back to my own room, wearing clothes borrowed from Cannon, and change. Luckily nobody saw me so I didn't have to make up any stories about where I'd gotten a Hard Rock Café T-shirt. I knocked on Margaret's door on time and more or less composed.

After a pause, Margaret slipped out into the hallway, closing the door behind her without letting me see any screens. I tried to hide my disappointment. She'd let me knock out a quick email reply to Thea, and I wanted to see if she'd written back. Even though she wasn't doing well, there was something reassuring about evidence of a world outside the show. It was beginning to feel like this tiny island was all there was, that everything and everyone beyond it had disappeared permanently.

That there was nowhere to escape, even if escape were possible.

But "I left my medication in my study," Margaret said as she clunked painfully down the hall with her cane. "I'm afraid I can't do without it any longer."

"I can get it for you," I offered, chafing at our slow pace.

"Nonsense," she replied. "Walking is good for me. I've become a couch potato with all these strangers in my house." She gave a little wheeze. "I need to keep myself fit, at least for a little while longer."

Down the hall, around the corner, and she paused in front of a door, fumbling for a large ring of keys in a deep pocket of her dress. Her hand trembled slightly as she inserted the key into the lock, and then the door opened with a loud pop. "After you," she said, and I ventured inside with her on my heels.

Furniture crowded the room, along with a plethora of embroidered cushions, haphazard stacks of books, and knick-knacks on every available surface. I wondered if some of these things were normally on display downstairs but hidden away up here for the duration of the show. Two Tiffany lamps gave the only light, a rosy glow that didn't reach the edges of the room. Margaret moved to an end table by the overstuffed sofa, picking up a plastic days-of-the-week pill case that didn't fit in with its old-fashioned surroundings, and poured the contents into her hand.

Except for some tall closed draperies and a fireplace, all the walls were lined with bookshelves, which made sense for a former editor. But instead of books, they all held dolls. So many dolls, packed in like dead little sardines in a can. Different hair styles, different skin tones, but all in elaborate dresses, all sculpted in unforgiving porcelain, they faced out, their chubby little arms reaching towards me. And every single one of them had empty sockets where their eyes should have been.

I drew back with a gasp. The dolls continued to stare sightlessly at me. "I know, aren't they horrible?" Margaret came to stand beside me. "I've had some of them since I was a little girl."

I swallowed. "What happened to their eyes?"

"One of the experts thought this would help exorcise Darwin." She reached out and fondled one of the doll's faces with a weird tenderness.

"Excuse me?"

"He said they were a reflection of what I'd wished for in my life and hadn't received. As such, they would be a potent sacrifice or some such bullshit. I've consulted with all the so-called authorities, trying to get rid of Darwin for good. I don't ask questions anymore. I simply do as they say and then brace myself for failure." Her fingers lingered on an empty eye socket. "In retrospect, this one was particularly insufferable. But none of them succeed, no matter how much money I pour into their greedy hands." She stroked another doll's curly hair. "You know why I don't hide these dolls away? It's the only outward display I allow myself of the horror I've been living my entire adult life. There's something cathartic about looking at them, at acknowledging what is rotten at the core."

The rows of empty sockets mesmerized me, and I shuddered with the knowledge that she actually found this display comforting.

"I kept all the eyes," she continued. "I couldn't bring myself to throw them away. They're in a bag over there on the mantle. Go look if you don't believe me."

It suddenly felt very important to be as far away from here as possible. "I...I believe you."

"No, you need to see them. Go on, they're right over there."

It seemed easier to do as she asked. I walked across the room and picked up the canvas bag, surprisingly heavy in my palm. I loosened the drawstrings. I opened the top. I peered inside into a blessed darkness.

Margaret appeared at my elbow. Funny, I hadn't heard her cane as she followed me. "So much destruction for so little purpose. It makes me sick. But then, I suppose that's the point." She grabbed the bag from me and spilled its contents all over the hardwood floor.

The eyes fell like thunder. They rolled across the floor in multiple directions, and it might have been a trick of the light, but it felt as though they were all looking up at me, staring with a heavy malice, furious that they'd been dropped with such abandon, or that they'd been plucked from their porcelain hosts in the first place, who can say.

So many eyes.

I knelt down to scoop them up, even though I had an irrational aversion to touching them, but Margaret put her hand on my shoulder with her usual strong grip. "Leave them," she said. As if cleaning them up would be a pointless exercise.

As I slowly rose to my feet, her amulet came into view, and it seemed to me as though it too had turned into a baleful eye, looking on my foolishness with a harsh judgment I couldn't escape. I looked away and told myself not to be silly. All the blank eyes rolling around the floor had rattled my nerves.

I followed her dutifully to the overstuffed couch and sat beside her. She gave a low little laugh. "Oh Zoe, you don't need to keep things from me." Before I could object, she shook her head. "No, no, save your breath. I've been watching you."

I sat ramrod straight, carefully not looking down at the eyes still staring up at us. "Oh?"

"Cannon is quite the white knight, isn't he? Noticing you covered with all that blood, taking care of you. Quite solicitous for a vapid reality host."

Was she implying she knew about our affair? "He's not vapid."

She shrugged. "Men. You can never trust them, my dear. But you'll learn that soon enough. You're still young." She patted my hand. "Don't worry, I won't tell anyone. Just remember, I'm not the only one watching."

How could I possibly forget? I desperately wanted to change the subject. "Do you know what happened to Lucy?"

"Oh, yes, you missed the hubbub." She gave me what I'd swear was a sly smile. "She was airlifted out, I'm afraid. They think she might have had a stroke."

"A stroke? But she's only twenty-three." A fact she'd repeated many times upon learning I'd be turning thirty-one soon.

Margaret grabbed my hands. "You need to leave this place, do you hear me? Take the other women and get out of here. This whole set-up—all the single young women vying for the affections of one man, the drama, the heartbreak—it's emboldened Darwin, made him more active than he's been in years. None of you are safe here."

I tried to be as gentle as I could in pulling my hands away. "I tried, but"—I shrugged—"you know how the producers are." You know how Kennedy is, I didn't say. Margaret already knew too much about me as it was. "And most of the other Gold Diggers don't want to leave. It's not like I can force them."

"Crazy old woman," Darwin whispered. *"When will she learn not to plot against me?"*

She kept hold of my hands. "You do realize, Zoe, things are spiraling out of control. The accidents aren't going to stop. And things could get worse. Much worse." She paused. "Those women—my friends from college—they didn't die in the fire, you know. It's funny, isn't it, how no one asks questions. It's almost like they don't want to know the truth. But a rampaging fire during a hurricane watch? Please. The fire didn't happen until later."

I caught my breath. "What happened?"

She closed her eyes. "Darwin turned them against each other, and they died fighting one another. The ones who were left, they killed themselves when they realized what they had done. I came back to face the aftermath, and believe me, it was...not pretty. So you must understand that what I'm asking you is a matter of life and death."

I looked down at her hands covering mine, the skin mottled against my perfectly pale fingers. Once her hands had looked just like mine. "I understand," I whispered. "But I don't know what I can do about it."

She sagged back into the couch, releasing my hands. "Me neither. Ever since this was first set in motion, it's had the terrible weight of inevitability. Even when I tried to drive him out, send him away with all your strength to help me during the séance, I was doomed to failure." She stared down at all those eyes. "I wish I'd never come back here," she whispered. "I resisted it for so many years, keeping myself busy, staying unattached, unemotional, rational. But I got so tired, and the older I got, the more he...crept in. I couldn't be perfect forever, it was too much to ask." It felt like she was asking me for forgiveness, but for what I wasn't sure.

The silence between us stretched out for several minutes, until I wondered if she'd forgotten I was still there. "Is there anything I can get for you?" I asked.

"When you get as old as I am, you come to a much deeper understanding of the truism that history repeats itself. You feel the predictable tragedy of it, all the way down to the marrow of your bones." She glanced over at me. "Perhaps dying young wouldn't be so bad after all."

I shivered. "I have to go." I fled for the door, but not before slipping on one of the rolling eyes. I careened into an armchair, jamming my knee against the side table with one of the Tiffany lamps. It teetered before slowly smashing to the floor.

"Leave it," she said, sounding wholly unconcerned. "This will all be gone soon enough."

I took her at her word, scrambling to get out of that room and its army of sightless dolls.

"Don't you see?" Darwin whispered. *"I'm the only one who has your best interests at heart."*

When I went downstairs, intent on scrounging a snack, Naomi was already in the kitchen making herself a sandwich. "When's tonight's group hangout?" I asked her, rummaging through the fridge. If there wasn't already an organized activity, the producers tended to encourage us to get together in a group in the evenings to see what drama, if any, they could get started between us while pulling us aside one by one for our Hot Seats.

"Oh, haven't you heard?" The mustard bottle made a rude sound. "No hangout. The producers are all in a huff because of Elaine."

Ugh. I still hadn't forgiven her for betraying me to Kennedy. "What about her?"

Naomi shook her head. "I guess she's leaving the show. I heard Leo saying he thought she might have been fired. But Giselle said Elaine completely lost it, started speaking in tongues or something and wouldn't shut up. Giselle says she talked for something like four hours straight before she was given a sedative. Like, without stopping at all."

Four hours straight? My throat hurt just thinking about it. Still—"How does Giselle know that?"

Naomi slapped the two pieces of bread together. "Haven't you noticed she and Jen are tight? Whenever Jen deigns to visit us, she always talks to Giselle. Every single time. Get with the program, girlfriend: they've already chosen their winner."

I looked around for the room's camera, and Naomi laughed at me. "You think they'd air me saying something like that? Can't have the audience thinking this whole circus is rigged. Relax, Zoe. You don't want to be the next one to crack up. There's some weird shit happening on this show, that's for sure." With that, she picked up her sandwich and took a huge bite.

Elaine speaking in tongues, blood gushing from Lucy's nose, all these women leaving and not because Emerson was sending them home.

"They're not worthy. But you, Zoe, you're different. You're special."

Darwin's whispers had become almost normal to me by that point, and I wanted to believe him so badly, that I mattered, that I was on the path to something better. But I couldn't help remembering the dolls' eyes still rolling blank and cold two floors above my head.

Darwin's lies were much more palatable than the truth.

Thirty-Seven

Last entry in Adelaide Vance's journal:

October 31, 1974

A storm is brewing, I can taste it in the air. The house is complete, and Darwin says it is almost time for me to join him. I can hardly wait. Everything has changed for me. My struggles are in the past. I look at the house blueprints, and the straight lines and precise dimensions don't matter to me anymore. After caring about them for so long, it's strange to cast them aside, just as I once discarded my childish pursuits for something more worthy of my time.

Leland is supposed to arrive in a few days to see the new house in all its glory. I won't be here waiting for him.

All I think about, all I care about, is Darwin. I spend hours sitting on the ground by the cliff side, legs crossed, eyes closed, simply communing with him. He is all I could ever want, the man of my dreams.

Finally I will be complete, and my emptiness will overflow.

Thirty-Eight

The next morning I went on the hunt for a producer. I had to stop this madness if I could.

But crew members were in short supply. I finally cornered Leo in the kitchen, where he was getting a coffee refill. "I need to talk to you," I said.

He gave an over-the-top sigh. "Not now, Zoe, okay? Unless it's an emergency. All of Elaine's responsibilities have been dumped on me, and what with the hurricane coming...."

"Hurricane?"

He swore under his breath. "Look, we're going to announce it to the group later today so keep it under your hat till then, okay? We don't want anyone to freak out."

He gave me an endearing grin, but I refused to be distracted. "Should we be freaking out?"

"Nope." He took a big gulp of coffee. "Do I look worried to you? Overworked, yes, but it's gonna be fine. We might lose power, and we're stuck on the island until the worst passes, no boats coming or going at this point, the final one left last night, but we have plenty of supplies. We just need to ride it out, that's all. You know we'd be evacuating if we expected any major problems."

Shit. This could have been the perfect excuse for me to get all these women off the island. But now we were trapped. "Are you sure?" I tried. "Better safe than sorry."

"You're not getting cabin fever now, are you, Zoe?" His smile showed too much tooth. "Because if so, we can sit down and do a Hot Seat right now."

"Not at all," I said. "But I need to see Kennedy."

He shook his head. "No can do. She's busy in production. We're all slammed now that we're short-handed. Just wait out the storm, that's my advice, and then we can sort out whatever you need. Sound good?"

I gave him my camera-ready smile. "Sure thing." I'd just have to find Kennedy for myself.

Kennedy was alone in the production room, staring intently at two screens, one with video streaming and one showing some kind of flow chart. Huge headphones covered her ears, but her eyes flickered when I came in. "Hold on," she said, and I waited. Interrupting her wouldn't help get her on my side.

Finally she pulled her headphones off, leaving them around her neck. "What is it? And keep it short please."

She didn't look good. Her ponytail had acquired the slightly greasy sheen that meant she hadn't had time to wash it in too long, and the bags underneath her eyes were darker and more pronounced than usual. The nails on her left hand had been chewed to the quick, an old habit I thought she'd broken years before.

My anger was already at a low boil. If it weren't for her I'd be long gone, and this wouldn't be my problem anymore. "I heard about the hurricane," I began.

"Well, shit." She sat up straighter in her chair. "Which idiot told you so I can have him fired?"

I refused to be deterred. "I think we need to evacuate the island as soon as possible. Before the storm hits if we can."

She swiveled her chair back around. "Don't worry about it, we have everything under control."

"No, I'm serious." But she had already slipped her headphones back on. "Kennedy!" I put my hand on her shoulder. "Kenny!"

She spun back around, eyes blazing. "How many times have I told you to stop calling me that? Get it together, Zoe, and stop trying to sabotage my show. I gave you the first second date of the season and you flushed it down the toilet. I know you're a glutton for self-punishment, but don't take me down with you. This isn't some journey of self-discovery for me, this is my career. I'm not going home at the end of the season to do something completely different. Do you get that?"

I took a breath and tried to remain calm, but it wasn't easy in the face of Kennedy's wrath. "This isn't about you or me. You know something weird is going on. Something...not right. And it's not just me who thinks so, you can ask Margaret—Emerson's aunt—about it. She's the one who thinks we all need to leave the island."

"You want me to suspend production on the word of a crazy old woman? Please."

"First of all, she's been sick, so taking her wishes into account isn't totally unreasonable. But you know as well as I do it's not just her. What happened at that séance? We all experienced things we couldn't explain that night. And what about the hair loss, the teeth falling out, Lucy falling into a coma? She's twenty-three, you do know that, right? And now Elaine lost it too? All these accidents aren't ordinary."

"Next thing I know you'll be telling me there's some kind of supernatural conspiracy and we all need to flee for our lives." Kennedy launched herself from her chair and grabbed me by the shoulders, pulling me in until our foreheads were almost touching. "Listen to me, Zoe, you need to stop getting spooked by shadows. Being on reality TV can sometimes make people a little paranoid, and that's all that's happening to you, okay?"

She stared at me as though her eyes could bore holes into my brain. I should have never believed a word coming out of her mouth. She was lying to my face, and I was trapped into being the only one in this conversation constrained by reason. "Don't you think we should at least give the other contestants some kind of warning?"

She pushed me away with a groan. "You try that, you'll be forever labeled as the crazy one. You'd be doing the show a favor, but not yourself."

"But—"

She didn't even let me start making my next argument. "Enough, Zoe. I'm going to make this very simple. You need to put your head down and work with me, not against me. And if you can't do that, I'm prepared to make your relationship with Cannon a major plot of the season."

"You...you know about that?" Shock jolted through my body, followed by a profound embarrassment that this development had taken me by surprise.

She gave me a long-suffering look. "Jesus Christ, of course I do. I know everything that happens on the show. That's my job." She said the last as if I were particularly dense. "I have plenty of juicy footage: you two on that stupid boat, you two in his bedroom. You might be determined to be cavalier about your own future, in spite of my best efforts to convince you to take things seriously, but what about Cannon's? Are you willing to set his career in flames?"

I'd sunk to a new low, being blackmailed by my own sister. She'd been prepared for this. She'd been pulling my strings ever since I showed up at her apartment door in LA, and I'd let her do it, happy to cede responsibility for a life I'd so royally fucked up.

"Stop and think for a minute, Zoe. There's nothing you can do. You tell the women there's a problem, who do you think they're going to believe? Me or you? They don't want to leave. They want to win Emerson's heart on national television. This show is going full speed ahead, and you can either abandon ship and hurt people in the process or you can come along for the ride. But we're not stopping for you or anyone else."

"But—"

"Zoe, be practical! There's a fucking hurricane coming. It's not safe to evacuate, do you understand? That would be way more dangerous than staying put and riding it out. So if you actually care about your fellow castmates' well-being, consider that. Now, if there's nothing else, I have work to do."

What could I say? She was going to get what she wanted like she always did.

"See?" Darwin whispered. *"You can pretend all you want, but in the end, she's right about you. You're a follower, not a leader. You need someone in charge telling you what to do."*

The glaring conclusion of his line of argument? I needed someone just like him.

The morning was gray and rainy, and as a special treat Emerson joined the nine of us Gold Diggers for lunch: soup and paninis whipped up by the chef. I didn't jockey for position, so Vivian and Simone ended up next to Emerson, while I sat toward the end of the table.

Cannon sat right next to me. "Hey," he said under his breath. "How are you doing? I've missed you."

He was slipping. And even though Kennedy already knew, I didn't want the rest of the house to find out. We were in a bad enough situation as it was. "I'm fine," I said. I stared at the small green curls of onion floating in my tomato soup.

Margaret walked deliberately into the room, leaning heavily on her cane, impeccably dressed in black. She didn't blend in with the crew though; her shirt and trousers were too ironed, her posture too upright. She looked like she was a beatnik poet, the only touch of color the amber pendant glinting above her sternum. All the Gold Diggers except me gave fake delighted sounds at her presence. I couldn't get the image of her spilling all the eyes onto the floor out of my mind.

She stopped at the end of the table closest to me. "A serious hurricane is approaching, and we need to evacuate." Her voice was loud and clear, her executive voice. "As soon as possible."

In that minute I loved her as much as I'd loved the author of *This is the End* when I was a teenager.

The Gold Diggers looked from her to Emerson and back again. "It's fine, Aunt Margaret." He sounded tired. "We've talked about this. The weather reports don't show any cause for alarm. We're not in the direct path of the hurricane, and we have more than enough supplies if we're cut off from the other islands for a few days." He gave us a reassuring smile. "Really. A lot of fuss about nothing, I promise." He turned his smile on his aunt. "Are you joining us for lunch, Aunt Margaret? What a wonderful surprise."

"We need to evacuate," she repeated. "On this island a hurricane is never a joke. I've learned that from experience."

Emerson ran his fingers through his hair, and Leo stepped forward to intervene. "We have it all under control, ma'am. There's no need for anyone to leave." He pulled a chair from the table. "Why don't you have a seat and relax?"

She pressed her lips together. "I'm afraid I must insist. You are all under my roof, and I'm telling you to leave."

"Aunt Margaret, we've been through this." I'd never heard Emerson sound so harried.

"And you haven't listened to me! You're foolhardy and self-absorbed, just like your father, and *my* father before him. Trust me, Emerson, if you don't listen to me, you'll regret it for the rest of your life."

His mouth pulled down at the edges. "We're staying, and that's final." He turned to Vivian. "Now, weren't you telling me about the squall you and your father sailed through a few years back?"

Margaret continued to stand at the end of the table, glaring at us all. Leo spoke to her in a lowered voice. The other Gold Diggers clustered around Emerson so Cannon and I were the only ones close enough to overhear. "Ma'am, I appreciate your position on this, but it's actually too late for anyone to leave. The regular boat isn't coming today. It wouldn't be safe. The important thing at this juncture is to keep everyone calm. We really do have everything under control."

Still she stood there. The greater part of the room ignored her, but she refused to give in.

"Is there anything I can get for you?" Leo continued. "Some lunch? Or a drink? We want to make you feel as comfortable as possible."

She seemed to crumble inwards, and suddenly she looked very old indeed. Her skin paled, showing every vein, every liver spot, and her hand shook on the handle of her cane. "It's too late," she whispered, and her hand shook harder. "There's nothing I can do to stop him now. There's nothing any of us can do."

"Why don't I take you back upstairs? You look like you could use some rest."

Leo put a hand on her shoulder and began ushering her out. She stopped and turned at the entryway, looked over us, and shook her head. "We can never leave the past behind," she said. Everyone continued to ignore her, and she turned and dutifully allowed Leo to lead her away.

"What was that all about?" Cannon said. "Guess she's still not recovered from that night up on the hill."

"Don't pretend this isn't a big deal. We're trapped here." The words came out louder than I intended, and all conversation at the other end of the table came to an abrupt halt.

Emerson frowned at us. "Everything okay down there?"

Margaret was right. If there had been a chance to escape from whatever she thought was coming, it was too late now. So I did what was expected of me: I laughed and tossed my hair and pretended to be as carefree as anyone could wish. "Couldn't be better. This food is delicious." I put a spoonful of soup in my mouth even though my appetite was completely gone. Beside me Cannon nodded and smiled in sync, like we were a pair of friendly robots.

"What's going on, Zoe?" he hissed when everyone had turned back to their food.

I played on my hunch. "I know you've been hearing voices too," I whispered back. "Doesn't that give you pause? Something bad is happening here." He got very quiet before abruptly leaving the room, his lunch only half-eaten.

I fled for the bathroom soon afterwards, my gut churning, and there was blood on the toilet paper. My period had begun.

It's a myth that women's periods sync when they live together. There is no scientific evidence to prove this actually happens.

But the trashcan in the bathroom was full of tampon wrappers.

Thirty-Nine

BAHAMAS BRACE FOR BAD WEATHER AS HURRICANE GABRIELLE REACHES CATEGORY 4 STRENGTH

by Shirley Jansen, *Forecast*'s Senior Meteorologist

October 30, 2018

Hurricane Gabrielle became a major hurricane on Wednesday as Bahamas residents began preparing for the potentially devastating storm, with its strong winds and possibility of extreme flooding. Gabrielle poses a serious threat to lives and property for over 100,000 residents of the idyllic island chain.

A hurricane warning has been issued for portions of the northwestern Bahamas. Residents can expect major damage, widespread power outages, and a loss of most other utilities. The biggest danger of a hurricane in terms of lives lost is storm surge.

A Category 4 hurricane has sustained winds reaching from 130-156mph.

Forty

It must have been around ten at night when the power went out.

The storm had been increasing in strength all day, and after dinner, all the women had opted to stay together in the lounge. Surrounded by the lighting and sound equipment and the crew members with their blasé attitudes, we could more easily pretend the gusts of wind rattling the windows weren't that big a deal. The producers passed around Halloween candy, but that didn't energize the subdued air. We were all braced for the storm's impact.

Emerson didn't come down—I overheard a sound guy saying he was up with his aunt—so we could all relax. Kennedy was in the production room, working her magic. From her years of stories, I'd thought she spent a lot more time actively producing the contestants, but either I'd gotten the wrong impression or this season was different. Leo and Shep and Maisie were all in the room, ready to do their producer thing, but maybe the storm had them rattled too, because the three of them sat off to the side and mostly whispered amongst themselves.

Vivian had just announced her intention of going to bed early, looking over at the producers as if in challenge, when the room was suddenly plunged into darkness. The wind howled for blood outside, and my hands went cold as my dread, building inside me all day, began to uncoil.

The camera people switched on their backup lights, creating small pools of safety. "Everyone remain calm," Leo said loudly. "It's just a power outage, we knew this might happen." The camera people moved in closer so we'd be lit as they continued to film.

"Even more reason to go to bed early," Vivian said.

But Grace shook her head violently. "I think we should all stay together." She was trembling in the pink hoodie she wore. "Just until the storm calms down. Please."

Vivian rolled her eyes and stood up. "Honey, the storm could go on all night. I'm not giving up my sleep because you're afraid of a little wind." She looked over at Leo. "Please tell me you anticipated this moment and have flashlights for all of us so we don't kill ourselves going to the bathroom."

Leo held up a paper bag. "We have four for you contestants. You'll have to share."

Vivian gave a sigh. "Of course we will. Who's coming with me?"

We all exchanged glances. Everyone seemed to be in Grace's camp, not wanting to split up, not wanting to leave the reassuring light from the cameras. Plus nobody liked Vivian. "I'll go," I said.

"Great." She grabbed a flashlight from the bag and gave a challenging look to the camera people. "Any of you feel the need to film us while we brush our teeth and indulge in some riveting girl talk for the five minutes before I take an Ambien and fall into a deep and dreamless sleep?" Leo gave a small shake of his head to the camera people. "No? What a shock. I'll see you in the morning then. Unless the hurricane kills us all first." She laughed as she walked out, and I followed close behind.

We'd made it to the top of the stairs when the screaming began. Vivian kept walking. "Um, shouldn't we go check and make sure everything's okay down there?" I asked.

"You do what you want," she said. "But you know Grace just got scared because one of the crew dropped something or there was a particularly large gust of wind, and I have a date with my bed."

I kept following her, reluctant to be left alone in the dark. It did sound like it might be only one person screaming, and Grace had been extra jumpy. "Still...."

"Please. What are you going to do that a roomful of crew can't do themselves? There are three producers in there whose only job is to keep us all happy."

"I don't think they'd put it that way."

"Yes, well, they keep us happy now, and then they tell any stories they want about us later. A deal's a deal. Now do you want to brush your teeth or not?"

A few more screams, and then nothing but the wind. The crew had indeed taken care of the problem. Vivian and I brushed our teeth and removed our makeup in the near dark of the flashlight, then took turns going to the bathroom and dealing with our tampons while the other one stood quietly on the other side of the door. It was so dark I found myself straining my eyes to see and wishing for lightning. But it wasn't that kind of storm.

Vivian shone the flashlight into her room before handing it off to me. "See you in the morning." Coming from her, that was almost friendly. I kept the flashlight fixed on her bed until she reached it safely.

I'd made it to my own door when I heard the sounds downstairs, even above the gale outside. At first I thought it was more screaming, but as I listened, it resolved itself into...laughter? A high-pitched shrieking kind of mirth. What were they doing down there?

Looking back, there are innocuous moments that reveal themselves as pivotal decision points. I wish I'd done as Vivian had done: taken a pill and slept the night away, waking in the morning with my innocence intact.

But I didn't. I went back downstairs to see what all the noise was about. I expected they'd started handing out margaritas, that maybe the women were playing truth or dare or telling ghost stories that were alternately causing outbursts of hilarity and scaring them to pieces.

I wanted to be able to pretend at normalcy like the rest of them.

But normalcy was the opposite of what I found.

As soon as I stepped into the lounge, I was enveloped in a moist sticky heat, like entering a tropical seedpod almost ready to burst. The room was a puzzle of darkness and strange puddles of light, the ray of my flashlight crisscrossing the scene of confusion. Simone pushed by me, fleeing into the dark vastness of the rest of the house, and I moved forward as if in a trance. I felt I would die if I didn't see what was happening.

The first thing my flashlight found: Giselle huddled under the coffee table in a duck-and-cover position, eyes squeezed shut, hands clasped behind her neck. When I reached down to touch her shoulder, she didn't move a muscle. It was as if she were pretending to be dead.

I stopped there in the center of the room and tried to take stock of what was going on around me.

Several crew members lay still, collapsed in awkward black heaps on the floor. My light found blood oozing from Curtis's temple, his hungry eyes finally closed. I moved my beam to where the producers had been sitting, but the only one I could find was Shep, who looked like he had fallen asleep on the ground, his head cradled in his arms. The bag of flashlights had disappeared. A couple of cameras were set on tripods, as they'd been when I'd left, their red lights tiny pinpoints of inevitability in the darkness. We would always be monitored, they seemed to say with their steady glow. No escape was possible.

Eva crawled through the fallen bodies, pausing from time to time, and as she drew closer, I realized she was holding a liquid eyeliner pen. Her shorts and halter top were soaked through with sweat, her long hair plastered to her head and neck. She came to where I still knelt by Shep, flinging herself on top of him. He didn't wake up or make any protest, and she drew two big black X's on top of his closed eyes. Then she leaned so her nose was touching him and gave an ear-splitting scream.

He didn't move. I backed away from her and saw she'd done the same thing to the other bodies of crew members—unconscious? dead?—in the room. All of them had crossed-out eyes, and black scribbles uncoiled across some of their mouths. The sole female cameraperson had "SLUT" written in red lipstick across her forehead.

A burst of laughter broke from further in the house, and I followed it into the dining room. Someone had brought one of the camera lights in here and put it in the corner. Naomi stood by the entrance, one of the cameras balanced on her shoulder. She was the one laughing, a continuous peal coming from her mouth like some kind of demented bray. She trained the camera on Summer, Grace, and Lauren, who had all stripped down to their bras and panties in the heat. They appeared to be writing words on the wall with some kind of reddish brown paint. Grace had already spelled out "S-L-U-" and was obviously about to start on the "T." Lauren had only done an "L" so far. Summer had just finished "S-I-N." All of them had tears streaming silently down their cheeks.

Lauren reached between her legs before extending her hand to start painting an "I." Menstrual blood. They were using their menstrual blood as paint. Well, all except Summer, who had stopped her graffiti and begun sawing off her own hair with a steak knife. God, why was it so hot in here?

I'd set down the flashlight without realizing it, and a low moaning sound reverberated from inside my chest cavity, mimicking the wind battering against the house. The heat constricted my breathing, and my skin felt like it had shrunk until my organs strained against it, unable to fit inside its strict confines. The camera's red eye had turned on me. It stared at me without pity, revealing every single one of my flaws for the world to mock as it willed.

The camera spoke with Darwin's voice. "*You speak too much, you feel too much, you overwhelm every person you meet*," he said. "*But in the end, you're never enough, are you, Zoe? You drive love away, and you know you'll end up being alone forever. But it doesn't have to be that way, Zoe. I see you, I understand you. We have something special together, you and I. And if you're willing to fight for me, I'll stay with you forever.*"

It wasn't so much the words he spoke, it was the tone, the rhythm, the persuasiveness of his mere presence in my head. He felt like a god who had finally, after a lifetime of my confusion and struggle, deigned to speak directly to me. He was telling me what I was born to do.

I ran from the dining room, back through the lounge where Eva, streaks of red across her cheeks, was jumping up and down on the bar. Behind her, in bold black letters: "FALL AND YOU SHALL FINALLY RISE."

I dashed into the kitchen, where I pulled the largest knife from its block, weighing its solid wooden handle in my hand. Purpose made it beautiful.

Purpose made *me* beautiful.

Guttural cries called me back to the lounge, which smelled of earth and ozone and metallic blood. Someone had opened the French doors, and rain lashed down, a small puddle already forming on the hardwood floor. The doors rattled and shook with the force of the wind, banging repeatedly against the walls. In the middle of the room, partly taking over one couch, several of the women—Grace, Eva, Summer, Lauren, and Naomi—were writhing in a gigantic pile. It took me a moment to realize they were fighting each other. Summer punched Lauren in the eye, Eva tugged ferociously at Naomi's hair, Naomi tackled Lauren, Grace was sinking her teeth into Summer's ankle.

"Take hold of your own destiny," Darwin said. *"Grace first."*

Grace had her back conveniently presented to me as she held Summer pinned. Her long blonde hair seemed to curl into a makeshift bull's eye just slightly left of center. I raised the knife above my head, opened my mouth to scream to the heavens. Finally there would be justice, justice and an end to the incessant noise that filled my head to brimming. I wasn't the master of my destiny, I never had been, and it felt so damn good to surrender, to transfer my burden to someone older and wiser. I'd simply do whatever he said, and—

Someone ran full force into me. We both fell to the ground, away from the undulating mass of fighting bodies. I hit my head against the floor, and in that moment of bursting pain I dropped the knife.

I couldn't see clearly, my hair in my face, the light shifting uncertainly. I fumbled for the knife by touch, my hands stroking the floor uncertainly. I needed that knife, I needed to be washed clean once and for all. The rain beat down on my head and shoulders from the open door, but the water felt cool against my burning skin.

Someone grabbed me roughly by the shoulder, yanked up, and pushed me through the doors into the pitch black. Their dark silhouette blocked my way back inside and to the salvation of that knife planted just so in Grace's back. I rushed them, hoping to knock them aside. But they stood firm and pushed me further and further from the house until we finally fell back to the ground. They wrapped their arms around me in a fierce hug.

"Let...me...go!" Pure rage at being kept from my goal gave me strength in spite of the throbbing in my head. I struggled to release myself from their grip, my ribs aching from the constriction, but they held on with remarkable tenacity. Until I decided to get my teeth involved. A few yelps later and I was stumbling back to my feet.

The power returned with a blinding burst of light just as Grace hurtled down the path past me. She didn't slow as she reached the cliff's edge, and for a brief, beautiful moment she sailed in the air like a bird, her long blonde hair fanning out behind her like wings.

Then she plummeted out of sight, down to the beach below.

Blood pulsed through my veins as I stared at the spot she had been before she vanished. To soar through the air like that, to give yourself over to the laws of physics, that was something worth doing. I braced myself to take my own flight.

A hand clamped around my wrist with punishing strength. "Don't even think about it. You're not going anywhere."

It was Kennedy.

FORTY-ONE

LOVE STORY Plays the Switcheroo

—February 19, 2019 by lacey, www.dontcallmegirl.com

The people behind *Love Story* this season are either honest-to-God geniuses or completely fucking insane. The jury's still out on which.

They've subverted all our expectations, I'll give them that. We thought we were getting a season of yet another romance reality TV show, watching women being lightly tortured while being superficial and catty and making ill-advised comments on air while falling in love. As they move toward the inevitable happy ending, there can only be One, a foregone conclusion we are meant to applaud.

That is patently NOT what *Love Story* Season 2 is all about. This is a full-on horror extravaganza, and they're not making any apologies for it either. I can imagine the pitch session now: "It's like *The Blair Witch Project* but with romance and hot girls in bikinis." "Why not? Ratings are down, we need to shake shit up, ready set go!" One has to speculate that either the contestants weren't informed of this audacious genre switch, or they're all actually obscure professional actors. I'd give it even odds since my internet stalking continues to provide surprisingly little information about these women.

In the latest episode, we get the classic horror set-up of the manor house in a storm, completely cut off from assistance or interference from the outside world. And then the weird, which has been making guest appearances all season, suddenly erupts from within in all its magnificent spectacle. We have bad artistic lighting, we have strange camera angles, we have unconscious (drugged?) crew members with marked-up faces, we have disturbing writing on the walls, and we have several women who look like they've completely fucking lost it after the stress of being constantly judged on camera by today's impossible standards for women.

This episode is a primal scream to tear down the patriarchy and do it now. The male gaze is on full display here, shown in all its creepy dehumanizing glory, revealed, in other words, for what it really is: a tool that turns its objects into a freak show and alienates women from both each other and their own authentic selves. The producers also play with the tropes of the "crazy over-emotional" woman and the "oversexualized" woman used to discredit women's voices, robbing them of their ability to share their authentic experiences. I particularly appreciated the touch of using menstrual blood to illustrate the shock and repulsion we feel about such an ordinary biological process, and how this is weaponized against women and shown to be dirty instead of inherently natural.

They've crossed a line here though, in that the believability, however strained, of reality TV is one of its primary selling points, and at this point we've jumped off that track into straight up fantasy. So far the ratings are up, but the fans are confused. And that confusion only grew when, after last night's bacchanalian spectacle, the family of Grace Alexander made a statement this morning asking for privacy during this difficult time, meaning there really was some kind of accident on set. We don't get to witness it firsthand, for which I am grateful. This show has fetishized suffering enough as it is. All we see is Zoe being shoved headlong into the storm, and then a few moments later, Grace rushing after her. Both women look flushed, exalted, almost otherworldly. And then only Zoe returns, bedraggled, muddy, and monosyllabic, before the shot fades to black and we come to the end of the episode, without the usual teasers following.

We can speculate the cameras didn't follow Zoe and Grace out of doors, so we have no way of knowing what actually happened out there in that hurricane. Unless they have Zoe tell us during the next episode.

And have Zoe tell us they must. It's the only way out of this quagmire they've created, and the only way we'll get a clear signal as to what kind of show *Love Story* wants us to believe it is.

Xoxo Lacey

Forty-Two

I don't remember the rest of what happened that night. I've seen the footage. I've seen myself come back inside, alone, without Grace or Kennedy. I can still hear Kennedy's voice, refusing to let me go, and then next thing I knew I was waking up in the morning on a couch in the lounge, hopelessly confused, covered in mud, several scrapes on my legs, and with a splitting headache.

The storm had abated by then, and I was left to my own devices, too disoriented to figure out what all the bustle around me meant but not hurt enough to merit any attention. I found my way to the conservatory and sat staring at a group of potted ferns as my head began to gradually clear. I felt like I was waking from a nightmare. And not just from the night before, but from the last several months since I'd arrived in LA, a numb shell of myself.

After an indeterminate amount of time, Cannon came rushing into the conservatory, batting errant branches from his path. He stopped dead when he saw me, a look of relief transforming his face. "I've been looking everywhere for you. How are you feeling? Are you okay?"

"I think so." I wished I felt more confident about that.

Cannon sat beside me and wrapped me in his arms. "Thank God.

When I didn't see you in the main house...I wondered...." He held me tighter.

A kind of horror beat in my heart as he held me. The events of the night before slowly drifted into my mind. The crew all passed out on the floor. The blood, the words on the walls. Me doing my level best to kill Grace, and Kennedy stopping me in the nick of time. My head pulsed, and I moaned. It had all happened just as Margaret had said it would. I skittered away from considering the implications and turned to Cannon, hoping he'd give me good news. "Do you know what happened? My memory is...kind of fuzzy."

Cannon took both my hands in his larger, warmer ones, but his shaky voice was the opposite of reassuring. "I'm not sure. Kennedy says she's fixing everything. She's with the doctor and some of the women right now."

This news did nothing to alleviate my worry. "What about Jen?" Surely the no-nonsense showrunner was a better candidate for damage control and making the call to shut down the entire production than my increasingly erratic sister.

Cannon shook his head. "She left the island before we knew how hard the storm would hit. Said she had important business that couldn't wait. She'll be spitting mad when she finds out what happened. Heads will roll." He patted my hand, realizing how ominous that sounded. "But not our heads. Only Kennedy's."

"Thank you for your concern." Kennedy rounded the corner, and her very normalcy made my stomach lurch. She didn't look like she'd been up all night, her ponytail as jaunty as ever, her fresh gray T-shirt free from any lettering, completing her anonymous black jeans and black Converse uniform. "But since all communications are still down, I'm the one in charge. Best not forget that, Cannon. After all, you're just another pretty face on this show." She glanced down at our joined hands and rolled her eyes. "And can you please not openly hold hands with one of Emerson's top contenders? Is that too much to ask?"

It was as if the night before hadn't happened. Cannon tried to pull his hand away, but I caught it and squeezed his fingers tighter. "Why does it matter?" I asked. "It's not as if the show can go on."

Kennedy made a grimace that might have been her version of a smile.

"That's where you're wrong, dear Zoe. We've already invested too much in this season, and there's no way in hell I'm letting my career flush down the toilet because one of our psych screens missed something. We'll be continuing with all the women who are willing and able."

Cannon stood up at that, his nostrils flaring slightly. "You've got to be kidding me. We can't go on now, not with a death on our hands. The network won't stand for it."

A death on our hands. That's when I remembered Grace flying over the edge of the cliff like a huge white bird. I must have made a sound because Cannon sat back down beside me and put his arm around me. "I'm trying to help Zoe, who is obviously not okay, which is more than I can say for any of you producers who are getting paid to do this. So back the fuck off, okay? Zoe was the only witness, after all."

I opened my mouth to disagree, to tell him Kennedy was there too, but she shook her head at me slightly. "Well, I'm here now," she said instead. "Zoe and I need to discuss her next Hot Seat." She gave me a once over. "And Zoe needs to clean herself up."

Why did I suddenly feel cold? "I'm done with this," I said. I stared down at my hands curled up into tight little fists. I'd come so close to having them covered with blood. That weird frenzy that had come over me, that thirst for dominance, it lingered in the corners of my mind and made me hate myself more than I'd thought possible. The producers could get me washed and dressed with a face full of makeup and it wouldn't make any difference to how soiled I was on the inside.

"Yes, well, that's not an option right now. You're stuck here. So you might as well make the best of it."

I thought about leaving anyway. About somehow commandeering a boat, striking out to sea, doing anything to avoid staying on this island another cursed minute. *"Leave now, my sweet,"* Darwin crooned in my mind. *"Please. Go ahead. Through your voice, through your very breath, I will infect the world."*

A peal of hysterical laughter burst from my lips. Every escape had been denied me. "I'm not going to lie," I said abruptly. "Whatever bullshit you want me to spout in the Hot Seat, you can forget about it. I'm stuck here? Fine. But I'm telling things my own way." Grace deserved that much.

Kennedy rolled her eyes. "It's safer for you if you stick to the script I'll prepare for you. Don't worry, I won't make you a villain in all of this, but the integrity of the narrative is crucial right now. And then I want you to have a conversation with the other girls. Cry, bond, do whatever you have to do, but convince them all to cooperate. We don't have a show without our Gold Diggers."

I shook my head. "I won't do it." Sobs began to shake my shoulders. "I'll do a Hot Seat, fine, because Grace...because maybe that's the right thing to do. I don't know. But I won't talk about it with the others. We've all been through enough."

Kennedy drew a frustrated breath and tightened her ponytail like she was getting ready to go to war. Cannon pulled me closer. "I told you to back off," he told her. He'd dropped his easygoing drawl. "Leave her alone. You'll get your Hot Seat, isn't that enough?"

Kennedy narrowed her eyes. "I don't think you understand how this works."

"Oh, I think I do." Cannon tightened his jaw and looked her straight in the eyes. "You drop this right now, let Zoe do this her own way, or I'm quitting. You can't protect the integrity of your precious narrative without your host. Am I being clear enough for you?"

If I'd thought Kennedy would react with anger, I was wrong. Instead she burst out laughing. "Well, Cannon, I didn't think it was possible for you to genuinely care. Zoe has really gotten under your skin, hasn't she?" She turned to me. "Fine, have it your way, we'll make the Hot Seat work one way or another. Just remember, the American public will be judging you. You don't want to say anything that casts you in a less than sympathetic light, especially given the tragedy you'll be describing." She gave a little click of her tongue. "I really am watching out for you, Zoe. I have been this whole time. Play along with me, and we'll both get what we want. You'll see."

I waited until she'd left to rest my head on Cannon's shoulder. "You'd really quit for me?" I asked him.

"I guess I would." There was a wondering note in his voice. "Who knew I had it in me?" He kissed the top of my head. "Don't worry, Zoe, at least one person in this shit show has your back."

Darwin kept blessedly silent.

Forty-Three

Hot Seat transcript: Zoe Roberts, November 1, as aired in episode seven

You have to understand, the whole night feels like it never happened. I have to keep reminding myself.... (She shakes her head.) It was like a nightmare come to life. (She pauses to collect herself.)

After the power went out, I'd gone upstairs with Vivian to go to bed early. We heard some screaming from down below, but we figured it was just people getting into the whole slumber party vibe, you know? But after Vivian went to bed, I heard a bunch of laughing and felt like I was missing out. We've all bonded over the past few weeks, and I...I decided to go back down and join in.

(She pauses, looks down, shakes her head.) I don't know if I can do this. (Another long pause. A deep breath.) I went into the lounge, ready to, you know, have some fun, goof off with the girls, but it was immediately obvious something had gone terribly wrong because none of the crew were up. Like, their cameras were there, but they were all asleep or... unconscious or...I don't know. I was afraid they were dead.

(She swallows convulsively.) They weren't, though. Thank God. And then I found some of the other women, and they were...well, they weren't really themselves. I don't think any of us had been drinking all that much.

I'd only been gone about ten minutes, but maybe they did shots when I was upstairs because things got really weird. They were busy writing on the walls and there was some fighting, and...and Naomi had a video camera at one point, and everything, it just felt wrong. Off kilter. Like it wasn't really happening, or like those dreams when you're somebody else and you forget entirely who you actually are. I can't explain it. (She shakes her head.) It was like we became other people. Like we were possessed or something. It sounds crazy, I know, but that's the only explanation I have.

It was really hot, so I left the others behind and went outside into the storm. Or maybe I was pushed? (She pauses, looking confused.) I know it doesn't make any sense, it was absolutely pouring, but it felt better out there, less...suffocating. And then.... (Tears start trickling down her face.) And then Grace ran out, and I don't think she even saw me, she ran right past me, and the power had just come back on, so I could see her clearly. She was smiling. (The tears keep coming.) And she didn't hesitate, she ran straight off the edge of the cliff. Just like that. Before I could say a single word, or even try to catch up with her. She ran off, and she...disappeared.

I'm sorry, I can't do this anymore, I'm sorry. (Her voice shakes, she stretches out her hand to block the camera lens, and the clip ends.)

Forty-Four

In the end, only four of us Gold Diggers agreed to cooperate and continue with the show: myself, Giselle, Simone, and Vivian. The others moved back down to the bungalows without even a goodbye. The aftermath of the storm was still wrecking its havoc, meaning no boat service or indeed, communication off the island, so it was anyone's guess when they'd be able to actually leave. When I asked Cannon about them, he got a peculiar grimace on his face. "The sooner they can leave, the better," he said. "They're...not in great shape."

I don't know what Kennedy promised them, but a reduced crew was in evidence the next morning, and Leo gave the four of us a briefing, albeit without his usual perky presentation. "We told Emerson you girls had a party, and it went a little too far," he told us. "Feel free to offer him your support, but probably the less said, the better."

"A little too far?" Vivian gave him her death stare. "Is Emerson aware one of the women committed suicide? Is that what you'd call 'a little too far?'" She made ironic air quotes as she spoke.

"He knows, yes, and he is distraught, just like we all are. That's why we're taking the rest of the week off."

"Oh, it's for him, is it?" Vivian wasn't letting up. "Not for us, the people who actually knew the woman in question. Or Zoe, who, oh, I don't know, saw her die."

Leo's face took on a pinched look. "Dr. Poppy will be meeting with each of you a few times before we resume filming. If you have any concerns, you should feel free to discuss them thoroughly with her. I can assure you all sessions with Dr. Poppy will be one hundred percent confidential and will not be filmed or recorded in any way."

"Well, that's big of you," Vivian said. "We'll try not to say anything too juicy where you might miss it, isn't that right, girls?"

Simone continued the stoic silence I hadn't yet seen her break, but Giselle gave Leo her sweetest smile. "Thank you for all your efforts on our behalf."

"Well, look who went to charm school," Vivian muttered.

I waited until Leo left us alone to ask, "How'd they get you to stay?"

Simone just shrugged, but Giselle answered readily enough. "I didn't want to leave Emerson alone," she said. "I know he's depending on the success of this show. He's talked to me about what he wants to do afterwards, and I don't want to let him down."

I turned to Vivian. "My daddy taught me not to be a quitter," she said. "Besides, it's not like *I* have anything to be ashamed of. I was asleep when you all...did whatever it is you did." The judgment never ended with Vivian.

"What about you, Zoe?" Giselle asked.

I'm being haunted by a psychopathic ghost, I didn't say. I don't want to be responsible for unleashing him on the world. The show was crafted from sticky fly paper, and no matter how much I struggled, I remained trapped within its all-seeing eye. "I guess I haven't given up on love." Now there was a tagline for the producers. And I could tell from Vivian's sour look she knew exactly to whom I was speaking.

"That's my girl," Darwin whispered. *"We're meant to be together. You'll come to see that in time."*

I felt him crawling around my mind like an ant, small enough to squeeze into all my secret nooks and crannies. He knew what I was thinking without me even having to say. He made me complicit in my own imprisonment.

"Soon."

The threat lingered long after the voice had fallen silent.

When I left the lounge, Margaret was waiting for me. She sat rigid-backed in one of the hard chairs lining the wall next to the grand staircase, and she rose the minute she saw me. Today she wore a fabulous retro silk dress in dark plum. "We need to talk."

Even when taken out of a romantic context, those words are never good. And after our previous interlude, I wasn't eager to hear anything Margaret might have to say. "Maybe later."

I headed straight for the stairs, but she followed me. She took them slowly, one painful step at a time, the hand on her cane turning white with effort. I paused at the top, feeling like a jerk, and let her catch up. "Fine."

If she had tried to take me back to the room with the disfigured dolls, I might have rebelled, but she led me to her viewing room, sitting across from me on the unforgiving chair. She fingered the warm-colored amber stone that hung around her neck, Darwin's mark on her, as if it were a good luck charm. Darwin's warning echoed in my mind, that he would follow me and transform me into a source of contagion.

"That young woman." She shook her head. "Such a tragedy. And yet they continue to film."

"You know what they say. The show must go on."

"When they say that in show business, it's meant to sound so noble, but it's almost always about the money. Nothing so exalted about the bottom line, is there?"

"We all have our reasons for being here." I turned the chair so I could see the monitors.

Margaret cut right to the chase. "What happened the night of the hurricane? Emerson said you were the only one who saw that girl kill herself."

Kennedy had effectively written herself out of the narrative, leaving all the weight to fall on my shoulders alone. "I think you know exactly what happened." I still couldn't believe Grace was gone. "You warned me. You warned everyone. And you were right."

"When I discovered the massacre after that first hurricane, Darwin told me he was responsible. He'd orchestrated the whole thing: brainwashed those women, given them weapons, drugged them out of their minds, and set them against one another. He convinced the survivors their only recourse was suicide. He didn't even try to pretend to be innocent. He said he'd done the noble thing, that those women had needed to be purified, that their deaths paved his path to greatness. And I knew, as he was saying it, I knew the only reason I hadn't died too was because he needed my money, my connections. I hadn't come into my trust fund yet, so he was biding his time." She spoke rapidly, as if it were a relief to finally speak the words out loud.

"I knew what I had to do, and I didn't flinch. I made sure he'd never hurt another woman, that I would never again be partially responsible for such a travesty." She pushed my chair back around so I was forced to face her. "Do you understand what I'm saying?" She fixed me with her stare until I nodded. She'd killed him herself. I didn't know whether that made her a hero or a monster. "Even as his death has weighed on me more and more over the years, I never doubted I did the right thing. Not once."

"And the fire?" I asked.

She waved a hand vaguely. "Part of the cover-up. Daddy had people arrange it all and sent me off to Europe to recover." She sucked in a deep breath. "Not that it mattered. Darwin wasn't about to let me slip through his grasp. He started whispering to me as soon as I left the island."

"For a long time I tried to resist. I ignored it. I drowned it out. I fought against it. I even tried medication: lithium at first, then more modern anti-psychotics. Nothing touched the voice. As time passed, it grew stronger. He...found his footing. I kept all the people in my life at arm's length, terrified he'd find some way of hurting them. The toll it takes, having a scorned lover haunt you decade after decade, trying to fight against it, trying not to allow it to affect your behavior, suffering in complete isolation, knowing the entire world would call you sick, obsessed, insane." I'd had a small taste of what she must have experienced, and that alone had almost driven me off the edge of a cliff. This woman was stronger than I could fathom. "I've lived with a constant stream of invective and vitriol in my head. Every action judged, every cruel possibility uttered. The whole time he wanted me to return to this island, and at long last I became so exhausted I gave in."

"He wanted you to come here? Why?"

She shrugged. "To slowly drive me insane and watch me die? I don't know. He's not a human being, Zoe. Not anymore. He's...an unfathomable force. I hoped he'd limit himself to torturing me, that maybe he could only speak to me. But as it turns out..." She shudders. "History has been repeating itself. All of you beautiful young women in the new house, competing for the attentions of one Golden Boy. Seems he still has a taste for torturing single and vulnerable young women. Only this time, he has these bloodthirsty producers on hand to make things even worse."

Maybe it was time for us both to come clean. "He's been speaking to me," I told her. "You guessed, didn't you? That he was masquerading as my ex-fiancé?"

She nodded. "He's a chameleon at heart. He shows himself as your secret heart's desire." She grabbed my hands, and I winced at her strong grip. "As much as it pains me to admit it, this period of relative silence on his part has been something of a relief. His attention is now divided between so many targets, he leaves me alone for hours at a time. I am a selfish old woman. I should have done whatever it took to make sure this show never happened. But when it mattered most, I faltered."

"As you always will." Darwin's disembodied voice came from above, and we both jerked up our heads as if to catch a glimpse of him. *"Oh, my sweet twin loves, Margaret and Zoe, always trying to deny me. Watch and learn."*

I followed Margaret's gaze to the monitors above and behind me, swiveling around in time to see Giselle shaking behind the kitchen counter. Her skin looked particularly pale against the dark wood of the cabinets as she did her jerky dance. I flashed back to Margaret at the séance, unable to communicate in any way, the same quivering of the jaw, the neck, the hands. White foam began to emerge from Giselle's mouth, sliding lazily down her chin and marring the perfect marble countertop below. Her eyes looked as vacant as the porcelain doll eyes that haunted my dreams.

And then she went rigid and fell down to the floor like a plank of wood.

Margaret dropped her head in her hands. "Enough, Darwin! Enough."

A cameraperson ran forward into the frame and crouched behind the counter. "She's unresponsive," he yelled. "Somebody call the doctor!"

"It's time to start over, my loves." Darwin was almost humming in satisfaction. *"Do you remember, Margaret? Do you remember how you promised we'd be together forever? And now I have the sweet Zoe to take your place, and it's time to collect."*

Margaret straightened her spine. "Take me, Darwin." There was no hesitation in her voice. "Leave these others be. Zoe doesn't matter to you, it's me you want. I'll keep my promise to you, and then we can be done with this."

The voice laughed, and it was a horrible sound, disembodied and flat as if deliberately reminding us it wasn't coming from lungs and chest and breath. *"Why don't I take you all? Fill the emptiness one death at a time?"* he said. *"Was that how it was for you, my love, when you killed me? Did you feel satiated? Did my death complete you the way I never could in life?"*

Margaret shuddered. "Why didn't you leave when you had the chance? Why didn't you all leave?" She clutched her ears and squeezed her eyes shut. "It's too late now."

"Silly woman." Darwin laughed. *"Zoe will never leave my side. She's mine now, as you could never be."*

I tried to comfort Margaret, to tell her we'd figure something out, but she'd retreated into herself, rocking and moaning as though something essential had been ripped from her. I couldn't think, I couldn't watch, an acrid taste lingered on my tongue and all I could do was flee to some other part of that tragic house and think: Better her than me.

But Darwin's laugh wouldn't leave me alone.

Forty-Five

There was a moment, when we slept together that last time, Cannon and I, after the shock and the blood and the shower. We were staring into each other's eyes as he came, and he didn't look away. He didn't retreat to some distant place, somewhere I could never hope to follow. He didn't hide behind the intensity of his physical sensations. He stayed right there with me.

I think that was the only time I've ever had a lover remain so present.

He pulled me with him when he collapsed to lie beside me, as if he couldn't bear to have physical space separating us. I rested my head against his chest, my breathing gradually slowing, my limbs slightly shaky in the aftermath. His heart beat a reassuring tempo in my ear.

"Zoe." His voice was a deep rumble in his chest, and I knew what he was going to say. I knew, and I felt all the jaggedly broken pieces of myself shift and stab into me. I couldn't. He couldn't. We were filming a show draped in artifice, based on selling a shiny gold capitalist fantasy to millions of people, and nothing could be allowed to matter. It was too much.

I lifted my head and kissed him, covering his lips before he could say those three little words that would cut me to the quick. "Thanks for helping me out," I said. Changing the mood, redirecting his thoughts, managing the narrative.

"It was my pleasure," he replied.

We lay in silence for a long time.

Forty-Six

As dusk settled around the house Vivian and I huddled together without speaking. The lounge felt alien and dark with the powerful lighting rig shut off, and our voices echoed strangely in the empty space. Vivian had pulled off her mike pack and tossed it onto the coffee table, and nobody came to scold her and wire her back up.

It almost felt like we weren't being watched.

Cannon wandered in and gave me a weak smile. "How's Giselle?" Vivian asked.

"The same." She'd lapsed into a coma, and there was no airlift to bring her to safety, not until we regained our communications with the outside world. She was as trapped in this house as the rest of us, Emerson glued to her side, stewing in confused guilt.

Cannon settled onto the couch next to me, a plausibly deniable distance away, and we all lapsed back into our own contemplations. I found myself straining to hear within the pregnant silence. Eventually I caught some faint rhythmic contractions, the house breathing around us with slowly increasing volume. No, wait, it was just my own heart beating.

It was through this companionable madness that Kennedy walked, without pause or any acknowledgment of our presence, an odd focused look on her face. She didn't even mention the mike pack lying in full view, mocking the failure of this show, her baby. In one hand she carried a shovel, the metal rusted, and in the other, a camping lantern.

She paused at the French doors. "Zoe, come with me, I need your help. And grab a flashlight while you're at it. Cannon, go get Emerson and bring him outside." She scowled before Cannon could respond. "Yes, I know he doesn't want to leave Giselle, but it's not like she's going to know the difference. Tell him it's important. Remind him of his contract if you have to. Got it?"

Cannon hesitated, then gave her a mock salute. "Whatever you say, boss." He gave me a wink.

"I'll go sit with Giselle," Vivian said. Without the cameras constantly trained on us, we were all becoming more human again.

I took one of the flashlights left on the side table, remembering all too well the last night they'd been used, and followed Kennedy. She headed directly for the place on the cliffside where Grace had taken her final plummet, her shape obscured by the mist, and I hastened my steps. "What are we doing out here?" I eyed the shovel.

She set down the lantern and planted the shovel into the ground. "It's finally time," she said.

I didn't like the sound of that. "Okay, that's great, but don't you think there are some things we need to talk about?"

She didn't stop, putting the whole weight of her Converse-clad foot into the shovel to drive it deep into the ground. "Things have gotten a little out of control." She tossed a shovelful of dirt to the side. "There weren't supposed to be any deaths. Darwin agreed there wouldn't be any deaths. Except that old hag, but she's lived a good long life, and it's not like her hands are clean. Should have known better than to trust a bitter ghost."

So Darwin had been speaking to Kennedy too. I wished I felt surprised, but nothing Kennedy did shocked me anymore. "Why?"

"Liz was never going to promote me to showrunner. Not unless I forced her into it by taking complete credit for delivering the network a bona fide hit. With the right ratings I can go over her head, get my own show. I have friends at the network, they know I've worked my ass off, and I deserve this."

I watched her like she was a dangerous animal while she dug. I'd never seen Kennedy do that much manual labor in her life. "But the show is falling apart."

"I know," she spit out. "Because Darwin didn't live up to his side of the bargain. But it's all going to be okay, I'm getting things back on track, and then I'll work my magic in the editing room. It's not like I'm not used to being stabbed in the back when my career's on the line." She began to pant from her exertions, the hole expanding at an alarming rate.

I watched her dig for a while, but eventually I couldn't help myself. I had to ask. "What was your side of the bargain?" How long had they been working together? I tried to keep my voice calm, friendly, like this was a pleasant experience we were sharing. One false step on my part and the teeter totter, with Kennedy up high, would come plunging down.

"That I'd make sure Emerson was chosen for the show and we'd film here." She spoke through gritted teeth. "I'd get Darwin his new chosen body. In return he'd make sure I got the footage I needed."

I stared at her in horror. "His new body?"

"Oh yeah, and I promised him one other little thing." She paused in her digging and gave me a sly grin. "I'd told him all about my annoying little sister who couldn't get her shit together. How she was wasting her life and her talent in her neurotic search for some fucking savior. He was intrigued. Wanted to meet her."

Okay, she could still surprise me after all. "I was part of your deal with him?"

"Don't let it give you a big head." The gleam of mania showed in her smile as she threw another shovelful of earth to the side. "You were just the cherry on top. I couldn't let you waste the rest of your life now, could I?" She threw the shovel down with a gigantic sigh. "There." She dug a small flashlight from her pocket and shone it down into the pit, and I moved my own beam to join hers.

Straight onto some bones. The right size to be human. I took an involuntary step backwards, then crouched down to have a closer look. Fallen slightly to the side of the rib cage was an amulet, a dark amber color that seemed to suck in the light, the twin to the one Margaret always wore. I reached down to touch it. *"Don't touch, greedy girl. That's not for you."*

I recoiled from the amulet, struck by an unnatural aversion. I started skirting the hole, trying to reach Kennedy. "Listen, Kennedy, I'm not sure you've thought this through. Once you give Darwin a body, what reason will he have to do anything you want?"

She stepped closer to the hole, peered down, and frowned. "Once he has a body, he'll be anchored in place, and he'll have to give up his ghostly shenanigans. And he's already delivered the footage I needed."

I reached her side. "But Kennedy." We both stared down at the skull, unexpectedly vulnerable as it nestled in the dirt. "There's no camera crew here now."

"Not to worry, little sister, it's all part of my plan." She grinned wolfishly in the dark. "Not everything I do is for public consumption."

Before I could try to persuade her that cooperating with an unhinged ghost wasn't the most rational of plans, Emerson and Cannon came down the paved path towards us. "I thought you said I could have today off," Emerson said. "You have some nerve asking me for anything with the show in shambles." He stopped at the edge of the hole and put his hands on his hips. "What, no cameras? Unbelievable. This show has been mismanaged from start to finish. You promised me you'd make me look good, Kennedy, but you can't deliver, can you? How exactly do you expect this shitshow"—he made an emphatic gesture—"to launch my career in entertainment? People are going to think I'm bad luck!"

Cannon looked between Emerson fuming and Kennedy blinking lazily, her focus fixated on her prey, and gave his wide, genial smile. "How about we go back inside and talk everything through over some dinner?" He sent a nervous glance at the hole. "We can always...dig more later."

But Emerson wouldn't be soothed. "This entire thing has been a train wreck. We just regained cell service, and medical help for Giselle will be here as soon as they can spare a helicopter. And I was finally able to get in touch with Jen, and you know what she just said? The network is almost certainly going to throw the whole thing out. Call it a wash. You know what that means? No airtime for me. This has all been a colossal waste of my time."

Kennedy's eyes bugged out of her head. "Jen said that? To *you*? But she knows what this means, I can explain how I'll fix it...." She cut herself off and squeezed her eyes shut as if she were in great pain.

"Kenny?" I reached out to her. "Are you okay?"

And then she began to laugh, an unhinged, very un-Kennedy-like laugh. Her eyes snapped back open, and it was as if she didn't see me at all. "It doesn't matter," she chirped, and then she pulled her gun from the back of her waistband and trained it directly at Emerson. "You'll do as I say, lover boy. For the sake of my show."

Emerson froze, his face twisting into a peculiar expression I realized must be surprise. Cannon slowly rose his hands in the air. I stared at Kennedy, incredulous. "What the hell are you doing?" I asked her.

Darwin's voice boomed out as loud as I'd ever heard it. *"You will all burn."* Cannon jerked his head and looked around, trying in vain to find the source of the voice. Emerson kept his eyes trained on Kennedy.

"What's going on here?" he asked. An acrid smell began to fill the air.

More laughter from Kennedy. "He wants your body, don't you see? And then he can live the life your aunt stole from him. It's a fair exchange. The Courtlands owe him quite a debt." I looked my sister straight in the face, and I didn't recognize her. It was as if Darwin had overwritten her features with what had always been inside.

"Kennedy?" I whispered. She ignored me, and it didn't feel any different from all the times she'd overlooked me in the past.

"It's my debt to pay." Margaret came walking from the house, barefoot and bareheaded, her robe fanning behind her in the wind. I was sorry to see she held no weapon in her hands. Beyond her, pale smoke billowed in the air. Apparently Darwin hadn't been speaking metaphorically about us burning. She knelt by the hole, and I obligingly shone my light down for her to see. "I thought this amulet was destroyed in the fire." She fingered her own necklace.

"We all have our secrets, love." Darwin's laughter sounded unhinged, maddening in its intensity.

Margaret got slowly to her feet and moved as if to shield Emerson from the old grave. "Leave my nephew out of this, Darwin."

"He has what I want."

Kennedy gestured with the gun. "Take the amulet from the hole, Emerson." And when he hesitated—"Now!"

Margaret clutched Emerson's arm. "Don't do it," she said. "Whatever you do, don't touch that amulet. Promise me."

Kennedy's lips pulled back in a sneer, and then she pulled the trigger. The loud crack hurt my ears, and then Margaret was sagging, falling in slow motion to the ground, Emerson kneeling down beside her as if he couldn't believe what he was seeing. The strengthening smell of smoke made me feel like my throat was being cut from the inside.

"Now then," Kennedy said, her aim steady, "take the amulet like a good boy and put it around your beefy neck. We'll give the viewers a love story one way or another." She glanced at me. "I said you could win him in the end. And Darwin is oh so taken with you, Zoe. He can't get enough of you. Isn't that sweet?" She leaned towards me, lowered her voice. "I suspect you remind him of a certain old flame of his." Margaret leaned against her nephew, face contorted with pain, struggling for each breath. "Only without the blood and recriminations. Best stay on his good side, little sister."

Emerson was transferring Margaret over to Cannon's arms. I knew his next step would be to put on the amulet. My future flashed in front of my eyes. Trapped in another relationship, only a hundred times worse than Joe had ever been, we'd be the darlings of the media, everyone convinced in the veracity of my happy ending while I lived out my days being terrorized and manipulated by a ghost in sheep's clothing. No exit.

To hell with that. Better the devil I didn't know than going back to that kind of torture.

I jumped down into the hole, grabbed the amulet, and put it around my own neck.

"No!" But Kennedy reacted too late. The cord tightened, biting into my skin as it became a choker. A searing pain washed down my body. Emerson looked between me and my sister and took advantage of her distraction to bolt back up the path towards the burning house.

And then Darwin was there, not his voice toying with me, but his entire presence. He knew what I knew, and I knew what he knew, and I screamed as his poison flowed into my identity.

"This wasn't what I had in mind," he said to me. *"But it does have a certain charm to it, I have to admit. You and I, joined in true communion. Till death do us part."*

He began his fight for dominance, overwriting my sense of self and experience of reality with his own. Everything he thought, everything he contained, was the truth. Everything of mine? Just so many leftovers.

"Cannon!" I croaked. "Cannon! Help me!" I reached out to him instinctively, the one person here who I knew loved me, who would lend me the strength I needed to fight back against Darwin's assault. I scrabbled from the hole in the earth and fell into a heap next to where he crouched beside Margaret's prone form.

He looked down on me, and even in the dim light I could make out every curve and feature of his face. I saw no love in his eyes, only a mindless fear. He scrambled back from me like I had a disease that was catching.

I tried again. "Cannon. *Please.*" It took all my effort to keep my hand raised towards him where he could reach out and grab it, pull me out of the uncompromising darkness that was Darwin's soul.

He met my eyes for one brief moment, shook his head as if in denial, and ran away.

Darwin roared, part laughter and part rage that even a small part of himself would be so casually rejected.

I abandoned myself to him. What, after all, had I expected? Cannon didn't love me, couldn't love me even if he'd wanted to. That was just the way things went in my world.

As Darwin began to subsume all that I was, there was a curious sensation of release. I had done my best, but in the end it hadn't been enough —no surprise there—and now none of those things were my problems anymore. I could abdicate responsibility with a clear conscience.

Except...there was something still tethering me, holding me back from the full commitment Darwin so desperately craved. A prickling feeling kept rising to the top of the maelstrom of our combined thoughts.

It was anger. Anger that I was once more being compressed into a restricted space and identified as being weak and needy and unimportant. Anger that what I needed never mattered. Anger that this was how I was going to end, unable to save myself as I'd finally decided I wanted to do.

Once I'd identified the anger, it grew into something that felt more like rage. The taste of smoke in the air only stoked it further. If anyone was going to burn my world to the ground, I wanted to be the one to do it.

I wasn't going to capitulate to him without a fight. I pushed back against Darwin's advances: gently at first, hesitant in my own power, sending out little nudges from my most secret places, but as he resisted, the struggle became more desperate. *No*, I told him. *You can't have me this way.* He had complete control of my body by then, but I wouldn't give him my soul.

But he was greedy, and he wanted my soul too.

"Kennedy's gone," he told me. *"Cannon's gone, and Joe. Your mother, your father. Everyone you've ever loved is gone. You're all alone now. Come, let me love you."*

I was stripped bare in all my vulnerability, soaking in the reality of my final terror: of being alone. Forgotten, unwanted, abandoned, shut out, unmoored and solitary.

Human beings aren't meant to be alone. My resistance began to crumble.

Margaret, bony weak Margaret, leaned over me, her face so close to mine I could smell the mintiness of her breath. "Not so fast, you bastard," she said, and then she ripped the amulet from my throat.

First, silence. Absolute blessed silence in my head, and I stared up at her in a daze. "You can't control everyone else when you're trying to inhabit a body, can you?" she taunted, and then she wrapped the amulet around her own neck where it banged against its twin. Her body went rigid for a moment, and I knew the internal assault had begun anew, this time inside Margaret.

I looked around in confusion, not knowing how much time had passed. Kennedy was gone. It was just me and Margaret lying in the dirt by the edge of the cliff. I'd been breathing in time to the rhythmic crashing of the waves. A low glow came from the direction of the house. Still on fire then. My tongue felt like a dry wad of cotton jammed into my mouth, but blissful silence washed through my head. Margaret must have been right: Darwin needed his entire focus to try to wrestle away control of her body.

I rolled over onto my side with difficulty. My limbs had become foreign objects, and every muscle protested even such a slight movement. Margaret's eyelids flickered for an extended time. The smoky air stung my eyes no matter how many times I blinked. Where was Kennedy? Helping fight the fire?

Or was she helping things burn? Darwin had been talking to her all along. I'd seen it all when he'd been part of me. He'd been intrigued by this vision of me she'd painted, talented but undisciplined, eager to please but with a caustic edge, trailing a painful insecurity in my wake, and with a bright talent that was overshadowed by uncertainty. I'd reminded him of Margaret before everything went wrong.

And so he'd persuaded Kennedy to bring her little sister back with her in the hopes that everything that was wrong with poor little Zoe would find its solution here in Darwin's domain. She'd been happy to make the sacrifice. Saw it as a win-win.

We'd both played so easily into his hands.

I reached out and took Margaret's hand, tears leaking down my cheeks, whether from the smoke or the weird sick emptiness inside me, I couldn't say. Already her color looked better, as if Darwin could control her flesh and blood and force it to bow to his will.

Margaret's bright blue eyes snapped open. Who was looking at me: Margaret or Darwin? I dropped her hand. With a low groan, she levered herself up on her side. "This is my fault," she whispered to me. "I started this. And I'm going to be the one who ends it."

She began crawling towards the cliff edge, foot after torturous foot. I knew what she intended, and I didn't stop her. I don't know if I could have at that point, but it didn't matter. I didn't even try. She carried whatever was left of Darwin inside her, she had his toxic amulet around her neck now, and I wanted him gone. Annihilated. Whatever the cost.

Margaret had made it most of the way to the edge when Kennedy shot past me. She didn't pause to see if I was all right. She ran full speed to where Margaret labored and launched herself on top of her.

It wasn't a fair fight, a seventy-something with a gunshot wound pinned by a thirty-something with everything to lose. Margaret must have known she didn't stand a chance. But she fought in spite of that, using one arm to cover the amulet and prevent Kennedy from removing it. They struggled and rolled ever closer to that final precipice, and Margaret's flailing became weaker, her breath coming in painful wheezes.

I pushed myself up to my feet, staggering like a drunk person. I had to intervene. This one time I couldn't let Kennedy have her way, not and wreck Darwin onto the world.

I shambled up to them and waited until Kennedy was once again on top. The crashing of the waves drowned out everything around us. It was just me, Kennedy, and Margaret at the top of the world.

I tapped Kennedy on the shoulder, and she looked up at me, wild-eyed and confused. "Kenny! You have to let her go!" I shouted it. It seemed like the only way I might be heard over the intense pounding of the surf.

Kennedy narrowed her eyes and opened her mouth to say something, doubtless a sharp retort. She was always good at putting people into their places.

But whatever she'd wanted to say was lost. Margaret took advantage of her momentary distraction, and with a final great heave, she rolled both of them off the cliff and down, down, down, to the sharp rocks and the ocean below.

I stared into the black depths in horror, numbness spreading outwards from my heart. She couldn't be...they couldn't be.... I strained my eyes searching for any sign of either of them, but there was simply nothing.

The fire raged on behind me. With no fire department on the island, there was nothing to stop the house from burning into a dried-out husk of its former self.

Kennedy and Margaret...both dead. And Darwin's horrifying amulet with them.

I don't know how long I stood there, staring blankly into the dark. The ocean continued its ceaseless battery of the cliff. I started shaking uncontrollably.

What had we done?

"Did you miss me?" Darwin's voice slipped comfortably back into my mind, and I howled my despair into the night.

Forty-Seven

LOVE STORY: All's Well that Ends Well?

—March 5, 2019 by lacey, www.dontcallmegirl.com

And so *Love Season* season 2 comes to an end, and discerning viewers are left to wonder, what the hell happened here?

Granted, the show gave us the happy ending we were promised, if in higher soap opera style than anyone expected. Emerson rescues his damsel in distress—in a COMA, no less—from a rampant house fire, and when she wakes up a few weeks later, he is still at her side, ready to declare his undying love for her. Or at least, you know, make their romantic arrangement exclusive and become her one and only boyfriend. And some clever producer managed to get the whole thing on camera.

Even now, it's hard to distinguish the line between fact and fiction. It's a discouraging reality that my internet sleuthing can only get me so far. But it looks like that fire really did happen, and it really did result in casualties. When the show cuts to the iconic Aunt Margaret's memorial service, Giselle gripping Emerson's hand in support and lending him her embroidered handkerchief (sustainability even in grief, people!), they imply Margaret Courtland died from health problems she'd been struggling with for some time. But there are already rumors circulating that she died the night of the fire. And at least one crew member was also killed: supervising producer Kennedy Brown, although thus far no one at the network is commenting on that either.

The former contestants are presenting a uniform front of silence instead of engaging in the usual Instagram influencer free-for-all we all know and—well, we don't love it, do we? But we show up for it all the same. But not this time, and my Spidey sense tells me there must have been a payout involved to convince this many women to eschew their opportunity for fame and (mild) fortune. Not only that, but it's been a week since the finale aired, and none of the women have agreed to follow-up interviews or appearances. It's becoming clearer why almost all the promo for the show has been handled by the show's host Cannon Murphy. That's one way to stay strictly on message. (In related news, Leogami announced yesterday they've given the green light to a new celebrity gossip show hosted by none other than our boy Cannon. Apparently they think he's doing something right.)

In the end, I don't think this season of *Love Story* ever figured out what genre it wanted to be or what story it was trying to tell, which is why it reverted to its tried and true happily-ever-after formula, hitting a note of dissonance after the tonal hoops it made its viewers jump through. And this failure has repercussions: that's right, folks, *Love Story* is officially no more. It's been summarily canceled by the network. Showrunner and executive producer Jennifer diCardio has already taken over *Shopping Maniacs*, a lower-profile series, and so far under her reign the show has remained true to its original format.

And what about the future of yours truly and this blog? I'll be returning to my roots, so to speak, and you can expect commentary on *Her Engagement* when it starts airing in May. It's not going to be the same, but hopefully we can drown our sorrows with enough Chardonnay and Gouda.

Xoxo Lacey

Forty-Eight

To: theacmasters@goodmail.com
From: zoezoezoe@goodmail.com
Date: October 4, 2025
Subject: The Hardest Month

Thea! Congratulations! I know you and Vivian will be very happy together, and you suit each other perfectly. Also, congratulations to both of you for thwarting the Gold Diggers curse, which apparently is as heteronormative as the show it came from. Yours is the first marriage in our cohort, and I wouldn't be surprised if it were also the last. I want photographic proof the instant you both sign that wedding certificate because I won't entirely believe it until I see it.

You've truly outdone yourself with the guilt tripping this time around, and of course I would love to attend your wedding, which I'm sure will be the loveliest wedding in the history of weddings—Vivian would accept nothing less—but as you know all too well, I never leave Montana if I can help it. Hell, I might not even leave my house if it weren't for the dogs. You'll have Lucy there to cry the appropriate amount in my stead. But don't worry, I will send a tasteful gift and the next time you visit, I will gush an appropriate amount over all the photos.

You are very kind to wish the same love for me, but to be honest I'm more grateful for the curse than not, which is probably why I cling to it like I do. After everything that has happened, the thought of being with another man makes me break out in a sweat. Maybe someday I'll regret it, but I really do believe I am at my best when I am alone. In the end, the show did what Kennedy hoped it would do: it toughened me up to certain realities.

Thanks also for the latest gossip. No surprise that Emerson is getting divorced from his socialite or that everyone suspects there was infidelity involved. That man had the emotional intelligence of a jello salad, and he's too used to getting whatever he wants to make any sacrifices for the sake of a marriage. Even Giselle eventually had the good sense to see that. And yes, I noticed your sly hint about seeing Cannon at the wedding, but since I won't be attending, please don't pass him my number. Let's leave well enough alone. I'm sorry to hear he's unhappy, but that's nothing new. He's done well enough for himself when it comes to money, anyway, and that will have to be enough.

I'm pleased to say the publication date for the second book in the Sherlock Chronicles has been set for late spring. The school visits will be an effort of endurance, but I don't mind children the same way I mind adults. The kids ask such ridiculous questions, it eases my despair about humanity. It's cheap enough out here that I'm set for a long time from the settlement from Leogami, but it's still good to have some income coming in. I'm thinking of having solar panels installed next spring so I can go entirely off the grid.

You asked about the nightmares. Yes, I still have them. I take it you do too. Sometimes I drug myself into a stupor to avoid them, but if I do it too often, it stops working, and the nights once more become a battlefield.

Give my love to Vivian, and save some of it for yourself. I really am thrilled you're getting married. You both deserve the very best.

Love,

Zoe

Forty-Nine

I flew down to Los Angeles only once after the show aired. It must have been nearly fifteen years ago now. I was sixty-one. Cannon was some years older. And he was dying.

He was reclining in a hospital bed in the living room of his ranch house up in the hills, but he managed to look good in spite of everything, still solid, still a presence. He wore a luxurious robe in a rich green hue, and his goatee was trimmed as neatly as I remembered. I could almost ignore the tubes in his nose and the way he couldn't shift his body at all without giving small winces of pain.

I could see exactly why he'd made such an impression on me thirty years earlier. A different lifetime, that.

A young woman in her early twenties had opened the door to let me in, all honey maple hair and a pouty lower lip just like Cannon's. He opened his eyes when the two of us entered the room, sunshine pouring in through the floor-to-ceiling windows, a glimpse of a sparkling blue pool in the yard. "Ah, I see you've met Zoe," he said to me, and he gave me that wink of his. "I bet you didn't realize you had such a charming namesake running around."

Zoe. I'd known he'd had a daughter with yet another fiancée, that they hadn't gotten married in the end, but I'd never heard her name. Zoe. "It's a pleasure to meet you," I told her.

"Huh." She looked me up and down. "You're not what I expected."

I laughed gently. "I rarely am, these days." She was so young. I wondered what Cannon had told her about me.

"Well, thanks for coming to see my dad. He said you wouldn't come."

"Not the first time he's been wrong."

"I'm right here," Cannon complained. "And there's nothing wrong with my hearing."

"Yeah, yeah, let me know if you need anything." The younger Zoe picked up a magazine and left us alone.

"Let me see you," Cannon said. I came to the side of his bed, backlit by his huge windows. "You look like an avenging angel."

"All too human, I'm afraid." I faked a little laugh and wished I hadn't come. This was too fraught, too difficult. We had nothing left to say to each other. All our words had been exhausted on that blasted island. "How are you doing?"

"I'm dying." He met my eyes directly as he said it, an invective, but I didn't flinch. "I assume they told you something like that to get you to come."

"They did."

"Thank you for making the trip." He took my hand. "It feels like it's been an age, and also like I saw you just yesterday."

I didn't allow myself to wallow in sentiment, not at this late stage. "It's been a long time."

"I didn't forget you, you know." He grasped my hand tighter. "I never forgot. In a funny way, never getting to see you after that last night, it's like you've been frozen in my mind, just the way you were when I met you."

I sighed. "I'm an old recluse now, Cannon. Nothing special."

"I should have stayed that night. When you asked me. I never should have left."

Had there been times in the intervening years when I'd been angry that he'd abandoned me to my fate? Yes. But the anger never lasted. After all, how could I blame him? If things had been different, maybe I would have been the one to run. "I understand why you did what you did," I told him. It was the only peace I could give him.

"I should have come after you," he said. "After the fire. I should have gone out to Montana, convinced you to come home with me." He paused. "I thought about it. But I just couldn't face it, Zoe. It seemed so much easier to pretend none of it had ever happened. That the world was the way I'd always thought it was."

What luxury to be able to retreat to his Hollywood life and bury his head in the sand of his success. I'd never had that option. But he was an old man now, consumed by regret. He didn't understand we'd all been played, and I'd never be able to convince him. "It was a long time ago."

He didn't ask about my life. He didn't ask if I was happy. Even on his death bed he couldn't ask me if I was still haunted. Maybe it was just as well. I'm not sure I would have had the energy to lie. "But still." Such passion shone from his eyes, even now, and such belief in his own worthiness. I could see why so many women had almost married him, and also why none of them had gone through with their promises. He took every inch of space in the room, as if death were merely a minor inconvenience. "You came to say goodbye. You felt it too. I loved you like I've never loved anyone else, Zoe. And it's taken me until now to finally understand it."

I knew what he wanted to hear, and I wanted to tell it to him. Maybe he was right. Maybe if he'd showed up afterwards, if he'd joined in the fun of piecing Zoe back together into some semblance of humanity, maybe things would have turned out differently. Maybe we could have faced the truth together and been stronger for it.

Then again, there is the Curse. So maybe not.

But it didn't matter. He hadn't shown up.

"I know," I told him. "It's okay."

Nothing had changed. He had no idea who I was. I kept myself apart from him, then as before, and I tamped down the small feeling of loss that persisted in my heart.

He died three days later.

FIFTY

It is past three in the morning. A thunderstorm rages outside. The windows shake, the thunder booms its indignation, the jagged flashes of light illuminate my age-spotted hands, hands that remind me indelibly of Margaret. Both dogs are hiding underneath the bed, but the weather holds no fear for me. That is reserved for sleep, where I cannot avoid the reality that my mind is not entirely my own.

Some things are irreversible.

Sometimes Darwin comes into my dreams masquerading as Kennedy. Those are always the worst nights. She hasn't aged at all, of course, looks just as she did that last fall, ponytail and slogan T-shirts and earpiece. She still tries to produce me, and sometimes I can't tell if it's him—it's him, of course it is—or if she's come back to haunt me herself, spouting her own brand of toxicity. Impossible to say. I keep my life simple as a survival tactic; there's very little for her to produce, and at this point I can endure yet another rehash of the past.

I am the last person left from that ill-fated season of *Love Story*. Not that I am so very old, but tragedy has dodged our footsteps. I gain great personal satisfaction when I consider that Darwin will die with me. And soon. I can feel it coming, and I am not afraid. It's never been death that's haunted me: it's this infection growing inside me like a tumor. I've never wanted to spread my disease.

He speaks to me even now. *"Zoe dearest,"* he says, *"why do you work so hard? Why do you bother to write this down? The world grinds on without you, and it's never been interested in the truth."*

But I paid such a great price for my writing, didn't I? I lost everything, and then the universe laughed at me and gave me the career I'd so desperately craved. My dreams rang hollow after everything I'd been through: that's the joke. But I'll take what I can get.

And oh, Darwin, old friend, solitude has seared me clean. The great mechanisms of our blood-ridden nation will continue to crush whoever gets in the way, turning their remnants into profit and a false sense of progress. There's nothing I can do to stop the machine. But I can hold myself apart.

So sweet Darwin, do your worst. You may whisper your insidious poison in my ear, unrelenting and perverse, but I have chosen my course. I have my self-sufficiency, my dear dogs, my beautiful home, the many novels I've written over the years: all in spite of you.

It is something. It might not be enough. But in the end, my story remains my own.

Thank you!

Thank you for reading *Gold Diggers*!

If you enjoyed reading this book, I hope you'll consider telling a friend about it or leaving a review. And if you want to stay in touch and find out when my next book comes out, you can subscribe to my newsletter at www.amysundberg.com.

Until then, happy reading!

Acknowledgments

The idea of this novel was born because I was joking around with my dear friend Lee Harris about how terrible dating apps are and how I would write him a horror online dating novella.

This is not that book. But when I sat down to brainstorm ideas for the project, I came up with the idea for this book instead, and I couldn't get it out of my mind. So the next year I began to write it. Thank you, Lee, for accidentally setting me on this creative journey with your amazing sense of humor.

I also owe a debt of gratitude to one of my oldest friends, Francine Estrada Guerrero. It was during a visit with her a few months prior to my conversation with Lee that I saw the hometown dates episode of *the Bachelorette* (Rachel Lindsay's season). I was simultaneously fascinated and horrified by what I'd seen, and it served as the original inspiration for this book.

Big thanks to my beta readers Barbara Webb, Beth Dawkins, Kelley Skovron, and Mark Pantoja. Their feedback and insight was invaluable, and any remaining flaws are all my own.

Thank you to Mark Teppo for lending me John Clute's brilliant *The Darkening Garden* and supporting me through some business bumps in the life of this novel, thanks to Meg Sinoff for getting me through the extreme isolation of 2020, and thanks to my sister Heather, who is absolutely nothing like Kennedy, a fact for which I am eternally grateful.

Finally, my apologies to W.B. Yeats.

About the Author

Amy Sundberg is a novelist and journalist. Whether she is writing romping YA retellings of self discovery or psychological Gothic horror with trenchant social commentary, her novels feature intrepid heroines, high stakes, and questions of agency and power.

When she's not plotting how to someday have her very own library ladder or elaborate indoor reading tent, Amy is drooling over grand pianos and singing her heart out. She indulges her sweet tooth with some abandon (her favorite treat is pie, followed closely by ice cream). Driven by an insatiable curiosity, she has been lucky enough to travel to six continents. She can be easily coaxed into playing board games or going for a walk at a local park. She has a passion for theater, and she enjoys cooking a variety of delicious soups. She lives in Seattle with her adorable little dog.

For more information visit her website amysundberg.com or follow her on Instagram @sundbergamy, Twitter @amysundberg and Bluesky @amysundberg.bsky.social.

Also by Amy Sundberg

To Travel the Stars: a Retelling of Pride and Prejudice

My Stars Shine Darkly: Book 1 of the Satori Chronicles

www.ingramcontent.com/pod-product-compliance
Ingram Content Group UK Ltd.
Pitfield, Milton Keynes, MK11 3LW, UK
UKHW041634190726
13854UKWH00006B/2490